PRAISE FOR
THE RICHARD SHARPE SERIES

"Richard Sharpe has the most astounding knack for finding himself where the action is . . . and adding considerably to it."
—*Wall Street Journal*

"Excellently entertaining. If you love historical drama . . . then look no further."
—*Boston Globe*

"Cornwell's blending of the fictional Sharpe with historical figures and actual battles gives the narrative a stunning sense of realism. . . . If only all history lessons could be as vibrant."
—*San Francisco Chronicle*

"A hero in the mold of James Bond, although his weapons are a Baker carbine and a giant cavalry sword."
—*Philadelphia Inquirer*

"Eminently successful historical fiction."
—*Booklist*

"[The Sharpe novels] do what good historical fiction must do—bring the period to life, and teach the reader something without making him feel as if he is back in school. On both counts, Cornwell succeeds admirably."
—*American Way*

Kelly Campbell

About the Author

Bernard Cornwell, "the reigning king of historical fiction" (*USA Today*), is the author of the acclaimed *New York Times* bestsellers *Agincourt* and *The Fort*; the bestselling Saxon Tales, which include *The Last Kingdom, The Pale Horseman, Lords of the North, Sword Song, The Burning Land,* and *Death of Kings*; and the Richard Sharpe novels, among many others. He lives with his wife on Cape Cod.

SHARPE'S PREY

SHARPE'S ENEMY
Richard Sharpe and the Defense of Portugal, Christmas 1812

SHARPE'S HONOR
Richard Sharpe and the Vitoria Campaign, February to June 1813

SHARPE'S REGIMENT
Richard Sharpe and the Invasion of France, June to November 1813

SHARPE'S SIEGE
Richard Sharpe and the Winter Campaign, 1814

SHARPE'S REVENGE
Richard Sharpe and the Peace of 1814

SHARPE'S WATERLOO
Richard Sharpe and the Waterloo Campaign, 15 June to 18 June 1815

SHARPE'S DEVIL
Richard Sharpe and the Emperor, 1820–1821

The Grail Quest Series

THE ARCHER'S TALE
VAGABOND
HERETIC

The Nathaniel Starbuck Chronicles

REBEL
COPPERHEAD
BATTLE FLAG
THE BLOODY GROUND

The Warlord Chronicles

THE WINTER KING
THE ENEMY OF GOD
EXCALIBUR

The Sailing Thrillers

STORMCHILD
SCOUNDREL
WILDTRACK
CRACKDOWN

Other Novels

STONEHENGE
GALLOWS THIEF
A CROWNING MERCY
THE FALLEN ANGELS
REDCOAT

SHARPE'S PREY

*Richard Sharpe and the Expedition
to Denmark, 1807*

BERNARD CORNWELL

HARPER

NEW YORK · LONDON · TORONTO · SYDNEY

HARPER

A previous edition of this book was published in Great Britain in 2001 by HarperCollins Publishers.

A hardcover edition of this book was published in 2002 by HarperCollins Publishers.

HarperCollins books may be purchased for educational, business, or sales promotional use. For information please write: Special Markets Department, HarperCollins Publishers, 10 East 53rd Street, New York, NY 10022.

First Perennial edition published 2003.
Reissued in Harper paperback in 2012.

Map by Ken Lewis

The Library of Congress has catalogued the hardcover edition as follows:
Cornwell, Bernard.
Sharpe's prey : Richard Sharpe and the Expedition to Copenhagen, 1807 / Bernard Cornwell. — 1st American ed.
p. cm.
ISBN 0-06-000252-2
1. Sharpe, Richard (Fictitious character) — Fiction. 2. Great Britain — History, Military — 19th century — Fiction. 3. Copenhagen (Denmark) — History — Bombardment, 1807 — Fiction. 4. British — Denmark — Fiction. I. Title.

PR6053.O75 S538 2002
823'.914—dc21
2001046501

ISBN 978-0-06-008453-0 (reissue)

14   15   16   ❖/RRD   30 29 28 27 26 25 24

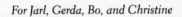

For Jarl, Gerda, Bo, and Christine

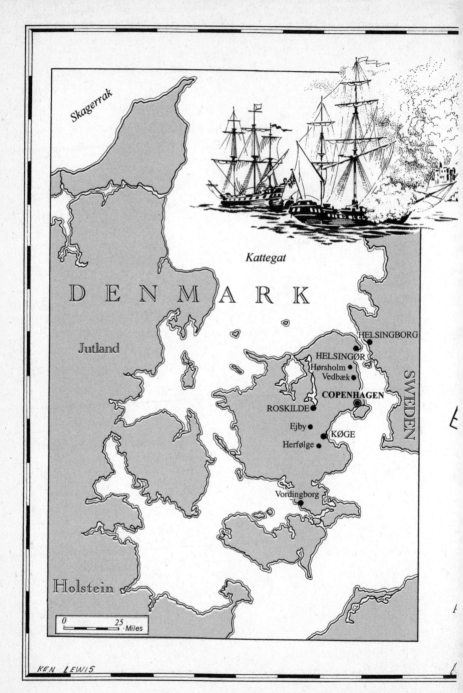

Skagerrak

Kattegat

DENMARK

Jutland

HELSINGBORG
HELSINGØR
Hørsholm
Vedbæk
COPENHAGEN
ROSKILDE
Ejby
KØGE
Herfølge

Vordingborg

SWEDEN

Holstein

0   25
         Miles

KEN LEWIS

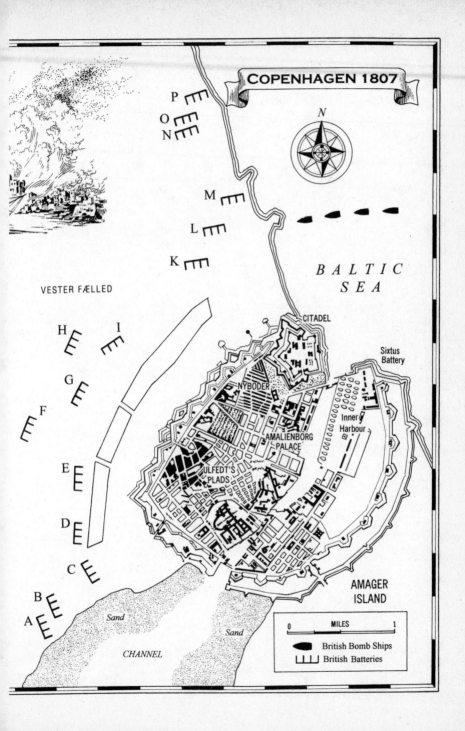

COPENHAGEN 1807

P O N

M
L
K

VESTER FÆLLED

N

BALTIC SEA

H   I
G
F
E
E
D
C
B
A

CITADEL

Sixtus
Battery

NYBODER

Inner
Harbour

AMALIENBORG
PALACE

ULFEDT'S
PLADS

AMAGER
ISLAND

0   MILES   1

British Bomb Ships

British Batteries

Sand

Sand

CHANNEL

SHARPE'S PREY

SHARPE'S PREY

CAPTAIN HENRY WILLSEN OF His Majesty's Dirty Half Hundred, more formally the 50th Regiment of West Kent, parried his opponent's saber. He did it hurriedly. His right hand was low so that his saber's blade was raised in the position known to the fencing masters as the *quarte basse* and the knowledgeable spectators thought the parry was feeble. A surprised murmur sounded, for Willsen was good. Very good. He had been attacking, but it was apparent he had been slow to see his taller opponent's counter and now he was in disorganized retreat. The taller man pressed, swatting the *quarte basse* aside and lunging so that Willsen skittered backward, his slippers squeaking with a staccato judder on the wooden floor which was liberally scattered with French chalk. The very sound of the slippers on the chalked wood denoted panic. The sabers clashed harshly again, the taller man stamped forward, his blade flickering, clanging, reaching, and Willsen was countering in apparent desperation until, so fast that those watching could scarce follow his blade's quick movement, he stepped to one side and riposted at his opponent's cheek. There seemed little power in the riposte, for its force all came from Willsen's wrist rather than from his full arm, but the saber's edge still struck the taller man with such might that he lost his balance. He swayed, right arm flailing, and Willsen gently touched his weapon's point to his opponent's chest so that he toppled to the floor.

"Enough!" the Master-at-Arms called.

"God's teeth." The fallen man swept his blade at Willsen's ankles in a fit of pique. The blow was easily blocked and Willsen just walked away.

"I said enough, my lord!" the Master-at-Arms shouted angrily.

"How the devil did you do that, Willsen?" Lord Marsden pulled off the padded leather helmet with its wire visor that had protected his face. "I had you on your damned ass!"

Willsen, who had planned the whole passage of the fight from the moment he made a deliberately soft *quarte basse*, bowed. "Perhaps I was just fortunate, my lord?"

"Don't patronize me, man," Lord Marsden snapped as he climbed to his feet. "What was it?"

"Your disengagement from the *sixte* was slow, my lord."

"The devil it was," Lord Marsden growled. He was proud of his ability with foil or saber, yet he knew Willsen had bested him easily by feigning a squeaking retreat. His lordship scowled, then realized he was being ungracious and so, tucking the saber under his arm, held out a hand. "You're quick, Willsen, damned quick."

The handful of spectators applauded the show of sportsmanship. They were in Horace Jackson's Hall of Arms, an establishment on London's Jermyn Street where wealthy men could learn the arts of pugilism, fencing and pistol shooting. The hall was a high bare room lined with racks of swords and sabers, smelling of tobacco and liniment, and decorated with prints of prize fighters, mastiffs and racehorses. The only women in the place served drinks and food, or else worked in the small rooms above the hall where the beds were soft and the prices high.

Willsen pulled off his helmet and ran a hand through his long fair hair. He bowed to his beaten opponent, then carried both sabers to the weapon rack at the side of the hall where a tall, very thin and extraordinarily handsome captain in the red coat and blue facings of the 1st Regiment of Foot Guards was waiting. The guardsman, a stranger to Willsen, tossed away a half-smoked cigar as Willsen approached. "You fooled him," the Captain said cheerfully.

Willsen frowned at the stranger's impertinence, but he answered politely enough. Willsen, after all, was an employee in Horace Jackson's Hall and the Guards Captain, judging by the elegant cut of his expensive uniform, was a patron. The sort of patron, moreover, who could not wait to prove himself against the celebrated Henry Willsen. "I fooled him?" Willsen asked. "How?"

"The *quarte basse*," the guardsman said, "you made it soft, am I right?"

Willsen was impressed at the guardsman's acuity, but did not betray it. "Perhaps I was just fortunate?" he suggested. He was being modest, for he had the reputation of being the finest swordsman in the Dirty Half Hundred, probably in the whole army and maybe in the entire country, but he belittled his ability, just as he shrugged off those who reckoned he was the best pistol shot in Kent. A soldier, Willsen liked to say, should be a master of his arms and so he practiced assiduously and prayed that one day his skill would be useful in the service of his country. Until that time came he earned his captain's pay and, because that was not sufficient to support a wife, child and mess bill, he taught fencing and pistol-shooting in Horace Jackson's Hall of Arms. Jackson, an old pugilist with a mashed face, wanted Willsen to leave the army and join the establishment full-time, but Willsen liked being a soldier. It gave him a position in British society. It might not be a high place, but it was honorable.

"There's no such thing as luck," the guardsman said, only now he spoke in Danish, "not when you're fighting."

Willsen had been turning away, but the change of language made him look back to the golden-haired Guards Captain. His first careless impression had been one of privileged youth, but he now saw that the guardsman was probably in his early thirties and had a cynical, knowing cast to his devil-may-care good looks. This was a man, Willsen thought, who would be at home in a palace or at a prizefight. A formidable man too, and one who was of peculiar importance to Willsen, who now offered the guardsman a half-bow. "You, sir," he said respectfully, "must be Major the Honorable John Lavisser?"

"I'm Captain Lavisser," Captain and Major Lavisser said. The Guards gave their officers dual ranks; the lower one denoted their responsibility in the regiment while the higher was an acknowledgment that any Guards officer was a superior being, especially when compared to an impoverished swordsman from the Dirty Half Hundred. "I'm Captain Lavisser," the Honorable John Lavisser said again, "but you must call me John. Please." He still spoke in Danish.

"I thought we were not to meet till Saturday?" Willsen said, taking off his fencing slippers and pulling on boots.

"We're to be companions for a fair time"—Lavisser ignored Willsen's hostility—"and it's better, I think, that we should be friends. Besides, are you not curious about our orders?"

"My orders are to escort you to Copenhagen and see you safe out again," Willsen responded stiffly as he pulled on his red coat. The wool of the coat was faded and its black cuffs and facings were scuffed. He strapped on his seven-guinea sword, unhappily aware of the valuable blade that hung from Lavisser's slings, but Willsen had long learned to curb his envy at the inequalities of life, even if he could not entirely forget them. He knew well enough that his captaincy in the Dirty Half Hundred was worth £1,500, exactly what it cost to purchase a mere lieutenancy in the Guards, but so be it. Willsen had been taught by his Danish father and English mother to trust in God, do his duty and accept fate, and fate had now decreed he was to be the companion of a man who was the son of an earl, a guardsman, and an aide to Prince Frederick, Duke of York, who was the second son of George III and Commander in Chief of the British army.

"But don't you want to know why we are going to Copenhagen?" Lavisser asked.

"I have no doubt I shall be informed at the proper time," Willsen said, his manner still stiff.

Lavisser smiled and his thin, saturnine face was transformed with charm. "The proper time, Willsen, is now," he said. "Come, at least allow me to buy you supper and reveal the mysteries of our errand."

In truth Captain Willsen was intrigued. He had served twelve years in the British army and had never heard a shot fired in anger. He yearned to distinguish himself and now, quite suddenly, a chance had arisen because an officer was needed to escort the Duke of York's aide to Copenhagen. That was all Willsen knew, though his commanding officer had hinted that his facility with small arms might be a great advantage. Willsen had been worried at first, fearing that he would be fighting against his father's people, but he had been assured that the danger in Copenhagen came from the French, not the Danes, and that assurance had permitted Willsen to accept the responsibility, just as it had piqued his curiosity.

Now Lavisser was offering to explain and Willsen, who knew he had been churlish, nodded. "Of course. It will be a pleasure to dine with you, sir."

"My name is John," Lavisser insisted as he led Willsen down the staircase to the street. Willsen half expected to find a carriage waiting, but it appeared Lavisser was on foot even though a small chill rain was falling. "Hard to believe it's July," Lavisser grumbled.

"It will be a bad harvest," Willsen remarked.

"I thought we might get a bite at Almack's," Lavisser suggested, "and maybe play a hand afterward?"

"I never wager," Willsen answered, and even if he did he could never have afforded the high stakes at Almack's.

"How very wise you are," Lavisser said. They were both speaking English again. "And I thought it might please you if we had a word with Hanssen before supper."

"Hanssen?"

"The first secretary at the Danish embassy," Lavisser explained. He gave his companion an earnest look. "I want to be quite certain that our activities are not prejudicial to Denmark. Hanssen's a decent man and I've always found his advice very sound."

Willsen shared the desire to avoid upsetting Denmark and so he rather liked the idea of talking to someone from the embassy, but his innate caution came to the fore. "Are we supposed to be revealing our purposes to the Danish government?"

"Of course we're not and of course we shan't." Lavisser stopped and unleashed his dazzling smile on Willsen. "Sir David told me you expressed scruples about visiting Denmark? Is that right? Believe me, my dear Willsen, I feel the same. My mother's family live there and I will do nothing, nothing, that places them in jeopardy." He paused, then his voice became, if anything, even more earnest. "If you and I cannot bring Denmark and Britain into a closer friendship, my dear Willsen, then we have no business going there, none. I merely seek general reassurances from Hanssen. I want news of the political situation in Denmark. I want to know what pressures the French are applying. The French are the irritants, but aren't they always? And of course Hanssen will want to know the purpose of our visit, but we shall merely say we are visiting families. What could be more innocent?" Lavisser smiled, walked on and Willsen, reassured, followed the tall guardsman across the street. A crossing sweeper, a skinny boy with a running sore on his forehead, sprinted to brush a horse dropping out of Lavisser's path. The guardsman spun a careless sixpence toward the lad, then led Willsen down an alleyway. "Would it offend you if we visited Hanssen by his servants' entrance?" Lavisser asked. "Only with the Baltic so tremulous you can be sure that the damned Frogs will be watching his front door."

"The French? In London?"

"They have agents everywhere," Lavisser said, "even London. But not, I think, in this alley."

The alley was noisome and dark. It culminated in a gate that stood ajar and led into a bleak narrow yard that was made even darker by the day's dense clouds and the surrounding walls. The yard's cobbles were half covered in rubbish that was being loaded onto a handcart by a tall, heavyset man who seemed surprised to see two red-coated officers invade his grubby domain. He hastily stood aside, snatched off his ragged hat and tugged his forelock as the two officers stepped gingerly through the yard's filth.

"Would you be averse to feminine company after supper?" Lavisser asked.

"I'm a married man, Captain," Willsen said severely.

"Do call me John, please."

Willsen was made uncomfortable by the invitation to such familiarity. "I'll not stay after supper," he said awkwardly, edging past the cart.

Henry Willsen was one of the finest swordsmen in the British army and his skill with a pistol would have been the envy of any duellist, but he had no defense against the attack which erupted as soon as he had passed the rubbish cart. The tall man kicked Willsen in the back of one knee and, as the officer fell, his assailant stabbed upward with a knife that slid between Willsen's ribs. The blade sank to the hilt and the man held it there, supporting Willsen who was gasping suddenly as his right hand groped for the hilt of his cheap sword. He managed to take hold of the weapon, though feebly, but Captain Lavisser, who had turned when the tall man attacked, just smiled and knocked Willsen's hand aside. "I don't think you need that, Harry," he said.

"You . . ." Willsen tried to speak, but his lungs were filling with blood. He began to choke and his eyes widened as he shook his head.

"I do apologize, my dear Willsen," Lavisser said, "but I'm afraid your presence in Copenhagen would be a most dreadful embarrassment." The Guards officer stepped hurriedly back as the big man, who had been supporting Willsen's weight with his knife, jerked the blade free. Willsen slumped and his attacker dropped beside him and slashed the knife across his throat. Willsen began to make choking noises as he jerked spasmodically on the cobbles. "Well done," Lavisser said warmly.

"Easy work," the big man grunted. He stood, wiping the blade on his dirty coat. He was very tall, very broad in the chest and had the scarred knuckles of a pugilist. His face was pitted with pox scars, his nose had been broken and ill set at least once, and his eyes were like stones. Everything about him declared that he was from as low a gutter as could bear life and just to look at him was to be glad that the gallows stood tall outside Newgate Prison.

"He's still alive." Lavisser frowned at Willsen.

"Not for long, he ain't," the big man said, then stamped hard on Willsen's chest. "Not now, he ain't."

"You are an example to us all, Barker," Lavisser said, then stepped close to the lifeless Willsen. "He was a very dull man, probably a Lutheran. You'll take his cash? Make it look like a robbery?"

Barker had already begun cutting the dead man's pockets open. "You think they'll find another bugger to go with us?" he asked.

"They seem tediously intent on giving me company," Lavisser said airily, "but time is short now, very short, and I doubt they'll find anyone. But if they do, Barker, then you must deal with the new man just as you dealt with this one." Lavisser seemed fascinated by the dead Willsen, for he could not take his eyes from him. "You are a great comfort to me, Barker, and you will like it in Denmark."

"I will, sir?"

"They are a very trusting people," Lavisser said, still unable to take his gaze from Willsen's body. "We shall be as ravening wolves among the woolliest of baa-lambs." He finally managed to look away from the corpse, raised a languid hand and edged past the handcart. He made bleating noises as he went down the alley.

The rain fell harder. It was the end of July 1807, yet it felt more like March. It would be a poor harvest, there was a new widow in Kent and the Honorable John Lavisser went to Almack's where he lost considerably more than a thousand guineas, but it no longer mattered. Nothing mattered now. He left worthless notes of hand promising to pay his debts and walked away. He was on his way to glory.

MISTER BROWN and Mister Belling, the one fat and the other thin, sat side by side and stared solemnly at the green-jacketed army officer across the table. Neither Mister Belling nor Mister Brown liked what they saw. Their visitor—he was not exactly a client—was a tall man with black hair, a hard face and a scar on his cheek and, ominously, he looked like a man who was no stranger to scars. Mister Brown sighed and turned to stare at the rain falling on London's Eastcheap. "It will be a bad harvest, Mister Belling," he said heavily.

"I fear so, Mister Brown."

"July!" Brown said. "July indeed! Yet it's more like March!"

"A fire in July!" Mister Belling said. "Unheard of!"

The fire, a mean heap of sullen coals, burned in a blackened hearth above which hung a cavalry saber. It was the only decoration in the paneled room and hinted at the office's military nature. Messrs Belling and Brown of Cheapside were army agents and their business was to look after the finances of officers who served abroad. They also acted as brokers for men wanting to buy or sell commissions, but this wet, chill July afternoon was bringing them no fees. "Alas!" Mister Brown spread his hands. His fingers were very white, plump and beautifully manicured. He flexed them as though he was about to play a harpsichord. "Alas," he said again, looking at the green-jacketed officer who glowered from the opposite side of the table.

"It is the nature of your commission," Mister Belling explained.

"Indeed it is," Mister Brown intervened, "the nature, so to speak, of your commission." He smiled ruefully.

"It's as good as anyone else's commission," the officer said belligerently.

"Oh, better!" Mister Brown said cheerfully. "Would you not agree, Mister Belling?"

"Far better," Mister Belling said enthusiastically. "A battlefield commission, Mister Sharpe? 'Pon my soul, but that's a rare thing. Rare!"

"An admirable thing!" Mister Brown added.

"Most admirable," Mister Belling agreed energetically, "a battlefield commission! Up from the ranks! Why, it's a—" he paused, trying to think what it was—"it's a veritable achievement!"

"But it is not"—Mister Brown spoke delicately, his plump hands opening and closing like a butterfly's wings—"fungible."

"Precisely." Mister Belling's manner exuded relief that his partner had found the exact word to settle the matter. "It is not fungible, Mister Sharpe."

No one spoke for a few seconds. A coal hissed, rain spattered on the office window and a carter's whip cracked in the street, which was filled with the rumble, crash and squeal of wagons and carriages.

"Fungible?" Lieutenant Richard Sharpe asked.

"The commission cannot be exchanged for cash," Mister Belling explained. "You did not buy it, you cannot sell it. You were given it. What the King gives, you may give back but you cannot sell. It is not"—he paused—"fungible."

"I was told I could sell it!" Sharpe said angrily.

"You were told wrong," Mister Brown said.

"Misinformed," Mister Belling added.

"Grievously so," Mister Brown said, "alas."

"The regulations are plain," Mister Belling went on. "An officer who purchases a commission is free to sell it, but a man awarded a commission is not. I wish it were otherwise."

"We both do!" Mister Brown said.

"But I was told . . ."

"You were told wrong," Mister Belling snapped, then wished he had not spoken so brusquely for Lieutenant Sharpe started forward in his chair as though he was going to attack the two men.

Sharpe checked himself. He looked from the plump Mister Brown to the scrawny Mister Belling. "So there's nothing you can do?"

Mister Belling stared at the smoke-browned ceiling for a few seconds as though seeking inspiration, then shook his head. "There is nothing we can do," he pronounced, "but you might apply to His Majesty's government for a dispensation. I've not heard of such a course ever being followed, but an exception might be made?" He sounded very dubious. "There are senior officers, perchance, who would speak for you?"

Sharpe said nothing. He had saved Sir Arthur Wellesley's life in India, but he doubted whether the General would help him now. All Sharpe wanted was to sell his commission, take the £550 and get out of the army. But it seemed he could not sell his rank because he had not bought it.

"Such an appeal would take time," Mister Brown warned him, "and I would not be sanguine about the outcome, Mister Sharpe. You are asking the government to set a precedent and governments are chary of precedents."

"Indeed they are," Belling said, "and so they should be. Though in your case . . . ?" He smiled, raised his eyebrows, then sat back.

"In my case?" Sharpe asked, puzzled.

"I would not be sanguine," Mister Brown repeated.

"You're saying I'm buggered?" Sharpe asked.

"We are saying, Mister Sharpe, that we cannot assist you." Mister Brown spoke severely for he had been offended by Sharpe's language. "Alas."

Sharpe gazed at the two men. Take them both down, he thought. Two minutes of bloody violence and then strip their pockets bare. The bastards must have money. And he had three shillings and threepence halfpenny in his pouch. That was it. Three shillings and threepence halfpenny.

But it was not Brown or Belling's fault that he could not sell his commission. It was the rules. The regulations. The rich could make more money and the poor could go to hell. He stood, and the clatter of his saber scabbard on the chair made Mister Brown wince. Sharpe draped a damp greatcoat round his shoulders, crammed a shako onto his unruly hair and picked up his pack. "Good day," he said curtly, then ducked out of the door, letting in a gust of unseasonably cold air and rain.

Mister Belling let out a great sigh of relief. "You know who that was, Mister Brown?"

"He announced himself as Lieutenant Sharpe of the 95th Rifles," Mister Brown said, "and I have no reason to doubt him, do I?"

"The very same officer, Mister Brown, who lived, or should I say cohabited, with the Lady Grace Hale!"

Mister Brown's eyes widened. "No! I thought she took up with an

Ensign!" Mister Belling sighed. "In the Rifles, Mister Brown, there are no ensigns. He is a Second Lieutenant. Lowest of the low!"

Mister Brown stared at the closed door. " 'Pon my soul," he said softly, " 'pon my soul!" Here was something to tell Amelia when he got home! A scandal in the office! It had been whispered throughout London how the Lady Grace Hale, widow to a prominent man, had moved into a house with a common soldier. True, the common soldier was an officer, but not a proper officer. Not a man who had purchased his commission, but rather a sergeant who had earned a battlefield promotion, which was, in its way, entirely admirable, but even so! Lady Grace Hale, daughter of the Earl of Selby, living with a common soldier? And not just living with him, but having his baby! Or so the gossip said. The Hale family claimed the dead husband had been the child's father and the date of the baby's birth was conveniently within nine months of Lord William's death, but few believed it. "I thought the name was somehow familiar," Brown said.

"I scarcely credited it myself," Mister Belling admitted. "Can you imagine her ladyship enduring such a man? He's scarce more than a savage!"

"Did you note the scar on his face?"

"And when did he last shave?" Belling shuddered. "I fear he is not long for the army, Mister Brown. A curtailed career, would you not say?"

"Truncated, Mister Belling."

"Penniless, no doubt!"

"No doubt!" Brown said. "And he carried his own pack and greatcoat! An officer doesn't carry a pack! Never seen such a thing in all my years. And he was reeking of gin."

"He was?"

"Reeking!" Brown said. "Well, I never! So that's the fellow, is it? What was the Lady Grace thinking of? She must have been quite mad!" He jumped, startled because the door had been suddenly thrown open. "Mister Sharpe?" he said faintly, wondering if the tall rifleman had returned to exact vengeance for their unhelpfulness. "You forgot something, perhaps?"

Sharpe shook his head. "Today's Friday, isn't it?" he asked.

Mister Belling blinked. "It is, Mister Sharpe," he said feebly, "it is indeed."

"Friday," Mister Brown confirmed, "the very last day of July."

Sharpe, dark-eyed, tall and hard-faced, stared suspiciously at each of the two men in turn, then nodded reluctantly. "I thought it was," he said, then left again.

This time it was Brown who let out a sigh of relief as the door closed. "I cannot think," he said, "that promoting men from the ranks is a wise idea."

"It never lasts," Belling said consolingly, "they ain't suited to rank, Mister Brown, and they take to liquor and so run out of cash. There is no prudence in the lower sort of men. He'll be on the streets within the month, rely upon it, within the month."

"Poor fellow," Mister Brown said and shot the door's bolt. It was only five o'clock in the evening, and the office was supposed to remain open until six, but somehow it seemed prudent to shut up early. Just in case Sharpe came back. Just in case.

GRACE, SHARPE thought, Grace. God help me, Grace. God help me. Three shillings, three pence and a bloody halfpenny, all the money he had left in the world. What do I do now, Grace? He often talked to her. She was not there to listen, not now, but he still talked to her. She had taught him so much, she had encouraged him to read and tried to make him think, but nothing lasts. Nothing. "Bloody hell, Grace," he said aloud and men on the street gave him room, thinking him either mad or drunk. "Bloody hell." The anger was welling inside him, thick and dark, a fury that wanted to explode in violence or else drown itself in drink. Three shillings and threepence bloody halfpenny. He could get well drunk on that, but the ale and gin he had taken at midday was already sour in his belly. What he wanted was to hurt someone, anyone. Just a blind, desperate anger.

He had not planned it this way. He thought he would come to London, borrow an advance from an army agent, and then go away. Back to India, he had thought. Other men went there poor and came back rich. Sharpe the nabob and why not? Because he could not sell his rank, that was why not. Some snotty child with a rich father could buy and sell his rank, but a real soldier who had fought his way up the ladder could not. Bugger them all. So what now? Ebenezer Fairley, the merchant who had sailed with Sharpe from India, had offered him a job, and Sharpe supposed he could walk to Cheshire and beg from the man, but he had no urge to start that journey now. He just wanted to vent his anger and so, reassured that it was indeed Friday, he walked toward the Tower. The street stank of the river, coal smoke and horse dung. There was wealth in this part of London that lay so close to the docks and to the Custom House and to the big warehouses crammed with spices, tea and silks. This was a district of counting houses, bankers and merchants, a conduit for the world's wealth, but the money was not displayed. A few clerks hurried from one office to another, but there were no crossing sweepers and none of the signs of luxury that filled the elegant streets to the city's west. The buildings here were tall, dark and secret, and it was impossible to tell whether the gray-haired man scuttling with a ledger under his arm was a merchant prince or a worn-out clerk.

Sharpe turned down Tower Hill. There was a pair of red-coated sentries at the Tower's outer gate and they pretended not to see the saber scabbard protruding from Sharpe's greatcoat and he pretended not to see them. He did not care if they saluted him or not. He did not much care if he never saw the army again so long as he lived. He was a failure. Storekeeper to the regiment. A bloody quartermaster. He had come from India, where he had received a commission into a red-coated regiment, to England, where he had been placed in the greenjackets, and at first he had liked the Rifles, but then Grace had gone and everything went wrong. Yet it was not her fault. Sharpe blamed himself, but still did not understand why he had failed. The Rifles were a new kind of regiment, prizing skill and intelligence above blind discipline. They worked hard, rewarded progress and encouraged the men to think for themselves. Officers trained with the men, even drilled with them, and the hours that other regiments wasted in pipe-claying and stock-polishing, in boot-licking and tuft-brushing, the greenjackets spent in rifle practice. Men and officers competed against each other, all trying to make their own company the best. It was exactly the kind of regiment that Sharpe had dreamed of when he had been in India, and he had been recommended to it. "I hear you're just the sort of officer we want," Colonel Beckwith had greeted Sharpe, and the Colonel's welcome was heartfelt, for Sharpe brought the greenjackets a wealth of recent experience in battle, but in the end they did not want him. He did not fit. He could not make small talk. Perhaps he had frightened them. Most of the regiment's officers had spent the last years training on England's south coast, while Sharpe had been fighting in India. He had become bored with the training, and after Grace he had become bitter so that the Colonel had taken him away from number three company and put him in charge of the stores. Which was where most officers up from the ranks were placed in the hidebound, red-coated regiments, but the Rifles were supposed to be different.

Now the regiment had marched away, going to fight somewhere abroad, but Sharpe, the morose quartermaster, had been left behind. "It'll be a chance," Colonel Beckwith had told Sharpe, "to clean out the hutments. Give them a damn good scouring, eh? Have everything ready for our return."

"Yes, sir," Sharpe had said, and thought Beckwith could go to hell. Sharpe was a soldier, not a damned barracks cleaner, but he had hidden his anger as he watched the regiment march north. No one knew where it was going. Some said Spain, others said they were going to Stralsund, which was a British garrison on the Baltic, though why the British held a garrison on the southern coast of the Baltic no one could explain, and a few claimed the regiment was going to Holland. No one actually knew, but they all expected to fight and they marched in fine spirits. They were the greenjackets, a new regiment for a new century, but with no place for Richard Sharpe. So Sharpe had decided to run. Damn Beckwith, damn the greenjackets, damn the army and damn everything. He had reckoned he would sell his commission, take the money and find a new life. Except he could not sell because of the bloody regulations. God damn it, Grace, he thought, what do I do?

Only he knew what he was going to do. He was still going to run. Yet to start a new life he needed money, which was why he had made certain it was a Friday. Now he edged down the greasy stairs at the foot of Tower Hill and nodded to a waterman. "Wapping Steps," he said, settling in the boat's stern.

The waterman shoved off, letting the river current carry him downstream past Traitor's Gate. The masts were thick on either side of the river where ships and barges were double-berthed against wharves crudely protected by bulging fenders made of thick, twisted, tar-soaked rope. Sharpe knew those fenders. The worn-out ones had been carted to the foundling

home in Brewhouse Lane where the children had been made to disman-
tle the matted remnants of tar and hemp. At the age of nine, Sharpe
remembered, he had lost the nails on four of his fingers. It had been useless work. Teasing out the hemp strands with small bare and bloody
hands. The strands were sold as an alternative for the horsehair that stiffened the plaster used on walls. He looked at his hands now. Still rough,
he thought, but no longer black with tar and bloody with ripped nails.

"Recruiting?" the waterman asked.

"No."

The curt tone might have offended the waterman, but he shrugged it
off. "It ain't my business," he said, deftly using an oar to keep the boat
drifting straight, "but Wapping ain't healthy. Not to an officer, sir."

"I grew up there."

"Ah," the man said, giving Sharpe a puzzled look. "Going home,
then?"

"Going home," Sharpe agreed. The sky was leaden with cloud and
darkened further by the pall of smoke that threaded the spires and towers
and masts. A black sky over a black city, broken only by a jagged streak of
pink in the west. Going home, Sharpe thought. Friday evening. The
small rain pitted the river. Lights glimmered from portholes in the
berthed ships which stank of coal dust, sewage, whale oil and spices.
Gulls flew like white scraps in the early dark, wheeling and diving about
the heavy beam at Execution Dock, where the bodies of two men, muti-
neers or pirates, hung with broken necks.

"Watch yourself," the waterman said, skillfully nudging his skiff in
among the other boats at the Wapping Steps. He was not warning Sharpe
against the slippery flight of stairs, but against the folk who lived in the
huddled streets above.

Sharpe paid in coppers, then climbed up to the wharf which was
edged with low warehouses guarded by ragged dogs and cudgel-bearing
thugs. This place was safe enough, but once through the alley and into
the streets he was in hungry territory. He would be back in the gutter, but
it was his gutter, the place he had started and he felt no particular fear
of it.

"Colonel!" A whore called to him from behind a warehouse. She
lifted her skirt then spat a curse when Sharpe ignored her. A chained dog
lunged at him as he emerged onto High Street where a dozen small boys

whooped in derision at the sight of an army officer and fell into mocking step behind him. Sharpe let them follow for twenty paces, then whipped round fast and snatched the nearest boy's shabby coat, lifted and slammed him against the wall. Two of the other boys ran off, doubtless to fetch brothers or fathers. "Where's Maggie Joyce?" Sharpe asked the boy.

The child hesitated, wondering whether to be brave, then half grinned. "She's gone, mister."

"Gone where?"

"Seven Dials."

Sharpe believed him. Maggie was his one friend, or he hoped she was, but she must have had the sense to leave Wapping, though Sharpe doubted that the Seven Dials was much safer. But he had not come here to see Maggie. He had come here because it was Friday night and he was poor. "Who's the Master at the workhouse?" he asked.

The child looked really scared now. "The Master?" he whispered.

"Who is it, boy?"

"Jem Hocking, sir."

Sharpe put the lad down, took the halfpenny from his pocket and spun it down the street so that the boys pursued it between the people, dogs, carts and horses. Jem Hocking. That was the name he had hoped to hear. A name from a black past, a name that festered in Sharpe's memory as he walked down the center of the street so that no one emptied a slop bucket over his head. It was a summer evening, the cloud-hidden sun was still above the horizon, but it seemed like winter twilight here. The houses were black, their old bricks patched with crude timbers. Some had fallen down and were nothing but heaps of rubble. Cesspits stank. Dogs barked everywhere. In India the British officers had shuddered at the stench of the streets, but none had ever walked here. Even the worst street in India, Sharpe thought, was better than this fetid place where the people had pinched faces, sunk with hunger, but their eyes were bright enough, especially when they saw the pack in Sharpe's left hand. They saw a heavy pack, a saber, and assessed the value of the greatcoat draped like a cloak over his broad shoulders. There was more wealth on Sharpe than these folk saw in a half-dozen years, though Sharpe reckoned himself poor. He had been rich once. He had taken the jewels of the Tippoo Sultan, stripping them from the dying king's body in the shit-stinking tunnel of the water gate of Seringapatam, but those jewels were gone. Bloody lawyers. Bloody, bloody lawyers.

But if the folk saw the wealth on Sharpe they also saw that he was very tall and very strong and that his face was scarred and hard and bitter and forbidding. A man would have to be desperately hungry to risk his life in an attempt to steal Sharpe's coat or pack and so, like wolves that scented blood but feared losing their own, the men watched him pass and, though some followed him as he turned up Wapping Lane, they did not pursue him into Brewhouse Lane. The poorhouse and the foundling home were there and no one went close to those grim high walls unless they were forced.

Sharpe stood in the doorway of the old brewery, long closed down, and stared across the street at the workhouse walls. On the right was the poorhouse that mostly held folk too old to work, or else they were sick or had been abandoned by their children. Landlords turned them onto the street and the parish beadle brought them here, to Jem Hocking's kingdom, where the men were put in one ward and the women in the other. They died here, husbands forbidden to speak with their wives, and all half starved until their corpses were carried in a knacker's cart to a pauper's grave. That was the poorhouse, and it was divided from the foundling home by a narrow, three-story brick house with white-painted shutters and an elegant wrought-iron lantern suspended above its well-scrubbed front steps. The Master's house. Jem Hocking's small palace which overlooked the foundling home which, like the poorhouse, had its own gate: a black slab of heavy timber smeared with tar and surmounted with rusted iron spikes four inches long. A prison, really, for orphans. The magistrates sent pregnant girls here, girls too poor to have a home or too sick to sell their swollen bodies on the streets. Their bastards were born here and the girls, as often as not, died of the fever. Those that survived went back to the streets, leaving their children in the tender care of Jem Hocking and his wife.

It had been Sharpe's home once. And now it was Friday.

He crossed the street and hammered on the small wicket door set into the foundling home's larger gate. Grace had wanted to come here. She had listened to Sharpe's stories and believed she could change things, but there had never been time. So Sharpe would change things now. He lifted his hand to hammer again just as the wicket door opened to reveal a pale and anxious young man who flinched away from Sharpe's fist. "Who are you?" Sharpe demanded as he stepped through the small opening.

"Sir?" The young man had been expecting to ask that same question.

"Who are you?" Sharpe asked. "Come on, man, don't bloody dither! And where's the Master?"

"The Master's in his house, but . . ." The young man abandoned whatever he had been trying to say and instead attempted to stand in front of Sharpe. "You can't go in there, mister!"

"Why not?" Sharpe had crossed the small yard and now pushed open the door to the hall. When he had been a child he had thought it a vast room, big as a cathedral, but now it looked squalid and small. Scarce bigger than a company's barrack room, he realized. It was supper and some thirty or more children were sitting on the floor among the oakum and the tar-encrusted fenders that was their daily work. They scooped spoons in wooden bowls while another thirty children queued beside a table that held a cauldron of soup and a bread board. A woman, her red arms massive, stood behind the table while a young man, equipped with a riding crop, lolled on the hall's low dais above which a biblical text arched across the brown-painted wall. Be sure your sin will find you out.

Sixty pairs of eyes stared at Sharpe in astonishment. None of the children spoke for fear of the riding crop or a blow from the woman's burly arm. Sharpe did not speak either. He was staring at the room, smelling the tar and fighting against the overwhelming memories. It had been twenty years since he had last been under this roof. Twenty years. It smelt the same, though. It smelt of tar and fear and rotten food. He stepped to the table and sniffed the soup.

"Leek and barley gruel, sir." The woman, seeing the silver buttons and the black braid and the saber, dropped a clumsy curtsey.

"Looks like lukewarm water to me," Sharpe said.

"Leek and barley, sir."

Sharpe picked up a random piece of bread. Hard as brick. Hard as ship's biscuit.

"Sir?" The woman held out her hand. She was nervous. "The bread is counted, sir, counted."

Sharpe tossed it down. He was tempted to some extravagant gesture, but what would it do? Upsetting the cauldron merely meant the children would go hungry, while dropping the bread into the soup would achieve nothing. Grace would have known what to do. Her voice would have cracked like a whip and the workhouse servants would have been scurrying to fetch food, clothes and soap. But those things cost money and Sharpe only had a pocketful of copper.

"And what have we here?" a strong voice boomed from the hall door. "What has the east wind blown in today?" The children whimpered and went very still while the woman dropped another curtsey. Sharpe turned. "And who are you?" the man demanded. "Colonel of the regiment, are you?"

It was Jem Hocking. Come like the devil to the heart of hell.

He was no devil to look at. See Jem Hocking in the street and a man might take him for a prosperous farmer up from the Vale of Kent. The years had whitened his hair and stretched his checkered waistcoat taut across a bulging belly, but he was still a bull of a man with wide shoulders, stout legs and a face as flat as a shovel. Thick jowls hung beneath bushy white side whiskers, a golden watch chain held a dozen seals, his tall boots were tasseled, his dark-blue coat was edged with velvet cuffs and he carried a varnished black staff with a silver knob. He was the Master and for a moment Sharpe could not speak. He was overwhelmed by hatred, by the memories of this man's cruelty, even by fear. Twenty years and a battlefield commission had not taken away that fear. He wanted to imitate the children; he wanted to freeze, pretend not to exist, not even breathe in case he was noticed.

"Does I know you?" Hocking demanded. The big man was frowning, trying to discern something familiar in Sharpe's scarred face, but the memory would not come. He shook his head in puzzlement. "So who are you?"

"My name is Dunnett," Sharpe said, using the name of an officer in the greenjackets who held a particular dislike of Sharpe. "Major Warren Dunnett," he said, promoting Dunnett from captain.

"A major, eh? And what kind of uniform is that, Major? Red coats I know, and blue I've seen, but bless me, I ain't seen green and black." He stepped toward Sharpe, pushing the children's skinny legs out of the way with his beadle's staff. "Is it a new-fangled uniform, eh? Some kind of coat that gives a man the right to trespass on parish property?"

"I was looking for the Master," Sharpe said. "I was told he was a man of business."

"Business." Hocking spat the word. "And what business do you have, Major, other than the killing of the King's enemies?"

"You want me to talk about it here?" Sharpe asked. He took one of the pennies from his coat pocket and spun it toward the ceiling. It glittered as it flew, watched by hungry, astonished children, then fell into Sharpe's hand and vanished.

The sight of the money, even a humble penny, was all the reassurance Hocking needed. The rest of his questions could wait. "I has business outside the poorhouse tonight," he announced, "it being a Friday. You'll take an ale with me, Major?"

"That would be a pleasure, Master," Sharpe lied.

Or perhaps it was not a lie, for Sharpe was angry and revenge was a pleasure. And this revenge had been simmering in his dreams for twenty years. He glanced a last time at the text on the wall and wondered if Jem Hocking had ever considered the truth of it.

Be sure your sin will find you out.

Jem Hocking should have taken note and been on his knees in prayer.

Because Richard Sharpe had come home.

CHAPTER 2

THE TAVERN DISPLAYED NO name. There was not even a painted sign hanging outside, nothing, indeed, to distinguish it from the neighboring houses except, perhaps, a slight air of prosperity that stood out in Vinegar Street like a duchess in a whorehouse. Some folk called it Malone's Tavern because Beaky Malone had owned and run it, though Beaky had to be dead by now, and others called it the Vinegar Alehouse because it was in Vinegar Street, while some knew the house simply as the Master's because Jem Hocking did so much of his business in its taproom.

"I have interests," Jem Hocking said grandly, "beyond those of the mere parish. I am a man of parts, Major."

Meaning, Sharpe thought, that Hocking persecuted more than the workhouse inmates. He had become rich over the years, rich enough to own scores of houses in Wapping, and Friday night was when the tenants brought him the rent. Pennies only, but pennies added up, and Hocking received them in the taproom where they vanished into a leather bag while a cowed white-haired clerk made notes in a ledger. Two young men, both tall, strongly built and armed with cudgels, were the taproom's only other customers and they watched every transaction. "My mastiffs," Hocking had explained the two young men.

"A man of responsibility needs protection," Sharpe had said, using two of his three shillings to buy a flagon of ale. The girl brought four tankards. The clerk, it seemed, was not to be treated to Major Dunnett's largesse. Only Sharpe, Hocking and the two mastiffs were to drink.

"It takes a man of authority to recognize responsibility," Hocking said, then buried his face in the tankard for a few seconds. "What you are seeing, Major, is private business." He watched a thin woman offer some coppers to the clerk. "But in my parish duties," Hocking went on, watching the clerk count the coins, "I have responsibility for the disbursement of public funds and for the care of immortal souls. I take neither duty lightly, Major." The public funds were fourpence three farthing a day for each pauper out of which Jem Hocking managed to purloin twopence, while the rest was grudgingly spent on stale bread, onions, barley and oatmeal. The care of souls yielded no profit, but did not require any outlay either.

"You have a Board?" Sharpe asked, pouring himself and Hocking more ale.

"I have a Board of Visitors," Hocking agreed. He watched the ale being poured. "The law says we must. So we do."

"So where is the responsibility?" Sharpe asked. "With you? Or the Board?" He saw the question had offended Hocking. "I assume it is you, Master, but I have to be sure."

"With me," Hocking said grandly. "With me, Major. The Board is appointed by the parish and the parish, Major, is infested with bleeding orphans. And not just our own! Some even gets stranded here by the ships. Only last week the mudlarks found a girl child, if you can imagine such a thing." He shook his head and dipped his nose into the ale's froth while Sharpe imagined the mudlarks, men and women who combed the Thames foreshore at low tide in search of scraps fallen overboard, bringing a child to Brewhouse Lane. Poor child, to end with Hocking as a guardian. "The Board, Major," Hocking went on, "cannot cope with so many children. They confine themselves to a quarterly examination of the accounts which, you may be sure, add up to the exact penny, and the Board votes me an annual motion of thanks at Christmas time, but otherwise the Board ignores me. I am a man of business, Major, and I spare the parish the trouble of dealing with orphans. I have two score and sixteen of the little bastards in the house now, and what will the Board of Visitors do without me and Mrs. Hocking? We are a godsend to the parish." He held up a hand to check anything Sharpe might say. This was not to deflect a compliment, but rather because a thin young man had come from the tavern's back door to whisper in his ear. A raucous cheer sounded from behind the door. The cheers had been sounding ever since Sharpe had arrived in the tavern and he had pretended not to hear them. Now he ignored the young man who tipped a stream of coins into the clerk's leather bag, then gave Hocking a pile of grubby paper slips that vanished into the big man's pocket. "Business," Hocking said gruffly.

"In Lewes," Sharpe said, "the parish offers three pounds to anyone who will take an orphan out of the workhouse."

"If I had such cash, Major, I could strip Brewhouse Lane of the little bastards in five minutes." Hocking chuckled. "For a pound apiece! A pound! But we ain't a rich parish. We ain't Lewes. We ain't got the funds to palm the little bastards off onto others. No, we relies on others paying us!" He sank half the ale, then gave Sharpe a suspicious look. "So what does you want, Major?"

"Drummer boys," Sharpe said. The 95th did not employ drummer boys, but he doubted Jem Hocking understood that.

"Drummer boys," Hocking said. "I've got lads that could beat a drum. They ain't much good for anything, but they can beat a drum. But why come to me for them, Major? Why not go to Lewes? Why not get three pounds with every lad?"

"Because the Lewes Board of Visitors won't let the boys go to be soldiers."

"They won't?" Hocking could not hide his astonishment.

"There are women on the Board," Sharpe said.

"Ah, women!" Hocking exclaimed. He shook his head in exasperation and despair. "They'll be the end of common sense, women will. There are none on our Board, I warrant you that. Women!"

"And the Canterbury Board insists the boys go before a magistrate," Sharpe said.

"Canterbury?" Hocking was confused.

"We have a second battalion at Canterbury," Sharpe explained, "and we could get the boys from there, only the magistrates interfere."

Hocking was still confused. "Why wouldn't the bloody magistrates want boys to be soldiers?"

"The boys die," Sharpe said, "they die like bloody flies. You have to understand, Mister Hocking, that the Rifles are the troops nearest the enemy. Under their noses, we are, and the boys have to serve as cartridge carriers when they ain't drumming. Back and forth, they are, and somehow they seem to be targets. Bang, bang. Always killing boys, we are. Mind you, if they live, it's a fine life. They can become Chosen Men!"

"A rare opportunity," Hocking said, believing every word of Sharpe's nonsense. "And I can assure you, Major, there'll be no interference from Boards or magistrates here. None! You can take my word for it." He poured himself more ale. "So what are we talking about here?"

Sharpe leaned back, pretending to think. "Two battalions?" he suggested. "Twenty companies? Say we lose four boys a year to the enemy and another six die of fever or manage to grow up? Ten lads a year? They have to be eleven years old, or near enough to pass."

"Ten boys a year?" Hocking managed to hide his enthusiasm. "And you'd pay?"

"The army will pay, Mister Hocking."

"Aye, but how much? How much?"

"Two pounds apiece," Sharpe said. He was amazed at his own glibness. He had dreamed of this revenge, plotting it in his imagination without ever thinking he would actually work it, yet now the lines were slipping off his tongue with convincing ease.

Hocking stuffed a clay pipe with tobacco as he considered the offer. Twenty pounds a year was a fine sum, but a little too obvious. A little too tidy. He drew a candle toward him and lit the pipe. "The magistrates will want paying," he observed.

"You said there'd be no trouble from magistrates," Sharpe objected.

"That's because they'll be paid," Hocking pointed out, "and there'll be other costs, Major, other costs. Always are other costs." He blew a stream of smoke at the ceiling. "Have you talked to your Colonel about this?"

"I wouldn't be here otherwise."

Hocking nodded. Which meant Sharpe had negotiated a price with the Colonel, and Hocking was damned sure it was not two pounds a boy. Five pounds, more like, with the Colonel creaming a pair off the top and Sharpe taking a single. "Four pounds," Hocking said.

"Four!"

"I don't need you, Major," Hocking said. "I've got chimney sweeps who like my lads, and those that don't sweep chimneys can shovel up the pure." He meant they could collect dog turds that they delivered to the city's tanners who used the feces to cure leather. "Some boys go to sea," Hocking said grandly, "some sweep chimneys, some scoop shit, some die, and the rest go to the gallows. They're all scum, Major, but they're my scum, and if you wants them then you pays my price. And you will, you will."

"I will, why?"

"Because, Major, you don't need to come to Wapping to get boys. You can find lads anywhere, magistrates or no magistrates." Hocking turned his shrewd eyes on Sharpe. "No, Major, you came to me on purpose."

"I came to you for drummer boys," Sharpe said, "and no awkward magistrates and no one caring that so many die."

Hocking still stared at him. "Go on," he said.

Sharpe hesitated, then seemed to make up his mind. "And girls," he said.

"Ah." Hocking half smiled. He understood weakness and greed, and Sharpe, at last, was making sense.

"We hear—" Sharpe began.

"Who's we?"

"The Colonel and me."

"And who told you?" Hocking asked fiercely.

"No one told me," Sharpe said, "but someone told the Colonel. He sent me."

Hocking leaned back and pulled at his bushy side whiskers as he considered the answer. He found it plausible and nodded. "Your Colonel likes 'em young, eh?"

"We both do," Sharpe said, "young and untouched."

Hocking nodded again. "The boys will be four pounds apiece and the girls ten a time."

Sharpe pretended to consider the price, then shrugged. "I want a taste tonight."

"Girl or boy?" Hocking leered.

"Girl," Sharpe said.

"You've got the money?"

Sharpe patted his pack which stood on the sawdust-strewn floor. "Guineas," he said.

Another cheer sounded behind the back door and Hocking jerked his head in that direction. "I've got business in there, Major, and it'll take me an hour or two to settle it. I'll have the girl cleaned up while you wait. But I want five pounds now."

Sharpe shook his head. "You'll see my money when I see the girl."

"Getting particular, are we?" Hocking sneered, though he did not insist on receiving any deposit. "What do you want, Major? A redhead? A blackbird? Fat? Skinny?"

"Just young," Sharpe said. He felt dirty even though he was merely pretending.

"She'll be young, Major," Hocking said and held out his hand to seal the bargain. Sharpe took the hand and suppressed a shudder when Hocking held on to it. Hocking gripped hard, frowning. "It's strange," he said, "but you do look familiar."

"I was raised in Yorkshire," Sharpe lied. "Maybe you were up there once?"

"I don't travel to foreign places." Hocking let go of Sharpe's hand and stood. "Joe here will show you where to wait, but if I was you, Major, I'd watch the dogs for a while."

Joe was one of the two young men and he jerked his head to show that Sharpe should follow him through the tavern's back door. Sharpe knew what to expect there, for when Beaky Malone had been alive Sharpe had helped in that back room which was little more than a long and gloomy shed raised above the yards of three houses. It stank of animals. There were storerooms at either end of the shed, but most of the space had been converted into a makeshift arena of banked wooden benches that enclosed a pit twelve feet in diameter. The pit's floor was sand and was surrounded by a barrier of planks.

"It's in there," Joe said, indicating one of the storerooms. "It ain't luxury, but there's a bed."

"I'll wait out here," Sharpe said.

"When the dogs are done," Joe explained, "wait in the room."

Sharpe climbed to the topmost bench where he sat close under the roof beams. Six oil lamps hung above the pit, which was spattered with blood. The shed stank of it, and of gin, tobacco and meat pies. There must have been a hundred men on the benches and a handful of women. Some of the spectators watched Sharpe as he climbed the steps. He did not fit in here and the silver buttons of his uniform coat made them nervous. All uniforms unsettled these folk, and spectators made room for him on the bench just as a tall man with a hooked nose climbed over the plank barrier. "The next bout, ladies and gentlemen," the man bellowed, "is between Priscilla, a two-year-old bitch, and Nobleman, a dog of three years. Priscilla is by way of being the property of Mister Philip Machin"—the name provoked a huge cheer—"while Nobleman," the man went on when there was silence, "was bred by Mister Roger Collis. You may place your wagers, gentlemen and ladies, and I do bids you all good fortune."

A boy climbed to Sharpe's bench, wanting to take his money, but Sharpe waved the lad away. Jem Hocking had appeared on a lower bench now and the wagers were being carried to his clerk. Another man, as thin as the ringmaster, threaded his way up the crowded benches to sit beside Sharpe. He looked about thirty, had hooded eyes, long hair and a flamboyant red handkerchief knotted about his skinny neck. He slid a knife from inside a boot and began cleaning his fingernails. "Lumpy wants to know who the hell you are, Colonel," he said.

"Who's Lumpy?" Sharpe asked.

"Him." The thin man nodded at the ringmaster.

"Beaky's son?"

The man gave Sharpe a very suspicious look. "How would you know that, Colonel?"

"Because he looks like Beaky," Sharpe said, "and you're Dan Pierce. Your mother lived in Shadwell and she only had one leg, but that never stopped her whoring, did it?" The knife was suddenly just beneath Sharpe's ribs, its point pricking his skin. Sharpe turned and looked at Pierce. "You'd kill an old friend, Dan?"

Pierce stared at Sharpe. "You're not . . ." he began, then checked. The knife was still in Sharpe's side. "No," Pierce said, not trusting his suspicions.

Sharpe grinned. "You and me, Dan? We used to run errands for Beaky." He turned and looked at the ring where the dog and the bitch were being paraded. The bitch was excited, straining at the leash as she was led about the ring. "She looks lively," Sharpe said.

"A lovely little killer," Pierce declared, "quick as a fish, she is."

"But too lively," Sharpe said. "She'll waste effort."

"You're Dick Sharpe, aren't you?" The knife vanished.

"Jem doesn't know who I am," Sharpe said, "and I want it to stay that way."

"I'll not tell the bastard. Is it really you?"

Sharpe nodded.

"An officer?"

Sharpe nodded again.

Pierce laughed. "Bloody hell. England's run out of gentlemen?"

Sharpe smiled. "That's about it, Dan. Have you got money on the bitch?"

"The dog," Pierce said. "He's good and steady." He stared at Sharpe. "You really are Dick Sharpe."

"I really am," Sharpe said, though it had been twenty years since he had last been in this rat pit. Beaky Malone had always prophesied that Sharpe would end up on the gallows, but somehow he had survived. He had run from London, gone to Yorkshire, murdered, joined the army to escape the law and there found a home. He had been promoted until, one hot day on a dusty battlefield in India, he had become an officer. Sharpe had come from this gutter and earned the King's commission and now he was going back. The army did not want him, so he would say goodbye to the army, but first he needed money.

He watched as the timekeeper held up a great turnip watch. A coin had been tossed and the bitch was to fight first. The dog was lifted out of the ring and two cages were handed across the planks. A small boy unlatched the cages, tipped them, then vaulted the planks.

Thirty-six rats scuttled about the sand.

"Are you up and ready?" the ringmaster shouted. The crowd cheered.

"Five seconds!" the timekeeper, a drunken schoolmaster, called, then peered at his watch. "Now!"

The bitch was released and Sharpe and Pierce leaned forward. The bitch was good. The first two rats died before the others even realized a predator was among them. She nipped them by the neck, shook them vigorously and dropped them promptly, but then her excitement overtook her and she wasted valuable seconds snapping at three or four rats in turn. "Shake them!" her owner bawled, his voice lost in the crowd's cheers. She ran into a knot of the rats and started working again, ignoring the beasts that attacked her, but then she would not let go of a big black victim.

"Drop it! Dead 'un!" her owner screamed. "Drop it! Drop it, you bastard bitch! It's a dead 'un!"

"She's too young," Pierce said. "I told Phil to give her another six months. Let her practice, I said, but he wouldn't listen. Cloth ears, that's his problem." He stared at Sharpe. "I can't believe it. Dick Sharpe a bloody jack pudding." He meant officer, for a jack pudding was a motley fool from the fairground, a clown dressed in fake finery and with donkey's ears pinned to his hair. "Hocking didn't recognize you?"

"I don't want him to either."

"I won't tell the bastard," Pierce said, then settled back to watch the bitch hunt the last few rats. The sand was speckled with fresh blood. A few of the rats were merely crippled and those who had wagered on the bitch were shouting at her to finish them off. "I thought when I first saw her," Pierce said, "that she'd hunt like her mother did. Christ, but that bitch was a cold-hearted killer. But this one's too young. She'll get better." He watched her kill a rat that had been particularly elusive. She shook it hard, spraying blood onto the customers closest to the barrier. "It ain't the teeth that kills 'em," Pierce said, "but the shaking."

"I know."

" 'Course you do, 'course you do." Pierce watched as the boy climbed into the ring and shoved the bloodied rats into a sack. "Lumpy's still trying to sell the corpses," he said. "You'd think someone would want to eat them. Nothing wrong with rat pie, especially if you don't know what it is. But he can't sell 'em." He looked down at Jem Hocking. "Is there to be trouble?"

"Would you mind?"

Pierce picked at a tooth with a long fingernail. "No," he said curtly, "and Lumpy will be pleased. He wants to run the book here, but Hocking won't let him."

"Won't let him?"

"Hocking owns the place now," Pierce said. "He owns every house in the street, the bastard." Two more cages had been tipped into the arena and the new rats, black and slick, scampered about the ring as a roar from the crowd greeted the dog. It was held above the skittering sand for a second, then dropped and began to fight. It went about its business efficiently and Pierce grinned. "Jem's going to lose his shirt on this one."

The bitch had been good and quick, but the dog was old and

experienced. It killed swiftly and the crowd's cheers got louder. Most, it seemed, had bet on the dog and the pleasure of winning was doubled by the knowledge that Jem Hocking was about to lose. Except that Jem Hocking was not a man to lose. The dog had killed about twenty of the rats when suddenly a spectator on the front bench leaned forward and vomited over the barrier and the dog immediately ran to gobble up the half-digested meat pie. The owner screamed at it, the crowd jeered and Hocking's face showed nothing.

"Bastard," Pierce said.

"Old trick that," Sharpe said, leaning back. He fingered his saber's hilt. He did not like the weapon's curved blade which was too light to do real damage, but it was the official weapon of Rifle officers. He would have preferred one of the basket-hilted broadswords that the Scots carried into battle, but regulations were regulations and the greenjackets had insisted he equip himself properly. A sword or saber, they said, was merely decorative and an officer who was forced to use one in battle had already failed so it did not matter that the light cavalry saber was unhandy, but Sharpe had used enough swords in battle and he had never failed. Go into a breach, he had told Colonel Beckwith, and you'll be glad enough of a butchering sword, but the Colonel had shaken his head. "It is not the business of Rifle officers to be in the breach," he had said. "Our job is to be outside, killing from a distance. That is why we have rifles, not muskets." Not that any of it mattered to Sharpe now. He would make his money, resign his commission, sell the saber and forget the Rifles.

Lumpy closed the entertainment by announcing that the next evening would be a mixture of cockfighting and badger-baiting. They would be Essex badgers, he boasted, as though Essex gave the animals special fighting skills, though in truth it was simply the closest source to Wapping. The crowd streamed out and Sharpe went back to the storeroom. Dan Pierce went with him. "I wouldn't stay, Dan," Sharpe said. "Likely to be trouble."

"Trouble for you, Dick," Pierce tried to warn his old friend. "He's never on his own."

"I'll be all right. You can buy me an ale afterward."

Pierce left and Sharpe went into the stinking room. The badgers were all in wire cages stacked against one wall while the rest of the room was occupied by a table on which a dim oil lamp burned, and by an incongruous bed that was plump with sheets, blankets and pillows. Lumpy's girls, the ones who sold gin and hot pies, used the room for their other business, but it would suit Sharpe perfectly. He put his pack and greatcoat on the table, then unsheathed the saber which he placed on the badger cages with the hilt toward him. The beasts, pungent and sullen, stirred behind their wire.

He waited, listening to the sounds fading in the shed. A year ago he had been living in a house with eight rooms that he and Grace had rented close to Shorncliffe. He had fitted in with the battalion well enough then, for Grace had charmed the other officers, but why should he have ever thought it could last? It had been like a dream. Except Grace's brothers and their lawyers kept intruding on the dream, demanding she leave Sharpe, even offering her money if she did the decent thing, and other lawyers had tied up her dead husband's will in a tangle of words, delay and obfuscation. Get her out of your head, he told himself, but she would not leave and when the footsteps sounded outside the storeroom Sharpe's sight was blurred with tears. He brushed his eyes as the door opened.

Jem Hocking came in with the girl, leaving the door ajar with the two young men just outside. The child was thin, frightened, red-haired and pale. She glanced at Sharpe then began to cry silently. "This is Emily," Jem Hocking said, tugging the girl's hand. "The nice man wants to play games with you, ain't that right, Major?"

Sharpe nodded. The anger he was feeling was so huge that he did not trust himself to speak.

"I don't want her hurt bad," Hocking said. He had a face the color of beefsteak and a nose erupting with broken veins. "I want her back in one piece. Now, Major, the money?" He patted the satchel that was hanging from his shoulder. "Ten pounds."

"In the pack," Sharpe said, nodding at the table, "just open the top flap." Hocking turned to the table and Sharpe edged the door closed with his shoulder as he moved to Emily's side. He picked her up and placed her on the bed, then whipped the blanket up over her head. She cried aloud as she was smothered in woollen darkness and Hocking turned as Sharpe pulled the saber off the cage tops. Hocking opened his mouth, but the blade was already against his throat. "Not a word," Sharpe said.

He shot the door bolt. "All your money, Jem. Put the satchel on the table and empty your pockets into it."

Jem Hocking, despite the saber at his throat, did not look alarmed. "You're mad," he said calmly.

"Money, Jem, on the table."

Jem Hocking shook his head in puzzlement. This was his kingdom and it did not seem possible that anyone would dare challenge him. He took a deep breath, plainly intending to call for help, but the saber's tip was suddenly hard in the flesh of his neck, drawing a trickle of blood.

"On the table, Jem," Sharpe said, the softness of his voice belying the anger in his soul.

Hocking still did not obey. He frowned instead. "Do I know you?"

"No," Sharpe said.

"You ain't getting a penny of mine, son," Hocking said.

Sharpe twisted the blade. Hocking stepped back, but Sharpe kept the saber in his neck. He had only broken Hocking's skin, nothing more, but he pushed a little harder and twisted again. "Money," he said, "on the table."

"Daft as a pudding, boy," Hocking said. "You ain't going anywhere, not now. I've got lads out there and they'll cut you into tatters."

"Money," Sharpe said, and reinforced the demand by whipping the saber's tip twice across Hocking's face to leave long thin cuts in his cheeks and nose. Hocking looked astonished. He touched a finger to his cheek and seemed not to believe the blood he saw.

There was a knock on the door. "Mister Hocking?" a voice called.

"We're just settling the money," Sharpe shouted, "aren't we, Jem? On the table or I'll bloody fillet you."

"You ain't an officer, are you? You dress up, don't you, but you picked the wrong man this time, son."

"I'm an officer," Sharpe said, and drew blood from Hocking's neck. "A real officer," he added. "Now empty your pockets."

Hocking dropped the satchel on the table, then thrust a hand into his greatcoat pocket. Sharpe waited to hear the chink of coins, but there was no such sound and so, as Hocking brought his hand out of the pocket, Sharpe slashed down hard with the saber. He slit the ball of Hocking's thumb, then slashed the blade again and Hocking, who had been drawing a small pistol from his coat pocket, let the weapon go to clutch at his wounded fingers. The pistol fell to the floor.

"Empty your damned pockets," Sharpe said.

Hocking hesitated, wondering whether to call for help, but there was an implacability about Sharpe that suggested he had best humor him. He flinched as he used his wounded right hand to pull coins from his pocket. The door rattled as someone tried the latch. "Wait!" Sharpe called. He saw gold coins among the silver and copper. "Keep going, Jem," he said.

"You're a dead man," Hocking grumbled, but found more cash that he piled on the table. "That's all," he said.

"Back against the cages, you bastard," Sharpe said and prodded Hocking toward the badgers. Then, still holding the saber in his right hand, Sharpe forced handfuls of the coins into the satchel. He could not look closely at the money, for he needed to watch Hocking, but he reckoned there was at least eighteen or nineteen pounds there.

The click saved Sharpe. It came from behind him and he recognized the sound of a pistol being cocked and he stepped to one side and risked a quick glance to see that there was a hole in the wooden wall. Lumpy's peephole, no doubt, and one of the young men outside must have seen what was happening and Sharpe stepped to the bed just as a pistol flamed through the hole to mist the room with smoke. Emily screamed from beneath her blanket and Jem Hocking snatched a badger cage and hurled it at Sharpe.

The cage bounced heavily off Sharpe's shoulder. Hocking was scrabbling for the pistol when Sharpe kicked him in the face, then slashed the saber across his head. Hocking sprawled by the table. Sharpe snatched up the small pistol and fired it at the wall beside the peephole. The timber splintered, but no shout sounded on the far side. Then he knelt on Hocking's belly and held the saber against the big man's throat. "You do know me," Sharpe said. "You bloody do know me."

He had not intended to reveal his name. He had told himself he would rob Hocking, but now, smelling the gun smoke, he knew he had always wanted to kill the bastard. No, he had wanted more. He had wanted to see Hocking's face when the man learned that one of his children had come back, but come back as a jack pudding. Sharpe smiled, and for the first time there was fear on Hocking's face. "I really am an officer, Jem, and my name's Sharpe. Dick Sharpe." He saw the disbelief on Hocking's face. Disbelief, astonishment and fear. That was reward enough. Hocking stared, wide-eyed, recognizing Sharpe and, at the same time, unable to comprehend that one of his boys was now an officer. Then the incomprehension turned to terror for he understood that the boy wanted revenge. "You bastard," Sharpe said, "you goddamned piece of shit." The anger was livid now. "Remember whipping me?" he asked. "Whipping me till the blood ran? I remember, Jem. That's why I came back."

"Listen, lad."

"Don't you bloody lad me," Sharpe said. "I'm grown now, Jem. I'm a soldier, Jem, an officer, and I've learned to kill."

"No!"

"Yes," Sharpe said, and the bitterness was unassuageable now, drenching him, consuming him, and the years of pain and misery were driving his right arm as he sawed the blade hard and fast across Hocking's throat. Hocking's last shout was abruptly cut short as a fountain of blood sprang up. The big man heaved, but Sharpe was snarling and still slicing down with the blade, cutting through muscle and gullet and a flood of blood until the steel juddered against the bone. Hocking's breath bubbled at his opened neck as Sharpe stood and stabbed the saber down so hard that the blade flexed as its tip drove into the back of Hocking's skull. "One in the eye, Jem," Sharpe snarled, "you bastard." The door shook as the men outside tried to force the bolt from its seating. Sharpe kicked the door. "We ain't done," he shouted.

There was a sudden silence outside. But how many men were out there? And the two pistol shots would have been heard. Men would be watching the rat shed, knowing that there would be pickings to be had from the violence. Bloody fool, Sharpe told himself. Grace had forever told him he had to think before he let his anger rule his actions, and he had not really meant to kill Hocking, only to rob him. No, that was not true, he had wanted to kill Hocking for years, but he had done it clumsily, angrily, and now he was trapped. There were still some coins on the table, one of them a guinea, and he threw them onto the bed. "Emily?"

"Sir?" a small voice whimpered.

"That money's for you. Hide it. And stay hidden yourself now. Lie down."

Still silence outside, but that meant nothing. Sharpe blew out the oil lamp, then pulled on his coat and pack. He hung the satchel across his chest, dragged the saber free of Hocking's face, then went to the door and slid the bolt back as silently as he could. He lifted the latch and eased the door ajar. He reckoned the two men only had one pistol between them, but both would have knives and cudgels and he half expected them to charge when they saw the door crack open, but instead they waited. They knew Sharpe had to come out eventually and so they were waiting for him. He crouched and felt for the badger cage that had been thrown at him. He placed the cage beside the door and slid its hinged flap open.

A small light came from the shed's far end, just enough to reveal a heavy dark shadow that crept out of the cage and snuffled its way forward. It was a big beast that tried to turn back into the storeroom's darkness, but Sharpe nudged it with his saber tip and the animal lumbered out into the larger space.

The pistol banged, flashing the dark with searing light. The badger squealed, then a club broke its spine. Sharpe had pulled the door open and was through it before the men outside realized they were wasting effort on an animal. The saber hissed and one man yelped, then Sharpe scythed the blade back at the second man who ducked away. Sharpe did not wait, but ran to the back of the shed where he remembered an alley that led to a noxious ditch up which small lighters could be dragged from the Thames. One of the two men was following him, blundering in the shed's darkness. Sharpe shouldered the door open and ran down the alley. Two men were there, but both stepped aside when they saw the saber. Sharpe twisted right and ran toward the big warehouse where tobacco was stored and where, in his childhood, a gang of counterfeiters had forged their coins.

"Catch him!" a voice shouted and Sharpe heard a rush of feet.

He twisted into another alley. The shouting was loud now. Men were pursuing him, not to avenge Hocking whom they did not even know was dead, but because Sharpe was a stranger in their gutters. The wolves had found their courage and Sharpe ran, the saber in his hand, as the hue and cry filled the dark behind. The pack, greatcoat and satchel were heavy, the lanes were foot-clogging with mud and dung, and he knew he must find a lair soon, so he twisted into a narrow passage that ran past the Mint's great wall, twisted left, right, left again and at last saw a dark doorway where he could crouch and catch his breath. He listened as men pounded past the alley's entrance, then leaned back as the noise of the hunt faded northward.

He grimaced when he realized his jacket was soaked in blood. That must wait. For now he sheathed the saber, hid the scabbard beneath his greatcoat and then, with the pack in his hand, he went westward through alleys and lanes he half remembered from childhood. He felt safer as he passed the Tower where yellow lights flared through high narrow windows, but he constantly looked behind in case anyone followed. Most of his pursuers had stayed as a pack, but some cleverer ones might have stalked him more silently. By now they knew he was worth killing, not just for the value of his saber and his coat's silver buttons, but for the coins he had thieved from Hocking. He was any man's prey. The city streets were empty and twice he thought he heard footsteps behind him, but he saw no one. He went on west.

The streets became busier once he passed Temple Bar and he reckoned he was safer now, though he still looked back. He hurried along Fleet Street, then turned north into a confusing tangle of narrow alleys. It had begun to rain, he was tired. A crowd of men streamed from a tavern and Sharpe instinctively turned away from them, going into a wider street he recognized as High Holborn. He stopped there to catch his breath. Had he been followed?

Yellow light streamed from windows across the street. Go to Seven Dials, he thought, and find Maggie Joyce. The rain was coming down harder now, drumming on the roof of a parked carriage. Another carriage splashed by and its dim lamps showed a green-and-yellow painted board on the building with the glowing windows. Two watchmen, buttons shining on blue coats and with long staves in their hands, walked slowly past. Had the watch heard the hue and cry? They would be looking for a bloodstained army officer if they had and Sharpe decided he should go to earth. The carriage lamps had revealed that the tavern was the French Horn. The place had once been popular with the musicians from the theater in nearby Drury Lane, but more recently it had been bought by an old soldier who was partial to any officer who happened to be in town, and throughout the army it was now known as the Frog Prick.

Beefsteak, Sharpe thought. Steak and ale, a bed and a warm fire. He had wanted to leave the army, but he was still an officer, so the Frog Prick could welcome him. He hefted the pack, crossed the street and climbed the steps.

No one took any notice of him. Perhaps half the patrons in the half-filled taproom were officers, though many of those in civilian clothes might also have been in the army. Sharpe knew none of them. He found an empty table in a shadowed spot by the wall and dropped his pack and took off his rain-soaked coat. A red-haired woman whose apron straps were decorated with the shako plates of a dozen regiments acknowledged that the tavern had a bed to spare for the night. "But you'll have to share it," she went on, "and I'll thank you not to wake the gentleman when you go up there. He went to bed early." She suddenly grimaced as she realized there was blood on Sharpe's green jacket.

"A thief tried to take this," Sharpe explained, patting the satchel. "You can give me a pail of cold water?"

"You'll want something to clean your boots too?" she asked.

"And a pot of ale," Sharpe said, "and a steak. A thick one."

"Haven't seen many riflemen lately," the woman said. "I hear they're going abroad."

"I hear the same."

"Where to?" she asked.

"No one knows," he said.

She leaned close to him. "Copenhagen, sweetheart," she whispered, "and just make sure you come home in one piece."

"Copen—" Sharpe began.

"Shh." She put a finger to her lips. "You ever got a question about the army, darling, you come to the Frog Prick. We know the answers two days before the Horse Guards ask the questions." She grinned and walked away.

Sharpe opened the satchel and tried to guess how much cash was inside. At least twenty pounds, he reckoned. So crime does pay, he told himself, and shifted his chair so that his back was to the room. Twenty pounds. A man could make a good start in a new life with twenty pounds.

Twenty pounds! A decent night's work, he thought, though he was angry at himself for having botched the killing. He had been lucky to escape unscathed. He doubted he would be in trouble with the law, for Wapping folk were reluctant to call in the constables. Plenty of men had seen that it was a Rifle officer who had been with Hocking and who, presumably, had done the murder in the back of Beaky Malone's Tavern, but Sharpe doubted the law would care or even know. Hocking's body would be carried to the river and dumped on the ebbing tide to drift ashore at Dartford or Tilbury. Gulls would screech over his guts and peck out his remaining eye. No one would hang for Jem Hocking.

At least Sharpe hoped no one would hang for Jem Hocking.

But he was still a wanted man. He had run out of Wapping with a small fortune and there were plenty of men who would like to find him and take that fortune away. Hocking's mastiffs for a start, and they would look for him in just such a tavern as the Frog Prick. So stay here one night, he told himself, then get out of London for a while. Just as he made that decision there was a sudden commotion at the tavern door that made him fear his pursuers had already come for him, but it was only a boisterous group of men and women hurrying out of the rain. The men shook water from umbrellas and plucked cloaks from the women's shoulders. Sharpe suspected they had come from the nearby theater, for the women wore scandalously low-cut dresses and had heavily made-up faces. They were actresses, probably, while the men were all army officers, gaudy in scarlet coats, gold braid and red sashes, and Sharpe looked away before any could catch his eye. "Good liquor, I stoutly maintain," one of the red-coated officers called, "gives genius a better discerning!" That odd statement provoked a cheer. Tables and chairs were shifted to make room for the party which was evidently known to a score of men in the room. "You look in the pink of perfection, my dear," the officer told one of the women, and was mocked for his gallantry by his fellows.

Sharpe scowled at his ale. Grace had loved the theater, but it was not his world, not any more, so damn it, he thought. He would not be an officer much longer. He had money now, so he could go into the world and start again. He drank the ale, gulping it down, suddenly aware of how thirsty he was. He needed a wash. He needed to soak his jacket in cold water. All in good time, he thought. Bed first, sleep or try to sleep. Try to sleep instead of thinking about Grace, and in the morning think what to do with the rest of his life.

Then a heavy hand dropped on his shoulder. "I've been looking for you," a harsh voice said, "and here you are."

And Sharpe, trapped, could not move.

CHAPTER 3

"I NEVER FORGET A FACE," Major General Sir David Baird said. He had taken a step back, alarmed by the ferocity of the scowl with which Sharpe had greeted him. "It is Sharpe, isn't it?" Baird asked, but was now met with a stare of incomprehension. "Well, is it or isn't it?" Baird demanded brusquely.

Sharpe, recovering from his astonishment, nodded. "It is, sir."

"I helped save you from a flogging once, and now you're an officer. The Lord's providences are incomprehensible, Mister Sharpe."

"They are, sir."

Baird, a huge man, tall and muscled, was in a red uniform coat that was heavy with epaulettes and gold braid. He scowled at his companions, the group who had just arrived with wet umbrellas and painted women. "Those young men over there are aides to the Duke of York," he said, "and His Majesty insisted they take me to the theater. Why? I cannot tell. Have you ever been forced into a theater, Sharpe?"

"Once, sir." And everyone had stared at Grace and talked of her behind their hands and she had endured it, but wept afterward.

"*She Stoops to Conquer*, what kind of name for an entertainment is that?" Baird asked. "I was asleep by the end of the prologue so I've no idea. But I've been thinking of you lately, Mister Sharpe. Thinking of you and looking for you."

"For me, sir?" Sharpe could not hide his puzzlement.

"Is that blood on your coat? It is! Good God, man, don't tell me the bloody Frogs have landed."

"It was a thief, sir."

"Not another one? A captain of the Dirty Half Hundred was killed just two days ago, not a hundred yards from Piccadilly! It must have been footpads, the bastards. I hope you hurt the man?"

"I did, sir."

"Good." The General sat opposite Sharpe. "I heard you'd been commissioned. I congratulate you. You did a fine thing in India, Sharpe."

Sharpe blushed. "I did my duty, sir."

"But it was a hard duty, Sharpe, a very hard duty. Good God! Risking the Tippoo's cells? I spent enough time in that black bastard's hands not to wish it on another man. But the fellow's dead now, God be thanked."

"Indeed, sir," Sharpe said. He had killed the Tippoo himself, though he had never admitted it, and it had been the Tippoo's jewels that had made Sharpe a rich man. Once.

"And I keep hearing your name," Baird went on with an indecent relish. "Making scandal, eh?"

Sharpe winced at the accusation. "Was that what I was doing, sir?"

Baird was not a man to be delicate. "You were once a private soldier and she was the daughter of an earl. Yes, Sharpe, I'd say you were making scandal. So what happened?"

"She died, sir." Sharpe felt the tears threatening, so looked down at the table. The silence stretched and he felt an obscure need to fill it. "Childbirth, sir. A fever."

"And the child with her?"

"Yes, sir. A boy."

"Good Christ, man," Baird said bluffly, embarrassed by the tears that dropped onto the table. "You're young. There'll be others."

"Yes, sir."

"You!" This peremptory demand was to one of the serving girls. "A bottle of port and two glasses. And I'll take some cheese if you've anything edible."

"Lady Grace's family," Sharpe said, suddenly needing to tell the story, "claimed the child wasn't mine. Said it had been her husband's, and so the lawyers baked me in a pie. Took everything, they did, because the child died after its mother. They said it was the heir to her husband, see?"

His tears were flowing now. "I don't mind losing everything, sir, but I do mind losing her."

"Pull yourself together, man," Baird snapped. "Stop sniveling."

"I'm sorry, sir."

"The Lord giveth and the Lord taketh away," Baird said, "and you don't piddle away your damned life because you don't like His dispositions."

Sharpe sniffed and looked up into Baird's scarred face. "Piddling away my life?"

"I've been keeping an eye on you, Sharpe," Baird said. "D'you know how many lives you saved by blowing that mine in Seringapatam? Scores! And my life among them. If it weren't for you, Sharpe, I'd be dead." He emphasized this by stabbing Sharpe's chest with a big forefinger. "Dead and buried, d'you doubt it?"

Sharpe did not, but he said nothing. Baird had led the assault on the Tippoo Sultan's stronghold and the General had led from the front. The Scotsman would indeed be dead, Sharpe thought, if Sharpe, a private then, had not blown the mine that had been intended to trap and annihilate the storming party. Dust and stones, Sharpe remembered, and flame billowing down a sunlit street and the air filling with smoke and the noise rolling about him like a thousand trundling barrels, and then in the silence afterward that was not silent at all, the moaning and screaming and the pale flames crackling.

"Wellesley made you up, didn't he?" Baird asked.

"Yes, sir."

"Not like Wellesley to do a man a favor," the General observed sourly. "Tight-fisted, he is." Baird had never liked Sir Arthur Wellesley. "So why did he do it? For Seringapatam?"

"No, sir."

"Yes, sir, no, sir, what are you, Sharpe? A bloody schoolboy? Why did the man promote you?"

Sharpe shrugged. "I was useful to him, sir. At Assaye."

"Useful?"

"He was in trouble," Sharpe said. The General had been unhorsed, was surrounded and doomed, but Sergeant Sharpe had been there and it was the Indians who died instead.

"In trouble?" Baird sneered at Sharpe's modesty. "It must have been desperate trouble if it persuaded Wellesley to do you a favor. Though how much of a favor was it?" The question was a shrewd one and Sharpe did not try to answer it, but it seemed Baird knew the answer anyway. "Wallace wrote to me after you joined his regiment," the General went on, "and told me that you were a good soldier, but a bad officer."

Sharpe bridled. "I tried my best, sir." Wallace had been the commanding officer of the 74th, a Scottish regiment, and Sharpe had joined it after he had been commissioned by Sir Arthur Wellesley. It had been Wallace who had recommended Sharpe to the 95th, but Sharpe was no happier in the new regiment. Still a failure, he thought.

"Not easy, coming up from the ranks," Baird admitted. "But if Wallace says you're a good soldier, then that's a compliment. And I need a good soldier. I've been ordered to find a man who can look after himself in a difficult situation. Someone who ain't afraid of a fight. I remembered you, but wasn't sure where to find you. I should have known to look in the Frog Prick. Eat your steak, man. I can't abide good meat getting cold."

Sharpe finished the beef as the General's port and cheese were put on the table. He let Baird pour him a glass before he spoke again. "I was thinking of leaving the army, sir," he admitted.

Baird looked at him in disgust. "To do what?"

"I'll find work," Sharpe said. Maybe he would go to Ebenezer Fairley, the merchant who had shown him friendship on the voyage home from India, or perhaps he would thieve. That was how he had started in life. "I'll get by," he said belligerently.

Sir David Baird cut the cheese which crumbled under his knife. "There are three kinds of soldier, Sharpe," he said. "There are the damned useless ones, and God knows there's an endless supply of those. Then there are the good solid lads who get the job done, but would piss in their breeches if you didn't show them how their buttons worked. And then there's you and me. Soldiers' soldiers, that's who we are."

Sharpe looked skeptical. "A soldier's soldier?" he asked.

"We're the men who clean up after the parade, Sharpe. The carriages and kings go by, the bands play, the cavalry prances past like bloody fairies, and what's left is a mess of dung and litter. We clean it up. The politicians get the world into tangles, then ask their armies to make things right. We do their dirty work, Sharpe, and we're good at it. Very good. You might not be the best officer in King George's army, but you're a bloody fine soldier. And you like the life, don't tell me you don't."

"Being a quartermaster?" Sharpe sneered.

"Aye, that too. Someone has to do it, and as often as not they give it to a man up from the ranks." He glared at Sharpe and then, unexpectedly, grinned. "So you've fallen out with Colonel Beckwith too, have you?"

"I reckon so, sir, yes."

"How?"

Sharpe considered the question and decided it could not be answered truthfully. He could not say he did not fit into the mess, it was too vague, too self-pitying, so he answered with a half-truth. "They've marched off, sir, and left me to clean up the barracks. I've fought more battles than any of them, seen more enemies and killed more men than all of them put together, but that don't count. They don't want me, sir, so I'm getting out."

"Don't be such a bloody fool," Baird growled. "In a year or two, Sharpe, there's going to be enough war for every man jack in this army. So far all we've been doing is pissing around the edge of the French, but sooner or later we're going to have to tackle the bastards head-on. We'll need all the officers we can get then, and you'll have your chance. You might be a quartermaster now, but ten years from now you'll be leading a battalion, so just be patient."

"I'm not sure Colonel Beckwith will want me back, sir. I'm not supposed to be in London. I'm supposed to be at Shorncliffe."

"Beckwith will do what I tell him," Baird growled, "and I'll tell him to kiss your bum if you do this job for me."

Sharpe liked Baird. Most soldiers liked Baird. He might be a general, but he was as tough as any man in the ranks. He could outswear the sergeants, outmarch the Rifles and outfight any man in green or scarlet. He was a fighter, not a bureaucrat. He had risen high enough in the army, but there were rumors that he had enemies higher still, men who disliked his bluntness. "What kind of job, sir?" Sharpe asked.

"One where you might die, Sharpe," Baird said with relish. He drained his glass of port and poured another. "We're sending a guardsman to Copenhagen. Our interest in Copenhagen is supposed to be secret, but I dare say every French agent in London already knows it. This fellow is going there tomorrow and I want someone to keep him alive. He's not a real soldier, Sharpe, but an aide to the Duke of York. Not one of those"—he saw Sharpe glancing at the table of theatergoers—"but the same sort of creature. He's a courtier, Sharpe, not a soldier. You won't find a better man for standing sentinel over the royal piss pot, but you wouldn't want to follow him into a breach, not if you wanted to win."

"He's going tomorrow?" Sharpe asked.

"Aye, I know, short notice. We had another man ready to hold his hand, but he was the fellow who was murdered two days ago. So the Duke of York tells me to find a replacement. I thought of you, but didn't know where you were, then God sent me to the theater and I find you guzzling ale afterward. Well done, God. And you won't mind slitting a few Frog throats?"

"No, sir."

"Our bloody guardsman says he doesn't need a protector. Says there's no danger, but what does he know? And his master, the Duke, insists he takes a companion, someone who knows how to fight and, by God, Sharpe, you know how to fight. Almost as well as me!"

"Almost, sir," Sharpe agreed.

"So you're under orders, Sharpe." The General gripped the port bottle by the neck and pushed back his chair. "Are you sleeping here?"

"Yes, sir."

"So am I, and I've got a carriage coming at seven o'clock to take us to Harwich." Baird stood, then paused. "It's a strange thing, Sharpe, but if you do your job properly you'll stop a war. Odd thing for a soldier to do, don't you think? Where's our advancement if we can't fight? But all the same I doubt we'll be beating our swords into ploughshares any time soon, not unless the Frogs suddenly see sense. So till tomorrow, young man." Baird gave Sharpe a brusque nod and went back to his companions, while Sharpe, with a start of surprise, realized he had not been told why the guardsman was being sent to Copenhagen, nor been asked whether he was willing to go with him. Baird, it appeared, had taken his assent for granted, and Baird, Sharpe reckoned, was right, for, like it or not, he was a soldier.

THE GENERAL was in a foul mood at seven o'clock next morning. His aide, a Captain Gordon, mimed the cause of Baird's ill temper by tipping an imaginary bottle to his lips, thus cautioning Sharpe to tact. Sharpe kept silent, settling on the carriage's front seat, while Baird grumbled that London stank, the weather was wretched and the coach seats lumpy. The vehicle lurched as the inn servants strapped the General's luggage on the roof, then there was a further delay as a final passenger appeared and insisted that his own luggage be secured alongside Baird's. The newcomer was a civilian who looked about thirty years old. He was very thin and had a frail, birdlike face on which, astonishingly, a black velvet beauty patch was glued. He wore a silver coat edged with white lace and carried a gold-topped stick from which a silk handkerchief hung. His hair, black as gunpowder, had been smoothed with a perfumed oil and tied with a silver ribbon. He climbed into the coach and, without a word, sat opposite Sharpe. "You're late, my lord," Baird snapped.

The young man raised a gloved hand, fluttered his fingers as if to suggest Baird was being extremely tiresome and then closed his eyes. Baird, denied sport with his lordship, frowned at Sharpe instead. "There's still blood on the coat, Sharpe."

"Sorry, sir. Tried to wash it out." The carriage jerked forward.

"Can't have you going to Denmark in a bloody coat, man."

"One supposes, Sir David," Captain Gordon cut in smoothly, "that Lieutenant Sharpe will not be wearing uniform in Denmark. The object is secrecy."

"Object, my ass," the General said helpfully. "He's my nephew," he informed Sharpe, referring to Captain Gordon, "and talks like a bloody lawyer."

Gordon smiled. "Do you have civilian clothes, Sharpe?"

"I do, sir." Sharpe indicated his pack.

"I suggest you don them once you're aboard your ship," Gordon said.

" 'I suggest you don them.' " Baird mimicked his nephew's voice. "Bloody hellfire. Doesn't this bloody carriage move at all?"

"Traffic, Sir David," Gordon said emolliently. "Essex vegetables for the Saturday market."

"Essex bloody vegetables," the General complained. "I'm forced into a bloody theater, Gordon, then subjected to Essex vegetables. I should have you all shot." He closed his bloodshot eyes.

The carriage, drawn by six horses, went first to the Tower of London where, after Sir David had sworn at the sentries, they were allowed through the gates to discover a cart guarded by a dozen guardsmen who appeared to be under the command of a very tall and very good-looking man in a pale-blue coat, silk stock, white breeches and black boots. The young man bowed as Baird clambered down from the carriage. "I have the gold, Sir David."

"I should damn well hope you do," Sir David growled. "Is there a jakes in this damn place?"

"That way, sir." The young man pointed.

"This is Sharpe," Baird said harshly. "He's replacing Willsen, God rest his soul, and this"—Baird was talking to Sharpe now—"is the man you're keeping alive. Captain Lavisser, or should I say Captain and Major Lavisser? The bloody Guards need two ranks. Bloody fools."

Lavisser gave Sharpe a rather startled look when he heard that the rifleman was to replace the dead Willsen, but then, as the General went to find the lavatory, the guardsman smiled and his face, which had looked sour and cynical to Sharpe, was suddenly full of friendly charm. "So you're to be my companion?" he asked.

"So it seems, sir."

"Then I trust we shall be friends, Sharpe. With all my heart." Lavisser thrust out a hand. Sharpe took it clumsily, embarrassed by Lavisser's effusive friendliness. "Poor Willsen," the Captain went on, clasping Sharpe's hand in both of his. "To be murdered in the street! And he leaves a widow, it seems, and a daughter too. Just a child, just a child." He looked pained, then turned to see his guardsmen struggling to move a great wooden chest from the cart. "I think the gold should go inside the carriage," he suggested.

"Gold?" Sharpe asked.

Lavisser turned to him. "You've not been told the purpose of our journey?"

"I'm to keep you alive, sir, that's all I know."

"For which I shall be eternally grateful. But our purpose, Sharpe, is to carry gold to the Danes. Forty-three thousand guineas! We travel rich, eh?" Lavisser hauled open the carriage door, motioned his men to bring the chest of gold, then noticed the carriage's last passenger, the pale civilian in the silver coat. Lavisser looked astonished. "God, Pumps! Are you here?"

Pumps, if that was his real name, merely fluttered his fingers again, then shifted his elegantly booted feet as the gold was manhandled onto the carriage floor. An escort of twenty dragoons took their places ahead of the carriage, then Sir David Baird came back and complained that the chest took up all the coach's leg room. "I suppose we'll have to endure it," he grumbled, then rapped on the coach's roof to signal that the journey could begin.

The General's mood improved as the coach jolted through the soot-grimed orchards and vegetable fields about Hackney where a fitful sun chased shadows over woods and low hills. "You know Lord Pumphrey?" Baird asked Lavisser, indicating the frail young man who still seemed to be asleep.

"William and I were at Eton together," Lavisser answered.

Pumphrey opened his eyes, peered at Lavisser as though surprised to see him, shuddered and closed his eyes again.

"You and I should have been to Eton," Baird said to Sharpe. "We'd have learned useful things, like which side of the pot to piss in. Did you have breakfast, Lavisser?"

"The Lieutenant of the Tower was very hospitable, thank you, sir."

"They like guardsmen in the Tower," Baird said, implying that real soldiers would not be so welcome. "Captain Lavisser"—he spoke to Sharpe now—"is an aide to the Duke of York. I told you that, didn't I? But did I tell you how useless His Royal Highness is? Bloody man thinks he's a soldier. He buggered up his campaign in Holland in '99 and now he's Commander in Chief. That's what happens to you, Sharpe, when you're the King's son. Fortunately"—Baird, who was plainly enjoying himself, turned to Lavisser—"fortunately for you royal camp-followers the army has still got one or two real soldiers. Lieutenant Sharpe is one of them. He's a rifleman in case you don't recognize that bloodstained green rag, and he's a thug."

Lavisser, who had taken no offense as his master was insulted, looked puzzled. "He's a what, sir?"

"You weren't in India, were you?" Sir David asked, making the question sound like an accusation. "A thug, Lavisser, is a killer; a brute, conscienceless and efficient killer. I'm a thug, Lavisser, and so is Mister Sharpe. You are not, and nor are you, Gordon."

"I nightly give thanks to the Almighty for that providence," Baird's aide said happily.

"Sharpe's a good thug," Baird said. "He came up from the ranks and you don't do that by being delicate. Tell 'em what you did in Seringapatam, Sharpe."

"Must I, sir?"

"Yes," Baird insisted, so Sharpe told the story as briefly as he could. Lavisser listened politely, but Lord Pumphrey, whose presence was still a mystery to Sharpe, opened his eyes and paid very close attention, so close that he unsettled Sharpe. His lordship said nothing, however, when the lame tale was done.

Lavisser spoke instead. "You impress me, Mister Sharpe," he said fulsomely, "you impress me mightily." Sharpe did not know what to say, so he gazed out of the window at a small wheatfield that looked rain-beaten. Beyond the damp wheat stood a haystack, reminding him that Grace had died between haymaking and the harvest a year before. He felt a lump in his throat. God damn it, he thought, God damn it, would it never go? He could see her in his mind's eye, see her sitting on the terrace with her hands on her swollen belly, laughing at some poor jest. Oh, Christ, he thought, but let it pass.

He became aware that Sir David Baird was now talking about Copenhagen. The Danish King, it seemed, was mad, and the country was ruled instead by the Crown Prince. "Is it true you know him?" Baird demanded of Lavisser.

"The Crown Prince knows me, sir," Lavisser said carefully. "My grandfather is one of his chamberlains, so I have that introduction. And my master, the Duke, is his first cousin."

"That will be enough?"

"More than enough," Lavisser said firmly. Lord Pumphrey took a watch from his pocket, fumbled with the catch, consulted it and yawned.

"Boring you, my lord?" Baird growled.

"I am forever entertained by your company, Sir David," Lord Pumphrey said in a very high-pitched voice. He pronounced each word very distinctly, which imbued the statement with an odd authority. "I am enthralled by you," he added, tucking the watch away and closing his eyes.

"Bloody fool," Sir David muttered, then looked at Sharpe. "We're talking about the Danish fleet," he explained. "It's a damn great fleet that's holed up in Copenhagen and doing bugger all. Just moldering away. But the Frogs would like to get their damned hands on it and replace the ships we took from them at Trafalgar. So they're thinking of invading little Denmark and stealing their ships."

"And if the French do invade," Lavisser smoothly continued the General's explanation, "then they will dominate the entrance to the Baltic and so cut off Britain's trade. Denmark is neutral, of course, but such circumstances have hardly deterred Bonaparte in the past."

"It's the Danish fleet he's after," Baird insisted, "because the bloody man will use it to invade Britain. So we have to stop him stealing it."

"How do you do that, sir?" Sharpe asked.

Baird grinned greedily. "By stealing it first, of course. The Foreign Office have a fellow over there trying to persuade the Danish government to send their ships to British ports, but they're saying no. Captain Lavisser is going to change their minds."

"You can do that?" Sharpe asked him.

Lavisser shrugged. "I intend to bribe the Crown Prince, Sharpe." He patted the wooden chest. "We are carrying Danegeld, and we shall dazzle His Majesty with glitter and befuddle him with treasure."

Lord Pumphrey groaned. Everyone ignored him as Baird took up the explanation. "Captain Lavisser's going to bribe the Crown Prince, Sharpe, and if the Frogs catch wind of what he's doing they'll do their best to stop him. A knife in the back will do that very effectively, so your job is to protect Lavisser."

Sharpe felt no qualms at such a task, indeed he rather hoped he would get a chance to tangle with some Frenchmen. "What happens if the Danes won't give us the fleet, sir?" he asked Baird.

"Then we invade," the General said.

"Denmark?" Sharpe was astonished. The woman at the Frog Prick had suggested as much, but it still seemed surprising. Fighting Denmark? Denmark was not an enemy!

"Denmark," Baird confirmed. "Our fleet's ready and waiting in

Harwich, and the Danes, Sharpe, ain't got no choice. They either put their fleet under our protection or I'll bloody take it from them."

"You, sir?"

"Lord Cathcart's in charge," Baird allowed, "but he's an old woman. I'll be there, Sharpe, and God help the Danes if I am. And your friend Wellesley"—he said the name sourly—"is tagging along to see if he can learn something."

"He's no friend of mine, sir," Sharpe said. It was true that Wellesley had made him into an officer, but Sharpe had not seen the General since India. Nor did he relish any such meeting. Grace had been a cousin of Wellesley's, a very distant cousin, but disapproval of her behavior had spread into the furthest reaches of her aristocratic family.

"I'm your friend, Mister Sharpe," Baird said wolfishly, "and I don't mind admitting I want you to fail. A fight in Denmark? I could relish that. No more talk of a man who can only fight in India." The bitterness was naked. Baird felt he had been unfairly treated in India, mostly because Wellesley had been offered the preferments that Baird believed he deserved. No wonder he wanted war, Sharpe thought.

They reached Harwich in the evening. The fields surrounding the small port were filled with tented camps while the damp pastures were crammed with cavalry and artillery horses. Guns were parked in the town streets and were lined wheel to wheel on the stone quay where, beside a small pile of expensive leather baggage, a man as tall and broad as Baird stood waiting. The man was dressed in servant's black and Sharpe at first took him to be a laborer wanting a tip for carrying the baggage onto a boat, but then the man bowed his head to Lavisser who clapped him familiarly on the shoulder. "This is Barker," Lavisser told Sharpe, "my man. And this is Lieutenant Sharpe, Barker, who has replaced the unfortunate Willsen."

Barker turned a flat gaze on Sharpe. Another thug, Sharpe thought, a hardened, scarred and formidable thug. He nodded at the servant who did not return the greeting, but just looked away.

"Barker was a footpad, Sharpe," Lavisser said enthusiastically, "before I taught him manners and morals."

"Don't see why you need me," Sharpe said, "if you've got a footpad on your side."

"I doubt I do need you, Sharpe," Lavisser said, "but our masters insist

I have a protector, so come you must." He gave Sharpe another of his dazzling smiles.

A small crowd had gathered on the quay to gape at the fleet of great warships that lay in the river's mouth, while transports, frigates and brigs were either anchored or moored nearer the small harbor where a falling tide was exposing long stretches of mud. Closest to the quay were some ungainly ships, much smaller than frigates, with low freeboards and wide hulls. "Bomb ships," Gordon, Baird's nephew, remarked helpfully.

"They've got damn great mortars in their bellies," Baird explained, then turned to look at the modest town. "A dozen well-manned bomb ships could wipe Harwich off the earth in twenty minutes," the General said with unholy relish. "It will be interesting to see what they do to a city like Copenhagen."

"You would not bombard Copenhagen!" Captain Gordon sounded shocked.

"I'd bombard London if the King demanded it," Baird said.

"But not Edinburgh," Gordon murmured.

"You spoke, Gordon?"

"I remarked that time is getting short, sir. I'm sure Captain Lavisser and Lieutenant Sharpe should be embarking soon."

Their ship was a frigate, newly painted and moored closer to Felixstowe on the river's northern bank. "She's called the *Cleopatra*," Baird's aide said, and it was apparent that the frigate's crew had seen the carriage's arrival, for a ship's boat was now pulling across the river.

A score of officers from the tented camps had gathered lower down the quay and Sharpe saw some green jackets among the scarlet. He did not want to be recognized and so he hid himself behind a great pile of herring barrels and stared down at the mud where gulls strutted and fought over fish bones. He was suddenly cold. He did not want to go to sea, and he knew that was because he had met Grace on a ship. It was made worse because a country gentleman, come in his open carriage to see the ships, was telling his daughters which of the far fleet had been at Trafalgar.

"There, you see? The *Mars*? She was there."

"Which one is she, Papa?"

"The black-and-yellow one."

"They're all black and yellow, Papa. Like wasps."

Sharpe stared at the ships, half listening to the girls tease their father and trying not to think of Grace teasing him, when a precise and high-pitched voice spoke behind him. "Are you content, Lieutenant?"

Sharpe turned to see it was Lord Pumphrey, the young and taciturn civilian who had spoken so little during the journey. "My lord?"

"I first heard you were involved in this nonsense very late last night," Pumphrey said softly, "and I confess your qualities were quite unknown to me. I apologize for that, but I am not very familiar with the army list. My father once thought I should be a soldier, but he concluded I was both too clever and too delicate." He smiled at Sharpe who did not smile back. Lord Pumphrey sighed. "So I took the liberty of waking one or two acquaintances to discover something about you and they informed me that you are a most resourceful man."

"Am I, my lord?" Sharpe wondered who on earth he and Lord Pumphrey knew in common.

"I too have resources," Pumphrey went on. "I work for the Foreign Office, though, for the moment, I am reduced to serving as a civilian aide to Sir David. It quite opens one's eyes, seeing how the military operate. So, Lieutenant, are you content?"

Sharpe shrugged. "It all seems a bit abrupt, my lord, if that's what you mean."

"Distressingly abrupt!" Pumphrey agreed. He was so thin and frail that it looked as though a puff of wind would blow him off the quay and dump him in the filth below, but that apparent weakness was belied by his eyes which were very intelligent. He took out a snuff box, snapped open its lid and offered some to Sharpe. "You don't use it? I find it calming, and we rather need calm heads at present. This alarming excursion, Lieutenant, is being encouraged by the Duke of York. We at the Foreign Office, who might be expected to know rather more about Denmark than His Royal Highness, profoundly disapprove of the whole scheme, but the Duke, alas, has gained the support of the Prime Minister. Mister Canning wants the fleet and would rather avoid a campaign that will inevitably make Denmark into our enemy. He suggests, too, that a successful bribe will spare the Treasury the expense of such a campaign. These are cogent arguments, Lieutenant, do you not think?"

"If you say so, my lord."

"Cogent indeed, and quite egregiously muddle-headed. It will all end in tears, Lieutenant, which is why the Foreign Office in its ineffable wisdom has attached me to the Danish expedition. I am deputed to pick up the pieces, so to speak."

Sharpe wondered why his lordship wore a beauty patch on his cheek. It was a woman's affectation, not a man's, but Sharpe did not like to ask. Instead he watched two gulls squabble over some fish offal in the mud under the quay. "You think it won't work, my lord?"

Pumphrey gazed at the ships. "Shall I just say, Lieutenant, that nothing I have heard suggests that the Danish Crown Prince is venal?"

"Venal?" Sharpe asked.

A ghost of a smile showed on his lordship's face. "Nothing I have heard, Sharpe, suggests that the Crown Prince is a man amenable to bribery, and in consequence the Foreign Office is acutely concerned that the whole sorry affair might embarrass Britain."

"How?"

"Suppose the Crown Prince is offended by the offer of a bribe and announces the attempt to the world?"

"That doesn't seem so bad," Sharpe said dourly.

"It would be clumsy," Lord Pumphrey said severely, "and clumsiness is the grossest offense against good diplomacy. In truth we are bribing half the crowned heads of Europe, but we have to pretend it is not happening. But there's worse." He glanced behind to make sure no one was overhearing the conversation. "Captain Lavisser is known to be indebted. He plays steep at Almack's. Well, so do many others, but the fact of it is worrying."

Sharpe smiled down at the birdlike Pumphrey. "He's up to his ears in debt and you're sending him off with a chest full of money?"

"The Commander in Chief insists, the Prime Minister concurs and we at the Foreign Office cannot possibly suggest that the Honorable John Lavisser is anything other than scrupulously honest." Pumphrey said the last word very sourly, implying the opposite of what he had just stated. "We merely must tidy things up, Lieutenant, when the enthusiasm has died down. Nasty thing, enthusiasm. And if things do turn out ill then we would appreciate that no one was to know what happened. We don't want the Duke and the Prime Minister to look like complete fools, do we?"

"We don't, my lord?"

Lord Pumphrey shuddered at Sharpe's levity. "If Lavisser fails,

Lieutenant, then I want you to bring him and the money out of Copenhagen to the safety of our army. We do not want the Danish government announcing a failed and clumsy attempt at a bribe." He took a piece of paper from his pocket. "If you need assistance in Copenhagen then this man may provide it." He held the paper out to Sharpe, then pulled it back. "I have to tell you, Sharpe, that I have worried greatly about revealing this name to you. The man is valuable. I devoutly hope you won't need his help."

"What treason are you talking, my lord?" Baird demanded loudly.

"I was merely remarking on the beauty of the scene, Sir David," Lord Pumphrey observed in his high-pitched voice, "and noting to Lieutenant Sharpe the delicate tracery of the ships' rigging. I should like a chance to depict the scene in watercolors."

"Good God, man, leave that to the proper bloody artists!" Baird looked appalled. "That's what the idiots are for."

Lord Pumphrey pressed the piece of paper into Sharpe's hand. "Guard that name, Lieutenant," he said softly. "You alone possess it."

Meaning, Sharpe thought, that Lavisser had not been trusted with the man's name. "Thank you, my lord," he said, but Lord Pumphrey had already walked away for the *Cleopatra*'s launch had come to the jetty that gave access to the deep-water channel. The chest was being loaded into the launch's belly and Baird held out a hand to Lavisser. "I'll bid you farewell, God speed and good fortune," Baird said. "I'll allow I won't mind if you fail, but there's no point in real soldiers dying if a handful of gold can keep them alive." He shook Sharpe's hand. "Keep our guardsman alive, Sharpe."

"I will, sir."

The two officers did not speak as they were rowed out to the *Cleopatra* which, in her haste to use a favorable wind and tide, was already hauling her anchor. Sharpe could hear the chant of the seamen as they tramped round the capstan and see the quivering cable shedding drops of water and lumps of mud as it came from the gray river. The topmen were aloft, ready to drop the high sails. Sharpe and Lavisser scrambled up the ship's side to be met by the dutiful squeal of bosuns' whistles and by a harassed lieutenant who hurried them aft to the quarterdeck while the hulking Barker carried the baggage down below and a dozen seamen hauled a line to bring the gold on deck. "Captain Samuels begs to be excused while we get under way," the Lieutenant said, "and requests that you keep to the stern rail, gentlemen, until the sails are set."

Lavisser grinned as the Lieutenant hurried away. "Meaning that Captain Samuels don't want us in the way while he makes a muck of getting under sail. And he's under the eye of the Admiral, no less! Rather like setting the guard at Windsor Castle. I don't suppose you've ever done that, Sharpe? Placed a guard at Windsor?"

"I haven't, sir," Sharpe said.

"You do it perfectly, then some decrepit old fool who last saw action fighting against William the Conqueror informs you that Guardsman Bloggs has an ill-set flint in his musket. And for God's sake stop calling me 'sir,' " Lavisser said with a smile. "You make me feel old, and that's dreadful unkind of you. So what was on that piece of paper little William gave to you?"

"Little William?"

"Lord Pumps. He was a pallid little worm at Eton and he's no better now."

"It's just his address," Sharpe said. "He says I should report to him when I get back."

"Nonsense," Lavisser said, though he did not appear offended that Sharpe had lied to him. "If my guess is any good then it's the name of a man in Copenhagen who might help us, a name, I might add, that the suspicious bastards at the Foreign Office refused to give me. Divide and rule, that's the Foreign Office way. Aren't you going to tell me the name?"

"If I remember it," Sharpe said. "I threw the paper overboard."

Lavisser laughed at that untruth. "Don't tell me little Pumps told you to keep it secret! He did? Poor little Pumps, he sees conspiracy everywhere. Well, so long as one of us has the name I suppose it don't matter." He looked upward as the topsails were released. The canvas shook loudly until the seamen sheeted the sails home. Men slid down shrouds and scrambled along spars to loose the mainsails. It was all so very familiar to Sharpe after his long voyage home from India. Captain Samuels, heavy and tall, stood at the white line which marked off the quarterdeck from the rest of the flush-decked frigate. He said nothing, just watched his men.

"How long a voyage is it?" Sharpe asked Lavisser.

"A week? Ten days? Sometimes much longer. It all depends on Aeolus, our god of the winds. May he blow us swiftly and safely."

Sharpe grunted an acknowledgment, then just stared ashore where the herring smokers made a haze over the land. He leaned on the stern rail, suddenly wishing he was anywhere but at sea.

Lavisser leaned on the rail beside him. "You ain't happy, Sharpe," the guardsman said. Sharpe frowned at the words, which struck him as intrusive. He said nothing, but was acutely aware of Lavisser so close beside him. "Let me guess." The Guards Captain raised his eyes to the wheeling gulls and pretended to think for a while, then looked at Sharpe again. "My guess, Sharpe, is that you met Lady Grace Hale on shipboard and that you've not been afloat since." He held up a cautionary hand when he saw the anger in Sharpe's eyes. "My dear Sharpe, please don't mistake me. I feel for you, indeed I do. I met the Lady Grace once. Let me see? It must be a dozen years or more ago and I was only a sprat of fifteen, but I could spot a beauty even then. She was lovely."

Sharpe said nothing, just watched Lavisser.

"She was lovely and she was clever," the Guards Captain went on softly, "and then she was married off to a tedious old bore. And you, Sharpe, forgive my being forward, gave her a time of happiness. Isn't that something to remember with satisfaction?" Lavisser waited for Sharpe to respond, but the rifleman said nothing. "Am I right?" Lavisser asked gently.

"She left me in bloody misery," Sharpe admitted. "I can't seem to shake it. And, yes, being on a ship brings it back."

"Why should you shake it?" Lavisser asked. "My dear Sharpe, may I call you Richard? That's kind of you. My dear Richard, you should be in mourning. She deserves it. The greater the affection, the greater the mourning. And it's been cruel for you. All the gossip! It's no one's business what you and Lady Grace did."

"It was everyone's business," Sharpe said bitterly.

"And it will pass," Lavisser said gently. "Gossip is ephemeral, Richard, it vanishes like dew or smoke. Your grief remains, the rest of the world will forget. They've mostly forgotten already."

"You haven't."

Lavisser smiled. "I've been racking my brains all day trying to place you. It only came to me as we climbed aboard." A rush of feet interrupted them as seamen came aft to secure the mizzen sheets. The great sail banged above their heads, then was brought under control and the frigate picked up speed. Her ensign, blue because the fleet's commander was an Admiral of the Blue, flapped crisply in the evening wind. "The grief will pass, Richard," Lavisser went on in a low voice, "it will pass. I had a sister who died, a dear thing, and I grieved for her. It's not the same, I know, but we should not be ashamed of demonstrating our feelings. Not when it is grief for a lovely woman."

"It won't stop me doing my job," Sharpe said stoically, fighting off the tears that threatened.

"Of course it won't," Lavisser said fervently, "nor, I trust, will it stop you from enjoying the fleshpots of Copenhagen. They are meager and few, I can assure you, but such as they are we shall enjoy."

"I can't afford fleshpots," Sharpe said.

"Don't be so dull, Richard! We're sailing with forty-three thousand of the government's guineas and I intend to steal as many of them as I decently can without getting caught." He smiled so broadly and with such infectious enjoyment that Sharpe had to laugh. "There!" Lavisser said. "You see I shall be good for you!"

"I hope so," Sharpe replied. He was watching the *Cleopatra*'s rippling wake. The tide was ebbing and the wind was out of the west so that the anchored ships presented their sterns to the frigate's quarterdeck. The ugly bomb ships sat low in the water. One was called *Thunder*, another *Vesuvius*, then there was *Aetna* with *Zebra* close by. The frigate sailed so close to *Zebra* that Sharpe could look down into her welldeck which was stuffed with what looked like coils of rope, put there to cushion the shock of the two great mortars that squatted in the ship's belly. The mortars were capped with tompions, but Sharpe guessed they threw a shell about a foot across and, because the flash of their firing would blast up into the air to lob the bombs in a high arc, the forward stays of the *Zebra* were not made of hemp, but of thick chain. Another eight guns, carronades by the look of them, were mounted aft of the mainmast. An ugly vessel, Sharpe thought, but a brute with massive teeth, and there were sixteen of the bomb ships moored or anchored in the river, along with a host of gun brigs that were shallow-draft vessels armed with heavy cannon. These were not ships designed to fight other ships, but to hammer targets ashore.

The *Cleopatra* was picking up speed now as the crew trimmed the big sails. She leaned to larboard and the water began to gurgle and seethe at her stern. The dusk was drawing in, shadowing the big seventy-fours that were the workhorses of the British fleet. Sharpe recognized some of the ships' names from Trafalgar: the *Mars*, the *Minotaur*, the *Orion* and the *Agamemnon*, but most he had never seen before. The *Goliath*, belying her name, was dwarfed by the *Prince of Wales*, a 98-gun monster which flew the Admiral's pennant. A gunport opened at the *Prince of Wales*'s bow to return the salute that the *Cleopatra* was firing as she passed. The sound of the guns was huge, the smoke thick and the tremor of the cannon, even though they were unshotted, shook the deck beneath Sharpe's feet.

Only one ship, another seventy-four, lay beyond the *Prince of Wales*. She was a good-looking ship and Sharpe had learned enough in his voyage home from India to recognize that she was French-built, one of the many ships that had been captured from the enemy. Water gushed from her pumps as the *Cleopatra* sailed by and Sharpe looked up to see men pausing in their work to watch the sleek frigate pass. Then the *Cleopatra* left the seventy-four behind and Sharpe could read the gold-painted name scrolled across her stern. *Pucelle*. His heart leaped. The *Pucelle*! His own ship, the ship he had been aboard at Trafalgar and which was captained by his friend, Joel Chase, though whether Chase was still a captain, or aboard the *Pucelle* or even alive, Sharpe did not know. He just knew that he and Grace had known happiness on board the ship that had been named by her French builders for Joan of Arc, *la pucelle* or the virgin. He wanted to wave at the ship, but it was too far for him to recognize anyone aboard.

"You're welcome, gentlemen." Captain Samuels, dark-faced, gray-haired and scowling, had come to greet his guests. "Lieutenant Dunbar will show you your quarters." He frowned at Sharpe, who had turned to stare at the *Pucelle* again. "You find my remarks tedious, Lieutenant?"

"I'm sorry, sir. I was aboard that ship once."

"The *Pucelle*?"

"Didn't she take the *Revenant* at Trafalgar, sir?"

"What if she did? There were easy pickings at that battle, Lieutenant." The envy of a man who had not sailed with Nelson was naked in Samuels's voice.

"You were there, sir?" Sharpe asked, knowing it would needle the Captain.

"I was not, but nor were you, Lieutenant, and now you will show me the courtesy of remarking my words." He went on to tell them the rules of the ship, that they were not to smoke aboard, not to climb the rigging and that they must salute the quarterdeck. "You will take your meals in the officers' mess and I'll thank you not to get in the crew's way. I'll do my duty, God knows, but that doesn't mean I must like it. I'm to put you and your damned cargo ashore by stealth and that I'll do, but I'll be glad to see the back of you both and get back to some proper sailoring." He left them as abruptly as he had come.

"I do love feeling welcome," Lavisser murmured.

Sharpe stared aft again, but the *Pucelle* was lost in the dark loom of the land. She was gone and he was sailing away again. Sailing to a war, or to stop a war, or to be tangled in treachery, but whatever it was, he was still a soldier.

SHARPE WAS a soldier without weapons. He had come aboard the *Cleopatra* with his official-issue saber, but nothing else. Nothing useful. He complained of it to Lavisser who said Sharpe could be amply supplied in Vygård. "It's the house where my mother grew up and it's rather beautiful." He sounded wistful. "My grandfather has anything you might need; pistols, swords, everything, though I truly doubt we'll encounter trouble. I'm sure the French do have agents in Copenhagen, but they're hardly likely to try murder."

"Where's Vygård?" Sharpe asked.

"Near Køge where our hospitable Captain is supposed to put us ashore." They were eleven days out of Harwich, sailing a sunlit sea. Lavisser was leaning on the stern rail where he looked as though he did not have a care in the world. He wore no hat and his golden hair lifted in the wind. He had blue eyes and a sharp-cut face, so that he looked like one of his Viking ancestors who had sailed this same cold sea. "You really won't need weapons, Richard," Lavisser went on. "We'll simply borrow a carriage from Vygård to carry the gold to Copenhagen, conclude our business with the Crown Prince and so have the satisfaction of preserving peace."

Lavisser had spoken confidently, but Sharpe recalled Lord Pumphrey's doubts that the Danish Crown Prince was a man open to bribery. "What if the Crown Prince refuses?" he asked.

"He won't," Lavisser said. "My grandfather is his chamberlain and he tells me that the bribe is the Prince's own suggestion." He smiled. "He needs money, Sharpe, to rebuild the Christiansborg Palace that got burned down a few years back. It will all be very easy and we shall go home as heroes. Where's the danger? There are no Frogs in Vygård, none in my grandfather's town house in Bredgade, and the Prince's own guards will keep the bastards well out of our way. You really do not need weapons, Richard. Indeed, I don't wish to offend you, but your own presence, though utterly welcome, is also superfluous."

"Things can go wrong," Sharpe said stubbornly.

"How very true. An earthquake could devastate Copenhagen. Maybe there will be a plague of toads. Perhaps the four horsemen of the apocalypse will ravage Denmark. Richard! I'm going home. I'm calling on a prince to whom I am distantly related. Like me, he's half English. Did you know that? His mother is King George's sister."

Lavisser was persuasive, but Sharpe felt naked without proper weapons, and other men who were senior to Lavisser had thought it wise to give the guardsman protection, and so Sharpe went below to the tiny cabin that he shared with Lavisser and there pulled open his pack. His civilian clothes were inside, the good clothes that Grace had bought for him, along with the telescope that had been a grudging gift from Sir Arthur Wellesley. But at the very bottom of the canvas pack, hidden and half forgotten, was his old picklock. He pulled it out, then unfolded the slightly rusting picks. Grace had discovered it once and wondered what on earth it was. She had laughed in disbelief when he told her. "You could be hanged for possessing such a thing!" she had declared.

"I keep it for old times' sake," Sharpe had explained lamely.

"You've never used it, surely?"

"Of course I've used it!"

"Show me! Show me!"

He had shown her how to pick a lock, a thing he had done scores of times in the past. He was out of practice now, but the picks still made brief work of the padlock which secured the great chest in which the government money was stored. There were plenty of weapons on board the *Cleopatra*, but to get some Sharpe knew he would have to cross some tar-stained hands with gold.

Sharpe had money of his own. He had taken twenty-four pounds, eight shillings and fourpence halfpenny from Jem Hocking and the bulk of that had been in coppers and small silver which Sergeant Matthew Standfast, the new owner of the Frog Prick, had been happy to exchange for gold. "At a price, sir," Standfast had insisted.

"A price?"

"Filthy stuff!" Standfast had poked the grimy coppers. "I'll have to boil them in vinegar! What have you been doing, Lieutenant? Robbing poor boxes?" He had exchanged the twenty-four pounds, eight shillings and fourpence halfpenny for twenty-two shining guineas that were now safely wrapped in one of Sharpe's spare shirts.

He could have used his own money to get weapons, but he did not see why he should. Britain was sending him to Denmark and it was Britain's enemies who threatened Lavisser, so Britain, Sharpe reckoned, should pay, and that meant taking gold from the big chest that half filled the cabin that Sharpe and Lavisser shared. Sharpe had to edge one of the hanging cot beds aside to open the chest's lid. Inside were layers of gray canvas bags secured with wire ties that were sealed with crimped lead tags blobbed with red wax. Sharpe lifted three bags from the top layer and selected a lower bag that he slit with his knife.

Guineas. The golden horsemen of Saint George. Sharpe lifted one, looking at the image of the saint lancing the writhing dragon. Rich, thick, gold coins, and the chest had enough to suborn a kingdom, but it could spare a little for Lieutenant Sharpe and so he stole fifteen of the heavy coins that he secreted in his pockets before restoring the bags. He was just putting the last one in place when there was the thud of feet dropping down the companionway ladder immediately outside the cabin. Sharpe closed the chest lid and sat on it to hide the absence of a padlock. The cabin door opened and Barker came in with a bucket. He saw Sharpe and paused.

Sharpe pretended to be pulling on his boots. He looked up at the hulking Barker who had to stoop beneath the beams. "So you were a foot-pad, Barker?"

"That's what the Captain told you." Barker put the bucket down.

"Where?" Sharpe asked.

Barker hesitated, as if suspecting a trap in the question, then shrugged. "Bristol."

"Don't know it," Sharpe said airily. "And now you're reformed?"

"Am I?"

"Are you?"

Barker grimaced. "I'm looking for Mister Lavisser's coat."

Sharpe could see the padlock in a corner of the cabin and hoped Barker did not notice it. "So what will you do if the French interfere with us?"

Barker scowled at Sharpe. It seemed as if he had not understood the question, or else he just hated talking to Sharpe, but then he sneered. "How will they even know we're there? The master speaks Danish and you and I will keep our gobs shut." He plucked a coat from a hook on the back of the door and left without another word.

Sharpe waited for his steps to fade, then restored the padlock to the hasp. He did not like Barker and the feeling was evidently mutual. On the face of it the man made a strange servant for Lavisser, yet Sharpe had met plenty of gentlemen who liked to mix with brutes from the gutter. Such men enjoyed listening to the stories and felt flattered by the friendships, and presumably Lavisser shared their taste. Maybe, Sharpe reflected, that explained why Lavisser was being so friendly to himself.

Next day he used two of the guineas to bribe the ship's Master-at-Arms who made the gold vanish into a pocket with the speed of a con-jurer and an hour later brought Sharpe a well-honed cutlass and two heavy sea-service pistols with a bag of cartridges. "I'd be obliged, sir, if Captain Samuels didn't know about this," the Master-at-Arms said, "on account that he's a flogger when he's aggravated. Keep 'em hidden till you're ashore, sir." Sharpe promised he would. There would be no diffi-culty in keeping the promise during the voyage, but he did not see how he was to carry the weapons off the ship without Captain Samuels seeing them, then thought of the chest. He asked Lavisser to put them with the gold.

Lavisser laughed when he saw the cutlass and heavy-barreled guns. "You couldn't wait till we reached Vygârd?"

"I like to know I'm armed," Sharpe said.

"Armed? You'll look like Bluebeard if you carry that lot! But if it makes you happy, Richard, why not? Your happiness is my prime concern." Lavisser took the chest's key from a waistcoat pocket and raised the lid. "A sight to warm your chill heart, eh?" he said, indicating the dull gray bags. "A fortune in every one. I fetched it myself from the Bank of England and, Lord, what a fuss! Little men in pink coats demanding signatures, enough keys to lock up half the world, and deep suspicion. I'm sure they thought I was going to steal the gold. And why not? Why don't you and I just divide it and retire somewhere gracious? Naples? I've always wanted to visit Naples where I'm told the women are heartbreakingly beautiful." Lavisser saw Sharpe's expression and laughed. "For a man up from the ranks, Richard, you're uncommonly easy to shock. But I confess I'm tempted. I suffer the cruel fate of being the younger son. My wretched brother will become earl and inherit the money while I am expected to fend for myself. You find that risible, yes? Where you come from everyone fends for themselves, so I shall do the same." He put Sharpe's new weapons on the gray bags, then closed the chest. "The gold will go to Prince Frederick," he said, securing the padlock, "and there will be peace on earth and goodwill to all mankind."

Next evening the frigate passed the northernmost tip of Jutland. The low headland was called the Skaw and it showed dull and misty in the gray twilight. A beacon burned at its tip and the light stayed in view as the *Cleopatra* turned south toward the Kattegat. Captain Samuels was plainly worried about that narrow stretch of water, in one place only three miles wide, which was the entrance to the Baltic and guarded on its Swedish bank by the great cannon of Helsingborg and on the Danish by the batteries of Helsingør's Kronborg Castle. The frigate had seen few other ships between Harwich and the Skaw, merely a handful of fishing boats and a wallowing Baltic trader with her main deck heavily laden with timber, but now, sailing into the narrowing gut between Denmark and Sweden, the traffic was heavier. "What we don't know"—Captain Samuels deigned to speak to Sharpe and Lavisser on the morning after they had passed the Skaw—"is whether Denmark is still neutral. We can pass Helsingør by staying close to the Swedish shore, but the Danes will still see us pass and know we're up to no good."

The Swedes, Sharpe gathered, were allied to the British. "Not that it means much," Lavisser said. "Their king is mad too. Strange, isn't it? Half the bloody kings of Europe are foaming maniacs. The Swedes won't fight for us, but they're on our side, while the Danes don't want to fight anyone. They're strictly neutral, poor darlings, but their fleet has complicated matters. They'll have to fight to protect it or else take the bribe. Of course, if the French have already sent a bigger bribe then they might already have declared war on Britain."

There was no alternative but to pass through the narrow strait. Lavisser and Sharpe were to be put ashore south of Køge, close to a village called Herfølge where Lavisser's grandparents had their estate, and Køge Bay lay south of Helsingør and Copenhagen. They could have avoided Helsingør by sailing west about Zealand, the island on which Copenhagen lay, but that was a much longer voyage and time was short. "We have to see the Prince before the British fleet and army arrive," Lavisser said. "D'you think they'd really bombard Copenhagen?"

"Why not?" Sharpe asked.

"Can you really imagine British gunners killing women and children?"

"They'll aim for the walls," Sharpe said, "for the defenses."

"They will not," Lavisser said. "They'll bloody pulverize the city! Cathcart won't want to, though. He's squeamish." Cathcart was the commanding General. "Let's hope the bribe works, eh?"

They passed Helsingør in the afternoon. Guns sounded from the fortress, but their noise was diffused for they were not loaded with ball or shell, but instead were merely responding to the salute that Captain Samuels ordered fired in honor of the Danish flag. Sharpe gazed at the flag through his telescope, seeing a white cross against a red field. Captain Samuels was also staring toward the fortress, but he was looking for the splashes of water that would betray the fall of round shot. None showed, which proved the Danes were merely saluting. "So they're still neutral," Captain Samuels grunted.

"They'll do all they can to stay neutral," Lavisser offered his opinion. "They're a small country, Captain, and they don't want to pick a fight unless they're forced to it." He borrowed Sharpe's telescope and stared at the massive Kronborg Castle which, from this distance, looked more like a palace than a fortress. The copper sheathing of its spires and steeply pitched roof glowed green above the drifting white smoke left by the guns. A frigate, anchored in the Helsingør Roads, was setting her sails in an evident attempt to follow the *Cleopatra*. "Does she mean trouble?" Lavisser asked.

Captain Samuels shook his head. "She'll not catch us," he said dismissively, "and besides, there's liable to be a fog with this wind."

Lavisser looked back to the castle. "Something is rotten in the state of Denmark," he intoned portentously.

"There is?" Sharpe asked.

The guardsman laughed. "It is from *Hamlet*, my dear Richard, which takes place in that very same castle. I was taken there as a child and I was quite convinced I saw the old king's ghost wandering the battlements, but alas, it was only my imagination. Then, years later, I acted the part at Eton. Bloody Pumphrey played Ophelia and a very convincing girl he made too. I was supposed to kiss him in one scene and he appeared to enjoy it so much that I squeezed his balls until he squealed like a pig." He smiled at the memory, then leaned on the rail to gaze at the low green shore. "I wish there really was something rotten in Denmark. It's a dull country, Richard, dull, religious, hidebound and cautious. It's inhabited by small people who lead little lives."

"We must all seem like that to you."

Lavisser was instantly contrite. "No, no. Forgive me. I was born to privilege, Richard, and I forget that others are not."

The *Cleopatra* stayed closer to the Swedish shore, making it seem to any who watched that she was on passage to Stralsund in northern Prussia where a British garrison was stationed, but on the night after they had passed Copenhagen the frigate left the well-traveled sea lane and turned west to beat her way into Køge Bay. She was alone now. The Danish frigate had long abandoned her stern chase of the British ship and Køge Bay was empty. The moon showed occasionally through spreading clouds and the low white chalk cliffs of the approaching coast seemed to shine with an unnatural brilliance. The frigate turned northward until the cliffs faded into long beaches and it was there that Captain Samuels hove to and ordered the launch to be lowered.

The heavy chest was slung overboard by a whip rove to a yardarm, then Sharpe, Lavisser and Barker climbed down to the waiting launch. Sharpe, like his companions, was in civilian clothes. He wore a brown coat, black breeches and boots, a white stock and a brown tricorne hat that Grace had always said made him look like a bad-tempered farmer. His rifleman's uniform was in the pack slung on his back.

The launch crew rowed through the dark. The moon was gone behind clouds that now smothered the sky, while well to the north, beyond Copenhagen, a thunderstorm roiled the night. Lightning split the blackness with snake tongues of fire, but no rain fell on Køge Bay and the sound of the thunder faded before it reached the launch. The only sounds were the creak of the muffled oars and the splash of water on the launch's hull.

There was no surf, just a gentle breaking of small waves on a shelving beach. The launch's keel grated on sand and a sailor leaped overboard to hold the boat steady while half a dozen men carried the chest of gold ashore. Sharpe, Lavisser and Barker followed, splashing through the shallows. The Midshipman in charge of the launch wished them good fortune, then the launch was heaved back from the beach and the sound of its muffled oars died swiftly away. A cold wind rattled grains of sand against Sharpe's boots.

He was in Denmark.

And Captain Lavisser drew his pistol.

CHAPTER 4

LAVISSER HESITATED. "WOULD THEY hear a pistol shot on the frigate?" he asked.

"Probably," Sharpe said. "Sound carries over water. Why?"

"I'm worried the priming got wet, but I don't want to alarm the *Cleopatra*. They might think we're in trouble."

"Priming didn't get wet," Sharpe said. "Water only came up to our ankles."

"You're probably right." Lavisser holstered the pistol. "I think it's best if you wait here, Richard. If Samuels landed us in the right place then Herfølge's at least an hour's walk. I'll see you at dawn and, with any luck, I'll bring a cart and horse to get this damn gold out of here." He climbed a dune. "You'll stay with Mister Sharpe, Barker?"

"I will, sir," Barker acknowledged.

"You know what to do," Lavisser said cheerfully, turning away.

"Do you have the key to the chest?" Sharpe called after the guardsman.

Lavisser half turned. He was nothing but a shadow on the dune's crest. "Surely you don't need it, Richard?"

"I'd like to get those pistols."

"If you must. Barker has the key. I'll see you in two or three hours." Lavisser waved and disappeared down the other side of the dune.

Sharpe peered at Barker's dark shape. "The key?"

"I'm looking for it." Barker's answer was surly. He began to rummage through a valise and Sharpe, as he waited, walked up the dune. It was cold for summer, but he supposed that was because the sea was so chill. From the dune's top he could just see the frigate as a tracery of dark rigging against the eastern sky while inland there was only a feeble and faraway scrap of hazed and flickering light. Captain Samuels had said that fog was likely in this weather and the smeared scrap of light suggested it was forming over the flat farmlands. The ground seemed to rock as Sharpe became accustomed to being on land again. He could smell hay, salt and seaweed. "Been to Denmark before, Barker?" he called down to the beach.

"No," Barker said.

"So where's the key?" Sharpe asked.

"I reckon he didn't give it me."

"It's customary, Barker, to address officers as 'sir.' " Sharpe could not conceal his dislike for the servant, who was plainly employed for his size and his capacity for violence rather than for any skills as a valet. Sharpe rooted through his pack until he found the picklock, then went back to the beach where he knelt beside the chest.

"What are you doing, sir?" Barker asked, putting a sarcastic stress on the last word.

"Fetching my pistols," Sharpe said, taking hold of the padlock.

A bang made him turn. The launch must have reached the frigate which was now sheeting home her foresails to turn away from land and the bang had merely been the wind slatting the canvas, but it saved Sharpe's life. He saw the gleam in Barker's hand, realized it was a knife that was about to bury itself in his neck and so threw himself to one side before scrambling away from the chest. He let go of the picklock, hurled a handful of sand into Barker's eyes and drew his saber, then heard the click of a gun being cocked and knew that Barker, careless of any noise, must have had a pistol hidden beneath his long coat. Sharpe just ran, going up the dune where he snatched up his pack and then down the sandy slope into the darkness behind the beach.

He had hardly thought since the banging sail had made him turn. He had just reacted, but now he crouched in the coarse grass and watched the crest of the dune for Barker's shadow. Sweet Jesus, he thought, but he had been fooled. He should have bloody known when Lavisser had claimed Barker possessed the chest's key. No man would entrust a fortune in gold to a servant like Barker.

So Lord Pumphrey had been right when he suggested there was something odd about this whole mission, but in his wildest imaginings Sharpe had not thought things were this warped. Lavisser wanted him dead. What else did Lavisser want? There was no way of knowing that, and now was not the time to speculate, for Barker had come to the dune's top and pointed the pistol into the shadows. He was waiting for Sharpe to move, just waiting, but the fog was thickening as the southern summer wind crossed the cold northern sea. Sharpe stayed motionless. Far inland a bell tolled four times. The small light had vanished, obscured by the growing fog.

Barker moved northward a few paces and Sharpe broke cover and ran southward. Barker heard him, and that was what Sharpe wanted, for he half hoped Barker would try a long shot. Once the gun was discharged it would take too long to reload and Sharpe would be on the servant like a terrier onto a rat, but Barker was no fool. He held his fire and instead followed Sharpe in hope of getting close enough for the pistol not to miss.

Sharpe went to ground in black shadows between two low dunes. The fog was blanching the first hint of dawn and muffling the small sounds of the wind and waves. Barker had lost him again, though the servant had a rough idea of where Sharpe was and now crouched on the sky-line. The man was no soldier, or else he would have sought the lower ground for at night it was impossible to see down into the hollows. A man could see upward against the sky, but not down. Sharpe watched the hulking servant, then raked his fingers through the sand and grass to come up with a scrap of wood and two pebbles that he flicked southward one after the other. They made tiny noises as they landed and Barker, hearing them, moved toward the small sounds.

Sharpe went back northward. He crept, feeling ahead of him to make sure he did not trample any stiff grass. He found two more pieces of wood that he hurled away into the misty dark, hoping to lure Barker far-ther south, and only when he had lost sight of the man did he stand and cross the dunes back to the beach. He needed to find the picklock, but it had vanished in the trampled sand about the chest. He searched quickly, sifting handfuls of sand, but he could not find it and suddenly he heard

Barker returning. The servant had given up his hunt and was coming back to guard the gold so Sharpe abandoned the weapons locked in the chest and went back across the dunes.

He headed inland until he reached a damp vegetable field edged with a ditch. He moved northward now, following the ditch which was half silted with blown sand. A bird flew up from a nest, startling him, then he saw he had come to a rough track, deep rutted by cartwheels, that headed inland. He was about to follow it, then heard hoofbeats and so he scuttled back to the ditch and lay in its damp grass.

The hoofbeats sounded like a whole troop of cavalry, but Sharpe could see nothing in the soft fog. He lay motionless, the hat shadowing his face from the wan early light. Then he saw a shape in the whiteness, another, and suddenly there were a half-dozen horsemen in sight. They all wore long red jackets with pale-blue collars and cuffs. Their breeches were black, edged with white piping, and their hats were black bicornes, elaborately plumed with white feathers. Their long straight swords hung from sashes of yellow silk and suggested they were dragoons. A second group appeared, all of them going slowly because of the fog, and then a shabby cart materialized. It was pulled by a plodding pony and was hung with remnants of seaweed. Sharpe guessed the cart was normally used to fetch weed from the beach to use as fertilizer and now it had come for the gold.

The horsemen and the cart vanished onto the beach. Sharpe darted across the track and found shelter in another ditch. He heard muffled voices and thought he detected anger. But who was angry, and why? Had the dragoons captured Lavisser, or had they been sent by him? Sharpe raised his head, but could see nothing. He crawled inland, staying low so that he did not appear as a dark patch in the lightening fog. What the hell was he to do? The clink of a curb-chain made him lie flat again. The horsemen had evidently spread into the fog to search for him, but they were looking too far to the south. They called to each other, sounding oddly cheerful now, and Sharpe sensed they were a group of friends rather than a military unit. All were apparently officers, judging by the sashes, and none was shouting orders. They laughed as they kicked their horses through the wet soil of the vegetable field, then they were gone to the south and Sharpe kept crawling. Go inland, he thought, and find shelter. Find trees. Find anything that would hide him and then work out what to do. Maybe, he thought, he should just wait. A British army was supposedly coming to Denmark, but the thought of emerging from some barn or ditch to a welcoming committee of supercilious officers was more than he could bear. They would say he had failed again, but what else could he do?

The voices and hoofbeats sounded again and Sharpe dropped into the mud. He must have been closer to the track than he had thought, for he could hear the squeal and rumble of the cart. Then he heard Barker's voice. He was apologizing, but his apology was cut short when Lavisser interrupted him. "It's a pity, Barker," the guardsman said, "but it's not a tragedy. And what can he do to us? I quite liked the fellow, but he's still an encumbrance and quite useless. Pitifully useless."

Useless? Sharpe raised his head to see that Lavisser was wearing the Danish uniform. He must have gone back home to his grandfather, changed into the uniform, joined his waiting friends and so become wealthy. All in an hour or two. Then damn him, Sharpe thought. Damn him. He watched the cart and the cavalrymen fade into the fog.

Get to Copenhagen, he thought. He felt in his pocket and found the piece of paper that Lord Pumphrey had given him in Harwich. There was just enough light to read the elegant handwriting. "Ole Skovgaard, Ulfedt's Plads," it read, and Sharpe stared at it. Was that a name? Or an address? Then he guessed the comma meant that Ole Skovgaard was the man's name and Ulfedt's Plads was where he lived, and that, Pumphrey had said, was in Copenhagen, so get there fast. Be useful.

He pushed the scrap of paper back into his coat pocket, checked that Lavisser and the other horsemen were truly gone from sight, then stood.

And that was when the dragoon sprang the trap.

It was an old trick. The cavalrymen had left one horseman behind, reckoning that Sharpe would think himself safe when he saw the riders leave and so come out of hiding.

Which Sharpe dutifully did and the last dragoon, waiting by the dunes, saw the rifleman appear as a dark shape in the field.

The dragoon should have shouted immediately. He should have called his companions back, but he wanted all the credit for capturing the missing Englishman and so he drew his sword and raked his spurs back. Sharpe heard the hooves, turned and saw the big horse being spurred across the muddy field. He cursed himself for falling for such an old ruse, but saw, too, that the horseman was right-handed, understood that the horse would therefore go to his own right and knew that the dragoon would lean from the saddle to chop with the sword, and knew, too, that there was no time to draw his own saber. Or perhaps he knew none of that, but instinctively realized it in the space of a heartbeat and understood how to react.

The cavalryman shouted, more to frighten Sharpe than summon his companions, but the horseman was too confident and too inexperienced. He believed Sharpe would stand like a scarecrow and be beaten down by the flat of his sword and the last thing he expected was for the rifleman to swing the heavy pack hard into the side of his horse's head. The horse slewed away and the dragoon, already swinging his heavy sword, found his horse going one way while he was leaning the other. Lavisser had cautioned him that the Englishman was dangerous so he had intended to stun Sharpe with the weight of his heavy straight blade, but instead he flailed for balance. Sharpe let go of his pack, seized the dragoon's sword arm and simply tugged. The man yelped as he was jerked from the saddle, then the breath was thumped out of him as he fell into the mud. He yelped again as Sharpe dropped onto his belly. "Bloody fool," Sharpe said.

The horse, shaking its head, had stopped. There was a pistol holstered on its saddle.

Sharpe was angry. It did not take much to make him angry, not since Grace died, and he hit the man hard. Too hard. He found a fist-sized stone in the field's mud and used it to break the dragoon's jaw. The man moaned as blood trickled into his long fair mustache. "Bloody fool," Sharpe said again. He stood and kicked the man. He thought about taking the sword, for a heavy cavalry sword was a much better weapon than a light saber, but the blade had fallen some feet away and the scabbard was secured by a complicated buckle and meanwhile the man's shout must have been heard by the other dragoons, for a voice called urgently out of the fog. Lavisser and his companions were coming back so Sharpe rescued his pack and ran to the horse. He put his left foot in the stirrup, hopped clumsily as the horse sidled nervously away, then managed to haul himself into the saddle. He fiddled his right foot into the second stirrup, turned the horse north and kicked his heels back. The fallen man watched him sadly.

Sharpe swerved back to the beach. He could hear hoofbeats and knew the other dragoons would soon be in full pursuit. Once across the dunes and on the beach he turned south and kicked the horse into a gallop. Sharpe clung on for dear life, the pack bouncing against his right thigh and the saber scabbard clanging like a cracked bell. He rode past the jumble of hoofprints where he and Lavisser had come ashore, then turned inland again. He was riding in a circle, hoping that the changes of direction would confuse his pursuers. He crossed the dunes, let the horse find its own way over the ditch, then curbed it in the field. He listened, but could hear nothing except his horse's harsh breathing.

He kicked the beast on. He crossed two more ditches, then turned northward again until he came to the rutted track where he turned west, then north again where a path branched away between windbent trees. His instinct told him he had lost his pursuers, but he doubted they would have given up the chase quite yet. They would be looking for him and, as the sun rose, the fog began to thin. The horse would be a liability soon, for Lavisser and his companions would be searching for a horseman in this flat, featureless landscape and so, reluctantly, Sharpe slid out of the saddle. He unbuckled the girth and took the saddle off the beast, then slapped its rump to drive it into a pasture. With any luck the other horsemen would simply see a grazing horse, not an abandoned cavalry mount.

He threw away the pistol. It had not been loaded and its ammunition must have been with its rider, so Sharpe tossed it into the ditch where he had hidden the saddle and walked on north. He hurried now, using the last vestiges of the fog to cover his escape. By midmorning, when the sun at last burned the mist away, Sharpe had gone to earth in a ditch from where he could just see his pursuers. They were far off, staring across the fields. He watched them for an hour or more, until at last they abandoned the search and rode inland.

Sharpe waited in case another man had been left behind. He was getting hungry, but there was nothing he could do about that. The sky was clouding over, threatening rain. Still he waited until he was certain there was no one looking for him, then he climbed from the ditch and walked through drab fields in a flat land. He kept the dunes to his right to make sure he was going north. He passed white-painted farms with red-tiled roofs and big barns, crossed earth roads and waded wide drainage ditches and, in the afternoon, just as it began to rain, he had to cut deep inland to skirt a fishing village. He splashed through a stream and threaded through a wood of oak and ash to find himself in the park of a vast mansion with two lofty towers. The windows were shuttered and a dozen men, their heads protected from the rain by hoods of sacking, were scything the big lawn. He walked along the edge of the park, climbed a wall and was back in the drab fields, though ahead of him the sky was smeared with a haze of smoke, evidence of a town, and he prayed it was Copenhagen, though he sensed that he was still far to the south. He could only judge the distance by the time it had taken the *Cleopatra* to sail down the coast and he reckoned the city was probably a two- or three-day walk.

The town, though he did not know it, was Køge. He smelt it before he saw it. There was the familiar reek of a brewery and the pungent odor of smoking fish that made his hunger even more acute. He thought of going into the town to beg or steal food, but when he came close to Køge's southern edge he saw two men in dark uniforms standing beside the road. They were sheltering from the rain as best they could, but when a carriage rattled along the road they stopped it and Sharpe saw one of them climb onto the step and peer through the window. The man saw nothing suspicious, jumped down and made a brief salute. So they were searching for someone and Sharpe knew who it was. Lavisser had made him into a hunted man.

He told himself he had endured hunger before and so he struck inland again. The rain fell harder as night descended, but it hid him as he walked and walked, always keeping the smell of the town and its scatter of dim lights on his right-hand side. He crossed a major road, followed a track northward, then crossed more fields. His boots were clogged with mud, his clothes were soaked and the pack was biting into the small of his back and his shoulders. He walked till he could not endure another pace, then he slept in a wood where he was woken by a heavy rain that thrashed the trees just before dawn. His belly ached and he was shivering. He remembered the bedroom he had shared with Grace, its fireplace and the wide windows that led to a balcony. He had been careless, he now knew, in thinking that idyll could last forever. He had sold his Indian jewels and used the money to make a haven while the lawyers bickered over her dead husband's will, but then Grace died and the same lawyers pounced like weasels on the property Sharpe had bought. He had put the house in Grace's name, saying that she needed the safety of her own home while he soldiered abroad, and that quixotic gallantry had lost him everything. Worse, he had lost her. Grace, he thought, Grace, and the self-pity swept over him so that he tipped his face to the rain as if it could wash away his tears.

Bloody fool, he told himself. Be useful. Pull yourself together. The woman is dead and you do not help her memory by collapsing. Get up, he told himself, walk. Sniveling and feeling sorry for himself would do nothing. Be useful. He got up, pulled on the pack and went to the wood's edge.

And there his fortune changed. A farm lay just a hundred yards away. It had a long low white-painted house, two barns, a windmill and a dairy. It looked prosperous and busy. Two men were driving a big herd of cattle toward the dairy while a dozen laborers gathered in the yard. All had haversacks slung on their shoulders and Sharpe reckoned that was dinner; bread and cheese, perhaps. He watched from the wood's edge. The rain eased. Most of the men went westward with a small cart laden with spades and forks, but three vanished inside the smaller of the two barns. Sharpe waited, hunger biting. The bigger barn had wide-open doors. Get inside there, he reckoned, and he could scout the rest of the farm, maybe even sneak into the kitchen or dairy to steal food. He never once thought of the guineas in his pack. He could have bought food, but his instinct was not to show himself. Live as he had learned to live before he met Grace.

The dairy herd was driven back to pasture and then no one moved in the farm for a while until two children, school bags swinging, walked down the lane. When they had gone from sight Sharpe broke cover and ran across the damp pasture, crossed a ditch and sprinted the last few yards into the big barn. He half expected a shout of protest or a dog to start barking, but he was unseen. He slipped through the doors to find a vast wagon loaded high with hay. A haversack, like the ones the laborers had been carrying, lay discarded on the wagon's seat and Sharpe scooped it up as he climbed the vehicle's high side which was a wooden grille designed to keep the hay in place. He scrabbled a hole for himself in the hay, took off his pack and greatcoat, then opened the stolen haversack to find bread, cheese, a big piece of ham, a sausage and a stone bottle which, uncorked, proved to hold ale.

He ate half the bread and all the cheese. He reckoned he could stay here for hours, but it was more important to reach Copenhagen and find

Skovgaard. He was about to clamber out of the wagon when a strange clatter sounded beneath him. He went still. The clattering was loud, wood against stone. The sound puzzled Sharpe until he recognized it as footsteps. Wooden shoes, Sharpe finally realized, banging on the barn's flagstones. Then a man's voice shouted a protest, presumably for his stolen dinner, another man laughed, and Sharpe heard the heavy sound of hooves and the clink of chains. A team was being hitched to the hay-wain. The voices went on, and a woman said something soothing that provoked more laughter. It all seemed to take forever. Sharpe stayed where he was, half buried in the wagon's high load.

Then, at last, the driver flicked his whip and the haywain eased forward as the horses took its vast weight on their harnesses. The wagon went out from the barn's shadow and creaked and groaned and rattled as it gained speed over the yard. A man and a woman called what Sharpe presumed was a farewell.

The cloud was shredding so that strips of blue showed as the wagon lurched along a farm track. It was going inland and Sharpe was happy to let it carry him, but where would it go once it reached the road? He prayed it would turn north. He ducked down as more voices sounded, then peered from the hay to see that it was a group of men clearing a ditch who had called to the driver. A field of wheat grew beyond, very close to harvest.

The wagon turned north. It splashed through a deep ford, groaned up a slope and then the horses settled into a plodding walk on a well-surfaced road that was wide and empty. A drift of tobacco smoke came to Sharpe. The driver must have lit a pipe. So where was he going? Copenhagen seemed as good an answer as any for the city, like London, surely had an insatiable demand for hay, but even if the wagon was bound elsewhere it was going in the right direction and Sharpe burrowed deeper, settled himself and fell asleep.

He woke close to midday. The wagon, so far as he could judge, was still going northward through a gentle countryside of small villages with painted houses and plain churches, all with roofs of bright red tiles. The road was busier now, mostly with pedestrians who called out greetings to the driver. Another haywain ambled a half-mile behind. The road led directly toward a blur of dirty smoke on the horizon and that told Sharpe the wagon was heading for a city. He reckoned it had to be Copenhagen.

But Lavisser, he warned himself, could have reached the city the day before.

Lavisser. How Sharpe was to revenge himself on Lavisser he did not know, but he would. The anger was in him again because he had been fooled by the guardsman's attentive friendliness on the boat. Sharpe had believed the man's sympathy and so revealed his own feelings, and all the while Lavisser had been plotting his death. So Lavisser would suffer. By God he would suffer. Sharpe would eviscerate the bastard and have him screaming. Sharpe might not know how he would do it yet, but he did know where. In Copenhagen.

SHARPE REACHED the city as evening was falling. The wagon creaked through a district of lavish houses, each standing in its own wide garden, then skirted the end of what looked like a wide canal that protected the city's walls. A causeway led over a smaller moat to one of the city's gates, this one a massive pair of metal-studded doors set in a wide tunnel that led through the layered ramparts. The haywain stopped among a group of other carts and more elegant carriages. Voices sounded close. Sharpe suspected soldiers were searching all the traffic, but if so they were content merely to ask the driver some questions. None bothered to clamber up the wagon's high sides and after a while the driver clicked his tongue, the horses took the wagon's weight and the vehicle lurched on through the long dark tunnel to emerge into the heart of the city.

Sharpe, bedded down in the hay, could only see gables, roofs and spires. The sun was low in the west, gleaming on red tiles and green copper. The evening wind billowed a white curtain from a high window. He smelled coffee, then an organ sounded from a church, filling the air with great chords. Sharpe pulled on his greatcoat, took hold of his pack and waited until the wagon turned into a narrower street, then he climbed over the wooden trellis at the vehicle's rear and dropped down to the cobbles. A girl watched him from a doorway as he tried to rid himself of the wisps of hay that smothered his clothes. A woman, leading a child by the hand, crossed the narrow street rather than go close by him and Sharpe, looking down at his muddied trousers, was not surprised. He looked like a tramp, but a tramp with a saber.

It was time to find Lord Pumphrey's man so Sharpe buttoned his greatcoat and walked toward the wider street. It was almost dark, but it looked a prosperous city. Shopkeepers were shuttering their premises while yellow lamplight spilled from hundreds of windows. A giant wooden pipe hung above a tobacco shop; laughter and the clink of glasses came from a tavern. A crippled sailor, his pigtail thick with tar, swung on crutches down the pavement. Big carriages rolled briskly down a wide street where small boys swept the horse dung toward wooden holding boxes. It was like London, but not like London. Much cleaner, for a start. Sharpe gaped at a soaring spire that was formed by the entwined tails of four copper dragons. He also saw, more usefully, that every street and alley was clearly marked with a name. That was not like London where a visitor found his way by guesswork and by God.

An elderly man, bearded and carrying a bundle of books wrapped in string, saw Sharpe gaping up at the street name. He said something in Danish and Sharpe just shrugged. "Vous êtes Français?" the man asked.

"American," Sharpe said. It did not seem wise to admit to being English at a time when a British fleet and army was sailing to assault Denmark.

"American!" The old man seemed delighted. "You are lost, perhaps?"

"I am."

"You seek a hostel, yes?"

"I'm looking for a place called . . ." What the hell was it? "Elfins Platz?" he guessed. "A man called Ole Stoveguard?" He knew he had got the names wrong and sorted though his pockets for Lord Pumphrey's scrap of paper. "Ulfedt's Plads," Sharpe read the unfamiliar name awkwardly. Two or three other passersby had stopped now, for it seemed that if someone was lost in Copenhagen then the citizens regarded it as their duty to offer help.

"Ah! Ulfedt's Plads. It is a short walk," the old man said, "but everything in Copenhagen is a short walk. We are not like Paris or London. Have you been to those cities?"

"No."

"Washington, now, is that big?"

"Pretty big," Sharpe said, who had no idea.

"Do all men carry swords in America?" The old man, not content with directing him to Ulfedt's Plads, was now walking with him.

"Most of us," Sharpe said.

"We have lost the habit in Denmark," the old man said, "except for the soldiers, of course, and a handful of our aristocracy who think it is a badge of rank." He chuckled, then sighed. "I fear, alas, we shall all have to wear swords soon."

"You will? Why?"

"We are warned that the British are coming again. I pray it isn't so, for I remember the last time when their Lord Nelson came. Six years ago! I had a son on the *Dannebroge* and he lost a leg."

"I'm sorry," Sharpe said awkwardly. He vaguely remembered hearing about Nelson's attack on Copenhagen, but it had happened when he was in India and the news had not provoked much interest in the regiment.

"It turned out for the best," the old man went on. "Edvard is a minister now, in Randers. It is safer, I think, being a minister than a naval officer. There are Lutherans in America?"

"Oh, yes," Sharpe said, having no idea what a Lutheran was.

"I am glad to hear it," the old man said. He had led Sharpe down a narrow street that emerged into a small square. "This is Ulfedt's Plads." He gestured to the square. "You will be all right now?" he asked anxiously.

Sharpe reassured and thanked the old man, then fished out the scrap of paper and read the name in the fading light. Ole Skovgaard. One side of the square was occupied by a gin distillery, another by a huge warehouse and between them were small shops: a cooperage, a wheelwright's and a cutlery store. He walked along the shops, looking for Skovgaard's name, then saw it painted in faded white letters high on the big warehouse wall.

The warehouse had a high archway and, next to it, a smaller door with a polished brass knocker. The smaller door belonged to a house that was evidently attached to the warehouse for the "S" of the Skovgaard sign was painted on its bricks. Sharpe rapped the knocker. He was nervous. Lord Pumphrey had made it plain that Skovgaard was a last resort, but Sharpe did not know where else he could seek help. He knocked again, heard a window being thrown up and stepped back to see a face peering down in the gloom. "Mister Skovgaard?" he called.

"Oh no," the man said unhelpfully.

"Are you Mister Skovgaard?" Sharpe asked.

There was a pause. "You are English?" the man asked cautiously.

"I need to see Mister Skovgaard."

"It is too late!" the man said disapprovingly, ignoring the lingering light in the summer sky.

Sharpe swore under his breath. "Is Mister Skovgaard there?"

"You will wait there, please." The window slammed down, there were footsteps on the stairs and, a moment later, the door was laboriously unbolted and unlocked. It opened to reveal a tall and lugubrious young man with long light-brown hair and a palely anxious face. "You are English?" the man asked.

"Are you Ole Skovgaard?"

"Oh no! No!" The young man frowned. "I am Aksel Bang. I am Mister Skovgaard's overseer. Is that the word? I dwell here now. Mister Skovgaard has moved to Vester Fælled."

"Where's that?" Sharpe asked.

"Vester Fælled is not far, it is not far. It is where the city is growing." Bang frowned at the mud and hay on Sharpe's clothes. "You are English?"

"My name's Sharpe. Richard Sharpe."

Bang ignored the introduction. "Mister Skovgaard insists the English are taken to him. It is his rule, you understand? I need a coat and then I shall take you to Vester Fælled. You will tarry here, please." He vanished down the hallway and returned a moment later with a coat and a wide-brimmed hat. "Mister Skovgaard did dwell here," he explained as he shut and carefully locked the door, "but he has bought a house outside the city. He went from this place a month ago. Not so long, I think, but Vester Fælled is not so far. It is where the new houses are. Not five years ago it was all meadow, now it is houses. You have just come to Copenhagen perhaps?"

"Yes."

"My English is not so good," Bang said, "but I practice. You know how I practice? By reading the Scripture in English. That is good, I think. There is an English church here, did you know that?"

"No."

"Is there a Danish church in London?"

Sharpe confessed ignorance. He was becoming increasingly nervous, for he knew he looked odd. His coat was filthy and his boots were caked

with mud, but it was the saber that seemed to attract most glances of disapproval, so Sharpe hitched the scabbard up into his left armpit and so
hid it under his coat. He had just done that when a man lurched from an
alley and startled Sharpe by trying to embrace him. Aksel Bang hurried
Sharpe on. "That man is a bibber of wine," he said disapprovingly, "a
drunkard. That is bad."

"You've never been drunk?"

"I abhor liquor. It is the devil's drink. I have never touched a drop and
with God's help I never will. Never! We have not so many drunkards in
Copenhagen, but there are some." He looked at Sharpe earnestly. "I trust
you are born again into Christ Jesus?"

"I trust so too," Sharpe growled, hoping that answer would deter
Bang. Sharpe did not much care about his own soul at that moment, he
was far more worried by the city gate that lay just ahead of them. He
brushed hay off his coat and hitched the saber up again. The gate was
inside the long tunnel that led through the thick walls and it was wide
open, but there were men in blue uniforms standing in the light of two
great lanterns suspended from the tunnel's roof. Were they searching for
Sharpe? It seemed likely, but Sharpe hoped they were only investigating
the incoming traffic.

"God so loved the world," Aksel Bang said, "that He sent His only
Son. You have surely heard that piece of Scripture?"

The tunnel was very close now. A uniformed man with a bushy mustache and a shouldered musket came from the guardhouse, glanced at
Bang and Sharpe, then struck flint on steel to light a pipe. He sucked on
the flame and his eyes, reflecting the small fire, stared hard at Sharpe.
"How do you say that verse in Danish?" Sharpe asked Bang.

"The således elskede Gud Verden, at han gav sin Søm den enbårne,"
Aksel Bang recited happily, "for at hver den, som tror på ham, ikke skal
fortabes, men have et evigt luv." Sharpe tried not to look at the mustached
guard, hoping that the sound of Danish would mislead the sentries. The
saber scabbard was high at his side, awkwardly trapped beneath his coat
by his left elbow. He kept his head down, pretending to be paying close
attention to Bang's fervent words. Their footsteps echoed under the arch.
Sharpe smelt the tobacco as he walked past the guard. He felt conspicu-
ous, sure that one of the men would reach out and take his elbow, but
none seemed to find him suspicious and suddenly he and Aksel Bang

were out of the gate tunnel and crossing a wide-open area that lay between the walls and the canal-like lakes that protected the city's landward ramparts. Sharpe sighed with relief.

"Beautiful words," Bang said happily.

"Indeed," Sharpe said, his relief making him sound fervent.

Bang finally abandoned Sharpe's soul. "You have met Mister Skovgaard before?" he asked.

"No." They were on a causeway that crossed the canal and Sharpe at last was feeling safe.

"I ask because it is rumored that England is sending an army to take our fleet. Is that true, do you think?"

"I don't know."

Bang glanced at the saber scabbard that Sharpe had let drop now that they were out of the city and in the less populated suburbs. "I think you are a soldier, perhaps," Bang said.

"I was," Sharpe said curtly.

"The buttons on your coat, yes? And the sword. I wanted to be a soldier, but my father believed I should learn business and Mister Skovgaard is a very able teacher. I am lucky, I think. He is a good man."

"And rich?" Sharpe asked sourly. They had left the road to walk through a cemetery, but beyond the graveyard's low wall he could see big houses standing in tree-shaded gardens.

"He is wealthy, yes," Bang said, "but in matters of the spirit he is poor. His son died, as did his wife, God bless their souls, as did his daughter's husband and her son. Four deaths in three years! Now all that is left is Mister Skovgaard and Astrid."

Something in Bang's voice made Sharpe glance at him. So that was how the land lay. Skovgaard had a daughter and no son, which meant the daughter would inherit. "And the daughter," Sharpe asked, "she hasn't married again?"

"Not yet," Bang said with studied carelessness, then he unlatched the cemetery gate and waved Sharpe through.

They walked up a street edged with trees until they reached a white-painted gate beyond which lay one of the big houses. Its bricks and red roof tiles were hardly discolored, suggesting the house was only a year or two old. Back in the city a church clock struck half past eight, the sound echoed by other church bells in the suburbs as Bang led Sharpe up the long carriage drive.

An elderly servant, soberly dressed in a brown suit with silver buttons, opened the door. He did not seem surprised to see Aksel Bang, though he frowned at the mud and hay on Sharpe's coat. Bang spoke in Danish to the servant who bowed and left. "You will tarry here, please," Bang told Sharpe, "and I shall tell Mister Skovgaard of your coming." Bang disappeared down a short paneled corridor while Sharpe looked around the tiled hall. A crystal chandelier hung above him, an eastern rug was underfoot and from one of the closed doors came the sound of tinkling music. A spinet or harpsichord, Sharpe was not sure which. He took off his hat and caught sight of himself in a gilt-framed looking glass that hung above a spindly table on which a china bowl held a pile of visiting cards. He grimaced at his reflection, picked some more hay off his coat and tried to smooth his hair. The music had stopped and Sharpe, still staring at the mirror, saw the door behind him open.

He turned and for the first time since Grace had died he felt his heart leap.

A girl dressed all in black stood looking at him with an expression of astonished delight. She was tall, very fair-haired and blue-eyed. Later, much later, Sharpe would notice she had a wide forehead, a generous mouth, a long straight nose and a quick laugh, but at that moment he just stared at her and she stared back and the welcoming look of pleasure on her face died to be replaced by a puzzled sadness. She said something in Danish.

"I'm sorry," Sharpe said.

"You are English?" she asked, sounding surprised.

"Yes, miss."

She stared at him oddly, then shook her head. "You look so like someone else"—she paused—"someone I knew." There were tears in her eyes. "I am Skovgaard's daughter," she introduced herself. "Astrid."

"Richard Sharpe, miss," he said. "You speak good English."

"My mother was English." She glanced down the corridor. "You are here to see my father?"

"I hope so."

"Then I am sorry to have disturbed you," she said.

"You were playing?" Sharpe asked.

"I am not good." She offered him a quick and embarrassed smile. "I have to practice." She gave him a last puzzled look, then went back into the room. She left the door ajar and, after a moment, a few solitary notes sounded again.

Two men came to fetch Sharpe. Like the servant who had answered the door, they were both dressed in brown, but these men were much younger. They also looked fit and hard. One jerked his head and Sharpe obediently followed them down the short passage. The door at the end squeaked alarmingly but opened into an elegant room where Aksel Bang was standing beside a thin man who was sitting at a desk, his head bowed. Sharpe dropped his pack, coat and hat on a chair and waited. The door squealed shut behind him, then the two young men, evidently guards, stood not far behind him.

The room was a study, but large enough to hold a small dance. Bookcases filled with forbidding leather volumes lined two walls, the third had tall glass doors opening onto a garden while the fourth was paneled in a pale wood that surrounded a carved marble hearth above which hung a portrait of a gloomy man dressed in preacher's black with Geneva bands. Then the man behind the desk laid down his pen, unhooked a pair of spectacles from his ears and looked up at Sharpe. He blinked with apparent astonishment when he saw his visitor's face, but hid whatever surprised him. "I am Ole Skovgaard," he said in a gravelly voice, "and Aksel has forgotten your name."

"Lieutenant Richard Sharpe, sir."

"An Englishman," Skovgaard said disapprovingly. "An Englishman," he said again, "yet you look just like my poor son-in-law, God rest his soul. You did not meet Nils, did you, Aksel?"

"I did not enjoy that privilege, sir," Bang said, bobbing his head with pleasure at being addressed by his employer.

"He looked exactly like that Englishman," Skovgaard said. "The resemblance is, what is the word? Extraordinary." He shook his head in wonderment. He had sunken cheeks, a tall forehead and an expression of severe disapproval. He looked to be in his fifties, though his fair hair had no gray yet. "Do you spell your name with an 'e'?" he asked and, when Sharpe confirmed the spelling, hooked the spectacles over his ears and made a note with a scratching quill. "And you are a lieutenant, yes? In the navy or the army? And what regiment?" His English was perfect. He wrote down Sharpe's answers, blew on the wet ink, then toyed with an ivory letter opener as he looked Sharpe up and down. After a while he gave a small shrug then turned to Bang. "Perhaps, Aksel, you would wait in the parlor with Miss Astrid?"

"Of course, of course." Bang looked absurdly pleased as he hurried from the room.

"Tell me, Lieutenant Sharpe," Skovgaard said, "what brings you to my house?"

"I was told you'd help me, sir."

"By whom?"

"By Lord Pumphrey, sir."

"I have never heard of Lord Pumphrey," Skovgaard said bleakly. He stood and crossed to a side table. He was dressed all in black and had a black crepe mourning band about his right sleeve. He was so thin he looked like a skeleton walking. He selected a pipe from a rack, filled it with tobacco from a jar that had a painted dragon circling its belly, then carried a silver tinderbox back to his desk. He struck the charred linen alight, transferred the flame to a spill and lit the pipe. He waited till the tobacco was burning evenly. "Why would this Lord Pumphrey believe I would help you?"

"He said you were a friend of Britain, sir."

"Did he now? Did he?" Skovgaard sucked on the pipe. The smoke curled to a ceiling that was lavishly molded in plaster. "I am a merchant, Lieutenant Sharpe," he said, somehow making the rank sound like an insult. "I deal in sugar, tobacco, jute, coffee and indigo. All those items, Lieutenant, must be carried here in ships. That would suggest, would it not, that I am in favor of the Royal Navy, for it helps our own navy protect the sea lanes. Does that make me a friend of Britain?"

Sharpe looked into the merchant's eyes. They were pale, unfriendly and unsettling. "I was told so, sir," he said awkwardly.

"Yet Britain, Lieutenant Sharpe, has sent a fleet to the Baltic. Ships of the line, frigates, bomb ships, gun boats and over two hundred transports—enough, I think, to convey twenty thousand men. That fleet passed the Skaw last night. Where do you think it is going?"

"I don't know, sir," Sharpe said.

"Russia? I think not. The little Swedish garrison at Stralsund, perhaps? But France can take Stralsund whenever she pleases, and throwing more men into its walls merely dooms them. Sweden? Why would Britain send an army to its friends in Sweden? I think that fleet is coming here, Lieutenant Sharpe, here. To Copenhagen. Do you think that is an unreasonable assumption?"

"I don't know, sir," Sharpe said feebly.

"You don't know." There was acid in Skovgaard's voice now. He stood again, agitated. "Where else can such a fleet be going?" He paced up and down in front of the empty hearth, trailing tobacco smoke. "Earlier this month, Lieutenant, a peace treaty was signed between France and Russia. The Czar and Napoleon met at Tilsit and, between them, they divided Europe. Do you know this?"

"No, sir."

"Then I shall educate you, Lieutenant. France and Russia are now friends while Prussia is reduced to a husk. Napoleon commands Europe, Lieutenant, and we all live under his shadow. Yet he lacks one thing, a fleet. Without a fleet he cannot defeat Britain, and there is only one fleet left in Europe that can challenge the Royal Navy."

"The Danish fleet," Sharpe said.

"You are not so ignorant as you pretend, eh?" Skovgaard paused to relight the pipe. "There was a secret article in the Treaty of Tilsit, Lieutenant, by which Russia agreed to allow France to take the Danish fleet. That fleet is not Russia's to give nor France's to take, but such niceties will not stop Napoleon. He has sent an army to our frontier on the mainland, hoping that we will surrender the fleet rather than fight. But we shall not surrender, Lieutenant, we shall not!" He spoke passionately, but Sharpe heard the hopelessness in his voice. How could little Denmark resist France? "So why," Skovgaard went on, "does Britain send ships and men to the Baltic?"

"To take the fleet, sir," Sharpe admitted, and he wondered how Skovgaard had learned of a secret article in a treaty signed by France and Russia. But then, if Lord Pumphrey was right, that was Skovgaard's business when he was not importing tobacco and jute.

"We are neutral!" Skovgaard protested. "But if Britain attacks us then she will drive us into the arms of France. Is that what Britain wants?"

"It wants the fleet out of French reach, sir."

"That we can manage without your help," Skovgaard said. But not if the French invaded, Sharpe thought, and broke the Danish army. The subsequent peace treaty would demand the surrender of the navy, and thus Napoleon would have his warships, but he said none of that aloud, for Skovgaard, he reckoned, knew that truth as well as he did.

"So tell me, Lieutenant," Skovgaard said, "what brings you to my house?"

So Sharpe told his tale. Told of Lavisser, of the chest of gold, of the mission to the Crown Prince and of his escape from the beach near Køge. Skovgaard listened with an expressionless face, then wanted to know more. Who had sent him exactly? When did Sharpe first know of the mission? What were his qualifications? What was his history? He seemed particularly interested that Sharpe had risen from the ranks. Sharpe did not understand why half the questions were even asked, but he answered as best he could though he resented the inquisition which felt uncomfortably like a magistrate's interrogation.

Skovgaard at last finished his questions, put down his pipe and took a clean sheet of paper from a desk drawer. He wrote for some time, saying nothing. He finally finished, sanded the ink, folded the paper and dropped a blob of wax to seal it. He then spoke in Danish to one of the two men who still stood behind Sharpe. The door squealed open and, a moment later, Aksel Bang returned to the room. Skovgaard was writing an address above the red sealing wax. "Aksel"—he spoke in English, presumably so Sharpe would understand—"I know it is late, but would you be so kind as to deliver this note?"

Bang took the letter and an expression of surprise showed on his face when he saw the address. "Of course, sir," he said.

"You need not return here," Skovgaard said, "unless there is a reply, which I do not expect. I shall see you at the warehouse in the morning."

"Of course, sir," Bang said and hurried from the room.

Skovgaard scraped out his exhausted pipe. "Tell me, Lieutenant," he said, "why you, an army officer of no special distinction, are here? The British government, I assume, employs men to fight the war of secrets. Such men will speak the languages of Europe and have the skills of subterfuge. Yet they sent you. Why?"

"The Duke of York wanted someone to protect Captain Lavisser, sir."

Skovgaard frowned. "Captain Lavisser is a soldier, is he not? He is also grandson to the Count of Vygârd. I would hardly think such a man needs your protection in Denmark? Or anywhere else for that matter."

"There was more to it than that, sir." Sharpe frowned, knowing he was doing a bad job of explaining himself. "Lord Pumphrey didn't really trust Captain Lavisser, sir."

"They don't trust him? So they sent him here with gold?" Skovgaard was icily amused.

"The Duke of York insisted," Sharpe said lamely.

Skovgaard stared at Sharpe for a few seconds. "If I might summarize your position, Lieutenant, you are telling me, are you not, that Captain Lavisser has come to Denmark under false pretenses?"

"Yes, sir."

"You're quite right, Lieutenant," Skovgaard said, "you are so very right!" He spoke with force and an evident dislike of Sharpe. "The Honorable John Lavisser, Lieutenant, arrived in Copenhagen yesterday and presented himself to His Majesty, the Crown Prince. That audience is described in this morning's *Berlingske Tidende*." He lifted a newspaper from his desk, unfolded it and tapped a column of print. "The paper tells us that Lavisser came to fight for Denmark because, in all conscience, he cannot support England. His reward, Lieutenant, is a major's commission in the Fyn Light Dragoons and an appointment as an aide-de-camp to General Ernst Peymann. Lavisser is a patriot, a hero." Skovgaard threw down the paper and a new, bitter anger entered his voice. "And it is contemptible of you to suggest he was sent to bribe the Crown Prince! His Majesty is not corrupt. Indeed he is our best hope. The Crown Prince will lead our country against all its enemies, whether they be British or French. If we lost the Prince, Lieutenant, then lesser men, timid men, might make an accommodation with those enemies, but the Prince is stalwart and Major Lavisser, far from coming to corrupt His Majesty, is here to support him."

"He brought gold, sir."

"That is hardly a crime," Skovgaard said sarcastically. "So what is it, Lieutenant, that you want me to do?"

"My orders, sir, were to take Captain Lavisser and the gold back to the British army if the Prince refused the bribe, sir."

"And you came here expecting my help in that endeavor?"

"Yes, sir."

Skovgaard leaned back in the chair and stared at Sharpe with an expression of distaste. His long fingers toyed with the letter opener, then he tossed it on the desk. "It is true, Lieutenant," he said, "that I have, at times, been of assistance to Great Britain." He waved a hand as if to suggest that assistance had been trivial, though in truth there were few men in northern Europe more valuable to London. Skovgaard was a Danish patriot, but his marriage to an Englishwoman had given him a fond attachment to a second country that was now sorely tried by the expectation of a British fleet. Skovgaard had never intended to involve himself in the murky business of espionage. At first he had merely passed on to the British embassy whatever news he gathered from the skippers of the Baltic traders who came to his warehouse, and over the years that intelligence had grown until Skovgaard was paying the golden coins of Saint George to a score of men and women in northern Europe. London valued him, but Skovgaard was no longer sure he wanted to help London now that a British fleet was fast approaching Copenhagen. "This is a time," he said to Sharpe, "when all Danes must choose their allegiance. That is as true of me as it is of Major Lavisser, a man I am not inclined to doubt. He has risen high in your country's service, Lieutenant. He was a Guards officer, an aide to the Duke of York and a gentleman who, in all conscience, can no longer support what your country is doing. But you? What are you, Lieutenant?"

"A soldier, sir," Sharpe said bleakly.

"What kind?" The question was caustic. "How old are you? Thirty? And still a second lieutenant?"

"It's where you start that counts," Sharpe said bitterly.

"And where will you end?" Skovgaard did not wait for an answer, but instead picked up the *Berlingske Tidende*. "The newspaper, Lieutenant, tells us more than the mere facts of Major Lavisser's arrival. Yesterday afternoon, at the invitation of the Crown Prince, Major Lavisser addressed the Defense Commission and I think you should hear his remarks. He warned that Britain is desperate and that she will stoop to the lowest measures to weaken Denmark's resolve. 'If it is a matter of cutting off heads then Britain can do it as well as Madame Guillotine.' Are you listening, Lieutenant? These are Major Lavisser's words. 'I have heard, I cannot vouch for its truth, that an army officer whose career is close to an end, a ruffian promoted from the ranks who faces ruin because of scandal at home, has been dispatched to Denmark to assassinate the Crown Prince. I cringe from believing such a thing, but would still encourage every loyal Dane to be watchful,'" Skovgaard threw down the paper. "Well, Lieutenant?"

Sharpe stared at him in disbelief.

"And what are you, Lieutenant?" Skovgaard asked. "An aging lieutenant who started in the ranks, yet you wish me to believe that Britain would send such a man to treat with a prince? You?" He looked Sharpe up and down with utter disgust.

"I've told you the truth!" Sharpe protested angrily.

"I doubt that," Skovgaard said, "but it is easy enough to discover. I have sent a note to Major Lavisser asking him to come here in the morning to confirm or deny your account."

"You invited Lavisser here!" Sharpe protested. "That bastard tried to kill me!"

Skovgaard stiffened. "I deplore base language," he said. "So, Lieutenant, are you willing to wait here and face Major Lavisser?"

"Like hell I am," Sharpe said. He turned to fetch his pack and coat. "And damn you, Skovgaard," he added.

The two young men blocked Sharpe from the door and Skovgaard's voice turned him back toward the desk where the merchant now held a long-barreled pistol. "I am not willing to risk my Prince's life, Lieutenant," Skovgaard said. "You will either stay here of your own accord or I shall detain you until Major Lavisser can give me advice."

Sharpe was just gauging the distance to the desk and the likelihood that the pistol would be accurate, when one of the two men drew another gun. It was a big one, the kind of pistol that a man would employ to put down a horse, and its great black muzzle was pointed at Sharpe's head. Skovgaard said something in Danish and the other man, while his companion held the gun steady, took away Sharpe's saber, then searched his pockets. He found the gold Sharpe had stolen on board the *Cleopatra*, but Skovgaard sternly ordered him to return it, then the man discovered Sharpe's small folding knife which went into a drawer of Skovgaard's desk. Then, with the pistols still threatening him, Sharpe was pushed into the hall. Astrid, Skovgaard's daughter, watched in astonishment from her doorway, but said nothing.

Sharpe was thrust into a small room that opened from the hall. The door was shut and he heard a key turn in the lock and the sound reminded him that he had lost his picklock on the beach near Køge. There were no windows in the room, and thus no light, but he groped about to discover he was in a small dining room furnished with a wide table and six chairs. It was the kind of room where a small intimate dinner party could be held, warmed by a great fire that would burn in the now empty hearth. The room was now Sharpe's prison.

He was locked in and feeling like a bloody fool. Lavisser had anticipated him, trapped him and beaten him. The guardsman was forty-three thousand guineas richer and Sharpe had failed.

CHAPTER 5

IT WAS ON THE wide terrace of Kronborg Castle, at Helsingør, that the ghost of Hamlet's father had stalked the night and now, under the quarter moon of another night's sky, a score of big guns faced the narrow sea, their long barrels shadowed in the deep embrasures.

Beneath the terrace, in an arched crypt, two men pumped the handles of massive bellows to blast cold air into one of the fortress's three furnaces. Other men, using long-handled cradles, tongs and pokers, rolled iron shot onto the coals which, in the fire's deep heart, glowed white as the air hissed through the bellows' iron nozzles. The furnace, hidden in the crypt so that its light would not glow on the fortress walls at night, was like a glimpse of hell. Red light flickered on the stone arches and glistened on the naked torsos of the men laboring about the roaring, seething incandescence.

The first six shot, each one an iron ball weighing twenty-four pounds, glowed red. "It's hot, sir," a sweat-soaked man shouted through the crooked passage that led from the furnace crypt.

"We're ready!" an officer outside the crypt called up to the nearest battery.

The guns had already been charged with their bags of powder over which had been rammed thick layers of felt that had been soaked with water. The felt was there to stop the red-hot shot prematurely igniting the powder.

"Bring the shot!" a man shouted from the battery.

A dozen men manhandled the red-hot round shot onto their cradles. The cradles were like stretchers and, at their centers, were shallow iron dishes for holding the heated shot. "Quick now!" the officer said as the men hurried from the crypt and up the stone steps to the waiting guns. The round shot cooled quickly, losing their glow, but the officer knew the heat was deep in the iron's heart and, when the great guns fired, the redness would come back. A thoroughly heated twenty-four-pound shot could cool for an hour and still retain enough fire in its belly to ignite wood. They were lethal against ships.

"Wait!" a new voice called. The commander of Kronborg Castle, a lieutenant-general who had been hastily summoned from his bed, hurried up the battery steps. He wore a tasseled nightcap and had a black woollen gown over his long nightshirt.

"The shot's newly heated, sir," the battery officer, a captain, pointed out respectfully as the furnacemen lowered the cradles beside the waiting barrels where the gunners had giant pincers ready to maneuver the shot into the cannons' muzzles. The Captain wanted to ram the first six guns and hear the felt wadding hiss. He wanted to see the round shot glowing as they seared across the sea to leave six streaks of redness in the dark, but the fortress's commander would not give the order to load. Instead the General climbed onto the lip of an embrasure and just gazed out to sea.

Countless ships were entering the channel. They looked ghostly in the night for their white sails were touched by the wan moonlight. They seemed motionless, for there was small wind this night. The General stared. There were hundreds of ships out there, far too many for his handful of guns, and those spectral vessels were bringing guns, horses and men to Denmark. Beyond the fleet, on the Swedish shore, a scatter of glimmering lights showed in the town of Helsingborg. "Have they fired on us?" he asked the Captain.

"No, sir," the Captain said. The redness was fading on the waiting shot. "Not yet, sir."

But just then a dull boom sounded from the distant fleet and the General saw a flash of red illumine one of the black-and-yellow hulls.

"Sir!" The Captain was impatient. He wanted his guns to pour their red heat into the dark bellies of the British fleet. He imagined that fleet burning, saw its sails writhing with flame and the sea shivering with fire.

"Wait," the General said, "wait."

Another gun fired at sea, but there was no trundling sound of round shot in the air and no splash of a falling shot. There was just the cannon's dull boom fading in the night, then renewing itself as a third gun fired. "They're making a salute," the General said. "Return it. No shot."

"We salute them?" The Captain sounded incredulous.

The General wrapped his nightgown tighter against the night's chill, then stepped down from the embrasure. "We are not yet at war, Captain," he said reproachfully, "and they are offering us a salute, so we shall return the compliment. Fifteen guns, if you please."

The red-hot round shot cooled.

The ships ghosted southward. They carried an army that had come to crush Denmark.

And Denmark saluted it.

SHARPE COULD hear voices coming from the parlor across the hall, but the conversation was in Danish so he learned nothing, though he presumed Skovgaard was telling his daughter of Britain's perfidy. A clock in the house struck ten and was followed by the cacophony of the city's bells.

Light flared briefly under the small dining room's door as Skovgaard or his daughter carried candles upstairs, then Sharpe heard the house shutters being closed and their bolts slammed home. Someone tested the door of the room in which he was imprisoned and, satisfied that it was securely locked, pulled the key from the door and walked away.

Sharpe had not been idle. He had explored the room to discover a bureau with drawers, but they held nothing useful, merely linens. He had groped for firedogs in the hearth, thinking he might use them to break down the door, but the fireplace was empty. He had tried the door, but it was solid, locked and immovable.

So now he waited.

Lavisser would kill him. Skovgaard might think the renegade guardsman was a hero, but Sharpe knew better. The Honorable John Lavisser was a thief and a killer. He was escaping from debt in England and it was no longer any wonder that the first man appointed to accompany Lavisser had died, because Lavisser had doubtless wanted a clean start in his new country. Sharpe was nothing but dirt to be swept out of his way.

And Skovgaard was no help. The Dane was dazzled by Lavisser's patriotic gesture and absurdly impressed that Lavisser was a gentleman with royal connections. So get out of here, Sharpe thought. Get out before Lavisser brought Barker to do his dirty work.

But the dining room's door was locked and its walls were solidly paneled. Sharpe had tried to lift the floorboards, but they were firmly nailed and he could get no purchase. Yet there was a way out.

He did not want to try. But escape was there, and he had no choice. Or a bad choice. He could wait till morning and then be handed over to Lavisser's mercies. Or he could do what he feared to do.

Jem Hocking had once tried to sell the young Richard Sharpe to a chimney sweep, only Sharpe had run away. Sweeping was a death sentence. Some boys got trapped in chimneys and suffocated, while the rest were coughing up bloody scraps of their lungs long before they were full grown. So Sharpe had run away and he had never stopped running since, but now he must try and climb like a sweep. Be sure your sin will find you out. He thought of that text as he stooped into the wide hearth. It was clean, but he could smell the rank soot in the shaft above him. He pushed his hands up to find a brick ledge a couple of feet above the hearth's throat. He did not want to do this. He was frightened of becoming trapped in the narrow black passage, but it was the only way out. Or rather he hoped it was a way out, but he could not be sure. It was possible that the chimney served only the one hearth, in which case it would become ever narrower and he would be blocked, but it was far more likely that this flue would join another. Go up this shaft, he told himself, then drop down the other. It will be easy, he tried to reassure himself, a ten-year-old could do it.

He hauled on the ledge with his hands and scrabbled with his boots to find some purchase on the tiled hearth. He slipped a couple of times, then managed to push and pull his way up through the chimney's throat. The air stank, but this first bit was easy enough and he clambered onto the ledge and knelt there while he groped up again and felt the flue becoming narrower. The house was only a couple of years old but that had been long enough to leave a thick deposit of soot that crumbled under his fingers and fell into his hair and eyes. His mouth was full of it. He tried to spit, but half choked instead. He could hear the flakes of soot and clinker rattling down into the hearth. Suppose Skovgaard was still downstairs? Suppose someone lit a fire? Common sense told him that was unlikely, but the fear would not go away.

He tried to stand, but the chimney bellied in at the sides and at first he could not squeeze past the bulging bricks so he twisted sideways and tried again. He managed to force his way up into the black hole, but the masonry inside the chimney was crudely pointed and his clothes kept snagging on mortar. He heaved the first two times it happened and heard his coat rip, but then the fabric was caught again and he knew the shaft could only get narrower and so he dropped back to his knees, twisted around and fell back into the fireplace. He crawled into the room where he gasped for breath and pawed soot from his eyes.

If it were to be done, he thought, then it would have to be done naked. He stripped, then nerved himself and went back into the hearth. He climbed onto the ledge, twisted sideways and stood up. It was easier now, though the rough brickwork gouged and scraped his skin. The flue was so narrow that the masonry scraped against his shoulder blades and chest. It was like being buried alive, he thought. Every time he breathed he could feel the eddy of air on the bricks in front of his eyes and smell the rank fumes of old soot. He could see nothing, but the constriction of the chimney pressed black and filthy like the cold walls of a tomb. He shivered. The flue was barely wide enough from front to back, but it was a few inches wider than his shoulders and he used that space to push himself up. He could scarcely bend his legs. Each time he wanted to move he had to lift a foot a few inches to find a rough ledge in the chimney's pointing, then shove himself up. He hooked his fingers into the small spaces between the brick courses, scrabbling through the thick deposit of soot that cascaded thick onto his face. He tried to breathe through his nose, but soot clogged it and he was forced to half choke through his dry mouth. He could not look up because the chimney was too narrow for him to tilt his head back and so he reached up, desperate to find the place where another flue joined this shaft.

Inch by inch he climbed. He slipped once and only stopped himself sliding back to the ledge by ramming his shoulder into the wall. He scraped his foot down the flue, seeking any purchase, and found a space where the pointing had come out of the brickwork. He shoved himself another inch, then another, but the chimney's sides were narrowing. He had his arms above his head, but the sides of the shaft were touching his shoulders now and he had to fight for every inch. His eyes stung even though he kept them closed. His throat was dry, the soot was sour in his gullet and the stench made him want to retch. He lifted his left foot two inches, all he could manage, and found a rough piece of masonry. He put his weight on it and the mortar broke away, clattering down to the hearth below. He held on with his hands, found another tiny ledge and shoved himself up. The hair on the back of his head brushed against bricks and he sensed the shaft was narrowing even more and he felt a terrible despair because he would be blocked, maybe even stuck, but then, quite suddenly, his right hand groped in nothingness. He flailed for a heartbeat, then discovered that the bricks above him sloped steeply away and he knew he had come to the place where two flues joined. All he had to do now was wriggle up, then drop down into the second flue and pray it was as wide as the first. He found a foothold, then pushed and slid and wriggled until there was just empty black space in front of his face. He paused, stretching out his hand to explore the mound of bricks where the flues joined and felt a fierce elation. He would damn well do it! He hooked his hands over the breastwork, hauled himself up, twisted so his belly would slide over the mound and then rammed his head painfully against bricks.

The flues joined to make a chamber that was wide, but very low, and the chimney leading up to the roof was much too narrow to climb. He could feel a draft from that upper chimney, though he could still see nothing. He forced his eyes open even though they stung terribly, but through the tears he could see no glimmer of moonlight from the upper chimney and no light from the second flue. He groped in the dark. He had reckoned on climbing above the join and lowering himself into the second flue, but there was not enough space in the chamber. How the hell did they clean their chimneys here? Maybe small boys just scoured the lower flues and brushes were used from the roof to clean the higher shafts, for even the smallest child could not climb into that narrow upper chimney and Sharpe knew he could not clamber over the breastwork for there was scarce a foot of space above it. Which meant he would have to slither over it and dive head-first into the second flue.

Every breath was a mix of air and soot. He was desperate for clean air, for water. He sneezed, then went very still, fearing that someone would have heard him. He was making enough noise anyway, for every movement dislodged great chunks of soot that rattled down to the hearths below. But he heard nothing. Presumably father and daughter had gone to their rooms and the servants were either in the attics or the basement.

He forced himself over the breastwork, sliding on his belly while the bricks above scraped on his back. He could feel down into the second flue now, but suddenly he was stuck fast. He could bend his upper body over the joint in the shafts, but his legs would not follow. He tried to find handholds to jerk himself forward, but the mortar pointing just broke off in his fingers. He could not move his legs at all. He jerked and pushed himself from side to side, achieving nothing. He even tried to push himself back, desperate to free himself from the black grip of the shallow chamber, but he was stuck, jammed like a stick in the bend of a pipe.

So turn over, he told himself. Turn over so that his legs would bend at the knee and let him slide on his back into the second flue. He tried and there was just enough space to half twist himself, but then he jammed again. Yet it was the only way. He would die here otherwise, smothered by soot. He swore under his breath, then twisted again and this time he forced his hip against the brick above him and, when it stuck, he twisted again, using his weight to grind his hips round. Bricks and mortar cut into him. He could feel blood trickling down the lacerated skin, but he gritted his teeth and lurched again and again, each time gaining a fraction of an inch and cutting deeper into his flesh. Then suddenly he had made it, he had turned, and he was lying on his back with his belly up to the top chimney and he could let his head fall so that he was slanting down into the second flue. He slid down, and the weight of his head and chest pulled on his hips as the blood ran warm down his belly. He reached down with his hands, found a ragged joint in the bricks and pulled and then he was half falling, half twisting and his legs could at last bend over the flue's mounded joint.

He was falling, but he rammed his hands and spine against the bricks. He tore his palms, ripping skin and flesh away, but he checked his fall. He was going head-first down the second flue now, and it was much easier than climbing. All he had to do was use his bloodied hands to brake himself and so he let himself drop inch by inch until he came to the chimney's throat and then there was no way of stopping himself, so he just let go.

He fell into an empty hearth. The air felt cool and wonderful. He curled up, feeling the soot flake down on him, and just shuddered for a few seconds. He had thought he would die up there. He remembered the grip of the brickwork, the black shroud all about him and he wanted to stay curled up. "Grace." He said her name aloud as though her spirit could come and give him strength. "Grace." He did not believe she was gone forever. It seemed to him that she hovered about him, a guardian angel.

He crawled out of the hearth to find he was in Skovgaard's study. A very faint moonlight showed through the higher windows. The lower ones were shuttered. He crossed the room, flinching from the pain in his hips, and lifted the locking bar from one pair of shutters. The shutters were heavy, so heavy he realized they were made of iron. Skovgaard, he thought, was a very cautious man. The window served as a door to the garden and he unbolted it, then flinched as the hinges squealed. The cool night air felt wonderful.

There was just enough moonlight for him to see his pack, coat, hat and saber still on the chair in the study. His uniform was inside the pack and he reckoned he would have to wear the green jacket, for the key to the small dining room had been taken away and he did not see how he could get back into the room where he had left his torn clothes without waking the whole household. He would lose the guineas he had stolen on board the *Cleopatra* and he would have to manage without boots, but that was better than being Lavisser's victim. The thing to do, he told himself, was get the hell away from this place, but before he dressed he wanted to wash the filth off his lacerated skin. He walked into the garden and saw a great rain butt under a downspout. He lifted off the lid to find it almost full of water and so he climbed inside, lowering himself gently, for the water was cold and the sound of it spilling over the edge would be too loud if he just dropped.

He ducked under, rubbing his skin, his hair and the bleeding cuts on his hips. He gulped down the water, then just crouched in the huge barrel. He had to get away, he knew that, but then what? He supposed he had no option but to wait for the British army to arrive and then crawl back to Sir David Baird as a failure.

He climbed out of the water and, dripping, went back into the study. He opened his pack and took out a dirty shirt and his rifleman's uniform. It might not be sensible to wear such a uniform this close to

Copenhagen, but he could cover it with his greatcoat. He pulled on the black trousers, buttoned the green jacket, then tied the red sash and the saber belt about his waist. A soldier again, and it felt good. It felt truly good. God damn it, he thought, but he would make Lavisser pay.

Except he could see no way of getting revenge on the guardsman. For the moment he just had to escape, but he reckoned there was time to search Skovgaard's study for anything useful. He went to the side table where the Dane kept his pipes and struck a light with the tinderbox. He lit two candles, then crouched by the leather-topped desk.

The seven drawers were locked, but the poker from the hearth made a stout crowbar that easily shattered the first lock. It splintered noisily and Sharpe froze, waiting for evidence that the sound had woken someone. He heard nothing, so levered the other drawers open and brought the candles closer.

Six of the drawers held nothing but papers, but in the seventh he found his folding knife and the pistol which Skovgaard had used to threaten him. The gun was one of a pair and they were beautifully balanced weapons with long barrels chased with silver. He thought at first they were dueling pistols, but when he probed one barrel he found it was rifled. This was no aristocratic toy, but a killing machine; expensive and deadly. He opened a frizzen and saw the gun was primed. He drew out the ramrod and slid it down both barrels to check the pistols were loaded, then looked in the drawer for more ammunition, which he found in a tooled leather box that held a silver powder flask and a dozen spare bullets. The spout of the powder flask had a measuring chamber to ensure that the pistols were charged with exactly the right amount of powder. He put the flask and bullets into a pocket, then thrust the two pistols into his belt. "Thank you, Skovgaard," he said under his breath.

He pulled on the coat and hat. There was little left in the pack that he needed so he just put the twenty-two guineas, the sewing kit and his telescope into his coat pockets and left the pack where it was. A sudden noise made him turn in alarm, but it was only the clock on the mantel whirring itself ready to strike midnight.

He blew out the candles and went back into the garden. He closed the shutters and glass doors then crossed a terrace of flagstones and went down a grassy slope. There were a dozen other houses in view, but all were a good distance away and all of them dark. A brick wall enclosed

Skovgaard's garden, but there was a gate next to the stables which he guessed led to an alley. He turned and looked back to see a single light gleaming soft behind louvred shutters. For some reason he decided that must be Astrid's room and he had a sudden vision of her high pale forehead, golden hair and bright eyes. He felt guilty then, thinking of Grace.

Go, he told himself. Go west into the country, steal some boots and wait for the British forces to come. He did not want to do that, for it would mean slinking back to Sir David Baird with his tail between his legs, but what choice was there? Then he heard the small scuffling sound.

A cat? He crouched. Not a cat, for he could hear footsteps. Someone was prowling about the house and trying to make as little noise as possible. A servant, perhaps, checking that the house was secure? Some servants plainly lived in the carriage house by the stables and maybe, as a final duty, one of them patroled Skovgaard's house. Yet the steps sounded like more than one man, none of them carried a lantern and they were moving with a deliberate stealth. Sharpe moved to the dark shadow of a bush and waited. The quarter moon was misted and half hidden behind some tall pines, yet it cast just enough light for Sharpe to see six dark shapes appear at the side of the house. They came slowly, edging past the rain butt where one of them inadvertently kicked the butt's wooden lid which Sharpe had left on the path and all six went very still. They waited for what seemed a long time, then one of them tried the back door, found it locked and moved on to the study's tall windows. There they discovered the unlocked glass door and the unbarred shutters. They paused, suspecting a trap, but then, after a whispered consultation, they all went inside. Sharpe had seen no faces, but the size of one man had suggested Barker and the height of another might have been Lavisser. Yet why would Lavisser come like a thief in the night? He had an invitation. He could wait till morning. Sharpe could make no sense of it, so he just stayed where he was. He heard the muffled squeal of the study door opening. The men would discover his escape soon enough and then they would presumably leave. He doubted they would search the garden, but would probably look for him on the nearby roads so he reckoned he was safe in his hiding place. It would not be a long wait, he told himself, then he saw a glimmer of light in an upstairs window. It flickered briefly, then faded as though someone was carrying a candle down a passage.

Go now, he thought, while they were upstairs, but then he heard the scream. It was brief, a woman's voice, cut off as soon as it sounded. More lights showed in the upstairs windows. A man shouted peremptorily and Sharpe just listened in astonishment. They had not come for him, but for Skovgaard! Then it could not be Lavisser, but who? The Danes themselves? But why come in the night? And men who came in the night implied harm, which meant Skovgaard would need help, and Sharpe needed Skovgaard if he was not to fail utterly and so he abandoned his resolve to flee westward and instead moved toward the house, throwing off his greatcoat because it hampered him. He paused briefly at the study window, but could hear nothing beyond the shutters and so he stepped through. The room was dark, but a faint light showed at the door to the hall.

He crossed the room, wincing whenever a board squeaked beneath the rugs. The hall was empty and the light was coming from the upper landing where he could hear voices raised in anger. They spoke Danish and he had no idea what was being said. He crossed the hall to the parlor where Astrid had been playing the harpsichord. It was pitch black inside, but he flattened himself beside the door and listened.

It sounded as though the whole household, including the servants, was being herded down the stairs. Then someone kicked the parlor door wide open to let in a wash of yellow lamplight, but blessedly no one came inside and Sharpe had time to move behind a screen printed with windmills and ducks. He accidentally kicked a flower-painted chamber pot, but no one heard because of the racket outside. He waited again.

Then he heard Lavisser's voice. He was sure it was Lavisser, but he was not speaking Danish or English. French? Sharpe was almost certain it was French. He was giving orders and a moment later a lamp was brought into the parlor and Sharpe heard footsteps. There was a mirror between the shuttered windows and in its reflection he could see two maidservants, both in nightgowns and caps, being pushed into the room. The elderly manservant followed, then Astrid entered and, behind her, a man with a pistol. Lavisser spoke to him in French.

"You want me in there, sir?" a voice asked in English. It was Barker.

"No. Get Sharpe," Lavisser answered and then, still using English, he spoke to Astrid. "You will not be hurt, I promise."

"But my father!" Astrid sounded distraught, and no wonder. She was

in a long nightdress and her blond hair fell loose on her shoulders. "I
want to be with my father!"

"Your father has become rich by fighting France," a voice replied. It
was not Lavisser who spoke, but a woman. Another mystery on a night
gone askew. "And your father should have known the consequences of
such foolishness," the woman finished. She had an accent. French?

The door closed. Astrid sat on the harpsichord bench, weeping, as the
Frenchman waved the three terrified servants toward the sofa. Sharpe
should have been visible to him in the mirror, but the rifleman was in
deep shadow and the Frenchman suspected nothing. He did not even
look behind the screen, but just leaned against the closed door with his
pistol held low. He yawned. What did he have to fear? Three women and
an elderly man?

Sharpe pulled one pistol from his belt. So Lavisser worked with the
French? The idea was repugnant, but it made sense. The enemy must
have their agents in London and how better to snare fools than to find
them playing cards at Almack's and the other rich gaming clubs? And
they had snared a choice one in Lavisser, but if Lavisser was now planning on killing Skovgaard then Sharpe did not have much time. He
wrapped the pistol in the hem of his jacket to muffle the distinctive sound
of the flint being cocked. He had been out of his depth ever since he had
arrived in Denmark, enduring insult, religion and imprisonment, but
now he knew what he was doing. He was back where he belonged and he
was smiling as he stepped out from behind the screen.

He held the pistol at arm's length and it took the Frenchman at least
two seconds to register his presence and by then the gun was just three
feet from his head. Sharpe motioned with his left hand. "Put the gun
down, Monsewer." He spoke softly.

The man looked as if he was about to shout.

"Please," Sharpe said. "Make a noise so I can kill you, please." He was
still smiling.

The Frenchman shook slightly. There was something about the eyes
of the green-jacketed man that told him death was hovering very close in
this comfortable parlor and so, sensibly and very slowly, he laid his own
pistol on the floor. Astrid and the servants were staring wide-eyed. Sharpe
kicked the Frenchman's pistol across the polished floorboards. "Down,"
he told the man, indicating what he meant with his left hand.

The man lay on his belly, anxiously twisting his head to see what Sharpe was doing. "I wouldn't watch, miss," Sharpe said to Astrid, then put a finger to his mouth to show that she should be silent.

He had a problem now. The Frenchman had seen Sharpe put the finger to his lips and must have realized that noise was his best friend, which meant Sharpe was unwilling to shoot him because the sound of the pistol would bring the other intruders into the parlor. The man took a deep breath and Sharpe, desperate, kicked him brutally hard in the throat. He hurt his foot, for he had no boots, but he hurt the Frenchman even more. Astrid gasped and the man began to choke as he clutched his gullet and his feet drummed on the floor. Sharpe dropped on the man's back to hold him still. He needed to make the man senseless, but that would take a deal of violence and must inevitably make more noise. Skovgaard's expensive pistols, though deadly, were not heavy enough to use as clubs. The Frenchman, catching his breath, tried to heave Sharpe off his back so Sharpe hit him hard, bouncing the man's skull off the floorboards, but he still tried to twist Sharpe off. Sharpe hit him again, this time so hard that the man went momentarily still and so gave Sharpe a chance to put the pistol down. He took out his folding knife and pulled out the blade. "Eyes closed, miss," he said grimly.

"What . . ."

"Shhh," Sharpe said. "Tell the others to close their eyes. Quick now."

Astrid whispered something in Danish as Sharpe felt the man tense under him. The Frenchman was about to make another effort to dislodge Sharpe, but the rifleman stabbed once with the short-bladed knife. It only took one thrust, right into the base of the skull, and the Frenchman gave a surprisingly strong spasm and then seemed to sigh. That was the only noise he made and there was remarkably little blood. Sharpe pulled the dead man's collar up to conceal the wound, wiped the knife clean on the corpse's coat, then stood. "You can open your eyes now," he said.

Astrid stared at Sharpe, then at the dead man.

"He's just sleeping," Sharpe said. He picked up the man's pistol. It was a clumsy thing compared to Skovgaard's sophisticated weapons, but it was loaded and gave him three shots. Four men and one woman left. "Are there any guns in this room?" Sharpe asked Astrid.

She shook her head.

He knelt by the corpse and searched its clothes, but the man had no other weapons. So, three shots and five targets. He went to the door and put his ear to the wood. He could hear voices. Then he heard the sound of a key turning in a lock, there was a pause and sudden feet on the hall floor. Sharpe waited a heartbeat, then eased the parlor door open an inch.

"He's gone!" Barker said.

"He can't have gone." That was Lavisser's voice.

"He's gone!" Barker insisted.

Sharpe imagined Lavisser glancing at the shutters. That opportunely open window could only be explained by Sharpe's otherwise inexplicable absence. "Look outside," Lavisser said, "and be careful."

The woman spoke, using French, then Lavisser talked in Danish. There was a pause, then Skovgaard, for it could be no one else, gave a shout that turned into a terrible groan and a yelp of pain. Astrid gasped and Sharpe whipped round and put his finger to his lips.

Skovgaard shouted again. It was the sound men made on the battle-field when they were wounded and did not want to scream. It was invol-untary, a wordless exhalation of pain. Sharpe pointed at Astrid. "Stay here," he said firmly, then pulled open the parlor door. Barker was proba-bly in the garden by now, so that left four targets and three shots. What had Baird called him? A thug. So he would be a thug now, and a damned good one. He crossed the hall and saw that the study door was ajar. He dared not push it open further for the hinges squealed so badly, but he wished he could see more of what was going on in the study. He could just make out that Skovgaard had been tied to the chair behind his desk on which stood a lantern, and in its light Sharpe could see that the front of Skovgaard's nightshirt was drenched in blood. Then he saw a man lean forward and force the Dane's mouth open. The man held a pair of pliers. They were making him talk.

A second man came into view to help keep Skovgaard's mouth open. The Dane tried to clamp his jaws shut, but the second man used a knife to force his teeth apart. The woman spoke. Skovgaard shook his head and the pliers' jaws closed on one of his teeth. Skovgaard groaned and made a huge effort to shake his head, but one of the men struck him hard across the skull. Then the Dane moaned as the pliers began to exert pressure.

Sharpe fired at the man wielding the pliers.

He used one of Skovgaard's rifled pistols and it was as accurate as it was beautiful. He had expected the long-rifled barrel to give the gun a heavy kick and so he had aimed a little low, but the weapon was so exquisitely balanced that it hardly quivered. It jetted smoke halfway across the study as the ball struck the man in his neck. A jet of blood fountained up over Skovgaard's desk. Sharpe dropped the gun, plucked Skovgaard's second pistol from his belt and pushed the door fully open. The man who had been holding Skovgaard's head was quick, incredibly quick, and he was already bringing up a pistol and so Sharpe, who had reckoned to take Lavisser with his second shot, fired at him instead. Smoke thickened in the room, shrouding Sharpe's targets, but he had the third pistol in his grip now and he aimed it at Lavisser, who had seized the woman's hand and was pulling her toward the open window. Sharpe fired. The Frenchman's heavy pistol kicked like a mule and made far more noise than the expensive guns. He heard the crash of breaking glass.

Someone squealed in pain, then Lavisser and the woman disappeared into the night. Smoke writhed about the room as Sharpe ran to Skovgaard's side. The Dane stared in astonishment, blood trickling down his long chin. Sharpe ducked down behind the desk so that he offered no target to anyone in the garden. The second man he had shot was lying against the wall, twitching, and his pistol was on the floor. Sharpe picked the weapon up, then hurled the lantern into the fireplace. The lamp glass shattered and the study was plunged into darkness.

He went to the window, knelt and peered into the garden. He could see no one, so he closed the metal shutters and put the bar into place. Lavisser, it seemed, had fled. The three shots, coming in such quick succession, must have convinced him that he was up against more than one man.

"Mister Sharpe?" Skovgaard said from the darkness. His voice was slurred.

"Aren't you glad Britain sent an aging lieutenant?" Sharpe asked savagely. He crossed to the desk and leaned on it so his face was close to Skovgaard. "And damn you, you bloody fool." He spat the words. "Damn you to bloody hell and all the bloody way back, but I was not sent to kill the Crown Prince."

"I believe you," Skovgaard said humbly. His voice was thick because of the blood in his mouth.

"And that was your hero Lavisser, you fat-headed bastard."

Sharpe, still angry, went to the parlor. "Your father needs water and towels," he told Astrid curtly, then picked up the lamp and went back to the study.

There were shouts outside the house. The coachmen and stable boys had evidently been woken by the shots and were now asking for reassurance from Skovgaard or his daughter. "Are those the two men who were with you earlier?" Sharpe asked Skovgaard who was still tied to the chair.

Skovgaard jerked his head toward the shutters. "That is them," he said indistinctly.

"Are they guards?"

"A coachman and a groom."

Sharpe cut Skovgaard free and the Dane went to the window to reassure the men outside while Sharpe knelt beside the wounded Frenchman, except he was a dead man now. He had bled to death. Sharpe swore.

Skovgaard frowned. "Lieutenant . . ."

"I know, you hate base language and after what you did to me I don't give a bugger. But I hoped this one was alive. He could have told us who was with Lavisser. But the bastard's dead."

"I know who they were," Skovgaard said bitterly, then his daughter came into the room and screamed when she saw her father. She ran to him and he clasped her to his bloodied nightgown and patted her back. "It's all right, dearest." Skovgaard spoke in English, then he saw the sooty marks on the big rug. His eyes widened and he stared, first at the black footprints, then at Sharpe. "Is that how you escaped?"

"Yes."

"Good God," Skovgaard said faintly. A maid had brought water and towels and Skovgaard sat at the desk and rinsed his mouth out. "I only had six teeth left," he said, "and now there are just four." Two bloody teeth lay on the desk next to his ivory false teeth and the broken lenses of his reading spectacles.

"You should have listened to me when I first came here," Sharpe growled.

"Mister Sharpe!" Astrid chided him.

"It's true," her father said.

Astrid turned a troubled gaze on Sharpe. "The man in there"—she gestured toward the parlor—"He's still sleeping."

"He's not going to wake up," Sharpe said.

"Three dead?" Skovgaard sounded incredulous.

"I wish it had been five." Sharpe put the two good pistols on the desk. "Your guns," he said. "I was going to steal them. Why didn't you keep a pair in your bedroom?"

"I did," Skovgaard said, "only they took Astrid first. They said they'd hurt her if I didn't come out."

"So who were they?" Sharpe asked. "I know one is your patriotic Lavisser. But the others?"

Skovgaard looked weary. He spat a mix of blood and spittle into a bowl, then smiled wanly when a maid brought him a robe that he wrapped about the bloody nightshirt. "The woman," he said, "is called Madame Visser. She is at the French embassy. Ostensibly she is merely the wife of the ambassador's secretary, but in truth she seeks information. She collates messages from throughout the Baltic." He hesitated. "She does for the French, Lieutenant, what I do, what I did, for the British."

"A woman does that?" Sharpe could not hide his surprise, earning a reproachful look from Astrid.

"She is very clever," Skovgaard said, "and without mercy."

"And what did she want?"

Skovgaard rinsed his mouth out again, then patted his lips with a towel. He tried to put in his false teeth, but his raw gums were too painful and made him wince. "They wanted names from me," he said, "the names of my correspondents."

Sharpe paced the room. He felt frustrated. He had killed three men and wounded a fourth if the blood on the small rug by the shutters was any indication, but it had all happened too quickly and his anger was still high, still unslaked. So Lavisser was in French pay? And Lavisser had almost given Britain's Baltic spymaster to the enemy, except that a rifleman had been waiting. "So what now?" Sharpe asked Skovgaard.

The Dane shrugged.

"You tell the authorities about this?" Sharpe nodded toward the dead men behind Skovgaard's desk.

"I doubt anyone would believe us," Skovgaard said. "Major Lavisser is a hero. I am a merchant and you are what? An Englishman. And my erstwhile affection for Britain is well known in Denmark. If you were the authorities who would you believe?"

"So you'll just wait for them to try again?" Sharpe asked.

Skovgaard glanced at his daughter. "We shall move back to our house in the city. It will be safer there, I think. The neighbors are closer and it is next to the warehouse so I don't have to travel. Much safer, I think."

"Just stay here," Sharpe suggested.

Skovgaard sighed. "You forget, Lieutenant, that your army is coming. They will lay siege to Copenhagen and this house lies outside the walls. Within a week, I suspect, there will be British officers quartered here."

"So you'll be safe."

"If Copenhagen is to suffer," Skovgaard said with a trace of his old asperity, "then I will share it. How can I look my workmen in the face if I leave them to endure a siege alone? And you, Lieutenant, what will you do?"

"I'll stay with you, sir," Sharpe said grimly. "I was sent to protect someone from the French, and it's you now. And Lavisser's still living. So I've work to do. And to start I need a spade."

"A spade?"

"You've got three dead bodies in the house. Where I come from we bury them."

"But . . ." Astrid began to protest, but her voice trailed away.

"That's right, miss," Sharpe said, "if you can't explain them, hide them."

It took him most of what remained of the night, but he dug a shallow trench in the soft soil by the back wall of the garden and laid the three Frenchmen inside. He patted the earth down and covered it with some bricks he found beside the carriage house.

And then, in a gray and weary dawn, he slept.

ELEVEN MILES north of Ole Skovgaard's house was the insignificant village of Vedbæk. It lay on the sea, halfway between Copenhagen and the fortress at Helsingør. The village held a handful of houses, a church, two farms and a small fleet of fishing boats. Tarred sheds lined the beach where nets hung to dry on tall poles and the burning charcoal of the herring smokers shimmered the air above the sand.

Work started early in Vedbæk. There were cows to be milked and fishing boats to be hauled down to the sea, yet this morning, at dawn, no one worked. The herring fires were dying and the people of the village were ignoring their duties and standing instead on the low grassy ridge that backed the beach. They said little, but just stared seaward.

Where a fleet had appeared in the night. Closest to the beach were gun brigs and bomb ships that had moored so their great cannons and mortars could threaten any Danish troops who might appear on the shore. Beyond those small ships were frigates and, farther out still, the great ships of the line, all of them with their gunports open. There was no enemy threatening the fleet, but the guns were ready.

Between the ships of the line and the frigates was moored a host of transport ships around each of which was a smaller fleet of tenders, launches and longboats that nuzzled the bigger hulls like so many suckling pigs. Horses were being slung out of holds and lowered into the boats. No one in Vedbæk had ever seen so many ships, not at one time. At least a dozen of the village men had been sailors, yet even they had not seen such a fleet, not in Copenhagen, London, Hamburg or in any other great port.

Someone began ringing the church bell as an alarm, but the pastor hurried back into the village to silence it. "We have already sent a messenger," he told the enthusiastic bell-ringer. "Sven has ridden to Hørsholm." There was a police barracks in Hørsholm, though what use the police would be the pastor did not know. They could hardly arrest a whole army, though doubtless they would send a warning to Copenhagen.

Folk from Hørsholm and from the lesser villages nearby were already coming to Vedbæk to see the ships. The pastor worried that the spectators might resemble an army and he did his best to disperse them. "Jarl! Your cows are lowing. They must be milked."

"I have girls to do that."

"Then find them. There is work to do."

But no one moved. Instead they watched as the first small boats headed for the shore. "Will they kill us?" a woman asked.

"Only the ugly ones," someone answered and there was nervous laughter. The man who had made the bad joke had been a sailor and he had a great telescope that he had propped on his wife's shoulder. He could see a field gun being lifted out of a ship's belly and slung on a whip into one of the bigger launches. "Now they're sending a cannon to shoot

Ingrid," he announced. Ingrid was his mother-in-law and as big as a Holstein cow.

A young lieutenant in the blue uniform of the Danish militia arrived on horseback. He was the son of a wheelwright in Sandbjerg and the only shots he had ever heard fired had been volleys of musketry emptied in the sand dunes as the militia practiced. "If you are going to fight them," the pastor said, "then perhaps you should go down onto the beach. Otherwise, Christian, take off your jacket so they don't realize you are a soldier. How is your mother?"

"She's still coughing. And sometimes there is blood."

"Keep her warm this coming winter."

"We will, we will." The Lieutenant stripped off his uniform jacket.

No one spoke as the first few launches neared the shore. The sailors at the oars had long pigtails showing under their tarred hats and their passengers were all in red uniforms and had big black shakos that made them seem very tall. One man was holding a flag, but because there was so little wind the banner just hung limply. The launches seemed to be racing each other for the honor of being first ashore. They heaved in the small waves close to the beach, then the first keel scraped on sand and the red-coated men were leaping over the side. "Form them up, Sergeant!"

"Aye aye, sir."

"You're not a bloody sailor, Sergeant. A plain yes will do."

"Aye aye, sir."

More boats grounded. The soldiers came out fast and the sailors were already pushing the launches off the beach, turning and rowing them back to the transport ships. A lieutenant colonel in a black bicorne hat walked up the beach. He was accompanied by a major and four captains. The villagers moved politely aside as the Lieutenant Colonel pointed to a small hill a half-mile inland. "Three companies to picket that high ground, John. I'll send the first battery ashore to reinforce you. Colin, your men will stay here in case anyone disputes us."

Colin, one of the captains, looked at the villagers. "They seem well disposed, sir."

"Keep them that way. Make sure the men behave."

The Lieutenant Colonel turned to watch for the boat carrying his horse. The pastor approached him. "May I ask why you are here?" the pastor inquired in good English.

"Good morning!" The Lieutenant Colonel touched the tasseled tip of his bicorne hat. "A nice one, eh?"

"Do you mean us harm?" the pastor asked nervously.

"Nicolson!" the Lieutenant Colonel shouted at a surprised private standing in the front rank of a company drawn up on the beach. "Shoulder your piece! Aim at the sky! Cock! Fire!"

Nicolson obediently pointed his musket at a wisp of cloud and pulled the trigger. The flint fell on an empty pan. "Not loaded, Father," the Lieutenant Colonel told the pastor. "We ain't here to kill decent folk, not on a nice morning. Come to stretch our legs." He smiled at the pastor. "This your village?"

"I am pastor here, yes."

"I'm afraid you're going to have soldiery as company all day, so keep the kitchen fires hot, Father, because the rogues like their tea. And if any man gives you any trouble, any trouble at all, just see an officer and we'll have the bastard hanged. Good day." He touched his hat again and walked back down the beach to where his horse was being coaxed ashore. The beast had been afloat for over two weeks and it staggered as though it was drunk when it reached the sand. The Lieutenant Colonel's orderly led it up and down for a while, then held it still while his master mounted. "Inland!" the Colonel called.

The first three companies marched inland, going to the high ground. More boats were landing now. A battery of field guns was being manhandled ashore and more horses were taking their first unsteady steps. One horse, sprightlier than the rest, escaped its handler and trotted up the beach where it stopped, apparently surprised by the spectators. A gunner ran after it and seized its bridle. He winked at some girls standing just paces away. They giggled.

Two companies of soldiers in green jackets landed closer to the village and that prompted many of the inhabitants to hurry back in case their houses were being plundered, though when they reached the main street they just discovered the green-jacketed men standing guard on their front doors. An officer was striding up the sandy street. "This is all private property," he was shouting, "and General Cathcart has given orders that any man who steals anything, I do not care how small or valueless a thing it is, will be hanged. Are you hearing this? You will be hanged! You will dance in the air! So keep your hands to yourselves! You will show respect to all civilians! Rifleman! You, the tall fellow! What's your name?" He knew all the men in his own company, but the tall man was from another.

The rifleman, well over six feet tall, feigned astonishment that he should be singled out. "Me, sir? I'm Pat Harper, sir, from Donegal."

"What's in that sack?"

Rifleman Harper turned an innocent expression on a sack that was lying against a cottage wall a few feet behind him. "Never seen it before in my life, Captain Dunnett, sir. Must have been left by one of the villagers, sir."

Dunnett looked suspicious, but accepted the explanation. "You will stand guard here," he told the men, "until we are relieved. If you apprehend any man trying to thieve anything you will arrest him and bring him to me so that we can have the pleasure of hanging him."

Captain Dunnett walked on down the street, repeating the orders. Another rifleman looked at Harper. "What's in the sack, Pat?"

"Three pullets, Cooper, and they're dead and they're also mine, and if you lay your thieving hands on them I'll stuff their feathers down your gullet until you start shitting angels' wings." Rifleman Harper smiled.

"Where did you find them?"

"Where I looked for them, of course."

"D'you see that girl?" a man called Harris said. They all turned to stare at a young woman with hair like fine-spun gold who was walking up the street. She knew she was being admired so lifted her head high and swung her hips as she strutted before the riflemen. "I think they shot me," Harris said, "and I've gone to heaven."

"We're going to like it here, boys," Harper said, "so long as they don't hang us."

"Ten to one you'll be hanged, Harper." It was Captain Murray, Harper's company commander, who had appeared beside the house and now peered inside the sack.

"It's not mine, Mister Murray," Harper said, "whatever it is. And I wouldn't tell you a lie, sir."

"Perish the thought, Harper, perish the very thought, but I'll still expect a cold leg of what's not yours."

Harper grinned. "Very good, sir."

Three battalions were on the beach now. The first field guns, hitched to their horses, were going inland to the high ground and still more ships were ghosting in the light wind from the north. No shots had been fired and no one had offered any resistance. The first generals were ashore and their aides laid maps on the sand while a squadron of the 1st Light Dragoons led their unsteady horses into the village where a pump fed a long watering trough.

"Hey, missus!" A rifleman accosted a woman who just looked at him fearfully. "Tea?" the man said, displaying a handful of loose leaves. "You can boil water?"

Her husband, who had sailed aboard a Baltic trader that had made several voyages to Leith and Newcastle, understood. "Firewood costs money," he grumbled.

"Here." The rifleman offered a copper. "It's good coin that! English money, none of your foreign rubbish. Tea, eh?"

So the riflemen had their tea, the high ground was secured and the British army was ashore.

CHAPTER 6

THE CLOUDS AT LAST fled Copenhagen, leaving a rinsed blue sky. A late summer sun glossed the copper roofs and shimmered the harbor where scores of merchant ships, fearing the British fleet that had anchored ten miles to the north, had taken refuge.

The Amalienborg Palace lay west of the harbor. It was really four small palaces grouped about a courtyard and was gracious rather than grand, intimate instead of intimidating, and it was there, on an upper floor overlooking the harbor, that the Crown Prince made his farewells to the city's notables. His Majesty was returning to Holstein. He had been in that southern province all summer, but had returned to Copenhagen when he heard that the British fleet had sailed for the Baltic. He had come back to encourage the citizens. Denmark, he said, did not want to fight. It had not started the quarrel and bore no ill will toward Britain, but if the British persisted in their outrageous demand to take the Danish fleet then Denmark would resist. And that, the Crown Prince knew, meant that Copenhagen must suffer, for it was in the capital's secure inner harbor that the fleet was sheltered.

Yet the British, the Crown Prince insisted, could not succeed. It was late in the year to begin a siege. It would take weeks to make a breach in the great walls and even then there could be no certainty that an assault would succeed. Besides, long before any breach was practicable, the Prince would bring the Danish army back from Holstein and trounce the besieging forces. "So the British will not attack the city," the Prince said forcefully, "but merely threaten it. It is a bluff, gentlemen, a bluff. There is no time for a siege."

"Plenty of time for a bombardment," General Peymann, who had been appointed the commander of Copenhagen's garrison, noted gloomily.

"No!" The Prince turned on the General. "No, no, no!" The Prince knew well enough that the city feared a bombardment by mortars and howitzers that could loft their shells over the wall to leave the city a smoking ruin. "The British are not barbarians," the Prince insisted, "and they will not risk an action that will earn the condemnation of all civilized people. There will be no bombing. The British will threaten it, just as they threaten a siege, but it is all bluff." Instead, he forecast, the British would blockade the capital and hope that hunger would persuade the garrison to yield. "So we shall fill the city with food," he told General Peymann, "and you must endure their blockade until the late autumn. Then I shall lead the army back from Holstein." Holstein was where the bulk of Denmark's army was guarding the southern frontier, which was threatened by a French army.

Peymann, an old man, straightened ponderously. He was white-haired, corpulent and had never led troops into battle, but he had a reassuring presence. There was something about the 72-year-old Ernst Peymann that suggested he could not be broken and the Prince was sure that Peymann, above all the other generals, could give the city confidence, though Peymann's next words smacked of nervousness. "It would be better, Your Majesty, if you came sooner."

"It can't be done. Can't be done." The Prince went to a window that overlooked the harbor. Three small ships, all low in the water because of the weight of grain they were bringing to the city, were mooring among the swarm of Danish gunboats being readied for battle. The Prince looked down at a table on which a map had been spread to catch the window's light. A valet followed him, holding the Prince's hat, sword and sash, but the Prince ignored him. "The British navy," he explained, "will surely blockade Zealand and we cannot ferry the army back if British ships are waiting."

Peymann stared gloomily at the map as if seeking inspiration. He found it in the sheer size of Zealand, the island on which Copenhagen stood. "Three thousand square miles," he said. "They cannot watch the whole coast!"

"They only need watch the harbors, sir," Captain, now Major, Lavisser pointed out respectfully.

"And that they can do with ships to spare," the Prince added, "but they're not cats, Peymann, they're not cats."

"They are most assuredly not, sire," Peymann said. The General was plainly confused by the Prince's declaration, but did not like to admit his puzzlement.

"They cannot see in the dark," the Prince explained anyway, "which means that when the long nights of winter come we can bring the army back to Zealand." He lowered his head so the valet could drape the sash over his shoulder, then raised his arms for the sword belt to be buckled. "We must wait for the long nights," he declared, "which means you must defend Copenhagen for two months, General, just two months."

"We can hold two months," Peymann said firmly, "unless they bombard."

"They won't," the Prince said firmly. "The British will not want the deaths of innocent civilians on their conscience."

"I do know that General Lord Cathcart is opposed to bombardment," Major Lavisser said, "though doubtless some of his subordinates will urge it on him."

"Lord Cathcart leads the army, does he not?" the Prince asked. "So let us hope he exercises his authority."

"We could send the women and children away," Peymann suggested, his face brightening at the thought. "There would be fewer mouths to feed."

"Do that," the Prince said, "and you invite the British to bombard the city. No, the women stay and the British, I assure you, will not commit a slaughter of the innocents. Two months, General! Hold the walls for two months and I shall bring the army back and we shall crush them like lice! Like lice!" The Prince pulled on white gloves. His optimism was genuine. Until the British fleet had sailed, the biggest threat facing Denmark had been the French army on the southern frontier, but the arrival of the British would almost certainly deter any French attack. Why should the French assault Denmark when the British were turning

Denmark into France's new ally? So there would be no fight in Holstein and when the longer nights blinded the enemy fleet the army could be brought back to Zealand where it would hugely outnumber the British forces. "We shall win," the Prince told Peymann, "so long as you hold for two months. And you can hold, General. The walls are thick, the guns are plentiful!"

Peymann nodded agreement. Like all the others in the room he now wished that the government had spent more on Copenhagen's defenses in the last few years, but even so the ramparts were adequate. The walls were massive and reinforced by bastions, batteries and forts. To the west the city looked over its own wealthy suburbs, but between those houses and the city there was an open space for the guns to kill attackers and a ring of canal-like lakes that served as a wide moat. The walls were not in the best of repair, but they mounted nearly two hundred guns, while out in the suburbs, wherever high ground might offer British batteries a vantage point, new strongholds were being constructed of earth, stone and timber. The city had a garrison of five and a half thousand troops, which was not enough to man all those new forts, but Peymann had four thousand well-trained seamen who had been the crews of the warships secured in Copenhagen's harbor, and the militia was being overwhelmed by volunteers. "We can give a good account of ourselves for two months," Peymann declared.

"So long as we are not betrayed," the newly promoted Major Lavisser intervened. His words cut across the room's mood of optimism. He shrugged, as if to suggest that he was reluctant to be the bearer of bad news. "There are British spies in the city, Your Majesty," he explained, "and they should be dealt with."

"Spies?" The Prince's protuberant eyes exaggerated his look of alarm.

"I made inquiries before leaving London, sire," Lavisser lied, "and ascertained one name. I wish I could have discovered more, should more exist, but I still urge that this one man is arrested, put in the Gammelholm cells and interrogated."

"Indeed he should!" the Prince agreed vigorously. "Who is he?"

"A man called Skovgaard, sire," Lavisser said.

"Not Ole Skovgaard," Peymann boomed. "Do you mean Ole Skovgaard?"

"I do." Lavisser was taken aback by Peymann's sudden vigor.

"You can rest assured he's no spy." The General spoke confidently. "He wrote to me this morning"—Peymann was talking to the Prince now—"and confessed he has helped the British in the past, but only in their struggle against France and I dare say there are a dozen men in this room who have done the same."

The Prince looked down at the map. He had a British mother and had been well known for his pro-British sentiments, but he did not want to be reminded of those things now.

"Skovgaard assures me of his loyalty," Peymann went on stolidly, "and I believe him. He's known to me by reputation. A worthy man, he worships at Our Savior's, he's a Commissioner of the Poor and he is, as are we all, disgusted by the British behavior. Arresting such a man will not help morale in the city, sire. This attack should unite us, not divide us."

The Prince tapped his fingers on the map. "You are sure of his loyalty?"

"He worships at Our Savior's!" Peymann repeated, as though that answered the Prince's question. "He volunteered this information, sire. He is no spy, but merely a merchant whose business suffered from French depredations. He tried to protect himself by assisting the enemies of France. We would punish a man for that?"

"No," the Prince decided. "We shall leave him alone." He smiled at Lavisser. "Men are finding their true allegiances in these hard times, Major. You did! And the same is true of this man Skovgaard. So let us not worry about past loyalties, eh? We should join hands to fight the real enemy!" He led his entourage toward the wide stairs. "Hold for three months," he encouraged Peymann, adding a month to his expectations, "and don't forget we have Castenschiold!"

"Castenschiold," Peymann exclaimed. General Castenschiold was raising troops in southern Zealand, but Peymann doubted there would be enough to make any difference.

"I have great hopes of Castenschiold," the Prince declared. "He can raid the British lines. He can harry them. Our enemies have not reckoned on Castenschiold!" He smiled as he emerged from the palace door to be greeted by a great cheer.

A huge crowd of Copenhagen's citizens had come to bid the Prince farewell. They filled the quays and crammed every window that overlooked the harbor while some of the younger ones had even swarmed up the two mast cranes which towered above the tallest church steeples. Ole Skovgaard and his daughter had been offered a vantage point on the balcony of the West India Company warehouse from where they could look down on the Prince as he walked to the water's edge. Sharpe had insisted on accompanying the Skovgaards, dressed again in his civilian clothes that were torn, soot- and mud-stained. Ole Skovgaard had not wanted him to come. "This is Copenhagen," he said, "we are safe."

"You were safe two nights ago?" Sharpe had inquired acidly, then Astrid, a peacemaker by nature, had begged her father to let Sharpe come and Skovgaard had reluctantly given in.

Sharpe knew he had nothing to fear from Lavisser this morning, for the guardsman was among the uniformed dignitaries who accompanied the Prince. Sharpe watched the renegade through his telescope and could see no evidence that Lavisser was wounded, which meant, proba- bly, that his last bullet had struck the Frenchwoman. It was rumored that the French embassy staff had all left the city, going to Colding in Jutland where the mad Danish King and his royal court were living. Sharpe, star- ing through his glass, saw Lavisser laughing at some jest by the Prince. "Is Lavisser going to Holstein?" Sharpe wondered aloud.

"Not if he's Peymann's aide," Skovgaard said.

"Who's Peymann?"

"The tall man next to His Majesty. He's commander of the city."

Lavisser was evidently staying. He offered the Prince a salute, then leaned forward and shook the royal hand. The Prince turned to the crowd who cheered even louder, then walked down a flight of stone steps to where a launch waited to row him out to a frigate. The frigate, the fastest in the Danish fleet, would take him back to Holstein and the army. The rest of the Danish fleet was in the inner haven and Sharpe could see its masts and spars above the tiled roofs of some warehouses on the far bank. "What I don't understand," he said, "is why you don't just sail the whole fleet away."

"To where?" Skovgaard asked sourly. His face was still swollen and white with pain. "Norway? It has no harbors so well protected as Copenhagen. We could send it to sea, I suppose, but there it will be inter- cepted by a British fleet. No, this is the safest place." The harbor was not at the edge of the city, but hollowed out of its very center and to reach it the British would have to get past the forts, walls, redoubts, guns and bastions. "It is here," Skovgaard said, "because it is safe here."

Some nearby folk heard the language and frowned at Sharpe. "American," he claimed.

"Welcome to Copenhagen!"

The cannons of the Sixtus Battery boomed out a twenty-one-gun salute as the Prince climbed the side of the frigate. "Did you hear that your army is landed?" Skovgaard said. "They came yesterday morning, not so far away"—he gestured to the north—"so they will be here within a few days. I think you should join them, Lieutenant."

"And leave you to Lavisser?"

"This is my city, Lieutenant, not yours, and I have already taken steps to ensure my own safety."

"What steps?" Sharpe demanded.

"I have written to Peymann assuring him of my loyalty."

"I'm sure General Peymann will persuade the French to forget you," Sharpe said.

"There are men who can be hired." Skovgaard spoke icily. He was plainly irritated by Sharpe's constant company. On the previous morning, after Sharpe had buried the three Frenchmen, he had accompanied Ole Skovgaard to a dentist while Astrid and the maids had packed the household belongings onto a wagon that would carry them to their old house in Ulfedt's Plads.

The dentist had proved to be an obese man who shuddered at the ravaged state of Skovgaard's mouth. He had packed the empty sockets with shreds of sphagnum moss, then given him oil of cloves to rub on his tender gums and promised he would have some new false teeth made. It seemed there were plenty of real teeth on the market these days, imported in the wake of the war in which France had beaten Austria and Russia. Austerlitz teeth, they were called. The rest of the day had been spent in moving furniture, linens, books and papers into the old house. The elderly servant was left to look after the new house while the coachmen and stable boys went to join the militia, taking Skovgaard's horses with them. "I have no need of a carriage in the city," Skovgaard had explained to Sharpe, "and our government needs horses to haul ammunition wagons."

"You need protection," Sharpe said, "and you've just lost all your male servants."

"The city needs them more than I do," Skovgaard had answered, "and Aksel has promised to find me some men. They will be cripples, probably, but a one-legged man can fire a musket." Skovgaard had sounded bitter. "And there are plenty of cripples in Copenhagen, Lieutenant, thanks to your last attack."

The bitterness had intrigued Sharpe. "Why didn't you break with Britain then?" he asked.

Skovgaard had shrugged. "My dear wife was alive. Besides, when Nelson attacked, I could see some justice in the British cause. We were denying them trade and the lifeblood of a nation is trade. But now? Now we deny you nothing except what is undeniably ours. Besides, I have never done anything to jeopardize Denmark. I simply assisted Britain to combat France, that is all. Now, alas, we shall be France's ally."

Two men in black carrying valises stuffed with papers were waiting for Skovgaard when he returned from watching the Prince's departure. Sharpe was instantly suspicious, but Skovgaard evidently knew the men and hurried them into his office. "They are from the government," Aksel Bang told Sharpe.

"What do they want?"

"Perhaps they have come for you, Lieutenant?"

Sharpe ignored that jibe. He walked down the center aisle of the big warehouse. "Where does that lead?" He pointed to a staircase that vanished in the dusty rafters of the high roof. He wanted to check every door and window, looking for any place where men might break into the premises.

"It goes to my upper chamber," Bang said, meaning a loft, "where I sleep now that Mister Skovgaard has returned."

"Lost your house, have you?"

"I do not mind," Bang said unctuously, "it is not my house and it is a blessing to have Miss Astrid back."

"A blessing for you or for her?"

"For both of us, I think. It is like things were before they moved. It is good."

Sharpe could find no weaknesses in the warehouse. Too much of value was stored in the place and Skovgaard had made it virtually thief-proof to protect the sacks of indigo, piles of jute and barrels of pungent spices that reminded Sharpe of India. "So what does the government want with Skovgaard?" he asked Bang.

"They want to know if any of these goods belong to British merchants."

"Why?"

"Because they will confiscate them, of course. We are at war, Lieutenant."

Sharpe looked at the dusty bays filled with barrels, sacks and crates. "And is any of this stuff British?"

"No. We do not store goods for other merchants. It is all our own."

"Good," Sharpe said, meaning there was no excuse for any more visits from officials. He turned on Bang. "Tell me, when you delivered Mister Skovgaard's letter, did you meet Lavisser?"

Bang blinked with surprise at Sharpe's forceful tone. "I met Major Lavisser, yes. He was very gracious."

"Did he ask you questions?"

Bang nodded. "He wanted to know about Mister Skovgaard, so I told him he is a good merchant and a committed Christian."

"Is that all?"

"It is all God asks of us."

Sharpe wanted to hit Bang. The man was nothing but a trumped-up clerk, but he had a sly and prickly pride about him. "What else did he ask you about Skovgaard?"

Bang pushed his long hair out of his eyes. "He asked if Mister Skovgaard had much to do with England. I said yes. I said he had many friends there and that he wrote there. That he had been married to an Englishwoman. Does it matter?"

"No," Sharpe said. Lavisser must have guessed that Sharpe would get in touch with the man whose name had been given him by Lord Pumphrey, so when Skovgaard's letter arrived it simply confirmed that suspicion. And, with the French on the point of evacuating their diplomatic mission, it must have seemed imperative to act immediately.

"I don't understand why you ask me these questions," Bang protested. He was genuinely confused why Skovgaard had moved back into the city and the explanation that his employer merely wanted to avoid the imminent British was made inadequate by Sharpe's presence and even more inadequate by Skovgaard's swollen face. "I think," Bang told Sharpe, "that you have snared Mister Skovgaard in unseemly matters."

"All you need to know," Sharpe said, "is that Mister Skovgaard is in danger. So if any strangers come here, fetch me. Don't let them in. And if anyone asks you about Mister Skovgaard, tell them nothing. Nothing! Don't even say he's a Christian because it's none of their damn business."

Bang looked mournful at Sharpe's tone. "He is in danger? Then perhaps Miss Astrid is also in danger?"

"Miss Astrid too," Sharpe said. "So just be watchful. Watch and pray, eh?"

"But maybe I should accompany Miss Astrid?" Bang sounded cheerful suddenly. "She goes to the orphanage."

"To the where?"

"The orphanage! Every day she goes. I can go with her, yes?"

"You?" Sharpe could not keep the contempt from his voice. "And what will you do if she's attacked? Pray for her? Bloody hell, Bang, if anyone goes with her, it's me."

Bang made no protest, but there was resentment on his face when, later that afternoon, Sharpe and Astrid left the warehouse together. Sharpe had brushed his clothes and hidden Skovgaard's two fine pistols under his coat. He wore his saber. More men were wearing weapons, he noted. It had suddenly become fashionable since the British had landed.

He also carried a big basket which contained crushed barley, rice and herrings. "We're taking it to the orphanage," Astrid explained.

"Orphanage?"

"It is an orphanage," she said, "and a hospital for children as well. It is where my son died."

"I'm sorry."

"He was very little, not even a year. He was called Nils like his father." There were tears in her eyes, but she forced a smile and said they would walk the long way around, going along the harbor quay where the Prince had embarked that morning. Sharpe's first instinct was to protest that his job was to protect her and that he could do that best if she went straight to the orphanage and back home, then he realized he did not want to be in Skovgaard's gloomy warehouse. Skovgaard himself was safe enough. He was in his office, he had a musket and had testily promised that he would allow no strangers into the warehouse, which meant Sharpe need not hurry back. Besides, Sharpe would rather be walking with Astrid and so the two of them strolled in the sunlight, though they were forced to stop every few yards to greet Astrid's friends or acquaintances. She introduced him as an American seaman which prompted no surprise, only enthusiastic welcomes. "It is a very little city," she explained after another such meeting, "and most people know each other."

"It seems a good city," Sharpe said.

She nodded. "And I like living inside the walls. The house in Vester Fælled can be lonely." She paused to show Sharpe the scorched walls of what had once been a great building. "That was the Christiansborg Palace," she said sadly. "It was where the King lived before the big fire."

"Another war?"

"Just a fire. A great fire. Almost a third of the city was burned. And it is still not all repaired." The ruined palace was sheathed in a tracery of scaffolding while makeshift huts, built in the remnants of great rooms, showed where some folk evidently still sheltered. "Poor Copenhagen." Astrid sighed.

They walked on past the Amalienborg Palace from where the Crown Prince had made his departure. A public path led through the central courtyard and the handful of blue-coated guards took no notice of the folk strolling in the afternoon sunshine. A dozen farm carts, heaped with grain or turnips, were parked by the palace. The city was stocking itself for a siege.

A few hundred yards beyond the palace was a small public garden dominated by the great citadel that guarded the harbor channel. The garden, which was mostly lawn with a few scattered trees, was the fort's esplanade; the killing ground for the cannon that just showed in the high embrasures. The grass was piled with round shot and cluttered with ammunition tenders, but even here folk took the air, ignoring the soldiers who were sorting the round shot and shells according to their calibers. Sharpe suspected the Danes planned to make a new battery here, one that could fire across the harbor mouth where a small wooden jetty held a dozen men placidly fishing. "They are always here," Astrid said, "but I've never seen them catch anything." She pointed northward to where, on the horizon, a dirty gray mass showed like a low-lying cloud. Sharpe had seen just such a sight on the morning of Trafalgar. It was a fleet. "Your friends," Astrid said sadly, "and they're coming here."

"I wish they weren't."

She sat on a bench facing the sea. "You look so like Nils," she said.

"That must be hard."

She nodded. "He was lost at sea. We don't know how. He was a captain, you see? He called his ship the *Astrid* and he was carrying sugar from the West Indies. When he didn't come home I thought perhaps his ship was being mended, but it wasn't so. We heard he had sailed and then there was a big storm just a few days after. We waited, but he never came. But I used to see him every day. I would see a stranger in the street and think, that is Nils! He has come back, then the stranger would turn and it would not be Nils." She was not looking at Sharpe as she spoke, but staring out to sea, and Sharpe wondered if she had come here in her early widowhood to look for her husband. "Then I saw you in the house"—she turned her big eyes on Sharpe—"and I knew it was Nils. For a moment I was so happy."

"I'm sorry," Sharpe said awkwardly. He knew how she felt, forever since Grace's death he would see a dark-haired woman in the street and think it was Grace. He felt the same leap of the heart and knew the same dull ache that followed the disappointment.

Gulls cried above the harbor channel. "Do you think we're really in danger?" Astrid asked.

"You know what your father does?"

She nodded. "I've helped him in the last few years. Since Mother died. He corresponds, Lieutenant, that is all. He corresponds."

"With folk in Europe and in Britain."

"Yes." She stared at the British fleet. "He does business all over the Baltic and all through the north German states, so he has scores of men who write to him. If a French column of artillery passes through Magdeburg then he will know within a week."

"And he tells the British?"

"Yes."

"Dangerous work," Sharpe said.

"Not really. His correspondents know how to write safely. That's why I help my father, because his eyes are not so good as they were. Some of the best ones send him newspapers. The French do not mind newspapers going to Denmark, especially if they are from Paris and full of praise for the Emperor, but if you open the paper and hold it against a window you can see that someone had pushed a pin hundreds of times through the pages. Each pinprick is under a letter and I just read the letters off in order and that is the message." She shrugged. "It is not so dangerous."

"But the French know who he is now," Sharpe said. "They want to know who writes to him, who sticks those pins in the newspapers. They want to stop the messages and your father can give them the names. So it is dangerous."

Astrid said nothing for a while. She gazed at a gunboat that was being rowed out of the harbor. There was a heavy boom made from chained logs protecting the entrance, but it had been hauled aside to let the gunboat pass. The ship had a tall mast on which a sail was furled, but the small wind was against the ungainly craft and so a score of oarsmen were pulling on long sweeps to crawl out of the channel. The boat had an ugly bill of a bow on which two heavy and very long-barreled cannons were mounted. Twenty-four-pounders, Sharpe guessed. Guns that could fire a long way and hit hard, and there were a score of other gunboats tethered against the far quay where powder and shot were being unloaded from carts. Other boats were bringing food into the city. "I hoped the danger was past," Astrid said after a long while, "now that the French are gone. But at least it stops life being dull."

"Is life dull?" Sharpe asked.

She smiled. "I go to church, I do the accounts and I look after Father." She shrugged. "It must sound very dull to you."

"My life's become dull," Sharpe said, thinking of his job as a quartermaster.

"You!" She was teasing him, her eyes bright. "You are a soldier! You climb chimneys and kill people!" She gave a shudder. "Your life is much too exciting."

Sharpe stared at the gunboat. The rowers, stripped to the waist, were hauling hard, but the boat was making little progress. He could see the tide rippling against the piers of the jetty and the gunboat was fighting the flood, but the oarsmen pulled on as though every burning muscle would help turn back the British. "I'm thirty years old," he said, "and I've been a soldier for fourteen years. Before that I was a child. I was nothing."

"No one is nothing," Astrid protested.

"I was nothing!" Sharpe sounded angry. "I was born into nothing, raised into nothing, expected to do nothing. But I had a talent. I can kill."

"That is not good."

"So I became a soldier and I learned when to kill and when not to kill. I became something, an officer, but now they don't want me. I'm not a gentleman, see? I'm not like Lavisser. He's a gentleman." He knew he had sounded jealous and angry and was embarrassed. He had forgotten, too, the reason for being with Astrid and he guiltily turned and looked at the folk taking the summer air on the fort's esplanade, but no one appeared to be taking any undue notice of the two of them. No Frenchmen were lurking and there was no sign of Barker or Lavisser. "I'm sorry, ma'am," he said.

"Sorry, why?"

"Tide has turned," Sharpe said, changing the subject and nodding at the gunboat. "Those lads are making some progress now."

"We must make some progress too," Astrid said, standing. Then she laughed. "You make me feel very rich."

"Rich? Why?"

"To have a manservant carrying the basket! Only the folk living on Amaliegade and Bredgade can afford such luxuries." They walked westward, skirting the moat of the vast citadel until they came to a poorer quarter of the city, though even here the houses were neat and clean. The single-story homes had been built to a pattern, were brightly painted and in good repair. "This is the sailors' quarter," Astrid told Sharpe. "Nyboder, it is called. They all have ovens! One oven for every two houses. It is nice, I think."

"Very nice."

"My father was a sailor's son. He grew up in that street, Svanegaden. He was very poor, you see?" She looked at him with big eyes, evidently trying to reassure him that she was no better born than himself. But Svanegaden, Sharpe thought, was a paradise compared to Wapping.

"You reckon this is a poor area?" Sharpe asked.

"Oh yes," Astrid said seriously, "and I know about these things. Father is one of the Commissioners of the Poor and I help with the correspondence."

The orphanage was on the edge of Nyboder, close to the sailors' cemetery where Astrid's son was buried. Astrid tidied the little grave, then bowed her head and Sharpe wanted to embrace her when he saw the tears on her cheeks. Instead he stepped back, giving her privacy, and watched the gulls wheeling over the citadel's ramparts. He thought of Grace and wondered what birds flew above her grave. She had been buried in a Lincolnshire church among her dead husband's family and under a memorial tablet recording Lord William Hale's virtues. Sharpe imagined her spirit hovering over him. Would she approve that he was so drawn to Astrid? He turned and looked at the widow stooping over the tiny grave and knew he was falling in love. It was as though green shoots were coming from the hatred and fury that had obsessed him since Grace had died.

Astrid stood and smiled at him. "Come," she said, "you must meet the children." She led him to the hospital where her son had died and Sharpe could hardly believe it was also an orphanage. It was nothing like Brewhouse Lane. There was no high wall or spiked gate, though the upper windows were all equipped with iron bars. "That is to stop the boys being daredevils," Astrid explained. "Sometimes the older boys want to climb on the roof."

"So it's not a prison?"

"Of course not!" She laughed at the idea, and indeed the orphanage looked anything but a prison. The two-story building was painted white and built about a courtyard where flowers grew in neat beds. There was a small chapel with a pipe organ, a simple altar and a high stained-glass window that showed Christ surrounded by small, golden-haired children. "I grew up in a place like this," Sharpe told Astrid.

"An orphanage?"

"A foundling home. Same thing. Wasn't quite like this, though. They made us work."

"The children work here too," she said sternly. "The girls learn to sew and the boys must learn to be sailors, see?" She had led him back into the courtyard where she pointed to a tall flagpole that was rigged like a ship's mast. "The boys must learn to climb it, and the girls make all those flags."

Sharpe listened to the sound of laughter. "It wasn't like this," he said. A dozen children, all in gray dresses or breeches, were playing a complicated game of tag about the flagpole. Three crippled children and one idiot, a girl with her head cocked sideways who twitched and dribbled and made small mewing noises, watched from wicker chairs equipped with wheels. "They seem happy," Sharpe said.

"That is important," Astrid said. "A happy child is more likely to be given a home by a good family." She led him upstairs to where the hospital occupied two large rooms and Sharpe waited on the balcony while she delivered her food and he thought of Jem Hocking and Brewhouse Lane. He remembered Hocking's fear and smiled.

"Why are you smiling?" Astrid asked as she came back to the balcony.

"I was remembering being a child," he lied.

"So it was happy?"

"No. They beat us too much."

"These children are beaten," Astrid said, "if they steal or tell lies. But it is not frequent."

"They used to whip us," Sharpe said, "till the blood ran."

Astrid frowned as if she was not sure whether to believe him. "My mother always said the English were cruel."

"World's cruel," Sharpe said.

"Then we must try to be kind," Astrid said firmly.

He walked her home. Bang scowled when they came through the door and Ole Skovgaard, seeing his daughter's happiness, gave Sharpe a suspicious look. "We must find Danes to protect us," Skovgaard told his daughter that evening, but men were needed in the militia, and the militia was busy throwing up the new outworks in the suburbs and so, reluctantly, and mostly at his daughter's urging, Skovgaard allowed Sharpe to stay on in Ulfedt's Plads. On Sunday the rifleman went with the household to church where the hymns droned, the sermon was interminable and Sharpe fell asleep until Aksel Bang dug an indignant elbow in his ribs. Next morning Sharpe escorted Skovgaard to a bank and in the afternoon he accompanied Astrid back to the orphanage, and then to a sugar warehouse on Amager, the small island on which the eastern half of Copenhagen was built. They crossed a lifting bridge which spanned the narrowest part of the harbor and walked past the vast boom which protected the inner haven in which the endangered Danish fleet was stored. Sharpe counted eighteen ships of the line and as many frigates, brigs and gunboats. Two great ships were under construction in the yard, their great hulls rearing on the slipways like half-clothed skeletons of wood. These ships were Napoleon's last hope of invading Britain, which was why the British were in Denmark and the French were poised across the Holstein frontier. Sailors were busy taking the great guns from the ships of the line and ferrying them ashore where they would be added to the artillery already on the city's walls.

After Astrid had delivered a bill of sale to the sugar warehouse she led him to the seaward ramparts where they climbed to the firestep between two giant bastions. The wind ruffled the water and lifted the fair hair at Astrid's neck as she gazed northward to where the masts of the British fleet looked like a thicket on the horizon. "Why are they staying to the north?"

"Takes time to land an army," Sharpe said. "Lots of time. It'll be a day or two before they come here."

The dull boom of a gun sounded flat in the warm afternoon. Sharpe stared eastward and saw a smudge of gray-white smoke rise from the distant sea. The smoke drifted on the wind to reveal the low hull of a gunboat, then a second gunboat fired to make a new white cloud. The gunboats were strung across the wide channel that ran past the city and a ship had sailed into their clutches. A third gunboat fired, then a cluster of shots hammered like thunder across the sun-touched waves. Sharpe took the telescope from his pocket, extended the tubes and saw the trapped ship's sails shudder as her captain turned into the wind. Then her flag, a British ensign, came down from the mizzen.

"What is it?" Astrid asked.

"A British merchantman," Sharpe said. The skipper must have come from deep in the Baltic and probably had no idea that his country was at war with Denmark until the gun ships had pounced. The Danish boats, low in the water, had ceased firing as the British ship furled her sails.

He gave the telescope to Astrid who steadied it on the wall. "What happens now?" she asked.

"They bring it in. She's a prize."

"So we are at war?" She sounded incredulous. The British army might have landed, the city might be raising a militia and building forts, yet still war had been unimaginable to her. Not in Denmark, and certainly not against Britain.

"We're at war," Sharpe said.

On their way back to Ulfedt's Plads they made a detour to see the big houses in Bredgade. It was easy enough to spot which house belonged to Lavisser's grandfather, for a small crowd was waiting outside for a glimpse of their new hero. Women carried flowers and someone had hung a Danish flag from the lantern above the front door. Sharpe stood on the street's far side and gazed up at the windows, but there was no sign of the renegade. Lavisser had effectively vanished, as though the night at Skovgaard's house had never happened. Yet Lavisser and his French allies would be back, Sharpe was sure of it.

Next day the city was filled with the news that the British were at last marching south. It was that same day that Sharpe came back from the orphanage to discover Aksel Bang was now in uniform. He wore a plain blue coat with tarnished silver buttons and a single silver bar on each shoulder. "I am a lieutenant in the militia," Bang said proudly. He carried an ancient sword with a black cloth-covered scabbard. A half-dozen men, all with muskets, lounged in the warehouse shadows. They were elderly men, the remnants of Skovgaard's workforce, who had all joined the militia with Bang. "They are stationed here," Bang said, "because this is now an official food store for the city. We are on guard. And now that we have muskets we can provide protection for Mister Skovgaard."

Sharpe looked at the six men. "Properly trained, are they?"

"We shall give a good account of ourselves," Bang said confidently. "There is something else, Mister Sharpe."

"Go on."

"You are English, yes?"

"Go on."

Bang shrugged. "You are an enemy. Out of loyalty to Mister Skovgaard I have done nothing about it, but it cannot continue. I shall have to arrest you."

"Now?" Sharpe smiled.

"If you do not leave the city, yes. I am an officer now. I have responsibilities."

"What you've got, Aksel," Sharpe told him, "is an itch in your breeches." Yet Sharpe knew the man was right. He was surprised that no one had come to arrest him for it was surely no secret that Skovgaard had an Englishman in his house. Yet Copenhagen was so civilized, so ready to believe that no harm could come to it, that the authorities had tolerated him.

Next morning, when Sharpe woke in the warehouse, he heard the distant crackle of musketry. It was very far off, but unmistakable. And an hour later, when he was washing under the pump in the back yard, he heard the percussive thump of big guns firing. So the army had arrived at last. Ole Skovgaard, the swelling about his jaw much reduced, came into the yard and frowned at Sharpe. "I think you should leave us, Lieutenant."

"You feel safe with Aksel and his merry men?"

"Safe from whom?" Skovgaard looked up into the sky where bands of white cloud stretched from east to west. "From my friends, the British?" he asked sarcastically.

"From your new friends, the French."

"I shall stay here in the warehouse. And so will Astrid. Aksel and his men will be sufficient, I think." Skovgaard listened to the distant gunfire for a few seconds. "Aksel is an officer now," he went on, "and your presence is an embarrassment to him."

"I wonder why," Sharpe said, thinking of Astrid.

Skovgaard must have known what Sharpe was thinking, for he blushed slightly. "Aksel is a good Dane," he said hotly, "and you are an enemy, Mister Sharpe."

"Enemy?" Sharpe pulled on his shirt. "I spent the last two afternoons playing tipcat with children in an orphanage. Is that what an enemy does?"

Skovgaard frowned. "You are English and Aksel is right. You put me in a difficult position. You may keep the two pistols, but I insist you leave."

"And if I don't?"

For a moment Skovgaard looked angry, then he bowed his head as though he was thinking. "I have lost much in my life, Lieutenant." He spoke surprisingly softly, still looking at the ground. "My wife, my son, my son-in-law and my grandson. God has punished me. I have pursued worldly goals, Lieutenant"—he looked up at Sharpe now—"preferring success to His will. Your country has rewarded me greatly in return for my help. That is how I could buy the house in Vester Fælled, but it is the fruit of sin. I am sorry, Lieutenant, but to me you represent evil. Your country's desires, its actions, its ambitions, they are all wrong."

"You think the French—"

"I think the French are as bad if not worse," Skovgaard anticipated Sharpe's words, "but it is my soul I must worry about. I shall put my faith in God, where it should have been all these months. This is a godly family, Lieutenant, it always has been, and you, I think, are not godly. I see . . ." Skovgaard hesitated and frowned, then nerved himself to go on. "I see my daughter's interest in you. That does not surprise me, for you resemble Nils, but you cannot be good for her."

"I—" Sharpe tried to speak.

"No!" Skovgaard again interrupted. "Tell me, Lieutenant, are you saved in Christ Jesus?"

Sharpe stared at Skovgaard's thin face, then sighed. "No."

"Then you will leave us, for this is a godly house and your presence disturbs us."

"You think God will protect you from Lavisser?"

"He can do whatever He wishes, Lieutenant. He will hold us against all the world's evils if it is His will."

"Then you'd better pray, Mister Skovgaard, you'd better bloody pray."

There was nothing to be done. Sharpe changed into his uniform which he covered with his greatcoat. He put the telescope into one pocket, the guineas into another, belted the saber about his waist and thrust the good pistols into the belt, then went down to the kitchen where Astrid had just served Aksel Bang with a dish of barley porridge. "So you leave us, I hear?" Bang said happily.

"Isn't that what you wanted, Aksel?"

"We can manage without the English," Bang said cheerfully.

"You will have breakfast, Lieutenant?" Astrid asked Sharpe.

"I just came to say goodbye."

"I shall come to the gate with you." She took off her apron and, ignoring Bang who watched her like a dog eyeing a bone, led Sharpe into the yard. Sharpe had thought she meant she would see him to the warehouse's back gate which opened onto Skindergade, but she must have meant one of the city gates for she walked into the street with him.

"You shouldn't be out here on your own," Sharpe told her, for once she had said goodbye she would have to return to her father's house unescorted.

"No one is looking for me this morning," she said dismissively. "Everyone is watching the British." She led him past the cathedral, which lay close to the warehouse. "I am sorry you are going."

"So am I."

"And the children will miss their American friend." She smiled. "You like children?"

"So long as they're properly cooked. Can't bear them cold."

"You are a horrible man, Lieutenant."

"Richard."

"You are a horrible man, Richard." She put her arm into his elbow. "How will you get through the city gates?"

"I'll find a way."

They stopped close to the Nørre Gate. The ramparts above the tunnel were crowded with folk staring westward. Musketry still crackled in the city suburbs and every now and then a bigger gun hammered. A constant stream of militiamen was going through the gate and Sharpe reckoned he would lose himself among that crowd. Yet he did not want to go. He looked down at Astrid. "Be careful," he told her.

"We are a careful nation," she said with a smile. "When it is over . . ." She stopped.

"I shall come and look for you."

She nodded. "I'd like that." She held out a hand. "I am sorry it is like this. My father? He has not been happy since Mother died. And Aksel?" She shrugged as if she could find no explanation for Bang.

Sharpe ignored her hand. He leaned forward and kissed her cheek instead. "I'll see you soon."

She nodded again, then abruptly turned and hurried away. Sharpe stared after her, and to anyone watching it must have just seemed like another man saying farewell to his woman. She turned when she was twenty paces away and saw him gazing at her and he knew she did not want him to go, but what choice was there? He walked to the gate where his weapons made him look like any other militiaman. He turned a last time to look for Astrid, but she was gone. The crowd jostled him on and he emerged from the gate's tunnel to see a dirty cloud above the roofs and trees of the western suburbs. It was powder smoke.

He stopped outside and stared back through the tunnel, hoping for one last glimpse of Astrid. He was confused. He was in love with a woman he did not know, except he knew her loyalty was to the enemy. Yet Denmark did not feel like an enemy, though it was. And he was a soldier still, and soldiers, he reckoned, fought for those who could not fight for themselves, and that meant he should be fighting for Astrid's folk and not his own. But that was too great a wrench to contemplate.

So he was simply confused.

A SERGEANT grabbed Sharpe's elbow and shoved him toward a growing band of men who were being hurriedly assembled close to the moat-like lake. Sharpe let himself be pushed. An officer was standing on a low wall and haranguing around three hundred men, most of them confused militiamen though there was a core of sailors armed with heavy sea-service muskets. Sharpe did not understand a word, but from the officer's tone and from the man's gestures he gathered that the British were threatening some place to the southwest and this makeshift half-battalion was being asked to throw the invaders out. A roar of approval rewarded whatever the officer had said, then the whole group, Sharpe among them, streamed across the causeway. Sharpe made no effort to leave the group. He had no choice but to rejoin the British army and every step took him closer.

The officer led them across the moat, past a cemetery, a church, a hospital and then through streets of new houses. The sound of musketry grew louder. Bigger guns hammered to the north, clouding the sky with powder smoke. The officer stopped beside a high brick wall and waited as his ragtag followers gathered around him, then he spoke urgently, and whatever he said must have roused the men for they gave a growl of agreement. A man turned to Sharpe and asked him a question. "American," Sharpe said.

"You're American?"

"Sailor."

"You are welcome I think. You know what the Captain said?"

"No."

"The English are in the garden"—the man nodded toward the wall—"but there are not many of them and we shall throw them out. We are making a new battery here. You have fought before, perhaps?"

"Yes," Sharpe said.

"Then I shall stay with you." The man smiled. "I am Jens."

"Richard," Sharpe introduced himself. He took out one of the pistols and pretended to check its priming. The weapon was unloaded and he had no intention of charging it. "What do you do?" he asked Jens, who was a pleasant-faced, fair-haired young man with a snub nose and lively eyes.

Jens flourished his ancient musket. The lock was rusted, the stock was split and one of its barrel hoops was missing. "I kill Englishmen."

"And when you're not killing them?" Sharpe asked.

"I am a . . . what is it called? I make ships?"

"A shipwright."

"A shipwright," Jens agreed. "We work on a new warship, but we have left her unfinished. We do this first."

The Captain peered through the gate, then gestured that his men should follow him. They jostled through the gate and Sharpe found himself in a wide parklike garden. Gravel paths led to groves of trees, and an elegant white summerhouse, a confection of gables, verandahs and pinnacles, stood on a small hillock. The garden looked to be a more genteel version of the Vauxhall Gardens in London. A company of regular Danish soldiers was crouching by the summerhouse, but there was no musketry sounding nearby and no sign of any British soldiers. The militia Captain, unsure what to do, ran to consult the regular officer, and his men sat on the grass. Far off to the north smoke trails whipped across the sky. Shells, Sharpe assumed. A dull explosion sounded in the distance. "Even if they take these places," Jens said, waving his hand to show he meant the suburbs, "they will never get into the city."

"What if they bombard it?" Sharpe asked.

Jens frowned. "You mean with guns?" He seemed shocked. "They will not do that! There are women in the city."

The militia Captain came back, followed by two men on horseback, one a cavalry officer and the other a civilian. Sharpe stood with the others, then saw that the horsemen were Barker and Lavisser. The two men were only a few feet away and Sharpe turned his back as Lavisser began haranguing the civilian soldiers.

"We are to go forward," Jens translated for Sharpe.

Lavisser, his sword drawn, had taken his place at the head of the militia while Barker was behind them. Sharpe pulled his brown hat down over his eyes and wished he had loaded the pistol. It was too late now, for the militia was hurrying west toward the trees. They went in a bunch and if the British had cannon there would be a massacre.

"We are to attack their side," Jens said.

"Their flank?"

"I expect so. When it is over you can take an English gun, eh? Better than that little pistol."

Lavisser led them into the woodland. A twisting path went downhill and Lavisser, evidently confident that no British troops were close by, spurred his horse ahead. There was plainly a battle of sorts going on just to the north for the musketry was crackling in loud bursts, but nothing was happening in this part of the gardens where the militia, confident that they were hooking around the southern flank of the British, followed Lavisser down into a gentle valley where a small stream fed an ornamental pond. Lavisser shouted at the militia, evidently ordering them into ranks. The group of sailors, all in straw hats and pigtails, set an example by forming four ranks and the two sergeants pushed the rest into crude files. Lavisser, his horse pawing great gouts from the turf, shouted excitedly. "He says the enemy is not many," Jens translated.

"How does he know?" Sharpe wondered aloud.

"Because he is a proper officer, of course," Jens said.

Lavisser had not looked in Sharpe's direction and Barker was still trailing the three hundred men who now set off up the western slope where their cohesion was immediately broken by the trees. The sound of musketry was coming from Sharpe's right, but it was sporadic now. Perhaps this makeshift half-battalion of disorganized enthusiasts really could take the approaching British on the flank, but Sharpe was relieved that he was in the rear rank and at the left-hand side, farthest from both Lavisser and the sound of battle. He was trying to load the pistol as he walked and wondering if he could somehow seize Lavisser and carry him bodily into the British lines.

Then a musket shot sounded directly ahead. The Danes were among the trees still, but there was open ground a hundred paces in front of them. Sharpe saw a drift of musket smoke at the edge of that sunlit space, then more muskets sounded. Lavisser dug in his spurs and the unwieldy mass began to run.

Sharpe ran wide to the left. He could see redcoats now, but only a handful. He guessed there was a British skirmish line at the edge of the wood, and that meant a full battalion was not far away. The Danes were shouting excitedly, then Sharpe saw a redcoat clearly and saw the man's wing epaulettes. A light company then, so the other nine companies were close at hand, formed and ready to fire. The Danes, knowing nothing of what waited for them, only saw the British skirmishers retreating and mistook that for victory. Lavisser must have thought the same, for he was yelping as though he was on a hunting field and holding his saber ready to strike down a fugitive.

The redcoat light company fired and retreated. One man knelt, aimed and fired while his companion reloaded, then the man who had fired ran back a few paces to let his comrade cover him while reloading. A Dane was sprawling on the ground, twitching, another was leaning against a tree and staring at the blood pouring from a wound in his thigh. Others of the Danes fired their muskets as they ran, the balls going wild and high in the trees. A whistle sounded ahead, calling the skirmishers back to the British battalion's other nine companies. Lavisser must have seen those companies, for he turned his horse so hard that its eyes went white and its hooves scrabbled in the leaf mold. He frantically shouted for his men to halt at the wood's edge and level their muskets.

Then the British volley came.

The battalion had waited till the Danes were at the edge of the trees and then nine companies let fly. The balls splintered bark, ripped through leaves, thumped men down and hammered on musket stocks. Lavisser himself was miraculously untouched. "Fire!" he shouted in English, forgetting himself. "Fire!"

Most of the Danes ignored him. They still thought they were winning and so they ran farther into the open ground only to find there was a red line of men behind a ditch some fifty yards ahead. That line was reloading. Ramrods turned in the air and came scraping down. There were flickers of tiny flames in the grass where the British musket wadding had set fires. A red-jacketed officer, cocked hat low over his eyes, was riding straight-backed behind the line. Sharpe watched the muskets come up into the redcoats' shoulders. The militia was at last realizing its predicament and those who still had loaded muskets aimed at the British. Others kept running, then saw they were isolated and so hesitated. Lavisser's charge was already in chaos and the British had yet to loose their second volley.

"Platoon, fire!" Sharpe heard the British order clearly and he grabbed Jens by the shoulder and dragged him down to the ground.

"What!" Jens protested.

"Head down!" Sharpe snarled, then the first platoon fired and the next followed immediately. The noise was deafening as the dirty gray smoke rolled down the battalion's front and the balls whacked into the disorganized militia. Sharpe pressed his face into the grass and listened to the volleys, one after the other, each spitting about fifty bullets at the bewildered Danes. It was the first time Sharpe had been on the receiving end of British musketry and he flinched under it. Jens fired his musket, but his eyes were closed as he fired and the ball went wild and high.

Jens knelt to reload, but just then another regiment of British appeared from some trees on the right and they let loose a battalion volley that sounded like the splintering of hell's gates. One of the balls snatched the musket from Jens's hands, shattering the stock, then the new battalion settled into the machine-like platoon fire and the Danes could only cower under the twin flails. Sharpe scrambled backward, staying low, getting out of the tangling fire of the two battalions. He looked for Barker, but the man had vanished, though Lavisser was visible enough. The renegade was galloping his horse up and down behind the ragged militia, shouting at them to close ranks and fire back at the British. He fired both his own pistols at the cloud of smoke shrouding the nearest redcoat battalion, then Sharpe saw Lavisser's horse lurch and slew sideways as a bullet struck deep into its rump. The beast tried to stay on all fours, but more bullets flecked its glossy coat red and it sank onto its haunches as Lavisser kicked his feet free of the stirrups. Another bullet twitched the horse's head sideways in a spray of blood. Lavisser managed to throw himself clear of the dying beast, then dropped to the grass as a flight of bullets hissed overhead. Sharpe still slithered back, found himself in a small dip and so ran for the trees. He would take cover, wait for the fight to end, then join the redcoats.

Jens had followed Sharpe. The shipwright looked dazed. He flinched at the sound of each volley. "What happened?" he asked.

"They're real soldiers," Sharpe answered sourly. He saw the Danish sailors try to organize a rank that could return the British fire, but the second British battalion had marched ten paces forward and poured their platoon fire into the sailors' flank and the seamen crouched as though they sheltered in a storm. One man fired back, but he had left his ramrod in the barrel and Sharpe saw it cartwheeling across the grass. A wounded man crawled back, trailing a shattered leg. Two battalions of red-coated regulars were giving an undisciplined group of amateurs a ruthless lesson in soldiering. They made it look easy, but Sharpe knew how many hours of practice it had taken to make them so efficient.

Then Jens shoved Sharpe sideways. "What the hell—" Sharpe began, then a pistol fired close by and the bullet smacked into a tree beside Sharpe, who turned and saw it was Barker, behind him and on horseback. Sharpe leveled his own pistol, pulled the trigger and the weapon did not fire. He had still not primed it. He threw the gun down, whipped the saber from its scabbard and ran at Barker who turned his horse and spurred down the hill. The big man ducked beneath tree branches, then suddenly sawed on the reins to turn the horse back and Sharpe saw he had a second pistol. He twisted sideways, expecting a shot, but Barker held his fire.

Sharpe crouched in some bushes. He sheathed the saber and pulled out his own second pistol. It would take time to reload because the powder horn with its dispensary was a fiddly thing, but he started anyway. Barker was not far away. Sharpe risked a quick glance and saw only the riderless horse. So Barker was stalking him on foot. Move, he told himself. Move now, because Barker knew where he was and so he thrust the powder horn into a pocket and sprinted across a clearing, dodged into trees, jumped down a steep slope and went to ground again behind a stand of laurel. He heard Barker's footsteps above him, but he reckoned he had bought himself enough time to load the pistol. British volleys stunned the sky above him. Some shots, missing the Danes, whipped through the trees at the top of the slope.

Sharpe poured powder into the pistol, spat the bullet after, then heard the crashing feet and looked up to see Barker charging headlong down the slope. The huge man had spotted Sharpe in the laurels and wanted the confrontation over. Sharpe's pistol was still unprimed, but Barker could not know that so Sharpe stood, aimed the weapon and smiled.

Barker took the bait, raising his own gun and firing too quickly. The ball whistled past Sharpe, who tucked the pistol under his left arm as he opened the small slide that would let a trickle of powder into the horn's dispensary. Barker saw what he was doing and drew a sword and Sharpe, knowing he did not have time to prime the gun, let both pistol and powder horn drop. He drew his saber. "Reckon you can beat me with a blade, Barker?"

Barker whipped his sword back and forth. It was a slim weapon, one of Lavisser's old swords, and Barker looked disgusted at the steel's flexibility. He could use guns, he liked knives and was lethal with a cudgel, but the sword seemed flimsy to him. "I could never use the bloody things," he said. Sharpe just stared at the big man, wondering if he had heard right. Barker slashed the blade at the laurels, then frowned at Sharpe. "You been in the city all along?"

"Yes."

"He thought you'd left."

"He didn't look very hard," Sharpe said, "because I wasn't hiding."

"He's been busy," Barker said. "And now you're going back to the army?"

"Yes."

"Then bugger off," Barker said, jerking his head up the hill.

Sharpe, astonished, let his saber tip drop. "Come with me."

Barker looked offended at the invitation. "I ain't buggering off."

"Then why aren't you killing me?"

Barker gave a sneering look at the sword. "Not with this," he said. "I ain't any good with bloody swords. Never learned them, see? So you end up skewering me, don't you? Not much sense there. But I ain't frightened," Barker added earnestly. "Don't you think I'm frightened. If I sees you back in the city I'll do you. But I'm not a bleeding gentleman. I only fights when I knows I can win." He stepped back and jerked his head uphill again. "So bugger off, Lieutenant."

Sharpe backed away, readying to accept the unexpected invitation, but just then a voice hailed Barker from high among the trees. It was Lavisser. Barker shot a warning look at Sharpe, then the voice called again. "Barker!"

"Down here, sir!" Barker shouted, then looked at Sharpe. "He'll have a gun, Lieutenant."

Sharpe stayed. He had seen Lavisser fire both his pistols and he doubted that either would be reloaded. There was a chance, he thought, a very small chance that he could hold Lavisser here until the redcoats came.

The redcoats had to come soon for up on the hill top the Danes were dying. Only the sailors had the discipline to reload, but they also had the sense to retreat. They grabbed their wounded and dragged them back to the woods and, one by one, the remaining militiamen tried to follow them. The platoon firing punched the eardrums as smoke drifted thick and foul across the bloodied grass where the tiny fires burned. One of the two Danish sergeants tried to rouse the cowering men, but he was hit in the throat. He did a pirouette, feet tangling, as blood jetted from his gullet. He continued to turn as he sank down, then he crumpled and his musket slid along the grass. Bullets were thumping into corpses, twitching them.

"Hold your fire!" a voice called.

"Cease fire!"

"Charge bayonets!"

"Skirmishers forward!"

Lavisser had found Barker's discarded horse and rode it down the hill to see his servant facing Sharpe. The renegade looked surprised, then smiled. "What on earth are you doing here, Richard?" He sounded oddly cheerful.

"Came to get you."

Lavisser glanced up the hill. The remnants of his force were running and the British must have been approaching the trees, but he sounded quite unworried. "Bloody militia. Redcoats are good, though. How are you, Richard?"

"Taken up dentistry, have you?" Sharpe sneered. "Failed as a bloody soldier so you draw teeth now?"

"Oh, Richard." Lavisser sounded disappointed. "You should leave attempts at wit to the witty."

Sharpe raised the saber as Barker stirred, but the big man was just moving to stand between Sharpe and Lavisser. "You're not fighting for Denmark," Sharpe said to Lavisser, "but for the Frogs."

"Comes to the same thing, Richard," Lavisser said cheerfully. He drew a pistol, then pulled a cartridge from a pouch. "Denmark is a little country," Lavisser explained when he had pulled the cartridge open with his teeth, "and she was always going to be raped by either Britain or France. Britain has got her pleasure in first, but all she'll do is drive Denmark into France's arms, and I really can't imagine that the Emperor will want to leave dim Frederick as Crown Prince. No, he'll be looking for some splendid and vigorous young man to be his ruler here." He poured powder into the barrel. Barker took a step toward Sharpe who slashed the saber to drive the servant back. "It's all right, Barker," Lavisser said, "I shall take care of the Lieutenant."

"I told him he could go," Barker said. "He's been in the city, sir, but he's leaving."

Lavisser raised his eyebrows. "You are generous, Barker." He looked at Sharpe. "I don't really want to kill you, Richard. I rather like you. Does that surprise you? I suppose that's not important, is it? What's important is that Mister Skovgaard is now unguarded. Is that a safe assumption?"

"Assume what you like," Sharpe said.

"How very obliging of you, Richard." Lavisser rammed the bullet home, then paused and looked reflective. "A nauseatingly dull man, our Ole. He's the kind of fellow I really dislike. He's so upright, so hard-working, so bloody pious. He's an affront to me." He lifted the frizzen to prime the gun. "Pretty daughter, though."

Sharpe used the efficacious word. Lavisser laughed, then a shout up the hill made him turn. A skirmish line had appeared among the trees. Sharpe had been expecting it. "Down here!" he shouted. "Down here! Quick!"

A musket fired and the ball tore leaves to shreds above Lavisser. Men were coming fast and quick and Lavisser did not finish priming the pistol, but just turned the horse. "*Au revoir*, Richard!" he called.

The two men fled. Sharpe started to follow, then a dozen shots riddled the laurels and he crouched instead. Barker and Lavisser vanished.

Sharpe took off his greatcoat and rescued his discarded pistol. A group of redcoats came down the slope. Their coats had blue facings, Welch Fusiliers, and their muskets were tipped with bayonets that pointed toward Sharpe. Then a sergeant saw Sharpe's uniform and pushed the nearest gun down. He was a short man, his broad face incredulous as he stared at the green jacket. "I'm not drunk, Harry, am I?" he asked a private.

"No more than ever, Sergeant."

"Looks like a rifleman!"

Sharpe sheathed his saber. "Morning, Sergeant."

"Sir!" The Welshman gave a twitch that was a gesture toward standing to attention. "If you don't mind my bloody asking, sir, but what are the bloody Rifles doing here?"

"Got lost, Sergeant."

A captain came down the slope with a group of men who held Jens prisoner. "What the devil's happening, Sergeant Davies?"

"Got a lost rifleman, sir," the Sergeant said.

"Lieutenant Sharpe," Sharpe said, "reporting for duty, sir. You wouldn't know where Sir David Baird is, would you?"

"Sir David?"

"He's expecting me," Sharpe lied. "And that fellow's with me." He gestured at Jens. "We've been making a reconnaissance in the city. Nice morning, isn't it?" He began climbing the hill and the Captain followed him.

"You've been in the city?"

"It's a good place," Sharpe said, "but with very fat churches. You'd best pray God isn't tempted to take sides, Captain, because there are a terrible number of Danes battering His eardrums." He grinned at Jens. "Are you all right?"

"Yes." Jens, not surprisingly, looked bewildered.

"You were with the Danes?" the Captain asked.

"They were only militia," Sharpe said, "but there was a company of proper troops on the next hill. No artillery though." He emerged onto the hill top which was horrid with bodies. Welsh bandsmen tended the Danish wounded while a few miserable prisoners stood among the thinning smoke. "Would you know where Sir David is?" Sharpe asked the Captain.

"He's at brigade, I think. Over there." He pointed beyond the ditch. "Last I saw of him he was by some glasshouses."

"Are you coming, Jens?" Sharpe asked, and he sounded a lot more cheerful than he felt. For it was time to face the music.

And time to confess that he had failed.

CHAPTER 7

HARPE WALKED JENS away from the carnage. Once beyond the ditch and out of sight of the two redcoat battalions Sharpe pointed back toward the city. "Get into that lower ground"—he showed Jens how to sneak round the side of the fusiliers—"and then just keep walking."

Jens frowned. "You are not American?"

"I'm not."

Jens seemed reluctant to go. "Did you know what would happen back there?"

"No. But it wasn't hard to guess, was it? They're real soldiers, lad. Trained to it." Sharpe took the remaining pistol from his belt. "You know Ulfedt's Plads?"

"Of course."

"There's a man called Skovgaard there. Give this gun to him. Now hurry, before the British capture the rest of the gardens. Keep in those lower trees and then go straight to the gate. Understand?"

"You're English?"

"I'm English." Sharpe pushed the unprimed gun into Jens's hand. "And thank you for saving my life. Now go on. Hurry."

Jens gave Sharpe a bewildered glance then ran. Sharpe watched until the Dane was safely hidden among the trees, then slung his greatcoat over his shoulder and walked on. Failed, he thought. Failed utterly.

He climbed a low hill. The newly dug ditch where the fusiliers had

fired their volleys had evidently been the beginning of a new Danish out-
work that had been captured before they could throw up walls or mount
guns, and now red-coated engineers were standing on the hill's summit
from where they trained telescopes on the city walls. They were obviously
considering the hill as a place for a battery. The sea could be seen to the
south, while on the hill's northern side, in a gully, a gardener was carefully carrying plants into a greenhouse. Beyond the gully the land rose to
a low ridge where a group of mounted British officers watched another
battalion advance into the woodlands. Thick smoke smeared the eastern
air. The Danes, retreating from the suburbs closer to the city, had set
some houses on fire, presumably so that the British could not use them as
advance positions. Farther north, out of sight, there was some heavy
artillery at work, for the air was being punched by the percussive blasts
and the sky was streaked and silting with smoke.

Major General Sir David Baird had a musket wound on his left hand
and another rivulet of blood where a ball had grazed his neck, but he was
feeling ebullient. He had led a brigade into the gardens, ejected some
Danish regulars, massacred some brave idiots from the militia and now
watched as his men secured the southern ground that would finally iso-
late Copenhagen from the rest of Zealand. Captain Gordon, his aide and
nephew, had been wasting his breath by chiding the General for exposing
himself to unnecessary danger, but Baird was enjoying himself. He would
have liked to keep the advance going, right through the western suburbs,
across the lakes and into the city itself. "We could have the fleet by night-
fall," he claimed.

Lord Pumphrey, the civilian aide from the Foreign Office, looked
alarmed at the General's bellicosity, but Captain Gordon did his best to
restrain Sir David. "I doubt Lord Cathcart would want a premature
assault, sir," the aide observed.

"That's because Cathcart's a bloody old woman," Baird grumbled.
Cathcart was the General in command of the army. "A bloody old
woman," Baird said again, then frowned at Lord Pumphrey who was trying to draw his attention. "What is it?" he growled, then saw where his
lordship was pointing. A Rifle officer was coming up the path from the
greenhouse.

"It's Lieutenant Sharpe, Sir David," Pumphrey said.

"Good God." Baird stared at Sharpe. "Good God. Gordon? Deal with him." The General, not wanting to be associated with failure, spurred his horse farther along the ridge.

Gordon dismounted and, accompanied by Lord Pumphrey, walked to meet Sharpe. "So you escaped the city?" Gordon greeted him.

"I'm here, sir," Sharpe said.

Gordon heard the bitterness. He led Sharpe toward the back of the greenhouse where the General's orderly had a fire going and a kettle boiling. "We heard about Lavisser," he said gently. "We read the *Berlingske Tidende*."

"He implied you were an assassin," Lord Pumphrey said with a shudder. "So very distressing for you. We sent a letter to His Royal Highness denying the allegation, of course we did."

"It's all very distressing," Gordon said, "and I'm very sorry you became involved, Sharpe. But how were we to know?"

"You don't know any of it," Sharpe said angrily.

"We don't?" Gordon asked mildly. He paused to organize some cups of tea. "What we learned the day after you left England, Lieutenant"—Gordon turned back to Sharpe—"is that Captain Lavisser, as well as being in debt, faced a prosecution for breach of promise. A woman, of course. She claims the marriage date was settled. One suspects she is also pregnant. He was doubtless eager to flee the country, but was rather clever to persuade the Treasury to fund his escape."

"The Foreign Office advised against it," Lord Pumphrey put in.

"As you will doubtless remind us frequently," Gordon said. He shrugged. "I'm sorry, Sharpe. Had we known we should never have let him go."

"There's worse," Sharpe said.

"Ah! The tea," Gordon said, "nature's soft nurse. No, that's sleep, isn't it? But tea's the next best thing. Thank you, Boswell." Gordon took a tin mug from the General's orderly and handed it to Sharpe.

Lord Pumphrey ignored the offered tea. His lordship no longer sported a beauty spot and he had abandoned his white-laced jacket in favor of a simple brown coat, but he still seemed out of place. He took a pinch of snuff, then shuddered as a Danish prisoner came down the hill. The man was bleeding from a scalp wound and two fusiliers were trying to hold him still while they bandaged his head, but the man kept shaking himself free and staggering a few wild steps. "Tell me what we don't know," Lord Pumphrey said, turning his back on the wounded man.

So Sharpe told them how Barker had tried to kill him, how he had then gone to Skovgaard who had betrayed him to Lavisser, about the French and the battle in the house that did not lie so very far to the north. He told them about Madame Visser and the three dead men and Skovgaard's bloody gums and the teeth lying on the desk. "Lavisser is working with the French," Sharpe said. "He's a goddamn traitor."

Lord Pumphrey took the news surprisingly calmly. He said nothing for a while, but just listened to the heavy sound of the artillery to the north. "Gunboats," he said bleakly. "I am forever astonished by the military. Their budgets are raised each year, yet the weapons are never suitable. It turns out that the Danish gunboats are rather better than ours. They draw less water and carry heavier ordnance and the results are not at all pretty." He watched as the fusiliers at last wrestled the wounded Dane to the ground, then he walked a few delicate steps northward to escape the man's moaning. "So Captain Lavisser is still in the city?" he asked Sharpe.

"He was here in these gardens a minute ago," Sharpe said bitterly. "The bastard was telling me that Bonaparte will want a new ruler for Denmark. Someone like him, but the last I saw of the bastard he was running like a deer."

"Of course we shall deny that any of this happened," Gordon said.

"Deny it!" Sharpe spoke too loudly.

"My dear Sharpe," Gordon remonstrated, "we cannot possibly have it known that the Duke of York had an aide who was on the French payroll. It would be a disastrous revelation."

"Calamitous," Lord Pumphrey agreed.

"So I trust we can depend on your discretion?" Gordon asked.

Sharpe sipped the tea and watched the smoke trails in the northern sky. They were too thick to be the fuses of shells so he decided they had to be rockets. He had not seen any rockets since India. "If I'm still a Rifle officer," he said, "then I'll be discreet. You can order me to be discreet." It was an attempt at blackmail. Sharpe had abandoned his place at the Shorncliffe barracks and he could expect little mercy from Colonel Beckwith unless Sir David Baird spoke for him, but Baird had only promised him support if he succeeded in Copenhagen. And he had failed, but it was clear no one wanted that failure known.

"Of course you're still a Rifle officer," Gordon said forcefully, "and Sir David will be happy to explain the circumstances to your Colonel."

"So long, of course, as you keep quiet," Pumphrey said.

"I'll keep silent," Sharpe promised.

"But tell me about Skovgaard," Lord Pumphrey said. "You think he's in danger?"

"Bloody hell, yes, my lord," Sharpe said vigorously, "but he wouldn't let me stay because he's not happy with Britain at the moment. He's got half a dozen old men with even older muskets guarding him, but they won't last two minutes against Lavisser and Barker."

"I do hope you're wrong," Lord Pumphrey said quietly.

"I wanted to stay," Sharpe said, "but he wouldn't let me. Said he'd trust in God."

"But your part's over now," Gordon declared. "Lavisser's a renegade, the gold is gone and we've been thoroughly humbugged. But it's not your fault, Sharpe, not your fault at all. You behaved creditably and I shall so inform your Colonel. You know your regiment's here?"

"I guessed as much, sir."

"They're down south, near a place called Køge, I think. You'd best take yourself off there."

"And what of Lavisser?" Sharpe asked.

"I suspect we shall never see him again," Gordon said bleakly. "Oh, we'll capture the city, but I've no doubt the Honorable John will conceal himself from us and we're hardly likely to search every attic and cellar for him. And I suspect His Majesty's Treasury can afford the loss of forty-three thousand guineas, don't you? Is there much food in the city?"

"Food?" Sharpe was momentarily thrown by the change of subject.

"Well stocked up on victuals, are they?"

"Yes, sir. Carts and ships were arriving all the time I was there. Packed with grain."

"Tragic," Gordon murmured.

Sharpe frowned when he realized why Gordon had asked the question. If the city had plenty of food then it could hold out against a prolonged blockade. But there was an alternative to blockade or, indeed, siege and Sharpe shuddered. "You can't bombard the place, sir."

"No?" It was Lord Pumphrey who made the inquiry. "And why not?"

"Women and children, my lord."

Lord Pumphrey sighed. "Women, children and ships, Sharpe. Pray do not forget the ships. That is why we are here."

Gordon smiled. "The good news, Sharpe, is that we found the underground pipes that carry fresh water to the city. So we cut them. Maybe thirst will force a surrender? But we can't wait too long. The weather in the Baltic will have our fleet running for home before too many weeks. Fragile things, ships." He took a notebook from his pocket, tore out a page and scribbled some words. "There, Sharpe, your pass. If you walk north you'll find a large red-brick house that passes as our headquarters. Someone will know if there's a unit going south and they'll make sure you go with them. I do apologize, profoundly, for having involved you in this nonsense. And remember, do, that none of this ever happened, eh?" He tossed away the dregs of his tea.

"It was a bad dream, Lieutenant," Pumphrey said, then he and Gordon went back to Baird.

"Seen him off?" Baird asked Gordon.

"I sent him back to his regiment, sir, and you're going to sign a letter of recommendation that I shall forward to his Colonel."

Baird frowned. "I am? Why?"

"Because no one will then associate you with a man who has turned out to be the Duke of York's aide and a French spy."

"Bloody hellfire," Baird said.

"Precisely," Lord Pumphrey said.

Sharpe walked north and Jens went east, but the young shipwright did not take Sharpe's advice. He should have kept walking toward the city as Sharpe had advised him, but he could not resist going north through the trees to discover the source of some sporadic musketry. Some skirmishers of the King's German Legion saw him. They were *Jäger*, hunters, equipped with rifles, and they saw the pistol in Jens's hand and put three bullets in his chest.

Nothing was working well. But Copenhagen was surrounded, the Danish fleet was trapped and Sharpe had survived.

GENERAL CASTENSCHIOLD had been ordered to harry the southern flank of the British forces blockading Copenhagen and he was not a man to ignore such orders. He dreamed of glory and dreaded defeat and his moods swung between optimism and a deep gloom.

The core of his force was a handful of regular soldiers, but most of his fourteen thousand men were from the militia. A few of those were well trained and decently armed, but far more were new recruits, some still wearing their wooden clogs and most carrying weapons that belonged in farmyards rather than on battlefields. They were country boys, or else from the small Danish towns of southern Zealand.

"They are enthusiastic," an aide told the General.

That only made Castenschiold even more worried. Enthusiastic men would rush into battle with no knowledge of its realities, yet duty and patriotism demanded that he take his inadequate force north to attack the British troops encircling the capital and he tried to persuade himself that there was a real chance of surprise. Perhaps he could drive so deep into the British-held ground that he could reach the siege works about Copenhagen before the redcoats knew of his presence, and in his secret and slightly guilty dreams he imagined his men slaughtering the hapless enemy and throwing down their newly dug batteries, but in his heart he knew the outcome would not be so happy. But it had to be tried and he dared not allow his pessimism to show. "Are there any enemy south of Roskilde?" he asked an aide.

"A few," was the airy answer.

"How many? Where?" Castenschiold demanded savagely and waited while the aide sifted through the dozens of messages sent by loyal people. Those reports said that enemy troops had appeared in Køge, but not many. "What is not many?" Castenschiold inquired.

"Fewer than five thousand, sir. The schoolmaster in Ejby says six thousand, but I'm sure he exaggerates."

"Schoolmasters can usually count reliably," Castenschiold said sourly. "And who leads these troops?"

"A man called"—the aide paused as he sought the right piece of paper—"Sir Arthur Wellesley."

"Whoever he is," Castenschiold said.

"He fought in India, sir," the aide said, "at least the schoolmaster says he did. It seems some officers were billeted in the school, sir, and they said Sir Arthur gained a certain reputation in India." The aide tossed down the schoolmaster's carefully written letter. "I'm sure it isn't hard to beat Indians, sir."

"You are?" Castenschiold asked sarcastically. "Let us hope this Sir Arthur underestimates us as you underestimate him." Castenschiold's dream of piercing the British lines about Copenhagen was dying fast, for even a handful of British troops would be sufficient to detect his approach and warn their comrades. And if the five or six thousand men were under the command of an experienced general then Castenschiold doubted he would even get past them. But it had to be tried, the Crown Prince had ordered it, and so Castenschiold gave the order to move north.

It was a glorious late-summer day. Castenschiold's army marched on three roads, filling the warm air with dust. They had a handful of field guns, though all were very old and the Captain who commanded the battery was not at all sure their barrels would endure too much firing. "They've been used for ceremonial purposes, sir," he told the General. "For salutes on the King's birthday. Haven't had an actual ball up their gullets in fifteen years."

"But they should fire well enough?" Castenschiold asked.

"They should, sir," the Captain said, though his voice was dubious.

"Then make sure they do," the General snapped. The presence of the guns gave his men confidence, though they did little for Castenschiold himself. He would rather have had a battery of new artillery, but all the new field guns were in Holstein, waiting for a French invasion that now seemed unlikely to happen. Why should the French invade Denmark when the British were forcing the Danes to become France's ally? Which meant the best troops and guns of the Danish army were all stranded in Holstein and the British navy was blocking them from the island of Zealand, and General Castenschiold was realistic enough to know that the best Danish generals were also in Holstein, which meant that the hopes of Denmark were pinned on one middle-aged and punctilious general who had a single ancient battery of unreliable artillery and fourteen thousand inadequately trained troops. Yet still he dared dream of glory.

A squadron of cavalry trotted through the fields of stubble. They looked fine and the sound of their laughter was reassuring. Ahead, up on the northern horizon, there was the smallest gray cloud. Castenschiold fancied that was the smoke from the big guns at Copenhagen, though he could not be sure.

Castenschiold's hopes rose in the afternoon when his cavalry patrols reported that the British troops under Sir Arthur Wellesley had withdrawn from Køge. No one knew why. They had come, stayed for a night and marched away again and the road to Copenhagen was evidently open. Castenschiold's dream of slicing into the soft belly of the British troops was still alive, and it grew even stronger when his small army reached Køge that evening and discovered the cavalry's reports were true. The British were gone and the road was indeed open. The commander of the local militia, an energetic chandler, had spent the time since the British departure digging entrenchments all about the small town. "If they come back, sir, we'll pepper them, pepper them proper!"

"You have evidence that they'll come back?" Castenschiold inquired, wondering why else the chandler had dug such impressive trenches.

"I hope they come back! We'll pepper them!" The chandler said he had only seen three British regiments, two in red coats and one in green. "Hardly more than two thousand men, I should think."

"Cannon?"

"They had some, but so do we now." The chandler beamed at the Danish guns trundling into the town.

Castenschiold's men bivouacked that night at Køge. There were reports of horsemen in the fields to the west, but by the time the General reached the place where the strange riders had been seen, they were gone. "Were they in uniform?" he asked, but no one was sure. Perhaps they had been local men? Castenschiold feared it was an enemy patrol, but the pickets saw no more such horsemen. Most of the army camped in the fields where a small stream twisted between woods and fields of stubble or turnips, while the luckier troops found shelter in the town and the General himself was billeted in the pastor's house behind Saint Nicholas's church where he tried to reassure his host that all would be well. "God will not desert us," Castenschiold claimed, and his pious optimism seemed justified when, at midnight, he was woken by a return-ing cavalry patrol who had succeeded in riding as far as Roskilde where they had discovered that town's garrison to be intact. The General decided he would send a message to Roskilde in the morning, demanding that its defenders march east toward Copenhagen. That might divert the British while he lunged up the open coast road. He forgot the vague reports of unidentified horsemen in the previous dusk because the dream was again taking shape.

The General's breakfast of cold herrings, cheese and bread was taken long before dawn. The army was stirring, readying to march. One of the militia colonels came to the pastor's house with a gloomy report that his men had been issued with ammunition of the wrong calibre. "It will fit," the Colonel reported, "but the balls rattle in the barrels. Too much windage, I think it's called." The Colonel was a cheese-maker from Vordingborg and was not entirely sure he wanted to lead his wooden-clogged soldiers against British regulars.

Castenschiold ordered an aide to sort out the problem, then strapped on his sword belt and listened to the gulls crying on the long beach. Today, he thought, he would either become famous or infamous. Today he must march his men up that long coast road, ever flanked by the sea with its threat of the British navy, and he must hope to pierce deep into the enemy troops that were wrapped about the capital. "Hammers and nails," he told an aide.

"Hammers and nails, sir?"

"To spike the British guns, of course," Castenschiold snapped, wondering if he had to do all the thinking in the army. "Soft nails, if you can find them. And search the town for axes. To break the wheel spokes of the gun carriages," he added quickly before the aide could ask why he wanted axes.

"You have time for prayers?" the pastor asked him.

"Prayers?" Castenschiold had been wondering if the water anywhere along the coast was deep enough to allow the big British ships close enough inshore to use their terrible broadsides against the road.

"You would be most welcome at our family prayers," the pastor explained.

"I must be moving," Castenschiold said hurriedly, "but pray for us, do pray for us." He mounted his horse and, followed by a half-dozen aides, rode north in the thinning mist. The dawn was just showing above the eastern sea when he reached the northern edge of his encampment and there summoned his commanders. "I want your men on either flank today," he told the two cavalry officers. "Push patrols forward, of course, but keep the bulk of your men close. And there'll be no stopping today. Carry forage if you need it, and tell your men to put dinner in their saddlebags. Speed, gentlemen!" He spoke now to all the officers. "Speed is essential. We have to reach the enemy before they know we are coming!"

He talked to his officers atop a small ridge. To his right, surprisingly close, was the long beach, and ahead of him the road to Copenhagen led between wide fields that sloped toward a shadowed tangle of hedgerows and trees. The sun was still below the horizon, but far off, silhouetted against the blanching east, he could see a ship of the line. "The regular infantry will lead the march," Castenschiold decreed, "artillery next and then the militia. I want to be fighting by midday!" By noon he should be close to Copenhagen and he planned to keep his cavalry and regular infantry to fight any redcoats who might oppose him, but release his militia loose among the batteries. They would spike the guns, break the carriage wheels and burn the powder charges. He could see it now, see the smoke whirling up from shattered batteries, see himself a hero. "Right, gentlemen! Let us make ready! We march in thirty minutes!" He pointed dramatically northward, a gesture in keeping with his grand ambitions. Some of the officers turned to stare where he pointed and saw a dark patch of shadow move where the road vanished among some trees. Castenschiold also saw the shadow and thought it was a deer, or perhaps a cow, then he saw it was a man on horseback. "Who sent out patrols?" he demanded.

"Not one of ours, sir," a cavalryman answered.

There were six horsemen on the road now and they had stopped, probably because they had seen the faint glow of the Danish campfires showing above the ridge where Castenschiold had tried to inspire his men. Castenschiold took his telescope from his saddlebag. The light was still bad so he dismounted and had an aide stand in front of him so he could use the man's shoulder as a rest for the glass.

Cavalrymen. He could see saber scabbards, but the men were not Danes, their hats were the wrong shape. He stooped slightly, letting the glass go beyond the cavalrymen to where the road ran up beside the distant beach. For a time he could only see gray and black, mist and shadow, then the hidden sun's light grew and the General saw men marching. It was darkness moving, a mass of men, columns of men and they were trampling on his dream. He collapsed the telescope. "We're staying here," he said quietly.

"Sir?" One of the aides thought he must have misheard.

"Regular infantry here," Castenschiold said, indicating the low crest that dominated the road. "Dragoons on the beach, light dragoons to the left flank. The militia will form a reserve between here and the town. Artillery right here, on the road." He spoke decisively, knowing that any sign of uncertainty would destroy his men's morale.

Because the British were coming. There would be no attack on the siege works about Copenhagen, instead fate had decreed that General Castenschiold must fight in front of Køge. So let them attack us here, Castenschiold decided. It was not a bad position. His regular troops dominated the road, his right flank was secured by the sea, and the newly dug entrenchments were at his back if he should need to retreat.

The six enemy cavalry scouts had vanished, carrying the news of the Danish presence to the advancing British. The sun flared on the horizon to flood the wrinkling sea with gold. It would be a beautiful day, Castenschiold thought, a beautiful day for a killing. His gloomy thoughts were interrupted by the arrival of a small cart from Køge. The cart was pulled by a shaggy pony and escorted by a cheerful aide. "Hammers and nails, sir!" the aide reported. "And forty-three axes."

"Take them back," Castenschiold said, "just take them back."

"Sir?"

"Take them back!" he snarled. For the dream was dead. Castenschiold extended his telescope again and saw the enemy infantry coming from the woods. Some were in red jackets and some in green. Green? He had never heard of any British infantry wearing green. The enemy was spreading along his front now, too far away for any cannon to reach, but waiting for their own guns to arrive and for a few moments Castenschiold was tempted to attack them. He outnumbered the British, he could see that, and he toyed with the thought of releasing his men down the slope, but resisted the temptation. Inexperienced troops fought better when they defended a position, so he would let the outnumbered enemy climb the long hill into the teeth of his guns and perhaps, even if he could not raise Copenhagen's siege, he could give Denmark a victory.

The Danish guns unlimbered, the flag was raised and the infantry formed line.

They were ready to fight.

"WHAT THE devil are you doing here?" Captain Warren Dunnett inquired of the battalion's quartermaster. He had never liked the man. He was up from the ranks and, in Dunnett's opinion, had an inflated idea of his own competence and, worse, had served in India and believed, therefore, that he knew something of soldiering.

"The Colonel sent me, sir. He told me you were a lieutenant short."

"And where the hell have you been anyway?" Captain Dunnett stooped to the hand mirror that he had wedged in the split top of a fence post. He scraped a razor down his cheek, carefully avoiding the tip of his wiry mustache. "Haven't seen you in weeks."

"I was on detached service, sir."

"Detached service?" Dunnett inquired acidly. "What the hell's that?"

"I was working for General Baird."

And what the hell would Sir David Baird want with a man like Sharpe? Dunnett was not going to ask. "Just don't get in the way," he said curtly. He shook water off his razor and ran a hand over his chin. Bloody quartermaster, he thought.

The riflemen chopped wood from a thicket and made small fires so they could brew their tea. The greenjackets were spread along a series of hedgerows and fences that straggled either side of the coast road. Behind them, in fields where the harvest was shocked, two battalions of redcoats waited. Every now and then an officer from one of those two battalions would come to the riflemen's positions and stare up the shallow slope to where a Danish army was arrayed on the crest. The enemy flag, a white cross on a red field, stirred in the small wind that brought the smell of the sea. There were blue-coated cavalry on both Danish flanks and a battery of field guns in their center. Men made guesses about the enemy's strength, most reckoning there were ten to twelve thousand Danes on the hill while the British numbered about three thousand and most of the redcoats and greenjackets were happy with those odds. "What are we waiting for?" a man grumbled.

"We are waiting, Hawkins, because General Linsingen is marching about their flank," Captain Dunnett answered.

That, at any rate, was the plan. General Wellesley would pin the enemy down by threatening an attack and Linsingen, of the King's German Legion, would march around their backside to trap them. Except that a bridge had collapsed and Linsingen's men were still three miles away on the wrong side of a stream and no message had come and thus no one knew that the plan had already broken down.

A rumbling series of crashes announced the arrival of a battery of British nine-pounders that unlimbered on the road. "Fires out!" a gunner officer snapped at the men crouched about the small campfires. He was worried because he was about to stack powder bags beside his guns.

"Bloody gunners," a rifleman complained.

A captain of the 43rd, red-eyed and pale, begged a mug of tea from a group of riflemen. The 43rd was a Welsh regiment that had trained with the greenjackets at Shorncliffe barracks and the two battalions were friendly. "I shall give you boys some advice," the Captain said.

"Sir?"

"Avoid akvavit. Avoid it. The devil brews it and the Danes drink it, God knows how. It looks like water."

The riflemen grinned and the Captain flinched as a kilted piper from the 92nd began taming his instrument to produce a series of moans, yelps and squeals. "Oh God," the Captain moaned, "not that, please God, not that."

Sharpe heard the pipes and his mind flashed back to India, to a dusty field swirling with men, horses and painted guns where the Highlanders had ripped an enemy to ruin. "I don't know if that noise frightens the Danes," a voice behind him said, "but it terrifies me."

Sharpe turned to see that Sir Arthur Wellesley was examining the enemy through his telescope. The General was on horseback and had not been talking to Sharpe, but addressing two of his aides. Wellesley swept the glass left and right, then collapsed the tubes and found himself looking down at a Rifle officer. A look of mingled surprise and embarrassment showed on his face. "Mister Sharpe," he said flatly, unable to avoid acknowledging Sharpe's presence.

"Sir."

"Still with us, I see?"

Sharpe said nothing. He had not seen the General in three years, not since India, and he did not detect the General's embarrassment, for he was too acutely aware of his disapproval. Grace had been a cousin of Wellesley's. True, she had been a very distant cousin, but her family's enmity had spread wide and Sharpe was certain Sir Arthur must share it.

"Enjoying the Rifles, are you, Sharpe?" Wellesley asked. He was looking up the road as he spoke.

"Yes, sir."

"Thought you would," Wellesley said, "thought you would. And we shall see how useful your new weapons are today, eh?" The General, like most officers in the British army, had never seen the rifles in action. "Where the devil is Linsingen? Not even a damned message!" He looked at the Danes through his glass. "Would you say they're readying to move?" He had asked his aides the question and one of them said he thought he could see a baggage cart behind the enemy guns. "Then damn it," Wellesley said, "we'll manage without Linsingen. To your regiments, gentlemen." He was talking to the red-coated infantry officers who had gathered near the guns. "Good day, Sharpe!" He turned his horse and spurred away.

"Know him well, do you?" Captain Dunnett was jealous that the General had spoken to Sharpe and could not resist asking the question.

"Yes," Sharpe said curtly.

Damn you, Dunnett thought, while Sharpe was thinking he did not really know the General at all. He had spoken to him often enough, he had saved his life once and he had received the telescope as a reward for that favor, but he did not know him. There was something too cold and frightening about Sir Arthur, but Sharpe was still glad he was in charge today. He was good, simple as that, just plain good.

"Stay on the right," Dunnett ordered him, "with Sergeant Filmer."

"Yes, sir."

Dunnett wanted to ask why Sharpe was carrying a rifle, but managed to resist the question. The man probably still thought he was in the ranks. Sharpe, as an officer, should not have carried a longarm, but he liked the Baker rifle and so he had collected one from the regimental surgeon who had a small armory of weapons that belonged to his patients. The rifle was much less cumbersome than a musket, was far more accurate and had a squat, brutal efficiency that appealed to Sharpe.

Sergeant Filmer nodded a greeting to Sharpe. "Glad you're back, sir."

"Captain Dunnett sent me to look after you."

Filmer grinned. "Going to make us tea, sir, are you? Tuck us up in bed?"

"Just going for a walk with you, Lofty. Straight up the hill."

Filmer glanced at the distant enemy. "Any good, are they?"

"God knows. The militia aren't, but those look like regulars to me."

"Find out soon enough," Filmer said. He was a very short man and was thus known throughout the regiment as Lofty. He was also very competent. He scraped out the bowl of a clay pipe, then opened his pouch and offered Sharpe a scrap of honeycomb. "Fresh, sir. Found some hives in that last village."

Sharpe sucked the honey. "They'll hang you if they catch you, Lofty."

"Hung a couple of fellows yesterday, didn't they? Silly bastards got caught." He spat wax onto the grass. "Is it right there's a town over the skyline, sir?"

"Called Køge," Sharpe said, thinking that he must have been very near this place when he had escaped from Lavisser.

"Bloody daft names they've got here, sir." Filmer held his rifle's trigger and worked the cock back and forth. "I put some oil on her," he explained, "'cos I reckon she got a bit damp at sea." He glanced at his men. "Don't be bloody sleeping, you dozy bastards, there'll be work for you in a minute."

The artillerymen had loaded their guns and now stood ready to fire while the 92nd, over by the beach, was forming in line. The 43rd, immediately behind Sharpe, was doing the same. Two regiments of redcoats and one of greenjackets. It was a small force, much smaller than the enemy, but Sharpe knew what these regular soldiers could do and felt pity for the Danes. He gazed at their white cross on its red field. We should not be doing this, he thought. We should be fighting the French, not the Danes. He thought of Astrid and then felt guilty because of Grace. "We'll see if it all works now, sir," Filmer said cheerfully.

"We will," Sharpe agreed. They would see if the months of hard training at Shorncliffe had been worthwhile. The army had always employed skirmishers, men who ran ahead of the rigid formations to harry and weaken the waiting enemy, but now the army was employing riflemen to make those skirmishers more deadly. There were plenty who said the experiment was a waste of time and money, for rifles were much harder to reload than the smoothbore muskets and so a greenjacket could only fire one shot to a musket's three or even four. The sceptics claimed that the riflemen would be slaughtered while they recharged their expensive weapons, but those weapons could kill at four times the distance of a musket. It was accuracy against quantity.

Both armies waited. Two redcoat regiments were in line, the guns were laid, and the Danes were showing no sign of retreat. Captain Dunnett walked to the right of his line. "You know what to do, Lofty."

"Skin 'em alive, sir," Filmer said.

"Keep your head!" Dunnett called to the men. "Aim properly!" He was about to add some more encouragements, but just then a shrill whistle sounded in short urgent blasts. "Forward!" Dunnett shouted.

The greenjackets were spread right across the British front so that both battalions would have the benefit of their rifles. They walked forward and Filmer's men kicked down a low fence that divided a meadow from a field dotted with shocked wheat. The light companies of the 43rd and 92nd advanced with the riflemen, a scatter of red coats among the green. The skirmishers stayed well clear of the road for that was where the British guns would fire.

Sharpe climbed the shallow slope and saw the Danish skirmishers double forward from their positions. These were regular soldiers, not militia, and their white crossbelts showed against pale-blue coats. The Danes spread along the hillside, waiting for the British skirmishers to come within range.

"Bloody boots," Sergeant Filmer said to Sharpe. The sole of the Sergeant's right boot had just come loose and was flapping. "They were a bloody new pair too, sir! Bloody boots."

A whistle blast checked the skirmishers. They had only advanced a hundred paces, but now they knelt among the shocked wheat. They were far out of musket range, but well within a rifle's killing distance. Sharpe watched a Danish officer holding on to his hat as he ran down the slope. "They haven't got enough skirmishers," he said. Even if the British had not deployed rifles still the enemy had sent too few men forward, which meant, perhaps, that they were relying on the efficiency of their battalion volleys, but only the British army trained with live ammunition, and

Sharpe doubted that these Danish regulars could match the redcoats shot for shot. Poor bastards, he thought.

"We'll skin 'em alive, sir." Filmer tore the sole clean off his boot and pushed it into a pocket. He looked up the slope then cocked his rifle. "Skin 'em alive."

The British guns fired.

It had been as though both armies had been holding their breath. Now the smoke jetted and swelled above the road as the round shot screamed up the hill. The gunners were already sponging out the barrels as Sharpe saw a scrap of black turf arcing through the sky close to the Danish flag, then heard the whistle blasts again. "Right, lads," Filmer shouted, "put the bastards down!"

The greenjackets took the Danes by surprise. The enemy's skirmishers had been waiting for the British to advance into range, but suddenly the bullets were whistling about them and men were being plucked backward.

"Aim for the officers!" Filmer shouted. "And don't be hurried! Aim proper!"

The riflemen knew exactly what to do. They fought in pairs. One man aimed and fired, then the other protected the first as he reloaded. The Danish skirmishers were recovering from their surprise and coming downhill to get within musket range, but they were too few and the closer they came the faster they were hit. The rifles, unlike the smoothbore muskets, had sights and many of the riflemen wore merit badges because they were expert marksmen. They aimed, fired and killed and the Danes were being hit hard at a range no man would have thought to be lethal. Filmer just watched. "Good boys," he muttered, "good boys." The redcoat skirmishers were firing now, but it was the rifles that were doing the damage.

"It works, Lofty!" Sharpe called.

"Bloody well does, sir!" Filmer answered cheerfully.

The enemy officer who had been holding his hat was on the ground. A man ran to him and was struck by two bullets. Riflemen called targets to each other. "See that big dozy bugger with a limp?"

Sharpe was oddly surprised by the noise. He had been in bigger battles than this, far bigger, but he had never realized just how loud it was.

The ear-pounding blows of the field guns were overlaid by the crack of the rifles and the brutal coughing of muskets. And that was only the skirmishers. None of the main battalions had so much as fired a volley, yet Sharpe had to shout if he wanted Filmer to hear him. He knew he was sympathizing with the Danes. Most of them, the overwhelming majority of them, would never have been in a battle and the noise alone was an assault on the senses. It was hammering and echoing, unending, crashing gouts of dirty smoke riven with red fire and over it, like a descant, the screams of the wounded and dying. The round shot blasted great lumps of earth from the crest, ripped a Danish cannon wheel to splinters and took a man's head in an explosion of blood.

The Rifles were pressing forward, going from shock to shock. Little fires left by wadding burned in the stubble. The redcoat skirmishers were adding their fire, but it was not needed. The Rifles were winning and the Danish light troops were going back to their line.

"Forward!" Filmer called.

"Two on the right!" Sharpe shouted.

"See them! Maddox! Hart! Get those bastards!"

The trails of the British field guns were gouging ruts in the road as the weapons recoiled. Smoke thickened until the gunners were firing blind, but still the shots seared home. The greenjackets could shoot at the Danish ranks now. They looked for officers as they had been trained to do, took aim, killed and looked again. The Danish ranks shifted uncomfortably, unprepared for this kind of distant fusillade. Then, in the hell of other noises, Sharpe heard the savage flare of the pipes and saw that the 92nd was advancing up the long slope. The British guns were still hammering the enemy center. The Danish guns had stayed silent, but now a great blossom of smoke showed at the hill top, but the sound was all wrong. A gun had exploded.

"On! On!" Dunnett called. "Closer!" The 43rd was advancing now. There was to be nothing subtle here. The Welshmen and the Highlanders were in line and walking straight up the slope. They would march till they were in musket range, then loose a volley and fix bayonets. "Keep killing them!" Dunnett shouted. "Keep killing! I want their officers dead!"

A riderless horse galloped along the front of the blue-coated Danish troops. Men were being thrown back from the enemy ranks by rifle bullets and the file closers were pushing men to fill the gaps. The Rifles were working. God, Sharpe thought, but it was murder. His rifle was loaded, but he had not shot it.

"Bring on the Frogs, eh, sir?" Filmer said. "Bring on the bloody Frogs!"

Wellesley ordered his cavalry forward on the left flank beside the beach. They were German hussars and they streamed out of the dunes leaving a trail of dust, their drawn blades glittering, and the sight of them must have convinced the Danes that the position was lost, for, long before the advancing redcoat battalions came within range, they began to vanish from the crest. The firing died down as the targets vanished. There was a scatter of bodies higher up the field, but only one greenjacket was down. "Get his boots," Filmer told a man. "It was Horrible Hopkins," he told Sharpe, "smacked in the eye."

"Forward! Forward!" Wellesley's voice rose sharp. The gunners were limbering up again. The German hussars had gone back to the line's center, their mere presence having been enough to dislodge the enemy. The kilted Scots were already at the hill's crest and the riflemen on the right of the road ran up to the skyline to see Køge ahead of them. Low roofs, chimneys, church spires and a mill. It could have been a town back home if the roofs had not been so red, but what caught Sharpe's eyes were the entrenchments that scarred the fields at Køge's edge. The Danes had not run away, they had merely pulled back into fortifications. The British infantry was hurrying on, but Danish cavalry was suddenly streaming out of the trenches and threatening to curl round the right-hand end of Wellesley's line.

There was a clamor of bugle and whistle calls. The 43rd stopped. It did not form square, though every man was half expecting the order. The riflemen, vulnerable to a cavalry charge, hurried back toward the protection of the Welshmen's muskets, but then the German hussars appeared again, this time on the inland flank and the Danish horsemen, outnumbered, checked their advance. Sharpe, his rifle cocked ready to meet the cavalry charge, realized that Sir Arthur Wellesley must have anticipated the Danish maneuver and had his horsemen ready.

The pipes started again and Sharpe saw that the 92nd was being sent straight at the entrenchments. They were not even waiting for the artillery, just marching forward to the beat of their drums and the wild music of the pipes. "Heathen bastards," Filmer said in a tone of admiration.

Sharpe was remembering Assaye, remembering the Highlanders marching so calmly into the heart of the enemy. The Danes, he reckoned, would have been unsettled by their swift retreat from the crest and now they were being presented with an impudent assault that reeked of confidence. They could see the British artillery unlimbering and knew that the second redcoat battalion was readying to follow the first, yet in all probability it would not be needed, for there was something utterly implacable about the Highlanders. They looked huge in their black fur hats as they advanced toward an angle of the trenches. The defenders far outnumbered them, but the trenches had been too hastily dug and the Scotsmen were attacking one salient corner so that their massed musketry could drown a small portion of the defenses with fire. The men farther down the trenches were too far away to help. "They're going to run," Sharpe said.

"You reckon so?" Filmer was not sure.

"One volley and the bayonet," Sharpe said, "then the whole lot will bugger off."

The Danes opened fire. They had lost their artillery, but their musketry was heavy. "Close up! Close up!" Sharpe heard the familiar litany of battle. "Close up!" The Scots appeared to ignore the fire, but just walked toward the smoke-rimmed piles of earth. A few bodies lay behind the battalion. Yellow ribbons fluttered from the pipes.

"Halt!" The 92nd stopped dead.

"Present!" It seemed that every man took a slight turn to his right as the muskets came up into their shoulders.

"Fire!" One volley. One blast of foul-stinking smoke.

"Fix bayonets!"

There was an odd silence in which Sharpe could hear the click of the bayonets being locked onto smoking muzzles.

"Forward!" The line moved into their own smoke, showed again beyond the ragged cloud. "Charge!"

The Scotsmen, released, gave a cheer and Sharpe saw defenders scrambling from trenches and fleeing south. The air was suddenly alive with bugles and whistles.

"Don't let them go to earth!" Wellesley shouted at the 43rd's commanding officer. There were more troops appearing in the west and a Welsh officer called a warning, but the newcomers were the Germans under General Linsingen. Cavalrymen broke away from Linsingen's columns to start the pursuit.

"Bloody hell," Filmer said, "that was quick."

"Rifles!" a voice shouted. "Companies in column. On the road!"

The greenjackets, like every other man in Wellesley's army, had been hoping they could go into the town where there was food, liquor and women, but only two companies went with the Highlanders to clear Køge's streets while the rest were ordered south behind the scavenging cavalry. They marched for an hour, passing corpses left in the fields by the marauding horsemen and listening to the occasional crackle of far-away carbines. Some of the Danish dead were wearing wooden clogs. Scores of prisoners were being escorted northward. At noon the marching column approached a village and found they had at last caught up with the cavalry. The German horsemen had dismounted because a rear-guard of the enemy was stubbornly defending a church and graveyard. The horsemen were firing carbines and pistols at too long a range and wasting their bullets against stone walls that were wreathed with smoke from Danish muskets.

"It'll be a job for us," Sergeant Filmer said, "just you wait."

And wait they did. The battalion's senior officers wanted to gauge how many of the enemy were in the small village, and that took time. The riflemen lay in a field, smoking pipes or sleeping. Sharpe walked up and down. Every once in a while a musket would fire from the church or from one of the nearby houses, but the cavalry had pulled back out of range and the balls whistled uselessly overhead. Most incongruous of all was a group of civilian horsemen who were evidently watching the whole confrontation from a safe distance. They looked like the local gentry come to see a battle, though for much of the early afternoon they saw nothing, but then Sir Arthur Wellesley and his staff arrived and there was a flurry of shouts, whistle blasts and sergeants' curses.

"Told you it would be our job," Filmer said. He squinted at the church. "Why can't they just bugger off? Silly bastards have lost, ain't they?"

The greenjackets spread into a skirmish line then advanced until they were a hundred paces from the makeshift fortress. "Fire!" Dunnett shouted at his company and the rifle bullets cracked on stone. Sharpe watched the church, the closest cottages and graveyard wall and could see no answering musket smoke.

Dunnett must have seen the same. "Two Company! Forward! Forward!" Dunnett shouted and led his men to the churchyard wall, paused a second, then vaulted over. The riflemen followed, conscious that they were being watched by the civilian horsemen and by General Wellesley. Men crouched behind the gravestones, but it seemed the Danes had left. "Got bored waiting for us," Filmer said.

"Into the street!" Dunnett called. The other companies were wrapping round the village, while the cavalry, mounted again, was following.

Sharpe walked round the side of the church to find himself in a small, neat village. A score of men were at the far end of the street, running away. "Encourage them!" Dunnett shouted and some of his riflemen ran to the center of the street, knelt and fired a farewell volley at the fugitives.

Sergeant Filmer took out his pipe. "Got blisters on my heel," he said to Sharpe. "It's Hopkins's boots, see? They don't fit." He pushed tobacco into the clay bowl. "Kept their heads, the lads, didn't they? Did bloody well, they—" He never finished the sentence but just pitched hard forward onto the dusty road where blood splashed on the broken white clay of his pipe.

The shot had come from behind. Sharpe turned and saw smoke drifting from an opening in the church tower. A bell hung in the shadows.

"Don't just stand gaping!" Dunnett snarled at him. The Captain, like the rest of his company, had taken shelter between the cottages.

Then a man showed in the tower, outlined against the bell. He raised a musket as Sharpe raised the rifle. Filmer had been shot in the back and Sharpe felt nothing as he squeezed the trigger. The bullet clanged against the bell, but it had gone clean through the man first. The musket dropped, clattering onto the roof of the church porch, then the body fell to thump onto red tiles and slide down into the graveyard. "You said something, Captain?" Sharpe asked as he fished a new cartridge from his pouch.

Dunnett walked away. Sharpe finished loading the rifle then walked to the end of the street where a horse trough stood. He bent and drank. He splashed water on his face, then slung the rifle on his shoulder and stared southward. The ground fell gently away. Off to his left the sun winked a myriad reflections from the sea where a British warship's sails were heaped white. Sharpe wondered if it was the *Pucelle* with his old friends aboard. Ahead of him the cavalry herded the fugitives, while to the right, about half a mile away in a small valley that was shaded by heavy trees, was a house that struck him as utterly beautiful. It was large, but not grand, low and wide, white-painted with big windows facing a carriage drive, a lake and a garden. Dark bushes had been trimmed into neat squares and cones. It looked comfortable and friendly, and for some reason Sharpe thought of Grace and felt the tears prick his eyes.

An old man came from the nearest cottage. He looked nervously at the greenjackets, then decided they meant no harm and so walked to Sharpe's side. He looked up into the rifleman's face, nodded a greeting, then gazed at the house. "Vygård," he said proudly.

The name took a moment to register, then Sharpe looked at the old man. "This is Herfølge?" he asked, nodding toward the village.

"Ja, Herfølge," the old man said happily, gesturing to the village, then pointed to the house. "Vygård."

Lavisser's grandfather's house. Vygård.

And Lavisser had reached Copenhagen remarkably quickly, much too quickly for a man carrying a heavy chest of gold. And surely, Sharpe thought, Lavisser would not want the gold trapped in a city that might be captured by an enemy?

"*Tak,*" he said fervently, "*mange tak.*"

Many thanks. For he was going to Vygård.

CHAPTER 8

VYGÂRD'S GATES WERE closed, but not locked. At first Sharpe thought the house was deserted, it was so quiet, then he realized no one would leave an empty house with its shutters open. Red roses grew between the windows. The front lawn was newly scythed, the smooth green marked where the blade's tip had left almost imperceptible wide curves, and the afternoon air was filled with the scent of cut grass.

He walked around the side of the house, past the large stables and coach house, through a flower garden that buzzed with bees, then under an archway cut from a box hedge and found himself on a wide lawn that sloped to a lake. In the middle of the grass, beneath a spreading white parasol, a dark-haired woman lay in a chair. She wore a white dress. A straw hat, decorated with a white ribbon, sat with a discarded newspaper, a handbell and a work basket on a small wicker table. Sharpe stopped, expecting her to challenge him or to call for the servants, but then realized she was asleep. It seemed extraordinary: a woman dreaming away the somnolent afternoon while, not a mile away, cavalrymen were rousting terrified fugitives from ditches and hedgerows.

The back of the house was heavy with wisteria among which a white-painted door stood invitingly open. A basket of pears and crab apples lay on the threshold. Sharpe stepped over it into the cool of a long stone-flagged corridor hung with pictures of churches and castles. A rack held a dozen walking sticks and two umbrellas. A dog was sleeping in an alcove. It woke as Sharpe passed, but instead of barking it just thumped its tail on the floor.

He opened a door at random and found himself in a long, elegantly furnished parlor with a white marble chimney breast that made him shudder as he remembered his ordeal in Skovgaard's flues. The room's windows overlooked the sleeping woman and Sharpe stood between the thick curtains and wondered who she was. Lavisser's cousin? She was much too young to be his grandmother. She seemed to have an incongruous musket propped beside her chair, then Sharpe saw it was a pair of crutches. The newspaper on the wicker table, weighted down by the work basket, stirred in the wind.

So where would Lavisser put his gold? Not in this room with its well-stuffed chairs, thick rugs and gilt-framed portraits. Sharpe went into the main hall. A curving white staircase lay to his right and, beyond it, an open door. He peered through the door and found a small parlor that had been turned into a bedroom. Presumably the woman on crutches could not climb the stairs and so a bed had been placed under the window. Books were piled on the white-painted window seat while newspapers lay across the bed and on a heavy leather valise that was overflowing with discarded petticoats. There were initials gilded on the valise's lid. MLV.

He wondered if the "L" stood for Lavisser, then dismissed the idea, and just then the name Visser came to him. Lavisser, Visser, Madame Visser. And in Skovgaard's house his last pistol ball had struck someone, provoking a yelp of pain and leaving blood on the floor. The woman in the garden had crutches.

He looked through the valise and found nothing with a name on it. He opened the books, but none was inscribed with an owner's name, though all, he thought, were in French. He went back to the big parlor and stared through the window at the sleeping woman. She was Lavisser's accomplice, she was French, she was the enemy. Sharpe reckoned he could spend all day searching the house for gold, but why bother when Madame Visser could probably tell him where it was?

He went back into the passage where the dog thumped its tail in welcome for a second time, crossed the lawn and stood behind the chair where he unslung the rifle from his shoulder. "Madame Visser?" he asked.

"*Oui?*" She sounded startled, then went silent as she heard the weapon being cocked. She turned *very* slowly.

"We met last week," Sharpe said. "I'm the man who shot you."

"Then I hope you suffer all the torments of hell," she said calmly. She spoke English well. A disturbingly good-looking woman, Sharpe thought, with an elegant face, dark hair and the eyes of a huntress. Those eyes, instead of showing fear, looked amused now. Her white dress had delicate lace at its neckline and hems and looked so feminine that Sharpe had to remind himself of Ole Skovgaard's verdict on this woman: merciless, he had said. "So what do you want?" she asked.

"Where is Lavisser's gold?"

She laughed. Not a pretend laugh, but genuine laughter. "Lieutenant Sharpe, isn't it? Major Lavisser told me your name. Sharpe. Not very appropriate, is it?" She looked him up and down. "So were you fighting up the hill?"

"Wasn't much of a fight."

"I can't imagine it was. Proper troops against farm boys, what does one expect? But my husband will be very disappointed. He and his friend rode up to watch. Did you see them? Perhaps you shot two gentlemen on horseback while you were culling the peasantry?" She was still twisted awkwardly in the chair. "Why don't you stand in front of me," she suggested, "where I can see your face properly."

Sharpe moved, keeping the rifle pointed at her.

Madame Visser still seemed amused rather than frightened by the weapon's threat. "Did you really come to find the gold? Major Lavisser probably took it with him and if that's all you came for then you might as well go away again."

"I think it's here," Sharpe said.

"Then you are a fool," she said and reached out for the small hand-bell on the wicker table. She picked it up but did not ring it. "So what are you going to do, fool? Shoot me?"

"I did once, why not again?"

"I don't think you will," she said, then rang the bell vigorously. "There," she exclaimed, "I'm still alive."

Sharpe found her good looks unsettling. He lowered the rifle's muzzle. "Where did I shoot you?"

"In the leg," she said. "You have given me a scar on the thigh and I think I hate you."

"Should have been in your head," Sharpe said.

"But the wound does well," she went on. "Thank you for asking." She turned as a sleepy-eyed servant girl came from the house. She spoke to the girl in Danish and the maid curtseyed and then ran back indoors. "I've sent for help," Madame Visser said, "so if you have any sense you'll leave now."

She was right, Sharpe thought. He should leave, but the gold was a lure and finding it would be a sweet revenge on Lavisser. "I'm looking for the bastard's gold," he told her, "and you can send for all the servants you want." He used the rifle's muzzle to open the work basket that weighted the newspaper.

"You think I keep a thousand guineas in there?" Madame Visser asked with amusement.

Sharpe had been looking for a pistol, but the only things in the basket were folded papers and a lethally long hatpin. He backed away. "A thousand guineas?" he asked. "What about the other forty-two thousand?"

For the first time since he had woken her Madame Visser looked discomfited. "Forty-two thousand?"

"He stole forty-three thousand guineas," Sharpe said. "What did he tell you? That it was a thousand?" She said nothing and he knew he had surprised her. "So which room did he use here?" he asked her.

She shrugged. "Upstairs, I suppose." She frowned at Sharpe. "Forty-three thousand?" She sounded disbelieving.

"All except for fifteen guineas that I stole off him."

"I imagine he took it to Copenhagen," Madame Visser said.

"Or hid it here," Sharpe said.

She nodded. "There are cellars and attics." She shrugged. "What will you do with it?"

"Return it to the British."

Madame Visser smiled. "I think, Lieutenant, you will keep it. And my silence will cost you five thousand."

He backed away. "Cheap, aren't you?"

She just smiled and blew him a kiss. He still backed away, unsure whether she had a pistol hidden under her skirts, but she did not move, just watched as he went back into the house.

He went upstairs. He considered searching the bedrooms, but decided Lavisser would not leave a fortune where any servant could filch from it and so he looked for the attic stairs and found them behind a small door. The loft was dusty, but lit by small dormer windows, and it was also crammed with chests, valises and crates. His hopes rose.

There was no gold. There were chests filled with ancient papers, crates of old toys and piles of moth-eaten clothes. There was a child's sledge, a rocking horse and a model ship that was rigged with cobwebs. But no guineas. He could not search all the boxes, but he could lift them and detect from their weight whether gold was stored inside, and there was none. Damn, he thought. So search the cellars. Madame Visser had sent for help and even though no one had yet disturbed him he knew he did not have much time.

He ran down the narrow, uncarpeted attic stairs, then crossed the landing and went down the big curving stairs and there in the hall, of all people, was Captain Warren Dunnett. A half-dozen riflemen were with him, their grubby uniforms looking out of place in the elegant setting. Dunnett smiled as Sharpe came downstairs. "You're under arrest, Lieutenant."

"Don't be daft," Sharpe said. He saw the surprise on Dunnett's face, then pushed past the six riflemen who looked embarrassed.

"Sharpe!" Dunnett called.

"Go boil your head," Sharpe answered. He went down the passage, past the dog, and so out into the back garden where Madame Visser was now attended by Captain Murray and two black-coated civilians in breeches and riding boots. The maid, Sharpe guessed, must have run to the village and appealed to the British.

Captain Murray, a decent man who commanded a company of greenjackets, shook his head sadly. "What were you thinking of, Sharpe?"

"Thinking of nothing," Sharpe protested. Dunnett and his men had followed him onto the lawn. "Do you know who this woman is?" Sharpe asked Murray.

"She's my wife, Lieutenant," one of the two civilians answered, "and I am an accredited French diplomat."

"Last week," Sharpe said, "I watched that bitch pull a man's teeth because he was a British agent."

"Don't be ridiculous," Dunnett snapped. He stepped toward Sharpe and held out his hand. "Give me your pistol, Lieutenant, and your saber."

"Captain!" Madame Visser said reprovingly. "Perhaps Lieutenant Sharpe has been affected by battle? I am told it makes some men insane. I think you should place him in a hospital."

"We shall arrest him, ma'am," Dunnett said enthusiastically. "Give me your rifle, Sharpe."

"Bloody take it," Sharpe said. The anger was rising dangerously in him.

"Richard," Captain Murray said emolliently. He took Sharpe's elbow and showed surprise when his hand was shaken off. "This isn't the place, Richard," he said softly. "We can sort things out back at the village."

"There's nothing to bloody sort out! I didn't do anything here!"

"You trespassed, Richard, and it ain't a serious offense."

"Lieutenant Sharpe!" Dunnett was becoming impatient. "You will give me your weapons now or I shall order my men to take them."

"Parole, Warren, parole," Murray suggested.

Madame Visser watched Sharpe with mock sympathy and a half-smile. She had won and was enjoying his humiliation. Then a new voice sounded angrily from the arch in the box hedge. "What the devil is going on?" the voice demanded, and the group on the lawn turned to see that Sir Arthur Wellesley, attended by three aides, had come to the house. "Someone tells me an officer was plundering here?" The General was plainly furious as he strode across the grass. "My God, I will not abide plundering, especially by officers. How can you expect obedience from the men when officers are corrupt?"

"I took nothing!" Sharpe protested.

"It's you," Wellesley said in a distant tone. Madame Visser, struck by the General's good looks, was smiling at him while her husband bowed stiffly and introduced himself. Wellesley spoke to them in fluent French, Dunnett and Murray stood back and Sharpe stared down at the wicker table and cursed his impulsiveness.

Wellesley turned cold eyes on Sharpe. "Monsieur Visser tells me you were annoying his wife."

"I put a bullet through her leg, sir," Sharpe said, "if that's what he means."

"You did what?" Wellesley snapped.

"Last week, sir, in Copenhagen. She was pulling a man's teeth at the time, and he was one of our agents."

Wellesley stared at him, Madame Visser chuckled. "He's mad, sir," Captain Dunnett said.

"I fear the sun or else the strain of battle has gone to his head, Sir Arthur," Madame Visser said gently. "I hurt my leg falling from a horse. Otherwise I would have ridden with my husband to witness your great victory. Instead I stayed here and Lieutenant Sharpe threatened me with a rifle, then said he would search the house for gold." She shrugged. "It is sad, I think, but perhaps you do not pay your officers properly?"

"Is that true, Sharpe?" Wellesley's voice was as cold as Sharpe had ever heard it.

"Of course it isn't true, sir," Sharpe said. He was not looking at Sir Arthur, but at the work basket. A hatpin, he thought, she had a hatpin in the work basket. My God, it was a wild chance, but perhaps the only one he had. Sir Arthur, confronted with an attractive woman, was talking to her in French and doubtless believing everything she said and in a moment he would confirm Dunnett's order to have Sharpe arrested and so, while the General was distracted, Sharpe stooped and pulled the newspaper from beneath the work basket. It was a copy of the *Berlingske Tidende*, nothing strange about that, but Madame Visser still made an ineffectual lunge to grab it back from him.

Wellesley frowned. "What the devil . . ." he began, then watched as Sharpe unfolded the paper and held it up to the sun. Tiny dots of light sparked on the page. Monsieur Visser and the other civilian stepped back as if to suggest they had nothing to do with whatever happened next and Sharpe just gazed at the pricks of sunlight and felt a great surge of relief. He was safe. "Sir?" he said.

Wellesley came and stood beside him, then took the paper and held it high. He stared at the pinpricks for a very long while. Dunnett, not understanding what was happening, fidgeted. Madame Visser sat still, saying nothing. The General still examined the tiny dots of light. "I'm told, sir," Sharpe said, "that each pinprick beneath a letter is . . ."

"I know how the system works, thank you, Sharpe," Wellesley said coldly. He read off each letter to decipher the hidden message, then finally lowered the newspaper. "You were employed on some obscure business for Sir David Baird, am I right?"

"Yes, sir."

"And Lord Pumphrey was entangled in the affair, yes?"

"Yes, sir."

"He woke me in London to ask my opinion of you, Sharpe."

"He did, sir?" Sharpe could not hide his surprise.

"The message is in French, Sharpe," the General said, carefully folding the paper, "and so far as I can see, it instructs their agents in the city to obey the Crown Prince's instructions to burn the fleet. I imagine General Cathcart will be interested." Wellesley thrust the folded paper back to Sharpe. "Take it to him, Sharpe. It looks as if your business is unfinished. Can you still sit on a horse?"

"Yes, sir."

"You never did it well. Let us pray you have learned better." He turned to one of his aides. "You will arrange for Lieutenant Sharpe to go north now. Right now! Madame? You are a diplomat, so I must leave you inviolate."

"Such a pity," Madame Visser said, clearly entranced by Sir Arthur.

Captain Dunnett seethed, Murray smiled and Madame Visser just shook her head at Sharpe.

Who blew her a kiss.

Then rode north.

THE DINNER was held in one of the big houses in Copenhagen's suburbs, a house very similar to the one where Skovgaard had lost his two teeth. A dozen men sat about the table that was presided over by General Sir William Cathcart, tenth Baron Cathcart and commander of His Britannic Majesty's army in Denmark. He was a heavyset and gloomy man with a perpetual look of worry that was being exacerbated by the thin, intense man sitting to his right. Francis Jackson was from the Foreign Office and had been sent to Holstein to negotiate with the Crown Prince long before Cathcart's forces had left Britain. The Danes had refused Jackson's demands and now he had come to Copenhagen to insist that Cathcart bombard the city. "I don't like the notion," Cathcart grumbled.

"You don't have to like it," Jackson said. He peered at the lamb and turnips on his plate as if trying to work out precisely what he had been served. "We must just do it."

"And swiftly," Lord Pumphrey supported Jackson. The small, birdlike Pumphrey was seated to Cathcart's left, thus completing the Foreign Office's encirclement of the General. His lordship had chosen a white coat edged with gold braid that gave him a vaguely military look, though it was spoiled by the beauty spot that had been fixed to his cheek again. "The weather will become our enemy soon," he said. "Is that not true, Chase?"

Captain Joel Chase of the Royal Navy, seated at the table's far end, nodded. "The Baltic becomes very adverse in late autumn, my lord," Chase answered in his rich Devonshire accent. "Fogs, gales, all the usual nuisances." Chase had been invited ashore to dine with Cathcart, a courtesy that was extended every night to some naval officer, and he had brought his First Lieutenant, Peel, who had drunk too much and was now fast asleep in his chair. Chase, who had taken care to sit beside Sharpe, now leaned toward the rifleman. "What do you think, Richard?"

"We shouldn't do it," Sharpe said. He was sitting far enough from Cathcart for his comment to go unheard.

"We will, though," Chase said softly. The tall, fair-haired naval Captain commanded the *Pucelle*, the ship on which Sharpe had served at Trafalgar and he had greeted Sharpe with obvious delight. "My dear Richard! How good to see you. And I am so very sorry." The two men had not met since Grace's death and it had been aboard Chase's ship that Grace and Sharpe had loved so passionately. "I did write," Chase had told Sharpe, "but the letter was returned."

"Lost the house," Sharpe said bleakly.

"Hard, Richard, hard."

"How are things on the *Pucelle*, sir?"

"We struggle by, Richard, struggle by. Let me think, who will you recall? Hopper's still my bosun, Clouter thrives with a few fingers missing and young Collier has his lieutenant's exams next month. He ought to pass so long as he doesn't confuse his trigonometry."

"What's that?"

"Tedious stuff that you forget the day after the lieutenant's exam," Chase said. He had insisted on sitting next to the rifleman even though seniority should have placed him much closer to Lord Cathcart. "The man's a bore," he told Sharpe, "cautious and boring. He's as bad as the

Admiral. No, not quite. Gambier's a Bible-thumper. Keeps asking if I've been washed in the blood of the Lamb."

"And have you?"

"Bathed, sluiced, washed, drenched and soaked, Sharpe. Reeking of blood." Chase had smiled, now he listened to the conversation at the table's far end before leaning close to Sharpe again. "The truth is, Richard, they don't want to assault the city because it's too well walled. So we'll unleash the mortars. Not much choice. It's either that or have you fellows assault a breach."

"There are women and children inside," Sharpe protested too loudly.

Lord Pumphrey, who had been responsible for bringing Sharpe to the dinner, overheard the comment. "There are women, children and ships, Sharpe, ships."

"Aye, but will there be any ships?" Chase asked.

"There had better bloody be ships," Sir David Baird growled.

Cathcart ignored Baird, staring instead at Chase whose question had raised alarm around the table. Jackson, the senior diplomat, pushed a gristly scrap of lamb to one side of his plate. "The Danes," he said, "will surely be reluctant to burn their fleet. They'll wait till the very last minute, will they not?"

"Last minute or not," Chase said energetically, "they'll still burn it and ships burn fast. Remember the *Achille*, Richard?"

"The *Achille*?" Pumphrey asked.

"French seventy-four, my lord, burned at Trafalgar. One minute she was fighting, next minute an incandescent wreck. Incandescent." He pronounced each syllable cheerfully. "We risk a city full of dead women and children in return for a pile of damp ashes."

Cathcart, Jackson and Pumphrey all frowned at him. Lieutenant Peel woke himself up by snoring abruptly and looked about the table, startled. "The message concealed in the newspaper," Lord Pumphrey said, "is presumably addressed to Lavisser?"

"We can assume so," Jackson agreed, crumbling a piece of bread.

"And it grants him permission from his French masters to carry out the Danish orders to deprive us of the fleet."

"Agreed," Jackson said carefully.

"The good news," Cathcart intervened, "is that thanks to Mister"—

he paused, unable to remember Sharpe's name—"thanks to the Lieutenant's watchfulness, we intercepted the message."

Lord Pumphrey smiled. "We can be quite certain, my lord, that more than one copy was sent. It would be usual in such circumstances to take such a wise precaution. We can also be certain that, because Monsieur and Madame Visser are protected by diplomatic agreement, they are free to send more such messages."

"Precisely so," Jackson said.

"Ah." Cathcart shrugged and leaned back in his chair.

"And we shall look remarkably foolish," Lord Pumphrey continued mildly, "if we were to capture the city and find, as Captain Chase so delicately phrases it, a pile of damp ashes."

"Damn it, man," Cathcart said, "we want the ships!"

"Prize money," Chase whispered to Sharpe. "More wine?"

"But how to stop the ships being fired?" Pumphrey asked the table at large.

"Pray for rain," Lieutenant Peel suggested, then blushed. "Sorry."

General Baird frowned. "They'll have their incendiaries ready," he observed.

"You can explain that, Sir David?" Jackson asked.

"They'll have stuffed the ships with incendiaries," Baird said. "Canvas bales filled with saltpeter, mealed powder, sulphur, resin and oil"—Baird listed the ingredients with an indecent relish—"and once the fuses are lit those boats will be pure flames in three minutes. Pure flames!" He smiled, then used a candle to light a dark cigar.

"Dear God," Jackson murmured.

"It probably isn't sufficient then," Lord Pumphrey spoke very judiciously, "to remove Captain Lavisser from the city?"

"Remove him?" Cathcart asked, startled.

Lord Pumphrey, so small and frail, drew a finger across his throat, then shrugged. "The message suggests that our renegade is the officer charged with delivering the order to burn the fleet, but alas, if he is absent then someone else will surely give the order."

Everyone stared at the diminutive Pumphrey. Baird, approving the idea of killing Lavisser, smiled, but most of the other officers looked shocked. Jackson just shook his head sadly. "One devoutly wishes that such a simple solution would obviate our problem, but alas, the Danes will have other men ready to start a conflagration." He sighed and looked up at the ceiling. "It will be a terrible defeat," he mused, "if we were to come this far and lose the prize."

"But, damn it, the Frogs won't get the ships!" Cathcart protested. "That's the point, ain't it?"

"A most craven defeat," Jackson said, ignoring the General's words, "for all the King's horses and all the King's men to have come this far merely to provoke a bonfire. We shall be the laughingstock of Europe." He made the last observation to Cathcart with the obvious insinuation that his lordship would be the butt of the joke.

General Baird signaled a waiter to bring the decanter of port. "Will the ships be fully manned?" he demanded.

No one answered, but most looked to Chase for an answer. The naval Captain shrugged as if to suggest he did not know. Sharpe hesitated, then spoke up. "The sailors have been added to the garrison, sir."

"So how many men are left aboard?" Baird demanded.

"Two or three," Chase opined. "The ships aren't in danger where they are, so why have crews aboard? Besides, I'm sure they're *en flûte*."

"They're what?" Baird asked.

"*En flûte*, Sir David. Their guns will have been taken ashore to add to the garrison's ordnance, so their gunports are empty like a flute's finger-holes."

"Why didn't you damn well say so?"

"And ships *en flûte*," Chase went on, "won't need crews, or nothing more than a couple of fellows to keep an eye on the mooring lines, pump out the bilges and be ready to light the fuses."

"A couple of fellows, eh?" Baird asked. "Then the question is, I sup-pose, how do we get a few of our fellows into the inner harbor?" Cathcart just stared at him wide-eyed. Jackson sipped port. "Well?" Baird inquired belligerently.

"I was there last week," Sharpe said. "Walked in. No guards."

"You can't send men into the city! They won't last an hour!" Cathcart protested.

"Sharpe did," Lord Pumphrey said in his delicately high voice. He was staring at the chandelier, apparently fascinated by a lengthening strand of wax that threatened to drip into the dessert bowl. "You lasted a good few days, didn't you, Sharpe?"

"You did?" Cathcart stared at Sharpe.

"I pretended to be an American, sir."

"What did you do?" Cathcart asked. "Spit tobacco juice everywhere?" He had made his name in the war of American independence and reckoned himself an expert on the erstwhile colonies.

"But even if our fellows can survive in the city," Captain Chase said, "how do we get them inside?"

Francis Jackson, elegant in a black suit and white silk shirt, snipped the end from a cigar. "How do the Danes infiltrate their messengers into the city?"

"Small boats, close inshore, dark nights," Chase said shortly.

"There's a small jetty," Sharpe said diffidently, "a small wooden pier by the citadel where people go to fish. It's very close to the fort. Too close, maybe."

"And right under the guns of the Sixtus Battery," one of Cathcart's aides observed.

"But a dark night?" Chase was suddenly enthusiastic. "Muffled oars. Blackened boat. Yes, why not? But why land at the pier? Why not row all the way in?"

"There's a boom across the outer harbor," Sharpe said, "and across the inner, but the pier's outside the boom."

"Ah. The pier it is, then." Chase smiled, then looked down the table at Cathcart. "But we'd need the Admiral's permission to send a launch, my lord, and might I suggest, with all the humility at my command, that this is a service best done by sailors? Unless, of course, you have soldiers who can find their way around a darkened ship at night?"

"Cite a verse from the Bible," Lord Pumphrey observed quietly, "that justifies such an expedition and I am sure Lord Gambier will grant permission."

One or two men smiled, the others wondered whether the prickly Admiral really would authorize such a gamble. "He'll give permission when he knows his prize money depends on it," Baird growled.

There was an embarrassed silence. Prize money, though much appreciated, was rarely acknowledged openly. Every senior officer, army and navy, stood to make a small fortune if the Danes refused to surrender, for then the ships would be prizes of war and worth real money.

"I suspect Lieutenant Sharpe should go with your sailors," Lord Pumphrey suggested. "He has a certain knowledge of the city."

"I'm sure we'd welcome him," Chase said, then looked at his friend. "Would you come?"

Sharpe thought of Astrid. "Yes, sir," he said.

"But if it were done," Lord Pumphrey said, "then 'twere well it were done quickly. Your fellows will be ready to open the bombardment in a day or two, will they not?"

"If we bombard," Cathcart growled.

"We must," Jackson insisted.

The argument returned to its old course, whether or not to bomb the city. Sharpe sipped port, listened to Copenhagen's bells ring the hour, and thought of Astrid.

THE DEVIL lurched up the slope and stuck at the top. "For God's sake push, you heathen bastards!" A sergeant, muddied to his waist, snarled at a dozen men. "Push!" The devil's eight horses were whipped, the men heaved at the wheels and the devil threatened to slide down the heap of clay. "Put your bloody backs into it!" the Sergeant bellowed. "Push!"

"Much too painful to watch," Lord Pumphrey said and turned his back. It was the morning after Cathcart's dinner and his lordship was feeling distinctly fragile. He and Sharpe were on a dune not far from where the devil was stuck and his lordship had an easel on which a very small piece of paper was pinned. He also had a box of watercolor paints, a tumbler of water and a set of brushes with which he was making a picture of Copenhagen's skyline. "I do thank the Lord I was never intended for the army," his lordship went on, touching a brush to the paper. "So very noisy."

The devil inched over the heap of clay and trundled down to the battery. It was a grotesquely heavy cart made for transporting mortars. The mortar carriage rode on the cart while the barrel was slung beneath the rear axle. The battery already possessed six long-barreled twenty-four-pounder guns that had been fetched ashore from a ship of the line; now it was being equipped with as many mortars.

They were evil-looking weapons. Just metal pots, really, squat and fat and short. The carriage was a chunk of wood in which the pot was set so it was pointing high into the air with a wedge at its front to change the elevation, though most gunners preferred to adjust their weapon's range by varying the amount of powder in the charge. Sharpe, watching the men maneuver the devil beneath the three-legged gin that would lift the heavy barrel off the ground and onto the carriage, tried to imagine the gun being fired. There would be no recoil, for the carriage had no wheels or trails and the gun was not being fired horizontally, so instead of leaping back the squat mass of wood and iron would simply try and bury itself in the earth. The mortars being assembled in this battery were all ten-inch weapons, not the biggest, but he imagined the smoking balls arcing high into the clouding sky and thumping down inside Copenhagen.

Lord Pumphrey must have guessed his thoughts. "These guns will be firing at the citadel, Sharpe. Does that assuage your tender conscience?"

Sharpe wondered if he should tell Pumphrey about the orphans in the city, then decided such a description would be wasted on his lordship. "General Cathcart doesn't seem to want to bombard either, my lord."

"General Cathcart will do what his political masters instruct him to do," Pumphrey observed, "and in the absence of any Minister of the Crown he will have to listen to Mister Jackson whether he likes it or not."

"Not to you, my lord?" Sharpe asked mischievously.

"I am a minion, Sharpe," Pumphrey claimed, touching his brush to the paint and frowning at his picture. "I am a lowly figure of absolutely no importance. Yet, of course, I shall use whatever small influence I can muster to encourage Cathcart to bombard the city. Beginning tomorrow night, I hope."

"Tomorrow?" Sharpe was surprised it would be so soon.

"Why ever not? The guns should be ready and the sooner it's done the better so we can be spared this dreadful discomfort and return to London." Pumphrey looked quizzically at Sharpe. "But why are you squeamish? Your reputation doesn't suggest squeamishness."

"I don't mind killing men," Sharpe said, "but I never had a taste for slaughtering women and children. Too easy."

"Easy victories are the best ones," Pumphrey said, "and usually the cheapest. And cheapness, you must remember, is the greatest desideratum of governments. I refer, of course, to their expenditure, not to their emoluments. If a man in government cannot become rich then he doesn't deserve the privileges of office." He flicked the brush across the top of the paper, smearing clouds out of the grayish paint. "The trouble is," he said, "that I never know when to finish."

"Finish?"

"Painting, Sharpe, painting. Too much and the painting will be heavy. Watercolor should be light, suggestive, nothing more." He stepped back and frowned at the painting. "I think it's almost there."

Sharpe looked at the painting. "I think it's very good, my lord." He did, too. Pumphrey had wonderfully caught the city's near magical look with its green spires and domes and red roofs. "I think it's really good."

"How very kind you are, Sharpe, how very kind." Pumphrey seemed genuinely pleased, then shuddered as the Sergeant cursed the men hauling on the lines that would hoist the mortar barrel. There were now fifteen batteries ringing the city's western edge, the closest ones hard against the protective canal, while offshore the British bomb ships were anchored in an arc facing the citadel and the Sixtus Battery which together guarded the harbor entrance. The Danish gun ships were staying home. In the first few days they had done serious damage to the Royal Navy's gun ships, for they drew less water and carried heavier ordnance, but the establishment of British shore batteries had driven them away and the city was now effectively locked in a metal embrace.

The boom of the big guns was constant, but they were all Danish as the cannon on the city walls kept a steady fire on the closest British batteries, but the shots were burying themselves in the great bulwarks of earth-filled fascines that protected the guns and mortars. Sharpe, from his vantage point on the dune, could see the smoke wreathing the wall. The city's copper spires and red roofs showed above the churning cloud. Closer to him, among the big houses and gardens, the earth was scarred by the newly dug British batteries. A dozen houses were burning there, fired by the Danish shells that hissed across the canal. Three windmills had their sails tethered against a blustering wind that blew the smoke westward and fretted the moored fleet that filled the sea lanes to the north of Copenhagen. Over three hundred transport ships were anchored there, a wooden town afloat. The *Pucelle* was one of the closest big ships and Sharpe was waiting for its launch to come ashore so that tonight, if the clouds thickened to obscure the moon, they could try to enter the city. He looked at the spires again and thought of Astrid. It was odd that he could not conjure her face to his memory, but nor could he ever see Grace in his mind's eye. He had no portrait.

"The Danes, of course, might just surrender now," Pumphrey said. "It would be the sensible thing to do." He was touching little smears of lighter green to highlight the city spires.

"I've learned one thing as a soldier," Sharpe said, "which is that the sensible thing never gets done."

"My dear Sharpe"—Pumphrey pretended to be impressed—"we'll make a staff officer of you yet!"

"God forbid, my lord."

"You don't like the staff, Sharpe?" Pumphrey was teasing.

"What I'd like, sir, is a company of riflemen and to do some proper fighting against the Frogs."

"You'll doubtless get your wish."

Sharpe shook his head. "No, my lord. They don't like me. They'll keep me a quartermaster."

"But you have friends in high places, Sharpe," Pumphrey said.

"High and hidden."

Pumphrey frowned at his picture, suddenly unhappy with it. "Sir David will not forget you, I can assure you, and Sir Arthur, I think, keeps an eye on you."

"He'd like to see me gone, my lord," Sharpe said, not hiding his bitterness.

Lord Pumphrey shook his head. "I suspect you mistake his customary coldness toward all men as a particular distaste for yourself. I asked him for an opinion on you and it was very high, Sharpe, very high. But he is, I grant you, a difficult man. Very distant, don't you think? And talking of distance, Lady Grace Hale was an extremely remote cousin. I doubt he cares one way or the other."

"Were we talking of that, my lord?"

"No, Sharpe, we were not. And I do apologize."

Sharpe watched as the mortar was lowered into its carriage. "What about you, my lord?" he asked. "What's a civilian doing as an aide to a general?"

"Offering sound advice, Sharpe, offering sound advice."

"That's not usual, is it, my lord?"

"Sound advice is very unusual indeed."

"It's not usual, is it, my lord, for a civilian to be given a place on the staff?"

Lord Pumphrey shivered inside his heavy coat, though the day was not particularly cold. "You might say, Sharpe, that I was imposed on Sir David. You know he was in trouble?"

"I heard, sir."

Baird's career had suffered after India. He had been captured by a French privateer on his way home, spent three years as a prisoner, and on his release was sent as Governor to the Cape of Good Hope where he had foolishly allowed a subordinate to make an unauthorized raid on Buenos Aires, a whole ocean away, and the disastrous foray had led to demands for Baird's dismissal. He had been exonerated, but the taint of disgrace still lingered. "The General," Lord Pumphrey said, "has all the martial virtues except prudence."

"And that's what you give him?"

"The Duke of York was unwise enough to enroll Sir David's help in facilitating Lavisser's outrageous scheme. We advised against, as you know, but we also pulled a string or two to make certain that someone could keep an eye on matters. I am that all-seeing eye. And, as I said, I proffer advice. We want no more irresponsible adventures."

Sharpe smiled. "Which is why you're sending me back into Copenhagen, my lord?"

Pumphrey returned the smile. "If Lavisser lives, Lieutenant, then he will inevitably spread stories about the Duke of York, and the British government, in its infinite wisdom, does not want the French newspapers to be filled with salacious tales of Mary Ann Clarke."

"Mary Ann Clarke?"

"A very beautiful creature, Sharpe, but not, alas, the Duke's wife. The Duchess is a Prussian princess and has, I am sure, many merits, but she seems to lack Miss Clarke's more lubricious skills."

Sharpe saw a launch appear between two of the bomb ketches. "So you want Lavisser dead, my lord?"

"I would never presume to issue such an order," Pumphrey said smoothly. "I merely note that you have a reputation for resourcefulness and therefore rely on you to do what is needful. And might I remind you that several thousand guineas are missing? I understand you looked for them in Vygârd?"

"I was going to return them to you, my lord."

"The thought never once crossed my mind that you would not, Sharpe," Pumphrey said with a smile. He watched a round shot from the citadel skip across the small waves and finally sink just short of a British gunboat. "There is, as it happens, another service you could render us in Copenhagen. That message you so cleverly intercepted? It was about more than burning the fleet, Sharpe. There was a gnomic sentence at the end to the effect that Paris is still demanding the list of names. I suspect that means Skovgaard, don't you?"

"I'm sure it does."

"You tell me he's taken precautions?"

"He thinks so. He thinks God is looking after him. And he reckons I'm evil."

"I do so dislike religious enthusiasm," Pumphrey said, "but do call on him, if you would be so kind. Just to make sure he's alive." Pumphrey frowned. "What is most important, Sharpe, is not the gold. It is not Lavisser's miserable life, nor even the unhappy chance that the Paris newspapers will spread tittle-tattle about Miss Clarke. What is important is that the French do not discover the identities of Skovgaard's correspondents. It is a pity that they have even learned his identity, for I fear he cannot possibly be kept safe when we're gone from here, but once this business is over I shall attempt to persuade him to move to Britain."

"I doubt he'll want to."

"I find most men prefer living to dying," Lord Pumphrey said, then stepped back to look at his painting. He shook his head in disappointment, tossed the brush down, emptied the water tumbler and closed the box of paints, evidently abandoning his efforts. "It will be sad to lose Skovgaard's services, but doubtless another man can be found to receive messages. Do you think that's your launch? Then might I wish you joy of the hunt in Copenhagen?" Pumphrey offered Sharpe a hand.

"Is there a reward for a successful hunt, my lord?" Sharpe asked.

"The gold is not enough?" Pumphrey inquired. "Then perhaps your reward will be the joy of catching your prey."

"I'm tired of being a quartermaster, my lord."

"Ah! You look for advancement!" Pumphrey smiled. "Let me see what I can offer you, Sharpe, though you may not like it."

"Like it?" Sharpe asked, puzzled.

"After you left Harwich, Sharpe," Lord Pumphrey said with evident enjoyment, "and before we ourselves embarked on a most uncomfortable vessel, a strange report came from London. A distressing murder in Wapping, of all places. Nothing strange in that, of course, except that a dozen witnesses swear that the criminal was an army officer. What do you make of that, Sharpe?" He waited for an answer, but Sharpe said nothing. Pumphrey shrugged. "Look after my trivial errand, Sharpe, and I shall make certain you remain an army officer, even a despised quartermaster. As for staying a quartermaster, well, I'm sure that in the proper time your own merits will elevate you far above that station and I anticipate observing your career with pride, knowing that I preserved it at a time of crisis. And, I promise you, I shall do my trivial best to advance your interests." He looked up at the sky. "It clouds over very nicely. Forgive me if I don't wave you farewell. I shall catch my death of cold if I stay here."

"My lord—" Sharpe began.

Pumphrey silenced him by holding up a hand. Then he folded his easel and picked up the paint box. "The man in Wapping was decapitated, they say, quite decapitated! Do give my regards to John Lavisser, won't you?" He walked away.

Bastard, Sharpe thought, bastard. He liked him, though. Then he turned and walked to the boat. Midshipman Collier was in charge. He had grown since Trafalgar, and was now a young man who smiled with genuine pleasure to see Sharpe. "We knew we was in for some dirty work when we heard you were coming. You remember Hopper?"

"Hopper is unforgettable," Sharpe said, grinning at the bosun of the crew who tugged his forelock. "And Clouter!" Sharpe spotted the huge black man whose right hand was now a mangled claw of two fingers, a legacy of Trafalgar. "How are you, Clouter?"

"Right as rain, sir."

"Shall we go?" Collier asked. Sharpe was watching Lord Pumphrey pick his fastidious way across the dunes. Be sure your sin will find you out, Sharpe thought.

So now he must go back into the city and commit murder.

And find the gold. And look for Astrid. And that last task seemed the most important.

He stepped into the boat, still confused.

CHAPTER 9

THE LAUNCH, INSTEAD OF taking Sharpe to the *Pucelle*, carried him only as far as the *Vesuvius*, a bomb ship anchored much closer to the harbor mouth. Captain Chase was waiting aboard to the evident apprehension of the *Vesuvius*'s commander, a mere lieutenant, who was in awe of having a genuine post captain aboard his vessel. Sharpe and Collier, being officers, were formally whistled aboard at the bomb ship's waist while the launch's crew scrambled over the bows. "I thought we'd spend the day here," Chase explained. "I'm sending my crew into the city with you, Sharpe, and it's much less far to pull from here than from the *Pucelle*. I brought dinner with me."

"And weapons, sir?"

"Hopper has your arsenal."

Sharpe still had the rifle he had borrowed at Køge, but he had asked Chase for more weapons and Hopper had brought them from the *Pucelle*. There was a heavy cutlass, two pistols and one of the massive seven-barreled guns that Sharpe had used at Trafalgar. It was a naval weapon of stunning ferocity and limited usefulness. The seven barrels, each of a half-inch diameter, were clustered so they could be fired together, but the gun, which had been designed to fire down from the rigging onto an enemy deck, took an age to reload. Nevertheless, used once and used right, it was devastating. Sharpe hung the squat, heavy gun next to the rifle on his shoulder and strapped the cutlass round his waist. "Good to have a proper blade again. So you're coming into the city, Hopper?"

"Captain wanted the best, sir," Hopper said, then hesitated. "The lads and me, sir . . ."

"You're the best," Sharpe said.

"No, sir." Hopper shook his head to indicate that Sharpe had misunderstood him. He was a huge man with a tarred pigtail and a skin smothered in tattoos, who now blushed. "Me and the lads, sir," he said, shifting uncomfortably and unable to meet Sharpe's gaze, "we wanted to say how sorry we were, sir. She was a proper lady."

"She was." Sharpe smiled, touched by the words. "Thank you, Hopper."

"They were going to send you a gift for your child," Chase told him a few moments later when the two men were ensconced in the *Vesuvius*'s small after cabin. "They made a crib from some of the *Pucelle*'s timbers broken at Trafalgar. It was probably burned in the galley fire when they heard the news. Sad days, Richard, sad days. So. You're ready for tonight?"

"Yes, sir."

"Young Collier's in charge of the landing party," Chase said. "I wanted to go myself, but the Admiral refused me permission. The wretched man said I was too valuable!"

"He's right, sir."

"He's a tedious bore, Richard, who should be in charge of some canting little chapel instead of a fleet. But Collier knows his business." Sharpe was dubious that an officer as young as Collier should command the landing party, but Chase was blithely confident. The men, once ashore, were to go to the inner harbor and there board a ship. Any ship, Chase said, because once safely aboard they would hide on the lower decks. "Effectively the ships are laid up," Chase explained, "which means no one's aboard except possibly a few fellows who'll light the fuses and you can wager ten years' salary to a farthing that they'll be wallowing in the officers' quarters. Collier's fellows can wait down below and the only risk, frankly, is if the Danes are doing any work aboard. One carpenter down in the ship's well and we'll have to start cutting throats."

"When do you cut the fuses?" Sharpe asked.

"Collier will have to judge the moment," Chase said, and the careless answer worried Sharpe even though it was none of his business. He was going into the city to hunt Lavisser while the cutting of the Danish fleet's fuses was Collier's responsibility and again Sharpe wondered if the young Midshipman was really the right man, but Chase would not abide any doubts. "He'll do splendidly, Richard, just splendidly. Now, how about some dinner? I've brought chine, tongue and cold hog's puddings."

"Hog's puddings?"

"Devonshire food, Sharpe, real food! I do like a hog's pudding."

Sharpe slept that afternoon, rocked into dreams by the small waves. When he woke it was a rainy dusk and the ship was alive with shouts, the sound of a capstan creaking and the shuffle of men's feet. The ship, it seemed, was being adjusted. The two huge mortars in the *Vesuvius*'s belly were fixed, so to aim their shells the whole ship had to be pointed at the target and this was achieved by tightening or loosening the cables of four anchors that held the gun ship in a tensioned web. "There! No! Too far!" a midshipman shouted. "Larboard bow anchor let go two steps!"

"They must do it twice a day," Chase said. "The tide affects it, I gather."

"What are they aiming at?"

"That big fort." Chase pointed toward the citadel that loomed above the small fishing pier where Sharpe hoped to land that night. "They'll drop the bombs straight down its gullet. Shall we finish the tongue for supper? Then you'll leave at midnight."

The launch was being readied. The rudder pintles were greased so they would not squeak and the tholes, which held the oars, were wrapped in rags while the hull and oars were painted black with Stockholm tar. The launch crew looked like pirates for they were hung with weapons and all dressed in dark clothes. A Danish seaman from the *Pucelle*'s larboard watch had been made an honorary member of the launch crew for the expedition. "Can you trust the man?" Sharpe asked Chase.

"Trust him with my life, Richard. He's been a Pucelle longer than I have. And Collier needs a fellow who can talk the language."

The night fell. The clouds made it utter dark, so black that Sharpe wondered how the launch would ever find its way into the harbor mouth, but Chase reassured him. He pointed to a distant lantern that glowed a pale blue. "That's hanging from one of the *Pucelle*'s yardarms and we're going to put another lantern on the *Vesuvius*'s foremast, and as long as young Collier keeps the two blue lights in line then he'll go straight as an arrow. The navy does try to anticipate these problems." He paused.

"Would you very much mind, Richard, if I didn't see you away? I'm feeling somewhat sickly. Just something I ate. I need sleep. Do you feel well?"

"Very."

"I wish you joy, Richard," Chase said, clapped his shoulder and walked aft.

It seemed a strangely abrupt farewell, and it did not seem right that Chase should be sleeping when the launch crew left, but Sharpe suspected Chase's sickness was as much to do with nervousness as an upset stomach. Sharpe himself was nervous. He was about to try and pierce an enemy stronghold, and doing it in a launch that offered no hiding place if they were discovered. He watched Chase go to the after quarters, then went and waited in the *Vesuvius*'s well deck where the great mortars crouched and where Hopper and his men honed knives and cutlasses.

It seemed an age until Collier ordered the embarkation and then it took another long while for all the men, encumbered with their weapons and carrying bags of food and skins of water, to clamber down the bomb ship's side into the tar-stinking launch. The men were oddly excited, almost giggly, so much so that Collier snapped at them to be quiet, then sensibly checked that none of them had loaded weapons for he feared the accidental discharge of a pistol or musket. Rain had started to fall. It was not heavy, merely an insistent drizzle that found its way down Sharpe's upturned collar.

The launch was crowded. It usually had a crew of a dozen men, but now held fifteen. They had embarked over the side of *Vesuvius* that lay farthest from the city and, at Collier's order, the men now rowed a few strokes to take them clear of the bomb ship. The great oars were silent in the tholes, though once they were a few yards from the *Vesuvius* Collier ordered the men to stop rowing. "The tide will take us in," he whispered to Sharpe. There was no need to whisper for they were still more than half a mile from the shore, but already they were feeling vulnerable.

The launch drifted. Every now and then the stroke or bow side oars would pull a brief correction to keep the pale-blue lanterns in line. The blue was very pale, almost white, and Sharpe, twisting about on the rear thwart, marveled that the men could distinguish those two lamps from all the other lights in the fleet. Most of the time the crew stayed still and silent, listening for the telltale splashes and creaks that would betray the presence of a Danish guard boat. There was bound to be at least one enemy boat patroling the harbor boom to prevent just such an incursion as this one by the *Pucelle*'s darkened launch.

A few lights burned in the city, their reflections glimmering long and shakily on the black water. A wind gusted cold out of the east, splashing small waves against the launch. Sharpe shivered. He could smell the harbor now, its water made rank by all the sewage and rot that was penned up by the long quays. A small flame flared and died on the ramparts of the citadel and Sharpe supposed it was a sentinel lighting a pipe. He turned to see that the lanterns of the British fleet now looked very far away and were blurred by the rain, then a hiss from the launch's bows made everyone go still. Sharpe heard a splash nearby and the groan of an oar in its rowlock. An enemy guard boat was close and Sharpe waited, scarce daring to breathe, but the next splash was fainter. He thought he saw a flash of white water from an oar, but he could not be certain. Collier and his men were bending low as if they might hide from the patroling enemy in the dark of the sea's surface.

A reddish glow now showed above the citadel's ramparts, cast by the lanterns in its central courtyard. The launch was drifting faster now, carried in by the fierce tide. Sharpe could not see the pier and he tried not to think of the big Danish guns in the embrasures above him. Just one barrel, loaded with canister, could turn the launch into a mess of blood-stained kindling. The first of the city clocks struck one.

Then the launch bumped into an obstacle. Sharpe gripped the gunwale, sticky with its coating of tar. His first thought was that they had drifted into the boom, or perhaps struck a rock, then he realized that the bow men were clambering out of the launch. They had reached the pier, guided unerringly by the blue leading lights. He heard thumps as the big bags of food and ammunition were heaved upward. "We'll just leave the boat here," Collier whispered, "let it drift."

Sharpe groped his way forward, then scrambled awkwardly up to the wooden staging which smelt of fish. "So where now, Richard?" a low voice asked him.

Sharpe turned, astonished. "Sir?"

"Shh." Captain Chase grinned in the dark. "Admiral Gambier thinks I'm ill, but I couldn't possibly let these lads come without me." His lads were all grinning. They had known the Captain was coming, which was why they had been so excited when they left the *Vesuvius*. "So where to, Richard?" Chase asked.

"You shouldn't be here, sir," Sharpe said fiercely.

"Not you too, for God's sake. Besides, a little late to tell me, don't you think?" Chase was wearing his uniform, but now draped a boat cloak over his shoulders. "Lead on, Richard, lead on."

Sharpe took them along the pier, always aware of the huge guns not a hundred paces away, then left down the path where he had walked with Astrid. Their boots seemed loud. Then, not twenty paces from the pier, a voice challenged from the garden where a battery of field guns had been placed behind fascines.

Chase's Danish seaman answered. There was a brief laugh from the darkness, then another rattle of words. The other seamen had stopped, hands on weapons, but the tone of the exchange was reassuring and Chase led them on. "What did you tell him?" the Captain asked when they were clear of the battery.

"The truth," the man said. "I told him we were British sailors come to capture the fleet."

"You did?" Chase sounded alarmed.

"My mother said I'd go to hell if I lied, sir. Then I told him our boat had sprung a leak and we were walking back. He thinks we're the guard-boat crew."

Chase chuckled. There was just enough light seeping from lamps in the city to cast a damp shine on the road beside the harbor quay, which was heaped with barrels of food stockpiled for a siege. "Does this strike you as damned odd, Richard?" Chase asked.

"Yes, sir."

"My God, we're in an enemy fortress!" Chase peered down alleys, plainly disappointed that there was so little to see. The city seemed asleep, not just the civilians, but the garrison too. There was an inno-cence here, Sharpe thought. Copenhagen might be under siege, yet still the city wanted to carry on with its ordinary life. No one wanted war and Sharpe sensed that the folk perversely believed it would go away if they ignored it. All that Denmark asked was to be left in peace while Europe went mad, but the Danes had ships and so they must have war whether they liked it or not.

They passed the Amalienborg Palace. There must have been sentries there, but none challenged the group of men whose footsteps echoed from the palace walls. A cat squealed somewhere and rats skittered in the dark. The quay, which had been almost empty on the day the Crown Prince had left for Holstein, was now crowded with moored craft, most of them merchantmen that had taken refuge from the British fleet. The wind slanted the persistent rain through their high rigging. "I keep thinking I shall wake up and discover this is a dream," Chase said.

"We're not at the inner harbor yet," Sharpe warned. Surely the Danes would guard their fleet? Yet the bridge had no sentries. The masts and rigging of the warships tangled the dark, dimly lit by a brazier that glowed outside a guardhouse that stood close to the two half-built ships on the slipways. Sharpe assumed it was a guardhouse, for there was a small covered booth for a sentry, but the booth was empty.

Chase led them down the stone quay that separated the inner and outer harbors. It was suddenly all ridiculously easy. The Danes had packed their fleet into the basin, gunwale to gunwale, and the bows of the warships touched the quay so that their bowsprits soared above the stones. Chase gestured at the very first ship and his men, with a practiced ease, scrambled into the netting rigged under the beakhead. Then, one by one, they vanished inside the bows. Sharpe waited till the last bundle had been passed up, then followed more clumsily.

The ship was dark as a tomb. No one challenged them. They groped down companionways until they had reached the empty lower deck. And there, come like thieves in the night, they waited.

GENERAL PEYMANN peered at the letter which had been brought to the city by two British officers under a flag of truce. The officers were waiting outside one of the gates for his answer.

The letter was in English and the General's command of that language was not sufficient to understand the elaborate courtesies demanded by diplomacy so he gave the paper to Lavisser. "Perhaps you'd translate, Major?"

Lavisser read his translation aloud. He hurried through the flowery compliments, then slowed when he came to what was little more than a demand for the city's surrender. " 'We, the undersigned, at this moment, when our troops are before your gates, and our batteries ready to open, do renew to you the offer of the same advantageous and conciliatory terms which were proposed through His Majesty's ministers to your court.' Nothing new there, sir," Lavisser commented. " 'If you will consent to deliver up the Danish fleet, and to our carrying it away, it shall be held in deposit for His Danish Majesty, and shall be restored, with all its equipments, in as good a state as it is received, as soon as the provisions of the general peace shall remove the necessity which has occasioned this demand.' It's signed by both Admiral Gambier and General Cathcart, sir," Lavisser said, tossing the letter down.

Peymann sat at the table and gazed gloomily at the letter. "They don't say anything about bombarding the city?"

"Not in so many words, sir."

"But will they?" Peymann demanded.

"They daren't," another aide answered. "They will earn the scorn of all Europe."

"But if they do," a third aide put in, "we shall have to endure. The fire brigades are ready."

"What fire brigades?" Lavisser asked sarcastically. "There are just seven pumping engines in the whole city."

"Seven? Only seven?" Peymann was alarmed.

"Two are being repaired, sir."

"Seven isn't enough!"

"Burn the fleet," Lavisser suggested. "When they see the prize is gone, sir, they'll go away."

"We are here to protect the fleet," Peymann said. "We will burn it if we must, but only at the very last moment." He sighed, then gestured for a clerk to write a reply to the British demand. "My Lords," he dictated, then thought for a moment. "We remain convinced that our fleet, our very own indisputable property, is as safe in His Danish Majesty's hands as ever it can be in those of the King of England." That, he thought, was very felicitous. Should he mention the possibility of a bombardment? He decided, on balance, that he should try to jog the British conscience. "Our master never intended any hostilities against yours," he went on, "and if you are cruel enough to endeavor to destroy a city that has not given you the least cause for such treatment, then it must submit to its fate." He watched the clerk write. "They won't bombard," he said, almost to himself. "They won't."

"They cannot," an aide agreed.

"It would be barbarous," another said.

"It will be a siege, I'm sure," Peymann said, hoping he was right.

That would be the last thing that Chase and his men would want, for they must hide until the city surrendered and even the ever optimistic Chase did not believe their luck could hold through the weeks or months of a prolonged siege. Chase had only dared come into the city because he believed that the Danish surrender would come swiftly once the mortars began their work. "Mind you," he told Sharpe in the morning, "we could probably live here for months. The bottom's full of salt pork. There's even some water barrels. A bit rank, but nothing worse than we usually drink." Dawn had revealed that they were on board the largest ship in the Danish fleet, the 96-gun *Christian VII*. "She's almost new," Chase told Sharpe, "and beautifully built. Beautiful!" The ship had been emptied of her crew, guns and ammunition, though great canvas bundles of incendiaries had been placed throughout her decks with fuses leading up to the forecastle. There were no Danes aboard, though in the afternoon, when most of Chase's bored men were sleeping, there was the thump of footsteps. The men, concealed in the forward magazine, took hold of their weapons while an alarmed Chase put a finger to his lips.

The footsteps came down to the deck immediately above them. There seemed to be two people, perhaps come to check the fuses or maybe to sound the ship's well, but then one of the intruding couple laughed and sang a snatch of song. It was a woman's voice and a moment later new sounds betrayed why the couple had come aboard. "If they fight as hard as they—" Collier whispered, but Chase silenced the Midshipman.

The couple eventually left and Chase's men ate bread and hog's puddings. "Florence sends the puddings to me," Chase said, "and she tells me these ones are made from our very own pigs. Delicious, eh? So"—he cut another slice from the pale fat sausage—"what do you plan to do, Richard?"

"I have a man to hunt," Sharpe said. And a woman to see, he added to himself. He had been tempted to go to Ulfedt's Plads during the long day, but prudence had suggested he wait till dark.

Chase thought for a moment. "Why don't you wait till the city surrenders?"

"Because he'll be in hiding by then, sir. But I'll be safe enough tonight." Especially, Sharpe thought, if the bombardment began.

Chase smiled. "Safe?"

"When those shells begin to fall, sir, you could march the 1st Foot Guards stark naked through the city center and no one would notice them."

"If they bombard," Chase said. "Maybe the Danes will see sense first? Maybe they'll surrender?"

"I pray so," Sharpe said fervently, but he suspected the Danes would be stubborn. Their pride was at stake and perhaps they did not really believe the British would use their mortars and howitzers.

The sun came out that afternoon. It dried the rain-drenched city and glinted off the green copper roofs and cast filmy shadows from the smoke of the Danish guns. Those guns had hammered all day, churning the earth and fascines about the British batteries. The big naval guns, brought from the empty ships in the basin, were mounted *en barbette*, meaning there were not enough embrasures to protect them so the weapons were firing directly over the wall's parapet and British gunner officers hungrily watched those pieces through their telescopes. Guns *en barbette* were easily destroyed.

The British mortars squatted in their beds. Their shells had their fuses already cut. All that was needed now was a decision to use them.

The sun sank across Zealand to leave a flaming sky. The last ray of the sun shone on a white-crossed Danish flag that hung from the tallest of the city's mast cranes. The flag glowed, then the earth's shadow engulfed it and another day was gone. The Danish guns stopped firing and their smoke slowly dissipated as it drifted westward. In the church of Our Savior, which had a handsome staircase winding outside its soaring spire, a prayer meeting called on God to spare the city and to imbue General Peymann with wisdom. General Peymann, oblivious of the prayers, sat down to a supper of pilchards. Three babies, born that day in the Maternity Hospital that lay between Bredgade and Amaliegade, slept.

One of their mothers had the fever and the doctors wrapped her in flannel and fed her a mixture of brandy and gunpowder. More brandy and barrels of akvavit were being drunk in the city's taverns which were full of sailors released from their duties on the walls. The city's seven fire engines, great metal tanks mounted on four-wheeled carts with monstrous double-levered pumps on their tops, sat waiting at street corners. Another prayer meeting, this one in Holman's Church, the sailors' shrine, beseeched that the fire engines would not be needed, while in the arsenal on Tojhusgade the last refurbished muskets were handed out to the newest volunteers of the militia. If the British made a breach and assaulted the city then those brewery workers and clerks, carpenters and masons, would have to defend their homes. On Toldboden, in a small shop beside the Customs House Quay, a tattooist worked on a sailor's back, making an intricate drawing of the British lion being drowned by a pair of Danish seamen.

"There are rules of war," General Peymann told his supper guests, "and the British are a Christian nation."

"They are, they are," the university chaplain agreed, "but they're also a very disputatious people."

"But they will not treat women and children as combatants," Peymann insisted. "Not Christian women and children. And this is the nineteenth century!" the General protested. "Not the Middle Ages."

"These are very fine pilchards," the chaplain said. "You get them from Dragsteds, I assume?"

In fifteen British batteries and on board sixteen bomb ships and in ten launches that had been specially fitted to hold smaller mortars, the officers consulted their watches. Rockets, launched from triangular frames, were set up beside the land batteries. It was not quite dark yet, but dark enough to conceal the batteries from the watchers on the city wall who did not see the heavy fascines protecting the long guns being dragged aside.

The clouds were breaking and the first stars showed above the city.

A linstock glowed red in a forward battery.

"They threaten to behave abominably," General Peymann averred, "and hope we believe the threat. But common sense and humanity will prevail. Must prevail."

"Christianity must prevail," the university chaplain insisted. "A direct attack on civilians would be an offense against God himself. Is that thunder? And I thought the weather was clearing."

No one answered and no one moved. It had sounded like thunder, but Peymann knew better. A gun had fired. It was far off, but the sound was heavy, the gut-pounding percussion of a heavy-caliber mortar. "God help us," the General said softly, breaking the silence about his table.

The first bomb arced upward, its burning fuse trailing a thin red line of sparks and a tenuous trail of smoke. It was a signal, and from all around the city's western edge and from the boats moored in the sound the other mortars fired. Howitzers slammed back on their trails to send their shells after the mortar bombs.

The burning fuses of the bombs reached up, red sparks curving in the night.

The gunners were reloading. The first bombs looked like livid shooting stars. Then, as they began their shrieking fall, the bomb trails converged. God had not shown mercy, the British possessed none and Copenhagen must suffer.

THE FIRST bomb broke through a roof with a cascade of splintering tiles, drove down through a plaster ceiling and lodged on an upper landing where, for an instant, it lay with a smoking fuse. Then, bumping and smoking, it rolled down a flight of stairs to lodge on a half landing. No one was in the house.

For a moment it seemed the mortar shell would not explode. The fuse burned into the hole of the wooden plug and the smoke just died away. Flakes of plaster dropped from the shattered ceiling. The bomb, a thirteen-inch black ball, just lay there, but the fuse was still alive, burning down through the last inch of saltpeter, sulphur and mealed powder until the spark met the charge and the bomb ripped the top story apart just as the other bombs of the first salvo came crashing down into the nearby streets. A seven-year-old girl, put to bed without supper for giggling during family prayers, was the first of the city's inhabitants to die, crushed by an eleven-inch mortar shell that burst through her bedroom ceiling.

The first fires began.

Eighty-two mortars were firing. Their range was adjusted by varying the amount of powder in the charge and the gunners had specified the quantities of the different batteries to make sure the bombs all fell in the same areas of the city. In the north they were dropping the missiles into the citadel's interior, while to the south the bombs were crashing into the streets closest to the wall. The crews of the fire engines trundled their heavy machines toward the first fires, but were obstructed by people try-ing to escape the bombs. A thirteen-inch shell cracked into a crowd, miraculously touching no one. Its fuse glowed red and a man attempted to extinguish it with his boot, but the bomb exploded and the man's foot, trailing blood, arced over the screaming street. There was blood and flesh on the house fronts. Families tried to carry their valuables away from the threatened area, further congesting the alleys. Some folk took refuge in the churches, believing there would be sanctuary from the enemy in sacred walls, but the churches burned as easily as the houses. One bomb exploded in an organ loft, scattering pipes like straws. Another killed ten people in a nave. Some bombs failed to explode and lay black and malevolent where they fell. An artist, hurriedly assembling paper, pencils and charcoal, had a smaller shell plunge through his roof and lie smoking next to his unmade bed. He picked up the chamber pot, which he had still not emptied from the night before, and upended it on the missile. There was a hiss as the fuse was extinguished, then a vile stink.

A score of fires started. The fiercest broke up through the roofs as more bombs hammered down into the flames. The British had begun to fire carcasses now, hollow shells designed to burn rather than explode. The heaviest, fired from the big thirteen-inch mortars, weighed as much as a man and were stuffed with saltpeter, sulfur, antimony and pitch. They burned with a furnace-like intensity, the fire seething out of holes bored in their metal shells and no mere fire pump could quench such horrors. There was still a vestige of evening light in the watercolor sky through which the fuses of the plunging bombs left threads of smoke. The threads wavered, mingled in the wind and vanished, only to be renewed as more bombs and carcasses fell. Then the threads were touched with red as flame blossomed out of the thicker, boiling smoke that churned up from a city of cratered cobbles, broken rafters and burn-ing homes. Scraps of shell casing whistled in city streets. The first fire engines clanked, their leather hoses pulsing as desperate men seesawed the great pumps, but the streams of water were futile. And still the bombs came and the western edge of the city was ringed by the noise and flaring lights of the batteries. The bomb ships shuddered as their mortars fired, each flash illuminating the chain rigging with a deep red light shrouded in smoke. The British long guns fired at the wall, their targets conveniently outlined by the glare of the city fires, while the rockets flared and hissed to carry their explosive heads in wild trajectories that plunged indiscriminately into city streets.

Sharpe walked into the city. He carried the rifle on one shoulder and the seven-barreled gun on the other, but no one took any particular notice of him. Men were running toward the fires, families were fleeing them and the whole city reverberated to the thump of the bombs. Sharpe was going to Skovgaard's warehouse because he did not know what else he could do. There was little point in visiting Bredgade for he was certain Lavisser would be with his General or else on the city walls, and Sharpe did not know how to find him.

So Lavisser could live an extra day and Sharpe would go to Astrid. It was what he wanted, what he had been thinking of all day as he waited in the stinking and dark lower deck of the Danish warship. Sharpe could not be certain that Astrid would welcome him while British bombs were shaking the city, but instinct told him she would be pleased. Her father would almost certainly be disapproving, while Aksel Bang would seethe, but to hell with them both.

It was dark now, but the city was lit red. Sharpe could hear the crackle and roar of flames punctuated by the crash of bombs falling through rafters and floors, and by the belly-punching blows as the powder charges exploded. He saw a fallen rocket skidding up a street, spewing sparks and terrifying a horse that was dragging barrels of sea-water from the harbor. A spire was outlined in red and surrounded by smoke. Sharpe became momentarily lost in the tangle of alleys, then smelt the gin distillery and followed his nose to Ulfedt's Plads which was well clear of the district where the bombs were falling. He knocked hard on Skovgaard's door, just as he had on the first night he had arrived in Copenhagen.

He heard a window thrown up and he stepped back. "Mister Skovgaard!" he shouted.

"Who is it?" It was Astrid who answered.

"Astrid!"

There was a pause. "Lieutenant Sharpe?" There was disbelief in her

voice, but no disapproval. "Is it you?" she asked. "Wait!" Sharpe's instinct
had been right because she smiled when she opened the door, but then
she frowned. "You should not be here!"

"I am."

She stared at him for a heartbeat, then turned down the hall. "I will
get a coat," she said as she went to a cupboard. "My father is not here. He
went to a prayer meeting with Aksel, but I wanted to go to the orphanage
and I promised Father I wouldn't go alone. Now you're here." She smiled
at him a second time. "Why are you here?"

"To see you."

"I think you English are as mad as you are cruel. I must find a key."
She found the front door key. "Why are you bombing us?"

"Because they're all mad."

"It is wrong," she said fiercely. "I cannot believe it's happening. It is
awful! I must leave Father a message." She vanished into the warehouse
office for a moment, then reappeared wearing a coat and hat. She locked
the front door and then, as though they were old friends, put her arm
though his. "Come," she said, leading him toward the hellish red glow
and snarling noise of the fire. "I should be angry with you."

"I'm angry with them," Sharpe said.

"Don't they know there are women and children here?"

"They know."

"Then why?" She asked it fiercely.

"Because they don't want your fleet filled with Frenchmen trying to
invade England."

"We would burn the fleet before the French took it. Before you take
it as well," Astrid said, then gripped his arm tightly as three bombs
exploded in quick succession. "If the fire is near the hospital," she
explained, "we have to fetch the children out. You will help?"

"Of course."

The sound of the bombs grew louder as they neared the citadel. The
missiles were hurtling down into the Danish fort and turning its center
into a cauldron. The small nearby streets were untouched by the bombardment and were full of people who stared at the reddened smoke boiling out of the citadel's walls. The children's hospital was untouched.
Astrid took Sharpe inside, but no help was needed, for a dozen other

women had come to soothe the children who were now gathered in the dispensary listening to a story. Sharpe stayed in the courtyard, half hiding in the shadows under the balcony, and he was still there when a half-dozen Danish officers came through the orphanage's arched gate. They were led by an elderly, heavyset man in a dark cloak and a gilded cocked hat. It seemed he had come to check whether the hospital was damaged, nothing more. Some of his aides looked curiously at Sharpe for he still had the two guns on his shoulders and his greatcoat was plainly not a Danish uniform, but they seemed reassured when Astrid came back to the courtyard and joined him. "That is General Peymann," she whispered.

The General was talking with the hospital's warden while his aides stood beneath the mast-rigged flagpole. Lavisser was not among them. "Ask him where Lavisser is," Sharpe said to Astrid.

"I can't do that!"

"Why not? Tell him you want to congratulate Lavisser for changing sides."

Astrid hesitated, then did what Sharpe wanted. One of the aides accosted her and clearly wanted to know who Sharpe was, for he glanced at the rifleman as he spoke. Astrid told him something, then curtseyed to General Peymann who took off his hat and bowed to her. A long conversation followed and Sharpe had just enough experience of the city to understand they would be discussing common acquaintances, but at last it ended, the General bowed again and then led his men back into the street. "I told them you were from the American ship in the harbor," Astrid said.

"Is there an American ship in the harbor?"

"The *Phoebe* from Baltimore."

"And what else were you talking about?"

"His wife's cousin is married to our pastor's uncle," she told him, then saw she was being teased. "I asked him about Lavisser," she said, "and he is not on official duty tonight, but the General thinks he will be helping to put out the fires." She took Sharpe's arm and led him into the street where the women stood in front of their houses watching the fires and the falling bombs. They gasped when a carcass arched overhead. The sphere's contents had already caught fire and it spun as it flew, spewing great spirals of flame so that it looked like an enraged flying dragon as it plunged toward the citadel. Astrid flinched as a ready magazine in the fort exploded. A constellation of sparks seared up into the night, streaking the smoke livid. The sky stank of powder, the smell as thick as on any battlefield. The Danish guns on the walls were firing back, adding their noise and smoke to the night. Astrid took Sharpe into the sailors' graveyard where her small son was buried. "My father said that if the English bombed the city he would never work for England again."

"Whatever he does," Sharpe said, "he's still in danger. The French want his list of names."

"Aksel looks after him," Astrid said.

"Then he's in far more danger than he realizes," Sharpe said.

Astrid smiled at that. "You don't like Aksel?"

"No. Do you?"

"No," Astrid confessed, "but this morning my father suggested I marry him."

"Why?"

She shrugged. She was silent for a few seconds, flinching as a succession of big shells cracked apart in the citadel. Each explosion flashed livid light on the smoke and threw shadows from the gravestones. Sharpe could hear the scraps of shattered casing striking on the citadel's walls or whistling overhead to rattle on the roofs of Nyboden's small houses. "It's the warehouse," Astrid said at last. "If my father dies then I will inherit and he does not think a woman can run the business."

"Of course you can run it," Sharpe said.

"And he would like to know that the business is safe before he dies," she went on as though Sharpe had not spoken. "So he wants me to marry Aksel."

"Marry someone else," Sharpe said.

"It has not been so long since Nils died," Astrid said, "and I have not wanted anyone. Except Nils." She still had her arm in his elbow, though they were not walking anymore, but instead were standing under a tree as though its branches would shelter them from the bombs that whistled overhead. "It would be beautiful," Astrid went on, "if it were not so sad." She was talking of the northern sky which was lit by the intermittent flashes of the mortars aboard the bomb ships. Each discharge flooded the night like crimson summer lightning and the flaring displays flickered one after another, filling the sky. "It is like the winter lights," she said.

"So will you marry Aksel?"

"I want Father to be happy," she said. "He has not been happy for a long while."

"A man who loves his business more than his daughter," Sharpe said, "doesn't deserve to be happy."

"He has worked hard," Astrid said as though that explained everything.

"And it will all be for nothing if he stays here," Sharpe warned her, "because the French will come after him."

"What else can he do?" Astrid asked.

"Move to Britain," Sharpe said. "His old friends in the Foreign Office want that."

"They do?"

"So they tell me."

Astrid shook her head. "After this? No, he will not go to Britain. He is a loyal Dane."

"And you?"

"Me?"

"You must have relatives in Britain?"

Astrid nodded. "My mother's sister lives in Hampshire. I visited a long time ago. It was very nice, I thought."

"Then go to Hampshire," Sharpe said. A piece of shell tore through the branches above them. Birds were singing, disturbed from their sleep by the noise.

"And what would I do in Hampshire?" Astrid asked.

"This," Sharpe said, and kissed her. For a heartbeat she seemed to resist, then he realized it was merely her surprise, for then she put her arms about him and returned the kiss with an astonishing ferocity. They kissed again, then she put her head on his shoulder and said nothing, but just clung to him for a long while. Six more bombs fell. The flames were now showing above the citadel's walls, then a shell struck a second ready magazine and Astrid shuddered in Sharpe's arms as the whole city physically trembled.

"I could not go to England," Astrid said softly, "not while Father lives." She pulled herself back so she could look up into his eyes. "You could come here?"

"It's a good place," Sharpe said. What was left of it.

"You would be welcome," she said. Her face, serious-eyed, was lit by the flames. "You really would be welcome."

"Not by Aksel," Sharpe said with a smile.

"No, not by Aksel." She smiled back. "I should go home," she said, but did not move. "Would you really stay here?"

"I will," Sharpe said.

She frowned. "I don't know you, though, do I?"

He kissed her again, tenderly this time. "You know me," he told her.

"We must trust the heart, yes?"

"Trust the heart," Sharpe said and she smiled, then laughed. She pulled him away from the tree.

"I really don't know you," she said. She was holding his hand as they walked. "But you are like Nils. He swore terribly!"

"A Dane? Swearing?"

She laughed. "He made me laugh too." She swung on Sharpe's hand, suddenly unable to contain a joy that bubbled in her despite the city burning around her. "And you?" she asked. "You have never been married?"

"No."

"Not even close?"

"Close enough," he said, and he told her about Grace and that tale brought them near to Ulfedt's Plads, and when the story was told Astrid stopped and hugged him. "I think," she said, "we both need some happiness."

"Your father won't be happy," Sharpe said. "He doesn't like me. I'm not religious enough for him."

"Then you must tell him you are searching for God," Astrid said. She walked on a few paces, flinching as more bombs shook the night. "It isn't just religion," she went on. "Father thinks any man will take me away from him, but if I tell him you are staying here then he might not be angry."

"I will stay here," Sharpe said and was amazed that a decision that would change his life should be taken so easily. Yet why not, he wondered. What waited for him in England? He could return to Shorncliffe, but he would be a quartermaster again, despised by men like Dunnett because he had been born in the wrong place. And he liked Copenhagen. The folk were tediously pious, but that seemed a small price to pay for the happiness he wanted. And had he not considered working for Ebenezer Fairley in Britain? So why not work for Ole Skovgaard in Denmark and take his daughter into the bargain? And with a little luck he could bring a pile of golden English guineas to this new life.

A dim light shone from the windows of the house in Ulfedt's Plads. "Father must be home," Astrid said. The house and warehouse were safe, for they lay far enough from the great fires that burned in the city's west and in the citadel. Astrid unlocked the door, offered Sharpe a wry smile as if to say she knew they must endure some hostility from her father, then pulled him over the threshold. "Papa!" she called. "Papa!"

A voice answered in Danish, then a light appeared at the top of the stairs to cast wavering shadows from the balustrade, but it was not Ole Skovgaard who carried the lantern. It was Aksel Bang. The Dane was wearing his shabby uniform and had a musket slung on his shoulder and a sword at his side. He seemed to be reproving Astrid as he came downstairs, then he saw Sharpe and his eyes widened in disbelief. "Lieutenant!"

Sharpe nodded, said nothing.

"You should not be here!" Bang said sternly.

"Everyone's saying that tonight," Sharpe said.

"Mister Skovgaard would not want you here! He will be angry."

"Then Mister Skovgaard can tell me that himself," Sharpe said.

"He will not be back tonight," Bang said. "He is helping with the fires."

"And you're not watching him?" Sharpe asked.

"He's safe," Bang said. "He has other men with him."

Astrid tried to reduce the tension between the two men. "We shall make tea," she said. "You like tea, Richard?"

"I love tea," Sharpe said.

Bang had seen the look on her face as she spoke to Sharpe and he stiffened. "You must not go into the yard," he told Astrid.

"Why not?"

"When I came back there were men who had collected unexploded bombs. English bombs." He spat the last two words at Sharpe. "They wanted somewhere safe to put them, so I let them use the yard. In the morning we must pull their fuses out."

"Why would I go to the yard?" Astrid asked. She edged past Bang, who still glared at Sharpe. Sharpe followed and, as he pushed past the recalcitrant Dane, he smelt gin on his breath. Aksel Bang drinking? It was extraordinary what a bombardment would do.

They went to the parlor where Astrid rang a bell to summon a maid and Sharpe crossed to the window and pulled aside the curtains to stare at the burning city. The cathedral's dome reflected the flames that roared skyward from the black walls of broken houses. The sky pulsed with gun flashes, was laced by the red threads of falling fuses and crazed by the fierce trails of rockets. A church bell, incongruous among the turmoil, struck the half-hour and then Sharpe heard the musket lock click.

He turned. Bang, pale-faced, was pointing the musket at Sharpe's breast. It was an old gun, smoothbore and inaccurate, but at three paces even a drunken Bang could not miss. "Aksel!" Astrid cried in protest.

"He is English," Bang said, "and he should not be here. The authorities should arrest him."

"You're the authorities, are you, Aksel?" Sharpe asked.

"I am in the militia, yes. I am a lieutenant." Bang, seeing that Sharpe was calm, became more confident. "You will take the two guns from your shoulder, Mister Sharpe, and give them to me."

"You've been drinking, Aksel," Sharpe said.

"I have not! I do not take strong liquor! Miss Astrid, he lies! The truth is not in him."

"Gin's in you," Sharpe said. "You're reeking of it."

"Do not listen to him, Miss Astrid," Bang said, then jerked the musket. "You will give me your guns, Lieutenant, then your saber."

Sharpe grinned. "Don't have a lot of choice, do I?" He took the seven-barreled gun from his shoulder with deliberate slowness, holding it well clear of the trigger to show he meant no mischief. The bombs echoed about the city, their explosions rattling the windows. Sharpe could smell the powder smoke, which was like the stench of rotten eggs. "Here," he said, but instead of tossing the gun he threw it with all his force. Bang flinched and before he recovered Sharpe had taken two paces, pushed the musket barrel aside and buried his right foot in Bang's groin.

Astrid screamed. Sharpe ignored her. He pulled the musket from Bang's unresisting hand and kicked him again, this time in the face so that the Dane flew backward to thump onto the floor. Sharpe picked him up by the lapels and dumped him in a chair. "You want to play soldiers," he told Bang, "then learn to fight first."

"I am doing my duty," Bang said through gritted teeth.

"No, Aksel, you're swilling in gin." Sharpe took away the man's sword and quickly searched Bang for other weapons. There were none. "Bloody hell, man, I'm not here to fight you or Denmark."

"Then why are you here?"

"To stay," Sharpe said.

"This is true," Astrid said earnestly, "he will stay." She was standing at the door where she had ordered a maid to make tea.

Bang looked from Astrid to Sharpe and then, pathetically, began to cry. "He's rare drunk," Sharpe said.

"He does not drink," Astrid insisted.

"He took a bellyful tonight," Sharpe said. "You can smell it on him. He'll be throwing up soon."

Sharpe half carried and half led Bang downstairs and put him to bed on a pile of empty sacks in the warehouse. Back upstairs, in the parlor, he turned Bang's musket upside down and rapped it smartly on the floorboards. The ball and powder, after a moment's reluctance, simply fell out. "Poor Aksel," Astrid said, "he must have been frightened."

"It's hard if you're not used to it," Sharpe said, talking of the bombardment rather than the gin. He went to the window. The bombs were more sporadic now and he guessed the batteries were running out of ammunition. He saw a fuse streak the smoke cloud, heard the explosion and watched the flames roar hungrily. "It'll stop soon," he said, "and I'll be going out."

"You're going out?"

Sharpe turned and smiled at her. "I'm not a deserter. I'll write a letter to the British army and tell them they can have their commission back. Do it legal, see? But I've something to do first. And it's English business, not Danish."

"Major Lavisser?"

"If he's dead," Sharpe said, "then your father will be safer."

"You'll kill him?" Astrid seemed surprised.

"It's my job," Sharpe said, "for now."

"For now?" Astrid wondered. "You mean you will stop killing soon?"

"Not much opportunity for killing here. I'll have to find another sort of work, eh?"

But first he would find and kill Lavisser. The renegade was off duty tonight, but Sharpe doubted he was at home. He would be watching the fires and bombs, but he must eventually go back to his bed and Sharpe reckoned that was the time to find him. So Sharpe would be a house-breaker for Britain. He would wait for Lavisser in the Bredgade house, kill him when he returned and take the gold as a gift for his new life in Denmark.

The city clocks were striking midnight as he went down the stairs. He carried the two pistols and the seven-barreled gun, but he had left the rifle and cutlass upstairs. Bang was sleeping, his mouth open. Sharpe paused, wondering if the man would wake and decide to go into the city and find some soldiers who could help him arrest the Englishman who had so inconveniently returned, but he decided Bang was probably stupe-fied by the unfamiliar gin. He left him snoring, unlocked the front door with the key Astrid had given him, carefully locked it again, then turned north through streets smelling of battle. The bombs had ended, though the fires still blazed. He walked fast, following the directions Astrid had given him, but he still got lost in the shadowed alleys, then saw a crowd hurrying three wounded people northward and remembered she had told him that Bredgade was close to King Frederick's Hospital. "You cannot mistake it," she had told him. "It has a black roof and a picture of the Good Samaritan above the door." He followed the wounded folk and saw the hospital's black tiles shining in the flame light.

He went to the front of Lavisser's house first. He doubted he could get in that way, and sure enough the windows were shuttered. The Danish flag celebrating Lavisser's homecoming still hung from the lantern. He counted the houses, then doubled back into a wide alley that ran behind the rich houses. He counted again until he came to a gate that would let him into the backyard.

The big gate was locked. He glanced up and saw spikes on top of the gate and glints of light on the wall's coping. There was glass embedded there, but householders never did the job properly and Sharpe simply went to the house next door and found their gate unlocked. The party wall had no glass on its coping and a convenient store shed gave him access to the top of the wall. He climbed, paused and stared into Lavisser's backyard.

It was empty. There was a stable and coach house, then a short flight of steps leading into the house, which was dark as pitch. He dropped over the wall and unbolted Lavisser's back gate to give himself an escape route, then crouched by the stable and examined the house again. There was a dark hole under the stone steps and he suspected it led to the basement. He would start there, but first he stared up at the house again. The uppermost windows were not shuttered and three of them were cracked open, but no lights showed there except the flickering reflection of the fires on the glass. All was still and utterly quiet, yet suddenly his instincts were tight as a drum skin. There was something wrong. Three open windows? All open the same amount? And it had all been too easy so far and it was much too quiet. Those open windows. He stared up at them. They had been opened just enough to let muskets poke through. Were there men there? Or was he imagining things? Yet he sensed he was being watched. He could not explain it, but he was certain this was not nearly so easy as he had imagined.

The house no longer looked dark and vulnerable. It was a threat. One part of his mind told Sharpe he was imagining things, but he had learned to trust instinct. He was being watched, being stalked. There was one way to find out, he thought, and so he took the big gun off his shoulder, cocked it, and positioned himself so he could see only the right-hand window. If he was being watched then the man up there would be waiting for Sharpe to cross the yard, to be in the open space that would serve as a killing ground. But the man would also see death in the seven barrels of the big gun and Sharpe suddenly jerked the weapon up, aiming it at the window and he saw the spark of the flint deep in the room and then the cough of flame at the window sill and he was already rolling back into cover as a musket ball cracked against the brick just inches from his face. Two more guns fired almost immediately, venting smoke from the upper floors. A tile shattered on the stable roof, then a voice shouted and feet sounded on the stone stairs that led from the house. Sharpe leveled the pistol at the steps, fired, then saw more men spilling from the coach house. He dropped the pistol, leveled the seven-barreled gun and pulled the trigger.

The noise, in the confines of the yard, was like a cannon firing. The muzzle flames licked out six feet, filling the air with smoke that was wickedly tangled by ricocheting bullets. A man shouted in pain, but Sharpe was already at the back gate. He hauled it open, slipped into the alley and ran. Two musket balls followed him from the high windows and a few seconds later a pistol was discharged down the alley, but Sharpe was already out of sight. He ran to the front of the hospital where a crowd waited under the bas-relief of the Good Samaritan. Some of them, alarmed by the eruption of gunfire and seeing the big gun in Sharpe's hand, shouted a question, but he dodged into another alley, ran to its end, turned and twisted down two more and then slowed to catch his breath. God damn it, but they had been ready for him. Why? Why would a man keep a close guard on his house when he was supposedly among friends?

He paused in a deep doorway. If anyone pursued him they had taken the wrong turning, for no one looked in this alley. Sharpe reloaded the seven-barreled gun, doing it by touch, hardly thinking about the powder and shot, instead wondering why Lavisser would have his house manned like a fortress. To protect the gold? Yet if men stood sentry night after night they soon became bored. They dozed. They thought about women instead of watching for enemies and the men in the Bredgade house had been alert, waiting, ready. So there was something new there, something that had made Lavisser very cautious.

And there had been something else new in this strange night. Something that had seemed funny at first, but now struck Sharpe as sinister. He rammed the last bullet home, put the ramrod in its hoops and set off southward. Off to his right the fires still roared and tired men worked the feeble pumps. Brewery carts brought barrels of water from the harbor, but the pumps were hardly touching the fires, though as the church clocks struck one it began to rain and the men fighting the fires at last began to dare feel hope.

Sharpe unlocked Skovgaard's door. He very much doubted that Skovgaard was at home, and Astrid, he hoped, was sleeping. He went to the kitchen and rooted in the dark for a lantern and a tinderbox. He found both, then carried the light to the warehouse where he discovered Aksel Bang still snoring on his makeshift bed of empty sacks. Sharpe put the lantern and the seven-barreled gun down, then lifted Bang off the sacks, shook him like a terrier killing a rat and flung him hard against a crate of cloves. Bang yelped with pain and blinked up at Sharpe.

"Where is he, Aksel?" Sharpe asked.

"I do not know what you are saying! What is happening?" Bang was still waking up.

Sharpe stepped toward him, lifted him again and slapped his lugubrious face hard. "Where is he?"

"I think you are mad!" Bang said.

"Maybe," Sharpe said. He thrust Bang against the crate and held him with one hand while he searched the Dane's blue uniform pockets. He found what he had dreaded in the coat's tail pockets. Guineas. The golden cavalry of Saint George; new, shining and fresh from the Mint. Sharpe put the coins on the crate one by one while Bang just whimpered. "You bastard," Sharpe said. "You sold him out for twenty guineas, didn't you? Why didn't you make it thirty pieces of silver?"

"You are mad!" Bang said and made a grab for the coins.

Sharpe hit him a stinging blow on the jaw. "Just tell me, Aksel."

"There is nothing to tell." A trickle of blood ran down Bang's long chin.

"Nothing! You go to a prayer meeting with Skovgaard and come back without him? You're drunk as a judge and you've got a pocketful of gold. You think I'm a fool?"

"I trade for myself," Bang said, wiping the blood from his lips. "Mister Skovgaard approves. I sold some things."

"What things?"

"Some coffee," Bang declared, "coffee and jute."

"You do take me for a bloody fool, Aksel," Sharpe said. He drew out his pocket knife.

"I have done nothing!" Bang glared at him.

Sharpe smiled and unfolded the blade. "Coffee and jute? No, Aksel, you were selling a soul, and now you're going to tell me all about it."

"I have told you the truth!" Bang declared indignantly.

Sharpe pushed him against the crate, then held the blade just under Bang's left eye. "We'll take this one first, Aksel. Eyeballs just pop out. It's not even very painful at first. We'll have the left one, then the right, and after that I'll fill the sockets with salt. You'll be screaming then."

"No! Please!" Bang screamed now, and feebly tried to push Sharpe away. Sharpe pressed the cold blade into the flesh and Bang squealed like a gelded pig. "No!" he wailed.

"Then tell me the truth, Aksel," Sharpe said, pressing harder. "I'll exchange the truth for your eyes."

The tale was not told straight for Bang desperately wanted to justify himself. Mister Skovgaard, he said, was a traitor to Denmark. He had been supplying news to the British and were not the British the enemies of Denmark? And Ole Skovgaard was a mean, tight-fisted man. "I have worked for him two years now and he has not raised my wages once. A man must have prospects, he must have prospects."

"Go on," Sharpe said. He tossed the knife into the air and Bang watched it circle and glitter, then gave a start when the handle slapped back into Sharpe's hand. "I'm listening," Sharpe said.

"It is not right what Mister Skovgaard was doing," Bang said. "He is a traitor to Denmark." He gave a small whimper, not because of anything Sharpe had done, but because Astrid, in a swathing green robe, had come down to the warehouse. Bang's scream must have woken her and she was carrying Sharpe's rifle, half expecting a thief, but now laid the weapon down and looked inquisitively at Sharpe.

"Aksel's telling us a story," Sharpe said, "of how he sold your father for twenty pieces of gold."

"No!" Bang protested.

"Don't piss on me!" Sharpe shouted, frightening Astrid as much as Bang. "Tell the damned truth!"

The damned truth was that a man had approached Bang and persuaded him that his patriotic duty was to betray Skovgaard. "For Denmark," Bang insisted. He claimed to have agonized over his decision, but it seems the agony was helped by a promise of gold and when Skovgaard suggested that the two of them attend a prayer meeting Bang had let his new friend know where and when the prayers would be offered. A coach had been waiting beside the church and Skovgaard had been snatched from the street in an instant.

Astrid had gone pale. She just stared at Bang, scarce crediting what she heard. Sharpe put the knife close to Bang's eye again. "So you sold him, Aksel, then celebrated with gin?"

"They said it would make me feel better," Bang admitted sadly. "I did not know it was gin."

"What the hell did you think it was? The milk of human kindness?" Sharpe was tempted to thrust the knife home, but instead he stepped back. "So you've given Astrid's father to Lavisser?"

"I do not know Major Lavisser," Bang insisted, as though that made his offense less heinous.

"That's what you did," Sharpe said. "I was there an hour ago and the house was guarded like a newly built outpost. You gave him to the French, Aksel."

"I gave him to Danes!"

"You gave him to the French, you bloody fool. And God knows what they're doing to him. They pulled two teeth before."

"They promised me they would not hurt him."

"You pathetic bastard," Sharpe said. He looked at Astrid. "You want me to kill him?"

She shook her head. "No, no."

"He bloody deserves it," Sharpe said. But instead he took Bang out to the yard where there was a brick-built stable that had a solid door with a heavy padlock. Sharpe locked Bang inside, then investigated the hand-cart that had been placed beside the yard gate. Eight unexploded bombs lay on the cart. They were probably safe, but in the morning he would pull out the wooden fuse plugs and pour water into the charges just to make sure. He went back to the warehouse, pocketed the guineas, and then climbed the stairs. "I'm sorry," he said.

Astrid was shivering, though it was hardly cold. "Those men," she said falteringly.

"The same men as before," Sharpe said, "and they've got the house in Bredgade tight as a prison."

"What are they doing to him?"

"Asking him questions," Sharpe said. And he did not doubt that the questions would eventually be answered, which meant that those answers had to stay in Copenhagen. The list of names had to be kept from the French, but that meant getting into the house on Bredgade and Sharpe could not do that without help.

He put his hands on Astrid's shoulders. "I'm going out again," he told her, "but I'll be back, I promise I'll be back. Stay here. Can you keep the warehouse closed? And don't let Aksel out."

"I won't."

"He'll be weeping on you. He'll be claiming he's thirsty or hungry or dying, but don't listen. If you or the maids open that door he'll jump on you. That's what he wants."

"He just wants money," she said bitterly.

"He wants you, love. He thinks that if your father vanished then you'd cling to him. He wants you, the warehouse, the money, everything." He hefted the seven-barreled gun. "Keep the house locked," he warned her. "No one comes or goes except me. And I'll be back."

It was almost dawn. The fires were going out slowly, though the fiercest of the blazes still lit a darkness in which no bombs fell, just a greasy ash that dropped like black snow in the dying night. Houses burned white hot and the water spurted by the feeble pumps was turned to steam that joined the thick smoke smearing the sky all across Zealand. Water was scarce for the city's supply had been cut and the pumps had to wait for barrels to be fetched from the harbor and that took time, yet slowly the clanking pumps and the small rain contained the fires. The tired men could smell roasted flesh in the embers. Coffins were laid in the streets, while the hospitals were filled with whimpering people.

Sharpe headed toward the harbor.

To give John Lavisser hell.

CHAPTER 10

C APTAIN JOEL CHASE scarcely dared believe his luck. All night his men had scrambled from ship to ship and found not a living Danish soul aboard the great warships. The fleet had been stripped of its seamen who had been sent to serve the great guns on the city walls, stand guard on the ramparts or carry water to the fire pumps. Chase had worried that perhaps the laid-up ships were being used as dormitories for the crews, but there were no slung hammocks and Chase realized that no sailor would be allowed to live aboard in case some fool should drop a speck of glowing tobacco near a fuse. The crews had evidently been billeted in the city and the Danish fleet had become the kingdom of rats and of Chase's men, who worked in the dark to sever fuses and dump incendiaries overboard. Where the incendiaries were on open decks, easily visible to a casual inspection, they were left, but the bundles on the lower decks were eased through gunports and lowered to the harbor's stinking water.

Sharpe came back to the inner harbor just before dawn. A small mist drifted through the fleet's rigging as he crouched under the forepeak of the *Christian VII*. "*Pucelle!*" he hissed, "*Pucelle!*"

"Sharpe?" It was Midshipman Collier who, with two men, was serving as Chase's picket.

"Help me aboard. Where's the Captain?"

Chase was in the captain's cabin on board the *Skiold* where, in the small light of a shielded lantern, he combed through the charts of the

Baltic. "Extraordinary detail, Richard! Far better than our own. See this shoal off Riga? Not even marked on my charts. Tommy Lister, a splendid fellow, almost lost the *Naiad* on that shoal and the fools in Admiralty swore it wasn't there. We'll take these. You'll have a brandy? This captain does himself well."

"What I want," Sharpe said, "is two or three men."

"When people say two or three," Chase said, pouring the brandies, "they usually mean four or five."

"Two will do," Sharpe said.

"And for what?" Chase asked. He sat on the cushioned bench under the stern window and listened to Sharpe. The city clocks struck four and a thin gray light began to show at the *Skiold*'s stern windows as Sharpe finished. Chase sipped his brandy. "So let me summarize," he said. "There is a man, this Skovgaard, who may or may not be alive, but whose rescue would be in Britain's best interest?"

"If he's alive," Sharpe said dourly.

"Which he probably ain't," Chase agreed, "in which case you think there may be a list of names that can be retrieved?"

"I hope so."

"And whether there is or isn't," Chase said, "you'd still like this fellow Lavisser killed?"

"Yes, sir."

Chase listened to the gulls screaming overhead. "The trouble, Richard," he said after a while, "is that none of this is official. Lord Pumphrey took very great care, did he not, to make sure nothing was written down? No signed orders. That way he can't take the blame if anything goes wrong. It's dirty work, Richard, dirty work."

"If the French have got the list of names off Skovgaard, sir, then they've got to be stopped."

Chase appeared not to hear Sharpe. "And what authority does Pumphrey have to issue such orders anyway? He's not a military man. Anything but, in fact."

Sharpe had said nothing of Pumphrey's veiled threat about a murder in Wapping, nor did he think Chase would want to hear of it. "If it wasn't for Pumphrey, sir," he said instead, "you wouldn't be here."

"I wouldn't?" Chase sounded dubious.

"It was the newspaper, sir, that told us the Danes' plan to burn this fleet. I took it to Lord Pumphrey and he arranged the rest."

"He's a busy little fellow, isn't he?" Chase gazed fixedly out of the stern window, though the only thing visible there were the bows of another warship. He thought Sharpe's argument was weak and suspected there was something unsaid, but he did recognize the importance of safeguarding Skovgaard's correspondents. He sighed. "I do dislike dirty work," he said mildly, "and especially when it comes from the Foreign Office. They expect the navy to clean the world for them."

"I have to do it, sir," Sharpe said, "with or without your help."

"Have to?" Chase asked. "Truly?"

Sharpe paused. If he was to stay in Denmark, then what did it matter if he was suspected of a murder in far-off London? But if Skovgaard was dead, would he stay? Or would Astrid return to Britain? It was all too complicated. What was simple was that Skovgaard's names needed to be salvaged and Lavisser needed to be buried. That was simple enough to understand. "Yes, sir," he said, "I have to."

Midshipman Collier knocked on the cabin door, then entered without waiting to be bidden. "Sorry to interrupt, sir, but it looks like there's a pumping party beating the bounds."

"Then we'd best be moving," Chase said.

"Pumping party?" Sharpe asked.

"Ships leak, Richard!" Chase said cheerfully, getting to his feet. "Can't just leave 'em floating here. They'll all end up in the mud. So they're sending fellows to pump all the bilges. It won't take them long, but we should still hide."

"Won't they find your cut fuses?"

"They'll notice nothing. We took care. Thank you, Mister Collier. Everyone back to the rat hole!" Chase scooped up the charts and smiled at Sharpe. "Will Hopper and Clouter be enough for you?"

Sharpe hardly believed his ears for a second. "Hopper and Clouter, sir?"

"I'm not sure I approve, Richard, but I do trust your judgment. And those two are my best fellows so they should keep you out of harm's way. But do bring them back alive, I beg you."

"Thank you, sir."

"There's nothing else you need?"

"Quick fuse, sir."

"Plenty of that!" Chase said brightly.

It was past eight in the morning when Sharpe left. The pumping party was working its way down the row of bigger ships, but none of the Danes noticed the three men drop through the *Christian VII*'s hawsehole onto the quay. All three were armed. Hopper had another seven-barreled gun, two pistols and a cutlass, while Clouter had a boarding axe and two pistols. They crossed the bridge and no one remarked on them. Just a fortnight before, an armed man received curious glances in Copenhagen, but now a British rifleman and two British seamen could carry enough ordnance to fillet a company and be ignored. Nor was the sight of two pigtailed men, one with a face covered in tattoos and the other black, unusual, for Copenhagen was well used to sailors. It was simply thought they were going to the walls where the remaining Danish guns had opened fire on the British batteries. A few folk wished Sharpe and his companions good morning and received grunts in reply.

Sharpe unlocked Skovgaard's door. Astrid heard him and came from the office with her black sleeves protected from ink by white cotton sheaths. She looked alarmed at the sight of Hopper and Clouter, for both were huge men, but they snatched off their straw hats and tugged their forelocks.

"They're staying here today," Sharpe told her.

"Who are they?"

"Friends," Sharpe said. "I need them to get your father out. But I can't do it until the bombardment starts again. Is there somewhere they can sleep?"

"The warehouse," Astrid suggested. She told Sharpe she had sent the workers away when they had arrived just after dawn. She had promised the men their wages, but said her father wanted them to help look for survivors among the burned houses. She had then ordered the maids to clean the long-neglected attics, while she had gone to her father's office and pulled out the big ledgers. "There is never time to check the figures properly," she told Sharpe once Clouter and Hopper were settled in the empty warehouse, "and I know he wants it done." She worked in silence for a while, then Sharpe saw an inked entry in one of the columns suddenly dissolve as a tear splashed on it. Astrid cuffed her face. "He's dead, isn't he?" she asked.

"We don't know."

"And it will have been painful."

"We don't know," Sharpe said again.

"We do," she said, looking up at him.

"I can't go back there till the bombardment starts," Sharpe said bleakly.

"It is not your fault, Richard." She put the quill down. "I am so tired."

"Then go and rest. I'll take the boys something to eat."

She went upstairs. Sharpe found bread, cheese and ham, then ate with Hopper and Clouter. Aksel Bang rattled the door in the yard, but went silent when Sharpe growled that he was in a killing mood.

It was almost midday when Sharpe went upstairs. He opened the bedroom door silently to find thick curtains drawn and the room dark, yet he sensed Astrid was awake. "I'm sorry," he said.

"For what?"

"For everything," he said, "everything." He sat on the bed. Despite the dark he could see her face and the astonishing gold of her hair on the pillow.

He thought he ought to explain exactly who Hopper and Clouter were, but when he began she just shook her head. "I thought you would never come upstairs," she said.

"I'm here," Sharpe said.

"Then don't leave."

"Never," he promised.

"I have been so lonely," Astrid said, "since Nils died."

And I, Sharpe thought, since Grace. He hung his cutlass on a chair and eased off his boots. A cold wind spat rain from the east and drifted smoke from the city's ruins. The guns on the walls fired on and Sharpe and Astrid, eventually, slept.

THE GUNS on the city's western walls fired all day. They fired till the rain falling on their barrels turned to instant vapor. Shot and shell ploughed into the British batteries, but the earth-filled fascines soaked up all the violence and behind their screens and parapets the British gunners stacked more ammunition for the mortars.

The city smoldered. The last flames were put out, but embers glowed deep in ruined houses and churches, and every now and then those embers would spark the fuse of an unexploded bomb and the blast would rattle the city's windows and folk would duck into doorways and wait for the next missile to fall. They would peer anxiously skyward and see that no fuses left smoke trails in the sky. There was just silence.

General Peymann toured the damaged streets, shuddering at the sight of gaunt scorched walls and at the smell of roasted flesh buried in ash. "How many homeless?" he asked.

"Hundreds," was the bleak answer.

"Can they live on the ships?"

"Not if we have to burn the fleet," an aide answered. "It could take hours to get folk ashore."

"The churches are coping," another aide said, "and if you order it, sir, the university will open its doors."

"Of course it must! Of course it must!" Peymann watched as a group of sailors dragged charred rafters aside to retrieve a body. He did not want to know how many were dead. Too many. He knew he must visit the hospitals and he dreaded it, but it was his duty. For now, though, he must prepare the city for more horror, and he ordered that the breweries must donate their largest casks which should be placed at street corners and filled with seawater. The British had somehow cut the city's fresh water supply, which meant the fire pumps were ever running short, but the casks would help. Or he hoped they would help. In truth he knew it was a futile gesture, for the city had no real protection. It just had to endure. He walked the ruined streets, edging between the fallen piles of masonry and the smoking ruins that had been Studiestræde, Peder Huitfeldts Stræde, St Peters Stræde and Kannikestræde. "How many shells did they use last night?"

"Four thousand?" an aide estimated. "Five, perhaps?"

"And how many do they have left?" That was the question. When would the British guns run out of ammunition? For then they would have to wait for more to be fetched from England, and by then the nights would be longer and perhaps the Crown Prince would come from Holstein with an army of regular troops that would vastly outnumber the British force. This misery, Peymann thought, could yet be turned to victory. The city just had to survive.

Major Lavisser, his face drawn and somber, picked his way across a spill of fallen bricks. He stopped to pick up a child's petticoat that had somehow escaped the flames, then threw it away. "I'm late for duty, sir," he said to Peymann. "I apologize."

"You had a long night, I'm sure."

"I did," Lavisser said, though it had not been spent in fighting fires. He had employed the dark hours by questioning Ole Skovgaard and the memory gave him satisfaction, though he was still worried by the unexplained visitor who had wounded two of his men in the yard. A thief, Barker reckoned, probably a soldier or sailor using the bombardment as an opportunity to plunder the rich houses on Bredgade. Lavisser had worried at first that it might have been Sharpe, but had persuaded himself that the rifleman was long gone back to the British army. Barker was probably right, merely a thief, though a well-armed one.

General Peymann stared up at a shattered church tower where a single bell was suspended from a blackened beam on which a pigeon perched. The remnants of the church pews gave off a choking smoke. A child's leg protruded from the embers and he turned away, revolted. It was time to visit the hospitals and though he did not want to face the burn victims, he knew he must. "You're on duty tonight?" he asked Lavisser.

"I am, sir."

"What you might do," the General suggested, "is find a vantage point. The spire of the Exchange, perhaps? Or the mast crane in Gammelholm? But somewhere safe. I want you to count the bombs as well as you can."

Lavisser was puzzled. He also suspected that counting bomb flashes was a demeaning duty. "Count them, sir?" he asked with as much asperity as he could muster.

"It is important, Major," Peymann said emphatically, "for if they fire fewer bombs tonight, we'll know they're running out of ammunition. We'll know we can endure then." And if they fire more, he thought, but he shied away from that conclusion. A message had been smuggled into the city from the Crown Prince which insisted that the city hold, so Peymann would do his best. "Count the bombs, Major," he said, "count the bombs. As soon as the firing starts, count the bombs." There was a chance that the bombardment might be renewed during the day, but Peymann doubted it. The British were using the night. Perhaps they believed the darkness increased the terror of the bombardment, or perhaps they hid their deeds from God, but tonight, Peymann was sure, they would start their mischief again and he must judge from the intensity of their bombardment how long they could keep going. And Copenhagen must endure.

"WHAT DO I do with Aksel?" Sharpe asked Astrid that afternoon.

"What do you want to do?"

"Kill him."

"No!" She frowned in disapproval. "Can't you just let him go?"

"And he'll have soldiers back here in ten minutes," Sharpe said. "He'll just have to wait where he is."

"Till when?"

"Till the city surrenders," Sharpe said. Another night like the last, he reckoned, and Copenhagen would give in.

And what then, he wondered? Would he stay? If he did, then he would be joining a nation that was Britain's enemy and France's ally, and suppose they wanted him to fight? Would he take off the green uniform and put on a blue one? Or would Astrid go to Britain? And what would he do then, except fight and so strand her in a strange country? A soldier should not marry, he thought.

"What are you thinking?" Astrid asked.

"That it's time to get ready." He bent and kissed her, then pulled on his clothes and went down to the yard. The city had the horrid smell of spent powder and a thin veil of smoke still smeared the sky, but at least the rain had stopped. He took bread and water to Bang who watched him sullenly but said nothing. "You'll stay here, Aksel," Sharpe told him, "till it's all over."

He relocked the makeshift prison door, then woke Hopper and Clouter. The three of them squatted in the yard where they made new fuses for three of the unexploded bombs. The wooden fuse plugs had to be extracted, the old failed fuse stubs pushed out of the holes in the plugs, and the new quick match inserted. "When we get inside," Sharpe told them, "we kill everyone."

"Maids too?" Hopper asked.

"Not women," Sharpe said, "and not Skovgaard, if he's alive. We go in, we find him and we get out, and we kill all the men. We're not going to have time to be particular." He trimmed the quick fuse, leaving a tiny stub so that the bomb would explode within seconds of being lit.

"How many of the bastards?" Clouter asked.

Sharpe did not know. "Half a dozen?" he guessed. "And I reckon they're Frogs, not Danes." He had been wondering who shot at him the previous night, and he had concluded that the French must have left men behind when their embassy went south. "Or they might be Danes who've signed up for the Frogs," he added.

"Same thing," Hopper said, using his shoe to hammer the wooden plug back into the bomb. "But what are they doing here?"

"They're spies," Sharpe said. "There's a dirty secret war being fought all across Europe and they're here to kill our spies and we're here to kill them."

"Is there extra pay for killing spies?" Clouter asked.

Sharpe grinned. "I can't promise it, but with any luck you'll get as much gold as you can carry." He looked up at the sky. Dusk was close, but the late summer twilight would linger for a time. They must wait.

There was an air of exhaustion over the city. The British batteries were masked and silent. The Danish guns fired on, but slowly, as if they knew their efforts were being wasted on fascines and earthworks. Some howitzers had been brought from the battered citadel and placed behind the wall and their gunners tried to loft shells into the closest British batteries, but no one could see what effect the shots were having.

Darkness came gently to the cloud-filled sky. The wind was chill from the east as the whole city waited. It seemed, for a time, as though there would be no bombardment this second night, but then a great flash seared across the western dark and a streak of red, thin as a needle scratch, climbed toward the clouds. The red scratch reached its topmost height and there hovered for a heartbeat before it began to fall.

And then the other mortars fired, their sound joining to make a gigantic thunderclap that rolled about the city as the fuse trails whipped upward and the first bomb hurtled down toward the houses.

"We can go," Sharpe said.

The three men walked through streets lit by distant fire. Sharpe could tell from the trails of the fuses that the bombardment was sparing the citadel this night, instead dropping its bombs close to the streets that had already been burned. The missiles from the fleet streaked overhead, while rocket traces, thick and glowing, curved above the rooftops. Sharpe, like his two companions, carried a thirteen-inch bomb in a leather bag hung from his shoulder. It was surprisingly heavy.

He led Hopper and Clouter into the alley behind Lavisser's house. It was black dark between the high close walls, though the backs of the big houses on Bredgade were reddened by the far-off flames. No bombs had touched this quarter of the city that lay near the royal palaces.

Sharpe dropped his bomb beside the gate that led into Lavisser's courtyard. Then he knelt, took out the tinderbox and struck the steel on flint. The charred linen glowed and he blew on it until it burst into flames that he touched to the quick fuse, then he ran back down the alley and crouched beside Hopper and Clouter. He could see the tiny red glow of the fuse, then it vanished and he lowered his head as he waited, but no explosion came and he wondered if the bomb had some other fault. Perhaps its powder was wet? "Bloody thing," he snarled, looking up, and just then the bomb caught the fire and the alley was filled with screaming shards of metal that rattled and ricocheted from the brick walls. Flame and smoke boiled up, while Lavisser's gate was ripped from its hinges and, propelled by a blast of heated smoke, slammed across the yard.

"Yours, Hopper," Sharpe said, and the three men ran to the smoky gateway and Sharpe again lit the tinder. Hopper held his bomb out, Sharpe put the fire to the fuse, then the bomb was rolled like a bowling ball into the courtyard's center. The three men sheltered behind the wall. Someone shouted from the house. Sharpe suspected men were stationed in the carriage house and that they would be the first into the yard to investigate the first explosion, which was why he was sending them the second bomb. A voice shouted quite close, then Hopper's bomb cracked the night apart, searing the alley with sudden flame light and filling the yard with more thick smoke.

Clouter was already at the gate with the third bomb. Sharpe struck the flint, blew on the charred linen and lit the fuse. He took the bomb from Clouter, stepped through the gate and ran a few paces into the smoke until he could just see where the steps went down to the basement entrance. The fuse hissed by his belly. He stopped, gauged the distance and heaved the shell over the remnants of the shattered gate. The bomb landed on the stones short of the steps, wobbled for a second, then toppled over. Hopper and Clouter had their backs against the stable wall. Both were staring up through the smoke. A musket fired from an upper window and the ball smacked into the cobbles beside Sharpe, who stepped back and almost tripped on a body. So someone had been caught by the second bomb. Then the third exploded, blasting its flame straight up the back of the house. Glass shattered in a dozen windows.

"Come on!" Sharpe shouted. He had the rifle in his right hand as he ran down the steps and pushed through the ruins of the splintered door. He found himself in a kitchen lit by the flaming scraps of the blown door. No one was in sight. He jumped the burning wood, crossed the flagstone floor and pushed open the farther door to see a dark staircase going upward. Pistol shots sounded behind him and he snatched a glance to see that Clouter was firing up into the yard. "You need help?"

"They're dead!" Clouter said, then backed away from the doorway and started reloading. An oilcloth covering a table by the window had caught fire. Sharpe ignored it, running up the stairs instead. Hopper came with him. Sharpe pushed open the door at the top to find himself in a wide hallway. There was a man on the stairs above, but he turned and vanished before Sharpe could aim the rifle. Clouter came up from the kitchen and behind him the smoke thickened with alarming speed.

"Upstairs," Sharpe said. There were men up there, men who knew they were coming, men who would have guns, but he did not dare wait. The fire was flickering beneath him. "Wait here," he told the two sailors. He hung the rifle on his shoulder and took the seven-barreled gun instead. He did not want to charge the stairs, but if he gave the men upstairs any longer then they would barricade themselves. He swore, nerved himself, and ran.

He took the stairs three at a time. Up to the half landing where there were two closed doors. He ignored them. His instinct said that the house's inhabitants were higher up, so he swung round the corner of the landing and took the next stairs at a run and saw a half-open door ahead of him and saw a musket barrel there and he threw himself down just as the musket flamed. The bullet cracked into a portrait high on the stairwell wall and Sharpe heaved himself up, pushed the seven-barreled gun over the lip of the top stair and pulled the trigger.

The seven bullets shredded the lower half of the door. A man screamed. Sharpe pulled out a pistol and fired again, then Hopper and Clouter were behind him and each of them fired into the door before running past Sharpe. "Wait!" he called. He wanted to be first into the room, not out of heroism, but because he had promised Captain Chase to look after the two men, but Clouter, the axe in his hand, had already shoulder-charged the door and tumbled through. "*Pucelle*," the black man was shouting, "*Pucelle!*" just as if he was boarding an enemy ship.

Sharpe followed just as Hopper fired his seven-barreled gun inside the room. An enemy's bullet whipped past Sharpe's head as he went through the door. He slid on the polished floorboards, crouching as he moved and turning the rifle down the length of the room that was an elegant study with portraits, bookshelves, a desk and a sofa. A man was flopping by the desk, jerking in pain from one of Hopper's bullets. Another man was by the shuttered window with Clouter's boarding axe buried in his neck. "There's a live one behind the desk," Hopper said.

Sharpe gave his empty volley gun to Hopper. "Reload it," he said, then he stalked toward the desk. He heard the scrape of a ramrod in a barrel and so knew his enemy was effectively unarmed. He took three more quick steps and saw a man crouching with a half-loaded pistol. Sharpe had hoped to find Lavisser, but the man was no one he recognized. The man looked up and shook his head. "*Non, monsieur, non!*"

Sharpe fired. The bullet took the man in the skull, fountaining blood across the desk and onto the dying man at Sharpe's feet.

There was a fourth man in the room. He was naked and tied to a sofa in an alcove, but he was alive, though Sharpe almost gagged when he saw him. He was alive by a miracle, for Ole Skovgaard had been half blinded and tortured and he seemed oblivious of the fight that had filled the room with choking powder smoke.

Clouter, bloodied boarding axe in one big hand, crossed to the sofa and swore softly. Sharpe grimaced at the sight of the empty eye socket, the bloodied mouth and the raw fingertips where the nails had been pulled before the fingers' bones had been broken. He put down his rifle, took out his clasp knife and sliced the ropes that secured Skovgaard. "Can you hear me?" he asked. "Can you hear me?"

Skovgaard raised a tentative hand. "Lieutenant?" He could hardly speak, for his bloody mouth was toothless.

"We're taking you home," Sharpe said, "taking you home."

Hopper fired a pistol down the stairwell and Clouter went to help him. Skovgaard pointed feebly at the desk and Sharpe crossed to it and saw a pile of papers spattered with the blood of the man he had just shot. There were names on the sheets, names and names, a list of the correspondents that London wanted protected. Hans Bischoff in Bremen, Josef Gruber in Hanover, Carl Friederich of Königsberg. There were Russian names, Prussian names, seven pages of names and Sharpe snatched the papers up and thrust them into a pocket. Clouter fired down the stairs. Hopper had reloaded one of the seven-barreled guns and now shouldered Clouter aside, but it seemed no one was threatening for he held his fire.

There were velvet curtains hanging inside the closed shutters. Sharpe seized one and tugged hard, ripping it from its hoops. He wrapped the naked Skovgaard in the red velvet, then lifted him. Skovgaard moaned in pain. "You're going home," Sharpe said. Smoke was coming up the stairwell. "Who's down there?" Sharpe asked Clouter.

"Two men. Maybe three."

"We've got to go down," Sharpe said, "and out of the front door." He had not seen Lavisser or Barker.

Hopper was loading the second seven-barreled gun. He had given the first to Clouter. Sharpe could hear the flames downstairs. Bombs were detonating to the west. A maid, eyes wide with terror, ran down the stairs. She seemed not to notice the men in the study door, but just vanished round the half landing. There was a shot from the hallway and the maid screamed. "Jesus Christ," Sharpe swore.

Hopper had four of the barrels loaded and decided they were enough. "Do we go?"

"Go," Sharpe said.

Clouter and Hopper went first, then Sharpe carried Skovgaard after them. The two seamen jumped to the half landing and both fired their guns straight down into the smoke that filled the hallway. Sharpe went more slowly, trying to ignore Skovgaard's soft moans. The maid was lying beside the banisters, blood streaking her gown. Another body lay beside a table in the hall while flames were flickering at the door which led down to the kitchen. The front door was open and Clouter led the way out. Sharpe shouted a warning that Lavisser's men might be waiting in the street, but the only folk there were neighbors who believed the fire and smoke had been caused by British bombs. One of the women looked alarmed at the sight of the two huge men who burst from the door with their guns, then a murmur of sympathy sounded when the crowd saw Skovgaard in Sharpe's arms.

But one woman screamed at the sight of the injured man.

It was Astrid who ran to meet Sharpe. "What are you doing here?" he asked her.

"I knew you would be coming here so I came to make sure you were safe." She gave an involuntary grimace when she saw her father's face. "Is he alive?"

"He needs a doctor," Sharpe said. He reckoned Skovgaard must have resisted for hours before he broke.

"The hospitals are full," Astrid said, holding her father's wrist because his hand was nothing but a broken claw. "They made an announcement this morning," she went on, "that only the worst injured must go to hospital."

"He's badly injured," Sharpe said, then thought that Lavisser would know that and so the hospitals were exactly where Lavisser would look for Skovgaard. The bombs were thumping steadily, their explosions flashing in the smoky sky. "Not the hospital," he told Astrid. He thought about Ulfedt's Plads, then reckoned that was the second place Lavisser would search.

Astrid touched her father's cheek. "There's a good nurse at the orphanage," she said, "and it's not far."

They carried Skovgaard to the orphanage where the nurse took charge of him. Astrid helped her, while Sharpe took Hopper and Clouter out to the courtyard where they sat under the flagpole. Some of the smaller children were crying because of the noise of the bombs, but they were all safe in their dormitories which were a long way from where any missiles fell. Two women carried milk and water up the outside staircase and glanced fearfully at the three men. "Lavisser wasn't there," Sharpe said.

"Does it matter?" Hopper asked.

"He wants this list," Sharpe said, patting his pocket. "These names buy him favor with the French."

"There was no gold either," Clouter growled.

Sharpe looked surprised, then shook his head. "I clean forgot about the gold," he said. "I'm sorry." He rubbed his face. "We can't go back to the warehouse. Lavisser will look for us there." And Lavisser, he thought, would take Danish troops with him, claiming he was looking for British agents. "We'll have to stay here," he decided.

"We could go back to the ships?" Clouter suggested.

"You can if you want," Sharpe said, "but I'll stay." He would stay because he knew Astrid would remain with her father and he would stay with Astrid.

Hopper began to reload one of the volley guns. "Did you see that nurse?" he asked.

"I think he wants to stay here, sir," Clouter said with a grin.

"We can wait it out here," Sharpe said. "And thank you, both of you. Thank you." The bombs lit the sky. By morning, he thought, the Danes must surrender and the British army would come and Lavisser would hide, but Sharpe would find him. If he had to search every damned house in Copenhagen he would find him and kill him. And then he would have finished the job and he could stay here, stay in Denmark, because he wanted a home.

NEXT MORNING General Peymann called a council in the Amalien-borg Palace. Coffee was served in royal china to men who were dirty with soot and ash, and whose faces were pale and drawn from another night of fighting fires and carrying horribly burned people to the crowded hospitals. "I thought there were fewer bombs last night," the General observed.

"They fired just under two thousand, sir," Major Lavisser reported, "and that includes rockets."

"And the night before?" Peymann tried to remember.

"Nearer five thousand," an aide answered.

"They are running short of ammunition," the General declared, unable to conceal a triumphant note. "I doubt we'll receive more than a thousand missiles tonight. And tomorrow? Perhaps none at all. We shall hold on, gentlemen, we shall hold on!"

The superintendent of the King Frederick Hospital offered a sober-ing report. There were no more beds available, not even now they had taken over the Maternity Hospital next door, and there was a severe shortage of salves, bandages and fresh water, but he still expressed a cautious optimism. If the bombardment got no worse then he thought the hospitals would cope.

A city engineer reported that an old well in Bjornegaden was yielding copious amounts of fresh water and that three other abandoned wells, capped when the city began piping supplies from north Zealand, were to be opened during the day. The deputy mayor said there was no shortage of food. Some cows had died in the night, he said, but plenty were left.

"Cows?" Peymann asked.

"The city needs milk, sir. We brought two herds into the city."

"Then I think," General Peymann concluded, "that when all is said and done we might congratulate ourselves. The British have thrown their worst at us, and we have survived." He pulled the large-scale map of the city toward him. The engineers had inked over the streets worst affected by the first night's bombardment, and now Peymann looked at the light pencil hatching which showed the effects of the second night's assault. The newly penciled areas were much smaller, merely a short length of street near the Nørre Gate and some houses in Skindergade. "At least they missed the cathedral," he said.

"And there was also damage here." An aide leaned over the table and tapped Bredgade. "Major Lavisser's house was destroyed, and the neighboring houses lost their roofs to fire."

Peymann frowned at Lavisser. "Your house, Major?"

"My grandfather's house, sir."

"Tragic!" Peymann said. "Tragic."

"We think it must have been a rocket, sir," the first aide said. "It's so far from the rest of the damaged streets."

"I trust no one was hurt?" Peymann inquired earnestly.

"We fear some servants might have been trapped," Lavisser answered, "but my grandfather, of course, is with the Crown Prince."

"Thank God for that," Peymann said, "but you must take some time today to rescue what you can of your grandfather's property. I am so very sorry, Major."

"We must all share in the city's suffering, sir," Lavisser declared, a sentiment that brought murmurs of agreement about the table.

A naval pastor ended the council by thanking God for helping the city to endure its ordeal, for the manifold blessings that would doubtless flow from victory and begging the Almighty to shower His saving grace upon the wounded and the bereaved. "Amen," General Peymann boomed, "amen."

A weak sun was shining through the pall of smoke that smothered the city when Lavisser emerged into the palace courtyard where Barker was waiting. "They prayed, Barker," he said, "they prayed."

"Do a lot of that here, sir."

"So what do you make of it?"

Barker, while his master had been attending the council meeting, had done his best to explore the ruins of Bredgade. "It's still too hot to get into, sir, and it's a heap of rubble anyway. Smoking, it is, but Jules, he got out."

"Only Jules?"

"He was the only one I found, sir. Rest are dead or in hospital, I reckon. And Jules swears it were Sharpe."

"It can't be!"

"He says three men came out the house, sir. Two were sailors and the other was a tall man, black hair and scar on the cheek."

Lavisser swore.

"And," Barker went on implacably, "the man with the scarred face was carrying Skovgaard."

Lavisser swore again. "And the gold?" he asked.

"That's probably still in Bredgade, sir. Melted, probably, but it'll be there."

Lavisser said nothing for a while. The gold could be salvaged and it could certainly wait, but he could expect no advancement from the French if he did not give them the list of names that had been so painfully extracted from Skovgaard. That list would open the Emperor's largesse to Lavisser, make him Prince of Zealand or Duke of Holstein or even, in his most secret dreams, King of Denmark. "Did Jules say anything about the list?"

"He reckoned it was inside when the house burned, sir."

Lavisser used the efficacious word. "All that work wasted," he said. "Wasted!"

Barker stared up at the pigeons on the palace roof. He thought his own night had been wasted, for Lavisser had insisted that he watch and count the falling bombs with him. Barker would have preferred to guard Bredgade, but Lavisser had instructed Barker to count the gun flashes from the fleet while Lavisser counted the shots from the land batteries. A real waste, Barker thought, for if he had been in Bredgade then Sharpe would have died and Skovgaard might still be revealing names. "We have to find Skovgaard again, sir," Barker said.

"How?" Lavisser asked sourly, then answered his own question. "He has to be in hospital, doesn't he?"

"At a doctor's?" Barker suggested.

Lavisser shook his head. "All doctors were ordered to the hospitals."

So Lavisser and Barker looked for Ole Skovgaard in Copenhagen's hospitals. That search took them all morning as they went from ward to ward where hundreds of burn victims lay in awful pain, but Skovgaard was nowhere to be found. A morning wasted, and Lavisser was in a grim mood when he went to see what was left of Bredgade, but the house was a smoking ruin and the gold, if it was still there, was nothing but a molten mass deep in its cellars. But at least Jules, one of the Frenchmen left behind when the diplomats fled Copenhagen, was still in the undamaged coach house and Jules wanted his own revenge on Sharpe.

"We know where he is," Barker insisted.

"Ulfedt's Plads?" Lavisser suggested.

"Where else?"

"You, me and Jules," Lavisser said, "and three of them? I think we must improve those odds."

Barker and Jules went to watch Ulfedt's Plads while Lavisser went to the citadel where General Peymann had his quarters, but the General had been up all night and had now taken to his bed and it was midafternoon before he woke and Lavisser was able to spin his tale. "A child was killed playing with an unexploded bomb, sir," he said, "and I fear there'll be more such deaths. There are too many bombs lying in the streets."

Peymann blew on his coffee to cool it. "I thought Captain Nielsen was dealing with that problem," the General observed.

"He's overwhelmed, sir. I need a dozen men."

"Of course, of course." Peymann signed the necessary order and Lavisser woke a reluctant lieutenant and ordered him to assemble a squad.

The Lieutenant wondered why his men needed muskets to collect unexploded missiles, but he was too tired to argue. He just followed Lavisser to Ulfedt's Plads where two civilians waited beside a warehouse. "Knock on the door, Lieutenant," Lavisser ordered.

"I thought we were here to collect bombs, sir."

Lavisser took the man aside. "Can you be discreet, Lieutenant?"

"As well as the next man." The Lieutenant was offended by the question.

"I could not be frank with you before, Lieutenant. God knows there are too many rumors circling the city already and I didn't want to start more, but General Peymann has been warned that there are English spies in Copenhagen."

"Spies, sir?" The Lieutenant's eyes widened. He was nineteen and had only been an officer for two months and so far his most responsible duty had been making certain that the citadel's flag was hoisted at each sunrise.

"Saboteurs, more like," Lavisser embroidered his tale. "The British, we think, are running out of bombs. They will probably fire a few tonight, but we think they will be relying on their agents in the city to do more damage. The General believes the men are hiding on these premises."

The Lieutenant snapped at his men to fix bayonets, then hammered on Skovgaard's door which was opened by a frightened maid. She screamed when she saw the bayonets, then said that her master and mistress had disappeared.

"What about the Englishman?" Lavisser asked over the Lieutenant's shoulder.

"He hasn't come back, sir," the maid said. "None of them have, sir."

"Search the premises," Lavisser ordered the soldiers. He sent some of the men into the warehouse and others up the stairs of the house while he, Jules and Barker went to Skovgaard's office.

They found no list of names there. They did find a metal box crammed with money, but no names. The Lieutenant discovered an unloaded musket upstairs, but then the terrified maids told the Lieutenant that Mister Bang was locked in the old stables. The Lieutenant took that news down to the office.

"Mister Bang?" Lavisser asked, stuffing money into his coat pocket.

"The fellow who sold us Skovgaard," Barker reminded him.

The padlock was prized from the door and a startled Aksel Bang stumbled into the waning daylight. He was nervous and indignant, and so bewildered that he was hardly able to talk sense and so, to calm him down, Lavisser ordered the maids to make some tea, then he took Bang upstairs and settled him in Skovgaard's parlor where Bang told how Lieutenant Sharpe had come back to the city and how Bang had tried to arrest him. The story was a little tangled there, for Bang was unwilling to admit how easily he had been overpowered, but Lavisser did not pursue the details. Bang did not know how many men were helping Sharpe, but he had heard their voices in the yard and knew there must be at least two or three.

"And Mister Skovgaard's daughter was helping these Englishmen?" Lavisser asked.

"Not willingly, not willingly," Bang insisted. "She must have been deceived."

"Of course."

"But her father, now, he was always on the English side," Bang said vengefully, "and he made Astrid help him. She didn't want to, of course, but he made her."

Lavisser sipped his tea. "So Astrid knows as much as her father?"

"Oh yes," Bang said.

"She knows the names of her father's correspondents?" Lavisser asked.

"What he knows," Bang said, "she knows."

"Does she now," Lavisser said to himself. He lit a candle, for dusk was darkening the room. "You did well, Lieutenant," he said, careful to flatter Bang by using his militia rank, "when you handed Skovgaard to the police."

A small doubt nagged Bang. "Lieutenant Sharpe said that it was you who had taken Skovgaard, sir."

"He said what?" Lavisser looked astonished, then unleashed his charming smile. "Of course not! I have no authority in that area. No, Mister Skovgaard was taken for questioning by the police, but, alas, he escaped. The confusion of the bombing, you understand? And our problem is that Lieutenant Sharpe and his English helpers are somewhere in the city. They may already have rescued Mister Skovgaard. General Peymann thought we would find them here, but alas." He shrugged. "I suspect they are hiding, but you, Lieutenant, know Mister Skovgaard better than anyone."

"True," Bang said.

"And who knows how they are deceiving Astrid?" Lavisser asked in a worried tone.

"They are deceiving her!" Bang said angrily, and spilled out his resentment of Sharpe. The Englishman, he said, had promised Astrid he would stay in Denmark. "And she believes him!" Bang said. "She believes him! He has turned her head."

And a pretty head it was too, Lavisser thought, and filled with knowledge that he needed. "I fear for her, Lieutenant," he said gravely, "I truly do." He stood and stared out of the window so that Bang would not see his amusement. So Sharpe was in love? Lavisser smiled at that realization. The darkening sky was banded in black cloud and soon, he thought, the first bombs would start falling unless the British had exhausted their stocks, in which case the city would be spared until more could be fetched from England. "They are doubtless holding poor Astrid as a hostage"—he turned back to Bang—"and we must find them."

"They could be anywhere," Bang said helplessly.

"Mister Skovgaard was injured by a bomb when he escaped," Lavisser lied smoothly. "He needs a doctor, we think, but he's not in any of the hospitals."

Bang shook his head. "His doctor lives in Vester Fælled."

"And he certainly can't have gone there," Lavisser said, "so where would he hide? What is it?" He had been alarmed by a sudden wide-eyed look on Bang's face.

But Bang was smiling. "Mister Skovgaard needs medical help?" he asked. "Then I know where they are."

"You do?"

"You will give me a gun?" Bang asked eagerly. "I can help you?"

"I should expect nothing less from a loyal Dane," Lavisser said unctuously.

"Then I shall take you to them," Bang said.

For he knew exactly where they were.

To the west a red flash lit the sky and the first bomb climbed into the dark.

Then the other guns hammered, their discharge ringing the city with flame-shot smoke.

And the bombs were falling again.

CHAPTER 11

SHARPE SPENT MUCH OF the day in a cramped storeroom above the arch of the orphanage gateway. He told Hopper and Clouter he was watching for Lavisser, but he did not really expect to see the renegade. He was thinking instead. Thinking about leaving Britain, thinking about Grace and about Astrid. Thinking about the army and about Wapping, and while he brooded, Hopper and Clouter took turns standing guard near Ole Skovgaard's bed, which had been placed under the inside stairs because the orphanage was so crowded with folk made homeless by the bombardment. A Danish flag hung across the small space to make it private and the two seamen were there, not to protect the patient against Lavisser, but rather from the intrusion of children excited by the bombardment and its upheavals. Astrid tended her father, or else helped calm the children.

Hopper brought Sharpe some bread and cheese toward evening and the two men ate in the storeroom, which had a small barred window looking down the street toward the houses of Nyboden. "He's sleeping," Hopper said, meaning Ole Skovgaard. Skovgaard's fingers had been splinted and his wounds bandaged. "He ain't sleeping well," Hopper went on, "but he won't for a while, will he?" He pushed a jug of water toward Sharpe. "I was thinking, sir, that either Clouter or me ought to go and see Captain Chase."

Sharpe nodded. "He'll be worrying."

"Just to let him know we're still ticking," Hopper said. "Doesn't matter which of us goes, sir, but the Captain, sir, he'll want to know what's going to happen."

"If I knew, I'd tell you," Sharpe said.

"I thought we'd wait till the bombs start again, then go. No one takes a blind bit of notice when the bombs are dropping."

Sharpe gazed down the street where a lame sweeper was brushing litter toward a wheelbarrow. "What we do," Sharpe said, "really depends on what the Danes do. On whether they surrender or not."

"Have to drop a few more bombs than we did last night," Hopper said scathingly. "It's no good annoying them, is it? You have to bloody hurt them."

"If they surrender," Sharpe said, "then there isn't a problem. We'll just take Mister Skovgaard to a British surgeon. But if they don't surrender . . ." He left the thought unfinished.

"Then we'll be dodging this Captain Lavatory?"

Sharpe nodded. "Though I think we're safe enough here."

Hopper nodded. "So when it's dark, sir, and the bombs start up, I'll sneak back to the Captain."

"Tell Captain Chase I'll stay here till Mister Skovgaard can be moved." Sharpe did not know what else he could do. He knew he should hunt Lavisser down, but guarding Ole Skovgaard now seemed the more important task. "And when it's all over, Hopper, you, me and Clouter are going to go digging in that house. There ought to be forty-three thousand melted guineas somewhere under the ashes."

"Forty-three thousand?"

"Give or take a handful."

Hopper whistled. "Captain Lavatory will already be digging though, won't he?"

"It'll still be too hot," Sharpe said.

"So pray the buggers surrender, eh?" Hopper stared down the shadowed street. "Look at that silly bugger! Sweeping up a bombed city! You should get some sleep, sir, you look like a rag." He frowned at the small storeroom. "You ain't got room to make a proper cot in here, sir, why not go to the chapel? It's quiet enough there."

"Wake me before you leave."

"Aye aye, sir."

It was quiet in the chapel, though Sharpe could not sleep. He sat at the very back in a white-painted pew and stared at the stained glass window above the simple altar. It was getting darker outside and the details of the window were obscured, but the golden hair of the children and Christ's silver halo showed up brightly. There were words scrolled around the halo, but they were in Danish so he could not read them.

He heard the door open and turned to see that Astrid had come to join him. "You look very thoughtful," she said.

"I was just wondering what those words say," Sharpe said, "up on the window."

Astrid peered up at the dark glass. "*Lader de små Børn,*" she read, "*komme til mig.*"

"I'm none the wiser."

"Let the little children come to me," she translated. "It's from the Gospels."

"Ah."

Astrid smiled. "You sound disappointed."

"I thought it might be 'Be sure your sin will find you out.' "

"So you do have some religion?"

"Do I?"

She took his hand and held it silently for a while, then she sighed. "Why would anyone hurt another man so much?"

"Because it's war," Sharpe said.

"Because the world is cruel," Astrid said. She stared up at the window. Christ's halo and eyes were piercing white, the rest was darkening. "From now on," she said, "he will be half blind, toothless and never able to hold a pen again." She squeezed Sharpe's hand. "And I will have to look after him."

"Then I'll have to look after you, won't I?"

"Will you?"

He nodded. The question, he thought, was not would he, but could he? Could he live here? Could he deal with a querulous Ole Skovgaard, with a strange language and the stifling respectability? Then Astrid rested her head on his shoulder and he knew he did not want to lose her. He sat silent, watching the dark suffuse the window, and he thought of Lord Pumphrey's confidence that the next few years would bring enough war to guarantee promotion and he reflected that he had never proved himself as an officer. He had shown he was a soldier, but he was still floundering as an officer. A company of greenjackets, he thought, and a French enemy to be humbled, that was a dream that would be worth pursuing. But a man must make choices, and that thought made him squeeze Astrid's fingers.

"What?" she asked.

"Nothing," Sharpe said, and he saw Christ's dark-blue robe turn purple and His white eyes flash livid red. You must be dreaming, he thought, then the colors faded to darkness again and he heard the thump and he instinctively put his arms around Astrid and covered her body with his as the bomb exploded beyond the window and the stained glass, all its blues and golds and scarlets and greens, shattered into a thousand shards that screamed through the chapel. Smoke boiled after it, and then there was silence broken only by the skittering of broken glass across the chapel floor. It was like an indrawing of breath.

Before the other bombs began to fall.

THE BRITISH had fired close to five thousand bombs on the first night of the bombardment and they had watched the fires rage beyond the walls and had been certain that another night of pain would persuade the Danes to surrender the city. They fired far fewer bombs the second night, a mere two thousand, thinking that would be sufficient to satisfy the garrison's honor, but in the morning, when the smoke covered the city like a pall, no message came from the city, the Danish flag still flew above the citadel and the guns on the shot-scarred ramparts opened a defiant fire. So now, on the third night, they would drown Copenhagen in fire. All day they had replenished the magazines, hauling wagon after wagon of bombs to the batteries, and as soon as darkness fell the great guns began their battering until the very ground seemed to throb with the hammering of the mortars and the recoil of howitzers. The sky flickered with fuse traces and was tangled with smoke trails.

The gunners had changed their aim, planning to devastate new areas of the city. Bombs and carcasses rained onto the cathedral and the university, while other shells reached deeper into the maze of streets to punish the defenders for their stubbornness. The bomb ships quivered with each discharge and rocket trails whipped fire across the clouds. The seven fire engines did their best. The teams of men pumped the long handles to spurt sea-water on the flames, but as new fires sprang up so the men deserted the machines to go and protect their families. The streets were overwhelmed by panicked refugees. Bombs cracked down, the flames roared, walls collapsed, the city burned.

General Peymann stood on the citadel wall and watched the fires spring up in a dozen places. He saw spires and steeples outlined by fire, saw them fall and watched the sparks spew in pillars of red through which the bombs crashed down. Pigeons, woken from their nests, flew about the flames until they fell burning. Why, Peymann wondered, did they not fly away? A rocket struck the cathedral's dome and bounced up into the sky where it exploded just as a bomb crashed though the dome's tiles. The whole of Skindergade was alight, then a carcass broke through the roof of Skovgaard's warehouse on Ulfedt's Plads and the sugar caught fire. The flames spread with brutal speed, making the district as bright as day. A school in Suhmsgade that had become a home for refugees was struck by three bombs. The shops on Frederiksborggade and in Landemærket were burning and Peymann felt an immense and impotent anger as he watched the destruction. "Is Major Lavisser here?" the General asked an aide.

"I saw him a few moments ago, sir."

"Tell him to burn the fleet."

"Burn it?" The aide was horrified, for such an order meant that Peymann knew the city could not hold.

"Burn the ships," Peymann said grimly, flinching as a flight of bombs crashed into the university. The British, he realized, were not short of bombs. They were unleashing hundreds onto a city that could either surrender or be obliterated. The distillery opposite Skovgaard's warehouse was struck and the stills exploded blue fire that ran like burning quicksilver down alleys and gutters. Even from the citadel's walls Peymann could hear screams in the streets. "Tell Major Lavisser to light the fuses quickly!" he called after the aide. He hoped that the British, seeing the fleet burning, would stop their terrible bombardment, though he knew it would be at least an hour or two before the ships could be fired because hundreds of refugees had gathered around the inner harbor in the certain knowledge that the British would not aim their mortars at the district where the fleet was stored, and those folk would have to be persuaded to move away before the fierce heat of the burning ships made the area untenable.

The aide ran down the firestep to the scorched courtyard, but found no sign of Major Lavisser. The General's orderly said he thought the Major had gone to Bredgade and so the aide followed, but as he left the citadel a bomb landed five paces behind him and the shattering case broke his spine and threw him into the moat. The university was on fire, its library making a roaring sound as the flames devoured the shelves. The city's separate fires were joining now, becoming higher and brighter, larger and fiercer. "Come," the General gestured to the rest of his aides, "we shall do what we can." There was little he could do for the city had no defense against this horror, but he could not just watch. There were people to be rescued and survivors to be comforted.

The bomb ships were throwing their shells over the citadel and one crashed into the orphanage chapel to splinter the roof and explode among the organ pipes. Astrid screamed as flames began to flicker from the organ's shattered casing. Sharpe took her hand and dragged her into the courtyard. "The children!" she shouted.

"We'll get them out," Sharpe said, but where? He stood under the flagpole and stared up at the sky. The bombs, he thought, were going just to the south of the orphanage, which meant the graveyard to the north might be the safest place. "The cemetery!" he shouted to Astrid. "Take them to the cemetery!" She nodded just as a bomb slammed into the courtyard to make a small crater in which it sat malevolently, smoke hissing from its burning fuse until Hopper stepped to it and plucked the burning match clean out of the plug. "I'm going to the Captain, sir!"

Sharpe almost called Hopper back, but there were plenty of adults to help rescue the children and so he let the big man go. He ran into the building and found Clouter beside Ole Skovgaard's bed. "There's a cemetery that should be safe," he told Clouter. "Take him there. Can you carry the bed as well?"

"Aye aye, sir."

"The cemetery's that way." He pointed, then dropped his rifle and seven-barreled gun in a corner. "Then come back and help with the children," he shouted after Clouter.

Someone was ringing the orphanage bell as though people needed any warning. The chapel was burning and another bomb had exploded in the kitchens so that the whole building was now lurid with flame. There were screams as another bomb crashed into a dormitory. The children were panicking. Sharpe ran up the outer stairs and shouted in his sergeant's voice at a score of screaming children who were jostling on the balcony at the stairhead. They knew no English, but they froze, more scared of him than of the flames and noise. "You!" He grabbed a girl. "Downstairs. You next!" He made them go in single file down the stairs. More adults were coming to help and Sharpe ran into the burning dormitory. Two children were plainly dead, their small broken bodies laced with blood, but a third was crouching, screaming, her hands tight over her bloodied face and Sharpe picked her up and carried her to the balcony where he pushed her into a woman's arms. The fire in the kitchens had broken through the roof, but no more bombs had come, though a dozen or more exploded just to the south where a row of houses was burning.

Astrid had been directing people into the sailors' cemetery, but now ran back through the gate's archway and up the stairs. "There are still the cripples," she told Sharpe.

"Where?"

She pointed to a corner room and Sharpe ran round the open balcony to find six terrified children in their beds. Clouter had come back to the courtyard and Sharpe simply carried the children out to the balcony one by one and threw them down to the seaman who caught and handed them to other adults who had come to help. Sharpe tossed the last child down just as a bomb splintered through the remnants of the chapel and exploded in its doorway to slash metal fragments and slivers of wood across the yard. No one was touched. Sharpe had blood on his back where scraps of the stained glass window had slit through his coat and jacket, but he was unaware of it. "Is that all?" he shouted to Astrid over the thump of bombs and the sound of fire.

"That's all!"

The last of the children had been carried to the graveyard and Clouter was alone in the courtyard. "Get out!" Sharpe shouted to him, then he took Astrid's hand and led her around the balcony toward the stairhead. The burning dormitory was like a furnace as he passed, then a bomb crashed through the outside staircase, splintering its steps. A carcass followed, hissing tongues of white fire in the courtyard. Sharpe pulled Astrid into the main landing and ran down the inside stairs to find Clouter in the small hallway. "I told you to get out."

"Came to get this," Clouter said, brandishing Hopper's seven-barreled gun. Sharpe picked up his own weapons. Tiles were clattering into the courtyard as more bombs hit the building, and he hoped to God the gunners were not shifting their aim northward for then the cemetery would be under fire. "All we have to do now," he told Clouter, "is look after Mister Skovgaard." The orphanage shuddered as two new bombs exploded. A child's doll, its hair burning bright, skidded across the smoke-filled yard as Sharpe led Astrid and Clouter toward the gate, then he suddenly twisted to his right and shouted a warning.

He shouted because there were soldiers in the archway and Lavisser was with them, and the men were bringing their muskets up to their shoulders. Sharpe picked up the shell that Hopper had defused and hurled it one-handed toward the men who, seeing it, flinched away and Sharpe dragged Astrid back through the door. He slammed it shut, shot its bolt then took Astrid by the shoulders. "Do the windows on this floor have bars?"

She looked at him uncertainly, then shook her head. "No."

"Then find a window, climb out and go to the cemetery. Hurry!" Musket butts were already pounding on the bolted door.

Sharpe pushed Astrid down the corridor then he ran up the stairs and out onto the smoke-wreathed balcony. Clouter followed as Sharpe ran to the undamaged end of the building where he stopped, turned and aimed the seven-barreled gun at the soldiers trying to break the door down. Then he hesitated. His quarrel was with Lavisser, not with the soldiers, but he could not see Lavisser, or Barker, though he did see a man climbing through one of the windows that opened onto the courtyard. Was Lavisser already inside? Flames were flying high to his right, licking at the rafters of the dormitories. He and Clouter were going to be trapped here, Sharpe thought, burned to death. Then one of the soldiers saw them and shouted to his comrades and Sharpe, still unwilling to start a private war in the burning building, pulled Clouter back into the undamaged dormitory. A bomb smashed into the yard and he heard screams. "What are we going to do?" Clouter asked him.

"God knows." Sharpe slung the seven-barreled gun on his shoulder and went to the windows. They were barred to stop boys being daredevils and he shook the bars, hoping that they could be loosened and that he and Clouter could drop down into the orphanage garden and make their way unseen to the cemetery, but the iron bars felt frustratingly solid. He swore and tugged again. Clouter saw what he was doing and came to help and the big man gave a grunt as he heaved on an iron rod. It came away in his hand, splintering the wooden sill.

Then Lavisser called from the courtyard. "Sharpe! Sharpe!"

Sharpe turned and went back to the landing. He went cautiously, half expecting a volley, but instead saw that a half-dozen of the soldiers were on the ground, bloodied, twitching and scorched. A bomb had exploded in the group beside the bolted door. But then Sharpe saw that Lavisser was not alone. Astrid was beside him and she was in the grip of a tall, pale-faced man. It was Aksel Bang. God damn it, Sharpe thought, but he had bloody forgotten Bang! "Sharpe?" Lavisser called again.

"What do you want?"

"Just come down, Sharpe, and that's an end to it." The city was shuddering, flaming, incandescent. Above the burning chapel Sharpe had an impression of scores of falling bombs and a sky laced with fiery rocket trails. The smoke boiled. He stepped back into the shadow and took the rifle from his shoulder. He could see Lavisser, but not Barker. Was Barker inside? Stalking him?

"End of what?" he called to Lavisser.

"I'm told Miss Skovgaard knows the names I want."

"Let her go."

Lavisser smiled. Another bomb crashed into the orphanage and the blast of its smoke and flame whipped the skirts of Lavisser's coat, but he showed no fear. He just smiled. "I can't let her go, Richard, you know that. I want the names."

"I've got the names. I've got your list."

"Then bring it down, Richard, and I'll let Miss Skovgaard go."

Sharpe knelt and thumbed back the rifle's cock. Jesus wept, he thought, but this gun had better be accurate. Aksel Bang was no more than twenty paces away, but he was standing behind Astrid with his right arm about her waist. Sharpe could only see Bang's lugubrious face, the rest of him was hidden by Astrid, but on the range at Shorncliffe Sharpe had been able to put ten bullets out of ten through a target the size of a man's face at sixty yards.

"What are you waiting for, Richard?" Lavisser called.

"I'm thinking."

Clouter crouched beside Sharpe. "There's a big fellow prowling," Sharpe told him. "Watch out for him."

Clouter nodded. Sharpe aimed through the bars of the balcony's balustrade, lining the notch in the rifle's backsight and the leaf of the foresight on Aksel Bang's face. Then Sharpe suddenly worried about whether he had wrapped the ball in its scrap of greased leather when he had reloaded the gun. He remembered firing the rifle in the Bredgade house, but when had he reloaded it? He thought when he had arrived at the orphanage last night, but he had given it no thought. Why should he? Loading a gun was like breathing, not something a man thought about. But if he had not used the leather patch then the bullet would not be gripped by the seven spiraling grooves and lands that gave it spin and so made it accurate. And if the ball was unwrapped then it would be fractionally smaller than the barrel's width and when he fired it would fly out at a slight angle. Very slight, but enough to make it go wide and perhaps strike Astrid.

"Sharpe! I'm waiting!" Lavisser peered up at the dark doorway. "Bring me the list!"

"Let her go!" Sharpe shouted.

"Please don't be tedious, Richard. Just come down. Or do you want me to describe what I plan to do to the lovely Astrid if you don't come down?"

Sharpe fired. He could not see where the bullet went, for the doorway was immediately filled with a fog of powder smoke, but he heard Astrid scream and Sharpe immediately knew he had made a mistake. He should have fired at Lavisser, not Bang. Bang did not have the guts to do anything on his own initiative, but Sharpe had picked him because he was holding Astrid and now Sharpe dashed through the smoke to lean on the balustrade and he saw that Bang was on his back, spreadeagled, and where his face had been there was only a great patch of broken bone, cartilage and bloody flesh. Astrid had vanished. Lavisser was staring at Bang in disbelief, then Sharpe saw the movement to his right and he dropped to one knee as Barker fired the musket. The ball plucked at Sharpe's hair and scored a slash across the side of his skull and he was dazed, but not disabled, and he was screaming a war shout as he charged down the balcony and rammed the muzzle of the unloaded rifle into Barker's groin. Another musket flashed and Sharpe felt the wind of the ball passing and he saw there was a second man behind Barker, but Clouter shouted at Sharpe to drop, and he did, and the volley gun flamed and roared as loud as an exploding bomb. The second man was snatched backward as two shells cracked through the rafters of the dormitory where Sharpe and Clouter had sheltered.

Barker was writhing on the balcony. "No!" he shouted at Sharpe who had drawn one of his pistols.

"Yes," Sharpe said.

"I let you live!" Barker shouted.

"More bloody fool you," Sharpe said and aimed the pistol. He fired and the ball took Barker under the chin, and then a musket banged from the courtyard and tore a splinter from the balustrade beside Sharpe. Clouter fired back with both his pistols, then crouched to reload the volley gun. Sharpe slid his last pistol along the balcony to the black man. "Wait there," he told him.

"Where are you going?" Clouter asked.

"To find the bastard," Sharpe said. Lavisser had vanished, so Sharpe took the volley gun from his shoulder, stepped over Barker's corpse, and stalked along the landing. Flames were terrible to his right, threatening to roast him, but he ran past them into cooler air and came to the door leading to the inside stairs and saw Lavisser there, on the half landing, and Sharpe brought the volley gun to his shoulder, but Lavisser was quicker to raise his pistol and Sharpe ducked back. "I'm not going to shoot, Richard!" Lavisser called. "I just want to talk!"

Sharpe waited. His head was ringing and blood was dripping from his ear. A bomb exploded in the courtyard, twitching the bloodied bodies of the dead infantrymen. A carcass was burning there and its flames set fire to a soldier's ammunition pouch which crackled angrily. "I'm not going to shoot," Lavisser said again, closer now. "Talk to me. Are you there?"

"I'm here," Sharpe said.

Lavisser, the pistol held away from his body to show he meant no harm, stepped cautiously onto the balcony. "See?" He gestured with the pistol. "No more shooting, Richard."

Sharpe had the volley gun at his waist and its seven barrels were pointing at Lavisser. He kept it there.

Lavisser glanced at the gun, then smiled. "Your woman's safe. She ran out through the arch."

"My woman?"

"Mister Bang seemed to think she was sweet on you."

"Bang was an idiot."

"My dear Richard, they're all idiots. This is Denmark! Dull, insufferably dull. It threatens to be the most respectable country on God's earth." He flinched as a bomb fell into the storeroom over the archway, but he did not take his eyes from Sharpe. "Our gunners are showing rare form tonight. Mister Bang says you're going to stay here."

"So?"

"So am I, Richard, and I could do with a friend who isn't insufferably respectable."

Sharpe took a step forward for the heat behind him was growing intolerable. Lavisser stepped back. He still held the pistol out to one side. Clouter was walking down the far side of the balcony now, then he nimbly leaped off the balustrade onto the mast-rigged flagpole. The tarred ratlines were burning, but he scrambled down with such practiced speed that he came to no harm.

"So what's the price of your friendship?" Sharpe asked Lavisser. "The list in my pocket?"

"Do you really care about the men on that list?" Lavisser asked. "Who are they? Unknown merchants in Prussia and Hanover? Let the French have them and the French will look after us. What do you want to be, Richard? A general in the Danish army? It can be arranged, believe me. You want a title? The Emperor is remarkably generous with titles. Everything is new in Europe, Richard. The old titles mean nothing! If you can take power then you can be a lord, a prince, an archduke or a king." Lavisser glanced down into the courtyard where Clouter was threatening him with the reloaded volley gun. "Is your black friend going to shoot me?"

"Let him be, Clouter!"

"Aye aye, sir." Clouter lowered the weapon.

Sharpe again stepped forward, forcing Lavisser another pace back toward the burning chapel. Lavisser was worrying now and began to swing the pistol to face Sharpe, but Sharpe twitched his own volley gun and Lavisser obediently held the pistol out to his right side again. "I'm serious, Richard," he said. "You and me? We can be like wolves in a land of woolly baalambs."

"I'm still wearing British uniform," Sharpe said, "or hadn't you noticed?"

"And what will Britain do for you?" Lavisser asked. "You think it will ever accept you? Besides, you're staying here. You're going to need money, Richard, money and friends. I offer you both. You really think you could endure Denmark without either?" He smiled with sudden relief because Sharpe had at last moved the seven-barreled gun so that it no longer pointed at Lavisser's waist. Now, instead, it was aimed to the side. "I confess I would like your friendship, Richard," Lavisser said.

"Why?"

"Because you're a rogue," Lavisser said, "and I like rogues. I always have. And you're efficient, impressively efficient. Like our gunners tonight." The gunners had turned Copenhagen into hell. Great swathes of the city were burning, the flames leaping high above the remaining spires and it seemed to Sharpe, glancing above Lavisser's head, that a bow of fire like a rainbow of pure flame was arched across the city. It was a glimpse of the world's ending, of hell's vengeance. It was efficient, right enough.

"I'm a thug," Sharpe said, "remember?"

"I aspire to be the same," Lavisser said. "This world is ruled by thugs. What is the Emperor but a thug? What is the Duke of York but another thug? Albeit a dim one. Thugs win, Richard. To the powerful go the spoils."

"I just have one problem," Sharpe said. The heat was burning his back, but he stayed still. "You threatened Astrid."

"Don't be absurd, Richard," Lavisser said with a smile. "Do you really think I meant it? Of course not. I like her far too much. Not as you do, of course, though I must say I admire your taste." He glanced at the volley gun and saw it was still pointed away from him. "I would never have hurt her, Richard."

"You wouldn't?"

"No! What do you take me for, Richard?"

"A bastard," Sharpe said, "a lying bloody bastard," and he pulled the volley gun's trigger. The seven bullets whipped up into the smoke and snatched the pistol out of Lavisser's hand. They also ripped his hand and wrist into bloody shreds so that Lavisser gaped at it, then shrieked as the pain struck.

"You bastard," Sharpe said, "you utter bloody bastard," and he tossed the seven-barreled gun down to Clouter and drew the cutlass, which he shoved hard into Lavisser's chest to drive him back and Lavisser snatched at his own sword hilt with his left hand, but he could not draw the weapon across his body, and Sharpe speared his chest with the cutlass point again and Lavisser staggered back a further step, then saw that the balcony ended at a doorway that had once led to the chapel's gallery and now opened onto an inferno.

"No!" he screamed and tried to lurch forward, but Sharpe was quicker. He rammed the heavy blade at Lavisser's chest, jarring him hard back, and Lavisser teetered on the doorway's edge. Beneath him was the red-hot fire of burning pews and bibles. "No!"

"Go to hell," Sharpe said and pushed again, but this time Lavisser caught hold of the cutlass blade with his good hand and clung on to the steel to keep himself from falling.

"Pull me back," he said to Sharpe, "please. Please!"

Sharpe let go of the cutlass and Lavisser fell back into the burning chapel. He screamed as he fell, his arms outspread, then thumped into the flames.

The balcony lurched under Sharpe. He vaulted the rail and jumped down to the yard. The archway was filled with smoke and brilliant with flames, but Sharpe reckoned they could dash through safely enough. He took the seven-barreled gun from Clouter then looked at the fire that roared and boiled in the archway. "Are you feeling lucky, Clouter?"

"Luckier than that poor bastard, sir."

"Then go!"

They ran.

THE CITY surrendered next morning. Seven thousand bombs had fallen in the night and some of the streets blazed so fiercely that no one could get within a hundred paces. Charred pages of the university's library had rained across a hundred square miles of Zealand, while the cathedral was a gaunt frame of scorched stone in which a heap of embers smoked like the pit. Bodies lay in neat rows in parks, squares and on the harbor quays. There were not nearly enough coffins, so folk whose homes were undamaged brought their sheets and did their best to make the dead decent. The fleet was whole, unburned and captured. No one had come to light the fuses and even if they had the ships would not have burned for Captain Chase had stripped the incendiaries away.

British soldiers fought the flames while a redcoat military band played outside the Amalienborg Palace. General Peymann listened to the unfamiliar music and tried to pay attention to the flattering remarks made by the city's new masters, but he could not rid himself of a feeling of gross injustice. "There were women and children here," he said again and again, but he spoke in Danish and the British officers, who dined off the palace's finest porcelain plates, did not understand him. "We did not deserve this," he finally protested, insisting one of his own aides offered a translation.

"Europe didn't deserve the Emperor," Sir David Baird retorted hotly, "but we have him. Come, sir, try the ragout of beef."

General Cathcart, who had never wanted to bombard the city, said nothing. The smell of smoke filled the dining room, taking away his appetite, though every now and then he would glance from the windows to see the masts of the captured fleet and wonder how much of their value would be given him in prize money. More than enough to buy an estate in his native Scotland, that was for sure.

Not far away, in Bredgade, a dozen sailors had finished hauling blackened beams and scorched bricks from a gaping hole. Now they squatted in a circle and chipped away at dozens of curious black lumps that, when broken apart with a boarding axe, gleamed like a newly risen sun. Not all of the gold had melted, some of the coins were still in the charred remnants of their bags, and Captain Chase was making piles of guineas. "I'm not sure we got it all, Richard."

"Enough," Sharpe said.

"Oh enough, certainly enough, more than I ever dreamed!"

Lord Pumphrey was watching over the excavation. He had appeared unexpectedly, accompanied by a dozen soldiers, and announced that he was there to look after the Treasury's interests. "Though I shall do as Nelson did at Copenhagen," he told Sharpe, "and turn a blind eye. I do not, after all, have a great love for the Treasury. Who does? But we must return something to them."

"Must we?"

"I like to think they will owe me a favor, so yes. But do help yourself, Richard, while my blind eye is watching."

Sharpe gave Pumphrey the list of names. "Lavisser's dead, my lord."

"You cheer me, Sharpe, you do cheer me." Pumphrey peered at the papers. "Is that blood?"

"Yes, my lord."

Pumphrey looked up at Sharpe, saw the anger that was still in the rifleman, so said nothing more of the blood. Nor did he ask him about the blood in his hair or the scorch marks on the green jacket. "Thank you, Sharpe. And Skovgaard?"

"Alive, sir, barely. I'm going to see him now. Last night's bombs burned his warehouse, nothing left of it at all, but he's got a house outside the city walls in Vester Fælled. You want to come?"

"I think I shall wait before I pay my respects," Pumphrey said, then held out a hand to hold Sharpe back. "But tell me, will he move to Britain? He can hardly stay here."

"He can't?"

"My dear Sharpe, we shall stay here a month, at the most two, and then the French will be very firmly in the Danish saddle. How long do you think Mister Skovgaard will last then?"

"I think, my lord, that he would go to hell before he went to Britain," Sharpe said, "so you'll have to find another way to protect him. And his daughter."

"His daughter?"

"She knows as much as he does. What will you do, my lord?"

"Sweden, perhaps?" Lord Pumphrey suggested. "I'd prefer them both to be in Britain, but I do promise you, Sharpe, I do promise you upon my honor, that the French will not trouble them."

Sharpe looked hard at Pumphrey who almost shivered under the intensity of the gaze, but then Sharpe nodded, satisfied with the promise, and walked away. His pockets were heavy with gold. Chase and his men would become rich this day, and doubtless Lord Pumphrey would skim a share before he returned the gold to the Treasury, but Sharpe, despite the weight in his pockets, would not be rich.

Nor would he stay in Denmark. Ole Skovgaard had forbidden his daughter to marry the Englishman. Sick as Skovgaard was, he had summoned the force to utter the refusal and Astrid would not disobey him. Now, when Sharpe came to the big house in Vester Fælled, she looked close to tears. "He will not change his mind," she said.

"I know."

"He hates Britain now," she said, "and he hates you, and he says you are not a Christian and I cannot . . ." She shook her head, unable to go on, then frowned as Sharpe took lumps of blackened gold and handfuls of coins distorted by heat from his pockets. "You think that will change his mind?" Astrid asked. "Money will not persuade him."

"It's not for him. Nor for you, unless you want it," Sharpe said as he took the last guinea and added it to the rest on the harpsichord. The house had been a billet for British officers during the bombardment and the fine wooden floor was marked with boot nails and the rugs were smeared with dried mud. "You said you wanted to rebuild the orphanage," Sharpe said, "so now you can."

"Richard!" Astrid tried to push the gold back to him, but he would not take it.

"I don't want it," he said. He did want it, he wanted it badly, but he had stolen enough guineas in the last month and, besides, he wanted Astrid's dream to come true even more than he wanted this gold. "Give it to the children," he said, and then she just wept and he held her.

"I cannot go against my father's wishes," she said at last. "It would not be right."

"No," he said, and he did not really understand her obedience but he did understand that it was important to her. He stroked her hair. "Someone told me this was a very respectable society," he said, "and I reckon I wouldn't have fitted. I'm not godly enough, so maybe it's for the best. But one day, who knows, perhaps I'll come back?"

He walked away, going through the nearby cemetery where a great pit was being dug for the fire-shrunken dead.

That night, in the Amalienborg Palace, Lord Pumphrey carefully took part of the gold and stored it in his valise. The remaining gold—he reckoned it was worth about nine thousand pounds—would be returned to the Bank of England and the Honorable John Lavisser could conveniently be blamed for all that was missing. "You could let Sharpe take it back," he told Sir David Baird next day.

"Why Sharpe?"

"Because I want him out of Copenhagen," Pumphrey said.

"What's he done now?"

"What he has done," Pumphrey said in his precise voice, "is exactly what I asked him to do, and he has done it exceedingly well. I commend him to you, Sir David. But among the things I asked him to do was to keep two people alive, which he did, only it is no longer in His Majesty's interest that they should live." Pumphrey smiled and drew a delicate finger across his throat.

Baird raised a cautionary hand. "Tell me no more, Pumphrey. I don't want to be privy to your dirty world."

"How very wise you are, Sir David. But remove Sharpe quickly, if you would be so kind. He has an inconveniently gallant soul and I don't want to make an enemy of him. He could be useful to me again."

The city still spewed smoke when Sharpe left. Autumn was in the air, brought by a cold wind from Sweden, but the sky was clear, spoiled only by the great feathered smear of smoke that drifted across Zealand. The smoke stayed in Sharpe's sight even when the city vanished beneath the *Pucelle*'s horizon. Astrid, he thought, Astrid, and at least he no longer thought only of Grace, and he was still confused, except he did now know what he was doing. He was going back to the barracks, back to his quartermaster's duties, but at least with the promise that he would not be left behind when the regiment next sailed to war. And there would be war. France was beneath that smoke-filled horizon and she was the mistress of all Europe now, and until France was beaten there would be no peace. It was a soldier's world now, and he was a soldier.

Chase joined him at the stern rail. "You've got some leave coming, haven't you?"

"A month, sir. I'm not due at Shorncliffe till October."

"Then you'll come to Devon with me. It's time you met Florence, a dear soul! We can go shooting, perhaps? I won't take a refusal, Richard."

"Then I won't offer you one, sir."

"There, look! Kronborg Castle." Chase pointed at the green copper roofs that shone in the sunset. "Know what happened there, Richard?"

"*Hamlet.*"

"My God, you're right." Chase tried to hide his surprise. "I asked young Collier when we were coming the other way and he didn't have the first idea!"

"Did he die?"

"Who? Collier? Of course not, he's right as rain."

"Hamlet, sir."

"Of course he died. Don't you know the play? Maybe you don't," Chase added in a hurry. "Not everyone does."

"What's it about?"

"A fellow who can't make up his mind, Sharpe, and dies of indecision. A lesson to us all."

Sharpe smiled. He was remembering Lavisser's fulsome friendliness when they had sailed past Kronborg, and how Lavisser had quoted some words from the play, and how Sharpe had liked the guardsman then. And he remembered how tempted he had been on the burning balcony. Part of him had wanted to take Lavisser's friendship, to take the gold and the opportunity and the adventure, but in the end he had pulled the trigger because he had to live with himself. Though God alone knew where that would take him.

Night fell. The smoke of a broken city vanished in the dark.

And Sharpe sailed home, a soldier.

THE BRITISH ATTACK on Copenhagen in April 1801 is remembered (by the British), while the far more devastating attack of September 1807 is largely forgotten. Perhaps the former is distinguished by the presence of Nelson, for it was during the Battle of Copenhagen that he famously placed a telescope to his blind eye and declared he could not see the signal to discontinue the action.

The battle of April 1801 was between a British fleet and the Danish fleet which was reinforced by floating batteries and the formidable seaward defenses of the city. Some 790 Danish sailors and soldiers were killed and another 900 wounded, but all those men, like the 950 British casualties, were troops. In 1807 the British killed 1,600 Danish civilians inside Copenhagen (British losses in the whole campaign amounted to 259 men) and the Danish defeat was far more comprehensive, yet the campaign has been largely forgotten in Britain.

The cause of it was the 1807 Treaty of Tilsit between France and Russia which agreed, among many other things, that the French could take the Danish fleet. The Russians had no right to grant such a thing, nor the French to take it, but Denmark was a small country (though not so small as she is today; in 1807 she still possessed Holstein, now in northern Germany, and all of Norway). She did, however, possess the second largest merchant fleet in the world and, to protect it, a very large navy with powerful ships which the French wanted to replace those they had lost at Trafalgar in 1805. The British, whose intelligence service was remarkably efficient, heard about the secret clause in the treaty and, to prevent its implementation, demanded that the Danes send their fleet into protective custody in Britain. The Danes, quite properly, refused, and so the 1807 expedition was launched to force their hand. When the Danes still rejected the British demands the gunners opened fire and bombarded Copenhagen until the city, unwilling to take more casualties, surrendered. The Danish fleet, instead of being taken into protective custody, was simply captured.

It was not a campaign in which the British can take particular pride. The Danish army was mostly in Holstein so the only action of any note was the one described in the novel, the Battle of Køge, between Sir Arthur Wellesley's forces and the scratch army assembled by General Castenschiold. The Danes call it "the battle of the wooden shoes" because so many of their militiamen were wearing farm clogs. It seems rather tough luck on the Danes that at a time when the British army had many mediocre generals they should have run up against the future Duke of Wellington, not to mention the 95th Rifles. Companies from the regiment had served in a couple of actions before, but Køge was the first time that the whole 1st Battalion fought together. There was no attempt to bribe the Danish Crown Prince, though the "golden cavalry of Saint George" was one of Britain's most potent weapons in the long wars against France and was used to subvert, bribe and persuade countless rulers. Between 1793 and 1815 the British Treasury spent no less than £52,000,000 on such "subsidies."

It is a mystery why the Danes did not burn their fleet. The Crown Prince certainly sent orders that it should be done, for one of his messages was captured by the British. Copies probably reached the city, but the ships were not fired. There were no British seamen smuggled into the city to prevent such a fire; it simply seems that in the chaos of the bombardment the orders were overlooked, or else Peymann thought that the British would exact a terrible price if he so thwarted them. So the fleet was waiting, and the British, who occupied the city for a further six weeks, took home eighteen ships of the line, four frigates and sixteen other ships as well as twenty-five gunboats. They also stripped the dockyard of stores and destroyed the half-built ships on the slipways. One of the ships of the line was lost on the voyage home, but the rest were all deemed to be prizes, thus making the senior officers of the expedition indecently rich

(Admiral Gambier and General Cathcart alone divided about £300,000 between them, a fortune). The British did leave behind a small and rather beautiful frigate, really little more than a pleasure craft, which had been a gift from King George III to his nephew, the Danish Crown Prince. The Danes, with a macabre sense of humor, sent this ship to England later in the year, together with a handful of British prisoners and a message saying that the frigate appeared to have been inadvertently forgotten. One of the minor trophies of the expedition was the capture from the Danes of the island of Heligoland in the North Sea which stayed under British rule until 1890 when it was amicably handed over to Germany.

The 1807 campaign was a disaster for Denmark. It forced her into a French alliance and ruined her financially. She lost Norway (to Sweden) and those parts of Copenhagen that had been burned by the British were not rebuilt for a generation. Over three hundred houses were destroyed, a thousand more seriously damaged, the cathedral was burned as were a dozen other churches and the university. The small tale of the artist extinguishing a mortar shell with the contents of his chamber pot is true; his name was Eckersburg and he left some harrowing pictures of the city under fire. Today there is little sign that the destruction ever took place, though a few of the rebuilt houses have British round shot mortared into their facades. The city's great fortifications were demolished in 1867, though the citadel (now the Kastellet) remains. There was a small wooden fishing pier close to the citadel, not far from where the Little Mermaid now sits. Many of the street names have changed, thus Ulfedt's Plads (which was burned out) is now Graabodretorv.

The campaign does have one curious footnote. One of the British generals on the expedition was Thomas Grosvenor who took with him a mare, Lady Catherine. While in Denmark, he discovered Lady Catherine was pregnant, so he sent her home where she gave birth to a foal, a stallion, that was later sold to Sir Charles Stewart who became Adjutant-General in the Peninsular War. Stewart, in turn, sold the stallion to Sir Arthur Wellesley and it became his favorite horse. Indeed, when he was Duke of Wellington, he rode the horse throughout the Battle of Waterloo and afterward retired it to his estate at Stratfield Saye. The horse died in 1836 and was buried in the grounds of Stratfield Saye where its gravestone can still be seen. The name of the horse was, of course,

Copenhagen. "There may have been many faster horses," the Duke said of Copenhagen, "and no doubt many handsomer, but for bottom and endurance I never saw his fellow."

So, tenuous though it is, the road to Waterloo winds through Copenhagen, and Sharpe, like the Duke, must march every mile.

HISTORY COMES ALIVE
READ ALL OF
RICHARD SHARPE'S
ADVENTURES

"Excellently entertaining. If you love historical drama . . . then look no further."
—Boston Globe

ISBN 978-0-06-008453-0
(paperback)
978-0-06-179762-0 (e-book)

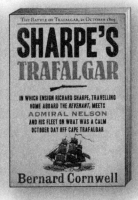

ISBN 978-0-06-109862-8
(paperback)
978-0-06-175173-8 (e-book)

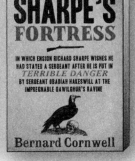

ISBN 978-0-06-109863-5
(paperback)
978-0-06-180957-6 (e-book)

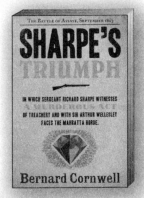

ISBN 978-0-06-095197-9 (paperback)
978-0-06-175175-2 (e-book)

ISBN 978-0-06-093230-5 (paperback)
978-0-06-180473-1 (e-book)

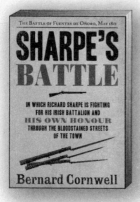

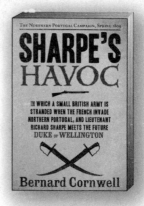